Deaf Sentence

DAVID LODGE

PENGUIN BOOKS

PENGUIN BOOKS

Published by the Penguin Group
Penguin Books Ltd, 80 Strand, London wc2r orl, England
Penguin Group (USA) Inc., 375 Hudson Street, New York, New York 10014, USA
Penguin Group (Canada), 90 Eglinton Avenue East, Suite 700, Toronto, Ontario, Canada m4p 2y3 (a
division of Pearson Penguin Canada Inc.)
Penguin Ireland, 25 St Stephen's Green, Dublin 2, Ireland (a division of Penguin Books Ltd)
Penguin Group (Australia), 250 Camberwell Road, Camberwell, Victoria 3124, Australia
(a division of Pearson Australia Group Pty Ltd)
Penguin Books India Pvt Ltd, 11 Community Centre, Panchsheel Park, New Delhi – 110 017, India
Penguin Group (NZ), 67 Apollo Drive, Rosedale, North Shore 0632, New Zealand
(a division of Pearson New Zealand Ltd)
Penguin Books (South Africa) (Pty) Ltd, 24 Sturdee Avenue, Rosebank,
Johannesburg 2196, South Africa

Penguin Books Ltd, Registered Offices: 80 Strand, London wc2r orl, England

www.penguin.com

First published by Harvill Secker, part of The Random House Group Limited 2008
Published in Penguin Books 2009

6

Copyright © David Lodge, 2008
All rights reserved

Lines from 'Clearing' by Tony Harrison (*Collected Poems*, Penguin, 2007)
are quoted by kind permission of the poet. 'Days' and four lines from 'Aubade',
by Philip Larkin (*Collected Poems*, Faber and Faber, 1988) are quoted by permission of
Faber and Faber Ltd. 'Inside Our dreams' by Jeanne Willis (*Toffee Pockets*,
Bodley Head/Red Fox, 1992) is reprinted by permission of
The Random House Group Ltd.

Set in Dante MT 11/13pt
Typeset by Palimpsest Book Production Limited, Grangemouth, Stirlingshire
Printed in England by Clays Ltd, St Ives plc

isbn: 978-0-141-03570-3

www.greenpenguin.co.uk

Dedication

Conscious that this novel, from its English title onwards, presents special problems for translators, I dedicate it to all those who, over many years, have applied their skills to the translation of my work into various languages, and especially to some who have become personal friends: Marc Amfreville, Mary Gislon and Rosetta Palazzi, Maurice and Yvonne Couturier, Armand Eloi and Beatrice Hammer, Luo Yirong, Suzanne Mayoux, Renate Orth-Guttmann, and Susumu Takagi.

D. L.

Sentence *noun*. Middle English [Old French from Latin *sententia* mental feeling, opinion, philosophical judgement, from *sentire* feel] **1**. Way of thinking, opinion, mind . . . **2b**. The declaration in a criminal court of the punishment imposed on a person pleading guilty or found guilty . . . **5**. A pithy or memorable saying, a maxim, an aphorism . . . **7** . . . A piece of writing or speech between two full stops or equivalent pauses.

The New Shorter Oxford English Dictionary

I

The tall, bespectacled, grey-haired man standing at the edge of the throng in the main room of the gallery, stooping very close to the young woman in the red silk blouse, his head lowered and angled away from her face, nodding sagely and emitting a phatic murmur from time to time, is not as you might think an off-duty priest whom she has persuaded to hear her confession in the midst of the party, or a psychiatrist conned into giving her a free consultation; nor has he adopted this posture the better to look down the front of her blouse, though this is an accidental bonus of his situation, the only one in fact. The reason for his stance is that the room is full of noise, a conversational hubbub which bounces off the hard surfaces of the ceiling, walls and floor, and swirls around the heads of the guests, causing them to shout even louder to make themselves heard. This is known to linguists as the Lombard Reflex, named after Etienne Lombard, who established early in the twentieth century that speakers increase their vocal effort in the presence of noise in the environment in order to resist degradation of the intelligibility of their messages. When many speakers display this reflex simultaneously they become, of course, their own environmental noise source, adding incrementally to its intensity. For the man now almost nuzzling the bosom of the woman in the red blouse, as he brings his right ear closer to her mouth, the noise reached some time ago a level that makes it impossible for him to hear more than the odd word or phrase of those she addresses to him. 'Side' seems to be one recurring word – or is it 'cider'? And 'flight from hell' – or was it 'cry for help'? He is, you see, 'hard of hearing', or 'hearing impaired' or, not to put too fine a point on it, deaf – not profoundly deaf, but deaf enough to make communication imperfect in most social situations and impossible in some, such as this one.

He wears a hearing aid, an expensive digital device, with little beige plastic earpieces that fit snugly in both ears like baby snails in their shells, which has a program for damping down background noise, but at the cost of also damping down foreground sounds, and at a certain level of decibels the former completely overwhelms the latter, which is now the case. It is not helpful that the woman seems to be an exception to the rule of the Lombard Reflex. Instead of raising the pitch and volume of her voice like everybody else in the room she maintains a level of utterance suitable for conversation in a quiet drawing room or a tête-à-tête in a sparsely peopled tea-shop. They have been talking, or rather *she* has been talking, for some ten minutes now, and strive as he may he cannot identify the conversational topic. Is it the art on the walls – blown-up coloured photographs of urban wasteland and rubbish tips? He thinks not, she does not glance or point at them, and the intonation of her speech, which he can just about register, does not have the characteristic declarative pattern of art-speak, or art-bollocks as he sometimes disrespectfully calls it to tease his wife. It has rather the tone of something personal, anecdotal and confidential. He glances at the woman's face to see if it gives a clue. She fixes him earnestly with her blue eyes, and pauses in her utterance as if expecting a response. 'I see,' he says, adjusting his countenance to express both thoughtful reflection and sympathy, hoping that one or the other will seem appropriate, or at least not grotesquely inappropriate, to whatever she has been saying. It seems to satisfy her, anyway, and she begins speaking again. He doesn't resume his former posture: there really is no point in aiming his right earpiece to receive her speech when the party babble is pouring into the left one, and if he should try to cover his left ear with his hand it would only produce a feedback howl from his hearing aid as well as an eccentric-looking posture. What to do now? What to say when she pauses again? It is far too late to confess, '*Look, sorry, I haven't heard a word you've*

4

said to me for the last ten minutes' (a quarter of an hour it might be by now). *'I'm deaf, you see, can't hear a thing in this din.'* She would reasonably wonder why he hadn't said so before, why he let her go on talking, nodding and murmuring as if he understood her. She would be annoyed, embarrassed, offended, and he doesn't wish to appear rude. She might be one of his wife's customers, for one thing, and for another she seems rather nice, a young woman maybe in her late twenties with bright blue eyes, a pale smooth complexion, shoulder-length flaxen hair centre-parted and straight-cut, and a naturally shapely figure – he can tell from the shadowy separation of her breasts just visible at the unbut-toned opening of her blouse that they are not artificially enhanced by silicone, or thrust forward and upward by under-wiring, but have the trembling plasticity of real unfettered flesh, with a faint surface transparency of the skin like good porcelain – and he doesn't wish to make a bad impression on a comely young woman who has taken the trouble to talk to an old fart like him-self even if it is a random encounter unlikely ever to be repeated.

She pauses again in her monologue and looks expectantly at him. 'Very interesting,' he says. 'Very interesting.' Playing for time, waiting to see if this will do, he puts his wine glass to his lips, only to discover that it is empty and that he has to tip it up into an almost vertical position and hold it there for some sec-onds in order to make the dregs of Chilean Chardonnay trickle down into his throat. The woman watches with curiosity as if she thinks he is going to perform some kind of trick, balancing the glass on his nose for instance. Her own glass of white wine is almost full, she has not taken even a sip from it since she started talking to him, so he cannot suggest they get themselves refills from the bar, while to go off on his own to recharge his glass, or to propose that she accompany him on this errand, seem equally discourteous options. Fortunately she seems to appreciate his plight – not his real plight, his total ignorance of what she has been saying, but his need for another drink – and smiling she says something with a gesture at his empty glass which he is fairly confident of interpreting as encouragement to go and get himself a refill. 'I think perhaps I will,' he says, 'Can I get you another?' Stupid question, what would she do with two glasses of white wine, one in each hand? And she is obviously not the kind of person who would eagerly gulp down one drink while you fetched her another. But she smiles again (a nice smile, disclosing a row of small even white teeth), declines with a shake of her head, and then to his dismay asks a question. He can tell it is a question by the rising intonation and the slight widening of her blue eyes and arching of her eyebrows, and it evidently demands an answer. 'Yes,' he says, taking a chance; and as she seems pleased he boldly adds: 'Absolutely.' She asks another question to which he also replies in the affirmative, and then, rather to his surprise, extends her hand. Evidently she is leaving the party. 'Very nice to have met you,' he says, taking the hand and shaking it. It is cool and slightly damp to the touch. 'What did you say your name was – I'm afraid with all this noise I didn't quite catch it.' She pronounces her name again but it is hopeless: the first name sounds faintly like 'Axe', which can't be right, and the surname is completely inaudible, but he can't ask her to repeat it *again*. 'Ah, yes,' he says, nodding, as if pleased to have pocketed the information. 'Well, it's been very interesting talking to you.'

'Who was that young blonde you were deep in conversation with?' Fred asked me in the car on the way home. She was driving because she hadn't had much to drink and I had had quite a lot.

'I've no idea,' I said. 'She told me her name, twice in fact, but I couldn't make it out. I didn't hear a word she was saying. The noise . . .'

'It's all the concrete – it makes the sound reverberate.'

'I thought she might be one of your customers.'

'No, I've never seen her before. What did you think of the exhibition?'

'Drab. Boring. Anybody with a digital camera could take those pictures. But why bother?'

'I thought they had a kind of interesting . . . sadness.'

That is a condensed account of our conversation, which actually went something like this:

'Who was that young woman you were deep in conversation with?'

'What?'

'You were deep in conversation with a young blonde.'

'I didn't see Ron. Was he there?'

'Not Ron. The blonde woman you were talking to, who was she?'

'Oh. I've no idea. She told me her name, twice in fact, but I couldn't make it out. I didn't hear a word she was saying. The noise . . .'

'It's all the concrete.'

'There's nothing wrong with the heating, in fact it's always too bloody hot for my liking.'

'No, *concrete*. The walls, the floor. It makes the sound reverberate.'

'Oh . . .'

(Pause.)

'What did you think of the exhibition?'

'I thought she might be one of your customers.'

'Who?'

'The young blonde woman.'

'Oh. No, I've never seen her before. What did you think of the exhibition?'

'What?'

'The exhibition – what did you think?'

'Drab, boring. Anyone with a digital camera could take those pictures.'

'I thought they had a kind of interesting . . . sadness.'

'Can badness be interesting?'

'Sadness, an interesting sadness. Are you wearing your hearing aid, darling?'

'Of course I am.'

7

'It doesn't seem to be working very well.'

She was absolutely right. I tapped the earpiece in my right ear with my fingernail and got a dull dead sound. The battery had packed up and I hadn't noticed. I don't know at what point in the evening it happened. Maybe that was why I didn't hear what the blonde woman was saying, though I don't think so. I think it must have happened when I went to the Gents, which was after she left. It was quiet in there and I wouldn't have registered the loss of volume, or I would have attributed it to the quietness of the Gents compared to the cacophony in the gallery, and when I went back to the party I didn't even attempt to have a conversation with anybody but pretended to be interested in the pictures, which were in fact not at all interesting, for their sadness or badness or any other quality, but merely banal.

'My battery's packed up,' I said. 'Shall I put a new one in? It's a bit tricky in the dark.'

'No, don't bother,' Fred said, as she often does these days. She'll come into my study, for instance, when I'm working on the computer, without wearing my hearing aid because it turns the soothing mutter of the keyboard into an intrusive clatter as loud as an old-fashioned upright Remington, and she'll say something to me which I don't hear, and I have to make a split second choice between either halting the conversation while I scrabble for my hearing aid pouch and insert the earpieces or trying to wing it without them, and usually I try to wing it, and a dialogue follows something like:

Fred: Murr murr murr.

Me: What?

Fred: Murr murr murr.

Me: (*playing for time*) Uh huh.

Fred: Murr murr murr.

Me: (*making a guess at the content of the message*) All right.

Fred: (*surprised*) What?

Me: What did you say?

Fred: Why did you say 'All right' if you didn't hear what I said?

8

Me: Let me get my hearing aid.
Fred: No, don't bother. It's not important.

We drove the rest of the way home in silence. I went to my study to put a new battery in my right earpiece, or 'hearing instrument' as the User's Guide rather grandiloquently calls it. I get through an amazing number of batteries because I frequently forget to switch off the hearing instruments when I put them away in their little zipped and foam-lined pouch, and then, unless Fred should happen to hear them making the high-pitched feedback noise they emit when thus enclosed and draws my attention to it, the batteries run down uselessly. This quite often happens at night if I take them out in my study or in the bathroom before going to bed and leave them there where Fred can't hear them whining to themselves like mosquitoes. It happens so often in fact, even after I have made a special effort to do the opposite, that I sometimes think there is some kind of hearing-aid imp who switches them on in the night after I have switched them off. I simply can't believe it when I open the pouch in the morning and find them switched on when I have such a clear memory of switching them off. There must be a kink in my neural pathways which makes me unconsciously switch them on again after consciously switching them off, a reflex motion of the thumb which slides the battery covers into the 'On' position even as I place them in their little nests of synthetic foam to sleep. The Bates Reflex, named after Desmond Bates, who established early in the twenty-first century that users develop an unconscious hostility towards their hearing aids which causes them to 'punish' these devices by carelessly allowing the batteries to run down. Actually it's self-punishment because the batteries are quite expensive, nearly four pounds for six. They come in a little round transparent plastic pack with six compartments, ingeniously mounted on a cardboard base like a carousel, which you rotate to expel a new battery through a hinged flap at the back. Each battery has a brown plastic tab adhering to it which stops the electricity leaking away, or so I understand, and which you must remove before inserting the battery into your hearing instrument. These sticky little wafers are quite difficult to detach from your fingers and dispose of. I tend to transfer them on to whatever surface is to hand, so my desktop, files, ringbinders and other home office utensils are covered with tiny brown spots, as if soiled with the droppings of some incontinent nocturnal rodent. The instructions on the back of the pack tell you to wait at least one minute after removing the plastic tab before inserting the battery into the hearing instrument (don't ask me why) but it often takes me longer than that to liberate myself from the tab.

When I had replaced the battery I went into the drawing room, but Fred had gone upstairs to read in bed. I knew that was what she was doing even though she hadn't said so, in the way married couples know each other's habitual intentions without needing to be informed, which is particularly useful if you happen to be deaf; in fact if she had informed me verbally of her intention I would have been more likely to get it wrong. I didn't want to join her because I can't read in bed for more than five minutes without falling asleep, and it was too early for that, I would only wake up in the small hours and lie there tossing and turning, not wanting to get up in the cold dark but unable to drop off again.

I thought about watching the *News at Ten* but the news is so depressing these days – bombings, murders, atrocities, famines, epidemics, global warming – that one shrinks from it late at night; let it wait, you feel, till the next day's newspaper and the cooler medium of print. So I came back into the study and checked my email – 'No New Messages'; and then I decided to write an account of my conversation, or rather non-conversation, with the woman at the ARC private view, which in retrospect seemed rather amusing, though stressful at the time. First I did it in the usual journal style, then I rewrote it in the third person, present tense, the kind of exercise I used to give students in my stylistics seminar. First person into third person, past tense into present tense, or vice versa. What difference does it make to the effect? Is one method more appropriate to the original experience than another, or does any method interpret rather than represent experience? Discuss.

In speech the options are more limited – though my step-grandson Daniel, Marcia's child, hasn't learned this yet. He's two years old, two and a half, and has quite a good vocabulary for his age, but he always refers to himself declaratively in the third person, present tense. When you say it's time for bed, he says, 'Daniel isn't tired.' When you say, 'Give Grandad a kiss,' he says, 'Daniel doesn't kiss granddads.' Pronouns are tricky for kids, of course, because they're shifters, as we say in the trade, their meaning depends entirely on who is using them: 'you' means you when I say it, but me when you say it. So mastery of pronouns always comes fairly late in the child's acquisition of language, but Daniel's exclusive use of the third person at his age is rather unusual. Marcia is anxious about it and asked me if I thought it was possibly a symptom of something, autism for instance. I asked her if she referred to herself in the third person when speaking to Daniel, like 'Mummy is tired', or 'Mummy has got to make the dinner', and she admitted that she did occasionally. 'You mean, it's my fault?' she said, a little resentfully. 'I mean he's imitating you,' I said. 'It's quite common. But he'll soon grow out of it.' I told her that Daniel's sentences were remarkably well-formed for his age, and that I was sure he would soon learn to use pronouns. I actually find it charming, the way he says, 'Daniel is thirsty,' 'Daniel doesn't tidy up,' 'Daniel is shy today,' with a perceptible pause for thought before he speaks. It has an almost regal gravity and formality, as if he were a little prince or dauphin. Dauphin Daniel I call him. But young parents, educated middle-class ones anyway, are very jumpy these days, they get so much information from the media about all the things that could be wrong with their child – autism, dyslexia, attention deficit disorder, allergies, obesity and so on – they're in a constant state of panic, watching their offspring like hawks for warning signs. And it's catching: I'm far more anxious about the baby Anne is expecting than I was about any of Maisie's pregnancies. Thirty-seven is late to give birth for the first time.

2

1st November, 2006. I rather enjoyed writing that piece last night, and re-reading it this morning. As aural-oral communication becomes more and more difficult, the total control one has over written discourse becomes more and more appealing, especially when the subject is deafness. So I'll go on for a bit.

I first discovered I was going deaf about twenty years ago. For some time before that I'd been aware that I was finding it increasingly difficult to hear what my students were saying, especially in seminars, with anything from twelve to twenty of them sitting round a long table. I thought it was because they mumbled – which indeed many of them do, being shy, or nervous, or unwilling to seem assertive in front of their peers – but it hadn't been a problem when I was younger. I wondered if perhaps my ears were blocked with wax, so went to my GP. He peered into my ears with a chilly steel optical instrument and said there was no build-up of wax, so I'd better have my hearing checked at the Ear, Nose and Throat department of the University Hospital.

They did an audiogram: you wear a pair of headphones and hold a press-button thingy which you squeeze when you hear a sound. The audiologist is using his apparatus out of your sight, so you can't cheat, not that there would be any point in cheating. The sounds are not words, or even phonemes, just little beeps, which get fainter and fainter, or higher and higher, until you can't hear them, like the cries of a bird spiralling up into the sky. Philip Larkin first discovered he was going deaf when he was walking in the Shetlands with Monica Jones and she remarked how beautiful the larks sounded singing overhead, and he stopped and listened but he couldn't hear them. Rather poignant, a poet finding out he's deaf in that way, especially when you think of Shelley's 'Ode to a Skylark', *'Hail to thee, blithe Spirit!'* one of the poems everybody learns by heart at school, or did before educational theory turned against memorising verse. A poet called *Lark*in, too – it's almost funny in a black way, deafness and comedy going hand in hand, as always.

Deafness is comic, as blindness is tragic. Take Oedipus, for instance: suppose, instead of putting out his eyes, he had punctured his eardrums. It would have been more logical actually, since it was through his ears that he learned the dreadful truth about his past, but it wouldn't have the same cathartic effect. It might arouse pity, perhaps, but not terror. Or Milton's Samson: *'O dark, dark, dark, amid the blaze of noon, / Irrecoverably dark, without all hope of day.'* What a heartbreaking cry of despair! *'O deaf, deaf, deaf . . .'* doesn't have the same pathos somehow. How would it go on? *'O deaf, deaf, deaf, amid the noise of noon, / Irrecoverably deaf, without all hope of sound.'* No.

Of course, you could argue that blindness is a greater affliction than deafness. If I had to choose between them, I'd go for deafness, I admit. But they don't differ only in degrees of sensory deprivation. Culturally, symbolically, they're antithetical. Tragic versus comic. Poetic versus prosaic. Sublime versus ridiculous. One of the strongest curses in the English language is 'Damn your eyes!' (much stronger than 'Fuck you!' and infinitely more satisfying – try it next time some lout in a white van nearly runs you over). 'Damn your ears!' doesn't cut it. Or imagine if the poet had written *'Drink to me only with thine ears . . .'* It's actually no more illogical than saying drink with thine eyes. Both metaphors are equally impossible concepts, in fact an ear is more like a cup than an eye, and you could conceivably drink, or at least slurp, out of an ear, though not your own of course . . . But poetical it isn't. Nor would *'Smoke gets in your ears'* be a very catchy refrain for a song. If smoke gets in your eyes when a lovely flame dies it must get in your ears too, but you don't notice and it doesn't make you cry. *'There's more in this than meets the ear'* is something Inspector Clouseau might say, not Poirot.

The blind have pathos. Sighted people regard them with compassion, go out of their way to help them, guide them across busy roads, warn them of obstacles, stroke their guide dogs. The dogs, the white sticks, the dark glasses, are visible signs of their affliction, calling forth an instant rush of sympathy. We deafies have no such compassion-inducing warning signs. Our hearing aids are almost invisible and we have no loveable animals dedicated to looking after us. (What would be the equivalent of a guide dog for the deaf? A parrot on your shoulder squawking into your ear?) Strangers don't realise you're deaf until they've been trying and failing to communicate with you for some time, and then it's with irritation rather than compassion. 'Thou shalt not curse the deaf, nor put a stumbling-block before the blind,' says the Bible (Leviticus, 19.14). Well, only a sadist would deliberately trip up a blind person, but even Fred lets out the occasional 'Bloody hell!' when she can't get through to me. Prophets and seers are sometimes blind – Tiresias for instance – but never deaf. Imagine putting your question to the Sybil and getting an irritable *'What? What?'* in reply.

It's a very unequal contest between the two organs. Eyes are the windows of the soul, they express feelings, they come in subtle, alluring colours and shades, they brim with tears, they shine and gleam and twinkle. Ears, well they're funny-looking things really, especially when they stick out, all skin and gristle, secreting wax, sprouting hair, no wonder women hang earrings on the lobes, men too of course in certain societies and periods, to distract the eye from the furry hole that leads to your brain. In fact what other function does the ear lobe have? Perhaps that's how it evolved, this otherwise useless flap of boneless tissue: prehistoric people with enough flesh on the lower rim of the ear to accommodate earrings had an advantage in the mating process, so got selected. But it would have been no advantage if the ears hadn't served their primary purpose.

> *Of all old women hard of hearing*
> *The deafest, sure was Dame Eleanor Spearing!*
> > *On her head, it is true*
> > *Two flaps there grew*
> *That served for a pair of gold rings to go through,*
> *But for any purpose of ears in a parley,*
> *They heard no more than ears of barley.*

Thomas Hood, 'The Tale of a Trumpet'. Not quite in Larkin's class – but Larkin never wrote a poem about being deaf, as far as I remember. Perhaps he found it too depressing to contemplate, though he wrote about a lot of other depressing things. I just looked up the anecdote about the larks in Andrew Motion's biography. It happened in 1959, so Larkin would have been only thirty-seven. Motion says: *'As his hearing grew weaker in the years ahead he felt more and more isolated, trapped in an incompetent body, foolish and pathetic . . . His deafness steadily darkened his melancholy.'* Yes, we know, we know. I was a bit older than him when I found out, in my mid-forties, but with more years ahead of me to feel foolish and pathetic in.

After my test I saw the ENT consultant, Mr Hopwood, a stout, moustached, bald-headed man with a slightly harassed manner, conscious no doubt of the long queue of patients sitting on moulded plastic chairs in the corridor outside. It was a hot day and he had taken off the jacket of his dark-blue pinstripe suit and was sitting in his waistcoat behind a cluttered desk. He showed me the charts the audiologist had made on graph paper, one for each ear. They looked a bit like diagrams of constellations, with straight lines joining the beeps, represented by crosses. The pattern was pretty much the same for both ears. Hopwood told me I had high-frequency deafness, the most common form of what they call 'acquired deafness' (as distinct from the congenital kind), caused by accelerated loss of the hair cells in the inner ear which convert sound waves into messages to the brain. Apparently everybody starts losing these cells from the moment they are born, but we have more than we need, some 17,000 in each ear, and it's only when we've lost about thirty per cent of them that it begins to affect our hearing, which happens to most people when they're about sixty, but to others, like Philip Larkin and me, much earlier.

This can be due to a variety of causes. The most common is trauma: exposure to excessive noise – gunfire, for instance. Lots of soldiers in the artillery suffer from high-frequency deafness in later life, especially if they were careless about wearing ear-protectors; likewise workers in very noisy industrial environments. Neither of these occupational hazards applied to me. I avoided National Service by deferring it till I'd finished my PhD, by which time it had come to an end, and I never worked in a factory. When I was attending a conference in San Francisco in the late Sixties I went to a rock concert at Fillmore West, just out of curiosity (modern jazz was my kind of syncopated music, Brubeck, the MJQ, Chico Hamilton, Miles Davis) because another chap at the conference told me it was a famous venue and he was going, so I went with him. I don't remember the name of the group, but their amplification was so loud it was actually painful. I moved back further and further in the hall and after about half an hour I walked out, I couldn't stand it any longer, and my ears buzzed for the rest of the evening. I asked Hopwood if that could have done the damage and he said he thought it was very unlikely from a single exposure, though regular clubbers and rock concert-goers were at risk from excessively loud music. So it may be a genetic weakness, though I'm not aware of any family history of premature deafness. Dad is nearly as deaf as me, but at eighty-nine he's entitled to be. When he was my age I don't remember it being a problem. In fact he went on working well into his seventies, the odd Saturday night gig in old-fashioned social clubs that still went in for ballroom dancing to a live band of elderly musicians, while the rest of the world was twisting and raving in discotheques. Though, come to think of it, being a bit deaf wasn't much of a handicap for playing in those bands – maybe it was even an advantage.

If it wasn't trauma, and it isn't genetic, the most likely cause of my deafness is some childhood illness, a virus or ear infection which irreparably damaged the hair cells. I did suffer from earache when I was a toddler, Mum told me later. 'You had mastoids,' she said – an ugly, sinister word I thought at the time, and still more now. And there were no antibiotics in the early Forties. The cause of my deafness is of academic interest, anyway (interesting that 'academic' should have that meaning of 'useless'), because it's incurable. Hopwood told me that. 'There's no cure,' he said cheerfully. 'The condition will get worse – but very gradually. You'll also experience some loss of volume at all frequencies as you get older.' 'Eventually, then,' I said, 'I'll be stone deaf?' 'Not *stone* deaf,' he said, frowning slightly as if this were a newly minted and excessively emotive metaphor. 'In theory you could suffer up to ninety per cent hearing loss, but you'll be lucky if you live that long. I wouldn't worry about it. Get yourself a hearing aid. You'll find it makes a great difference.'

I got my first hearing aid from the National Health Service, a rather clumsy device in two pieces, one about the size of a tangerine segment that fitted behind the ear, containing the microphone, amplifier, battery and controls, with a little transparent plastic tube attached which conveyed the sound to the other bit, a custom-made transparent plastic mould seated in the ear. Putting it all in place was tedious, and it was fairly visible unless you grew your hair very long over the ears, which would have been easy in the Sixties, but looked a bit eccentric by the mid-Eighties. Also if you wear glasses, as I do, the space behind your ear gets rather congested. The arm of the spectacles can squeeze the plastic tube so that the sound is cut off, or removing your glasses can inadvertently remove your hearing aid. Once I whipped off my spectacles in the street to put on a pair of prescription sunglasses and sent my hearing aid flying into the road, where it was run over by a Parcelforce van. The National Health Service would have replaced it, but I decided to go private and get one of the in-the-ear type, then something of a novelty, which are miracles of electronic micro-engineering, all the components being contained in a moulded earpiece not much bigger than an earplug. But you can still have misadventures with these, because they're so small. A year or two ago when Fred was driving the car I took out an earpiece to change the battery and dropped it down between the seat and the door. We were on a motorway so Fred couldn't stop. I groped for the earpiece under my seat and felt my fingers touch it but somehow I managed to push it through a small hole in the metal tracks on which the seat slides backwards and forwards and it disappeared into a cavity under the floor. I took the car into the service centre the next day and they had to remove the whole seat and part of the floor to recover it from the chassis. The man behind the counter in Reception was grinning from ear to ear as he gave me the bill and, sealed in a transparent sachet, the little plastic earpiece with a mechanic's oily finger-print on it. 'This job was a first for us,' he said. It cost me eighty-five pounds, but I had no option since each hearing instrument costs over a thousand. I use two, now, one in each ear. In the past I only needed one. My relationship with hearing aids has been a steady escalation of cost and technical refinement.

The first in-the-ear one I bought had a fiddly volume control like a tiny studded wheel which you twisted with the tip of your forefinger, as if trying to insert a screw into your head, but they got more and more sophisticated over the years, and my latest one is digital, has three programs (for quiet conditions, noisy conditions and loop), adjusts itself automatically on the first two, or can be manually adjusted with a remote control concealed in my watch (very James Bond). Unfortunately the technology seems to have hit a ceiling and it's unlikely that there's going to be a great improvement in the near future. I read a report in a newspaper a year or two ago which gave me a spasm of hope, about people having their hearing restored by new techniques of surgical implants, but when I asked my GP about this treatment he told me that it only worked with a different type of deafness from mine, otosclerosis, where one of the bones in the middle ear that transmit vibrations to the inner ear becomes fixed, and can be artificially replaced. He asked around and discovered that experimental work is being done with implants in the inner ear, but with limited success, and you'd have to be in a pretty bad way to even try it. In short, there's no cure for my kind of deafness, as Hopwood told me twenty years ago.

As soon as he said 'high-frequency deafness' I knew it was bad news. 'So that's why I'm missing consonants,' I said. 'That's right,' he said, looking impressed. 'How did you know?' 'I'm a linguist,' I said. 'Oh, are you? What languages?' 'Only the one,' I said. (It's a common mistake.) 'I'm in Linguistics. Applied Linguistics to be exact.' 'You understand the problem then?' he said.

I did. Consonants are voiced at a higher frequency than vowels. I could hear vowels perfectly well – still can. But it's consonants that we mainly depend on to distinguish one word from another. *'"Did you say* pig *or* fig?" *said the Cat. "I said* pig," *replied Alice.'* Maybe the Cheshire Cat was a bit deaf: it wasn't sure whether Alice had used a bi-labial plosive or a labiodental fricative the first time she pronounced the word, and being a well-brought-up Victorian middle-class little girl she would have spoken very clearly. 'F' is called a labiodental fricative because you produce it by bringing your top teeth into contact with your bottom lip and allowing some air to escape between them. It's also called a continuant because you can continue making the sound as long as you have breath: *ffffffffffffffffffffff* . . . though I can't imagine why you would want to, unless perhaps you started to say 'Fuck' and thought better of it. I have a smattering of phonetics, although it's not my field.

I was at a party a few years ago, not as noisy as the one last night, but bad enough, and I overheard a man enthusing about a book he was reading called *Being Deaf*. It sounded like just the book for me, a self-help manual I presumed, but I didn't like to barge into the conversation demanding the bibliographical details. The man was talking to a girl who was looking admiringly into his eyes and nodding eager agreement, and he left the party early (with the girl) before I had an opportunity to speak to him. So the next day I went to Waterstone's to try and get the book. 'What was the author's name?' the assistant asked. 'I think it was Grace,' I said. It turned out to be Crace, Jim Crace, and the book was a novel called *Being Dead*.

Often only the context allows me to distinguish between 'deaf' and 'death' or 'dead', and sometimes the words seem inter-changeable. Deafness is a kind of pre-death, a drawn-out intro-duction to the long silence into which we will all eventually lapse. *'To every man upon this earth, / Deaf cometh soon or late,'* Macaulay might have written. But not Dylan Thomas, *'After the first deaf, there is no other.'* There are lots of others, stages of auricular decay, like a long staircase leading down into the grave.

> *Down among the deaf men, down among the deaf men,*
> *Down, down, down, down;*
> *Down among the deaf men let him lie!*

3

2nd November. An odd thing happened this morning. I was sitting over the remains of my breakfast, in my dressing gown, reading the newspaper. It's one of the few perks of retirement I really enjoy, the leisurely breakfast, the unhurried perusal of the *Guardian* over a third cup of tea . . . After that the day tends to drag rather. Fred was bustling in and out of the kitchen, fully dressed, getting ready to go out. She had an early manicure appointment before going to the shop. I had taken in that information because I was wearing my hearing aid. I really prefer not to at breakfast because it amplifies the noise of eating corn-flakes and toast inside my head with an effect like dinosaurs crunching bones in Surroundsound, but I bear it, if we get up at the same time, for the sake of matrimonial harmony. Fred was making out a list of things for me to buy at the supermarket when the telephone rang. 'Answer that, would you, darling?' she said. She frequently addresses me as 'darling', though not neces-sarily with affection. In fact I don't know anyone who can utter that term of endearment with so many different tones of hos-tile implication, including impatience, disapproval, pity, irony, incredulity, despair and boredom. This, though, was a faintly ingratiating 'darling'.

'You know it's for you,' I sighed, folding the newspaper and getting reluctantly to my feet. I was in the middle of a rather interesting if depressing article about the ageing populations of the developed world, who combine increased life expectancy due to advances in medicine with a diminishing capacity to enjoy it because of physical and mental deterioration. 'Nobody phones *me* at this hour of the day,' I said. Very few people phone me at any hour, actually, since I retired.

'If it's Jakki, tell her I'm busy. And remind her I'll be late because I'm getting my nails done,' Fred said, frowning over her list. Jakki is Fred's business partner and one of the many things about her that irritate me is her propensity to make unnecessary phone calls. Another is the way she spells her name.

I lifted the wall-mounted phone off its cradle and put it to my ear, immediately producing a howl of feedback. I always forget that ordinary phones produce that effect if you're wearing a hearing aid, or else I forget I'm wearing a hearing aid when I pick up an ordinary phone. Which was the case this morning? I forget. I prised the earpiece out of my right ear and dropped it in my haste, exclaiming 'Fuck!' as it hit the vinyl-tiled floor. The last time I did that the hearing instrument was a write-off. My insurance policy covered it, but if I make another thousand-pound claim the company might refuse to renew it. Fortunately it seemed that no damage had been done on this occasion: the device whistled in the palm of my hand as I picked it up, indicating that it was still working. I switched it off, slipped it into my dressing-gown pocket and put the phone to my empty ear. I was conscious of Fred observing me impatiently like the teacher of a chronically clumsy infant pupil. 'Hallo,' I said.

'Is that how you usually answer the phone?' said a faint female voice. '"Fuck", and then "hallo"?'

'No, I'm sorry,' I said. 'I dropped my – I dropped something just as I picked up the . . . Is that Jakki?'

'No, it's . . .'

I didn't catch the name. 'I'm sorry – who?'

She said something that sounded like 'Axe'.

I said: 'Look, this phone's no good, I'll go into my study. Hang on.' I have a phone in my study specially designed for the deaf. You can use it while wearing a hearing aid in the loop mode, and you can increase the volume if necessary. I replaced the kitchen phone on its cradle and made for the door.

'Who is it?' Fred asked.

'I don't know – not Jakki.'

'You've cut them off anyway, darling.' (This was a faintly sarcastic 'darling'.)

'No, I haven't.' I have explained this before to Fred – that both parties have to put their phones down to break the connection – but she doesn't believe me.

'Well, if it's for me and it's urgent you can get me on my mobile,' Fred said. 'I simply must go this minute. I'll leave the list here on the worktop.' She added something about melons which I didn't catch because I had only one earpiece in place and was nearly out of the kitchen, with my back to her. I hoped it wasn't important.

I sat down at my desk, inserted my right earpiece, set it in the loop mode and picked up the phone. 'Hallo,' I said.

'Oh, I thought you'd cut me off,' said the voice. It was still faint, so I turned up the volume.

'No. Sorry about all the confusion. I have a hearing problem, it makes phones difficult. I'm afraid I didn't get your name.'

'It's Alex. We met at the ARC gallery the other evening.' She spoke with a perceptible transatlantic accent.

'Oh yes, I remember.'

'But you didn't remember our appointment.'

'What appointment?' I said, with an internal flutter of panic.

'You were going to give me some advice about my research.'

'Was I? Where? When?'

'Don't you remember *anything*?' she said, with understandable asperity.

'Well, to be honest, I didn't hear much. It was frightfully noisy, that room, it's all the concrete, and as I said, I have a hearing problem . . .'

'I see.'

'I'm terribly sorry. It must seem very rude of me but . . .'

'All right, I forgive you. When shall we meet then? Tomorrow?'

I said I couldn't meet her tomorrow because I was going to London to see my father, and then it would be the weekend, and she was tied up on Monday so eventually we agreed on the following Tuesday afternoon, at three.

'The same place?' she said.

'What was that?'

'The ARC gallery café,' she said.

'It's rather noisy,' I said. 'The tiled floor and those Formica-topped tables . . . What about the University? The Senior Common Room in the –'

'No, I don't want to meet you at the University,' she said emphatically. 'If you want somewhere quiet, I have an apartment just minutes away from the ARC.'

As I wondered and hesitated about this proposal, she gave me the address, and I wrote it down.

'What is your research about?' I said.

'You really do have a hearing problem, don't you? I'll tell you again on Tuesday,' she said, and terminated the call.

When I went back into the kitchen, Fred had gone. I brought the kettle to the boil, freshened the teapot, poured another cup and picked up the *Guardian* again, but I couldn't get back into the article about ageing, or into anything else. Marshall McLuhan said somewhere (McLuhan, how that dates me!) that we don't read newspapers in an orderly systematic way, like a book, we *scan* them, our eyes skipping from one column to another and back again, but mine were twitching all over the place, and my hands turned the pages restlessly until I found myself staring at the back page, a full-page ad for cheap broadband, without any memory of what had preceded it. The call had disturbed me, for several reasons. It was completely unexpected; and that I had apparently made an appointment to meet this woman to discuss her research without the slightest awareness of doing so was not only deeply embarrassing but also a depressing index of the extent of my deafness. What kind of research could it be – something to do with linguistics, presumably. But how did she know that was my field? I didn't recall telling her. I didn't even recall telling her my name, though I suppose I must have done so, since she found my telephone number. We are in the book and there is only one 'Bates D. S., Prof.' in it.

I was conscious that Fred had left the house without knowing the identity of the caller, and I am conscious now, as I write this late at night in my study, that she still doesn't know. If she had asked me on her return home this afternoon I would have told her of course, but she didn't. She asked me if I had remembered to get a Galia melon. I said, 'No, I got cantaloupe instead, they were two for the price of one.' That was my excuse, thought up on the spur of the moment, pretending that I overrode her instruction for reasons of economy, when in fact I hadn't heard the instruction, which had been, I inferred, '*Only get a melon if they have Galias.*' She said: 'We don't *need* two melons, darling, we'll never eat them before one goes bad, especially cantaloupes.' She had evidently forgotten all about the call in the morning, and in the ill-humour that followed this little dispute over melons I didn't feel like reminding her, or telling her who it was from. In fact, I knew who was calling as soon as I heard the voice on the phone say a name that sounded like 'Axe', but when Fred said, 'Who is it?' as I made for my study to take the call I replied, 'I don't know.' Why was that? Because I wasn't in fact absolutely sure? Or because I wanted to find out why 'Axe' was phoning, and have a little time to think about it, before telling Fred? Well, I've had all day to think about it and I still haven't told Fred. It seems to me that I have somehow compromised myself by agreeing to go to the woman's flat – not that I suppose she has amorous designs on me, I have no illusions on that score – but whatever favour she intends to ask will be more difficult to refuse in her own home than on neutral, public ground, and the ARC café is probably not all that noisy in mid-afternoon. I would have phoned her to change the venue back again if I knew her number – but I don't, nor do I have any way of discovering it. I tried dialling 1471, but '*The caller has withheld the number.*'

Apart from that unsettling little episode it's been an ordinary sort of retirement day. I did the shopping at Sainsbury's in the morning. When I'd unpacked the bags and put away the food I had my lunch (Covent Garden asparagus soup, bread and cheese with salad, and an apple) and listened to *The World at One* on Radio Four. I can only listen to the kitchen radio when I'm alone in the house because I have to have the volume turned up so high. Then I sat down in the lounge with the G2 section of the *Guardian*, habitually reserved for this time, and fell asleep over it for half an hour, as I usually do. Then I walked into the University for the exercise, and checked my mailbox in the Arts Faculty office, which contained a publisher's catalogue, an invitation to an Inaugural Lecture by a new professor in Theology, 'The Problem of Petitionary Prayer', and an appeal from a charity raising money for earthquake relief. I had a cup of tea in the common room and read last week's *TLS*, glancing up every time the swing doors creaked open, but nobody whom I recognised came in. It was the middle of the afternoon, when most people would be teaching or in meetings. There were just a few retired codgers like myself dotted round the room, slumped in armchairs, looking with mute resentment over their newspapers and magazines at a group of secretaries and technicians chatting and laughing in one corner. In the past they wouldn't have been allowed in here, but the passage of time has eroded the old caste distinctions of academic life.

It was my turn to cook the evening meal so I didn't linger in the common room. It was exactly four o'clock as I made my way out of the building, and doors opened behind and before me, discharging salvos of vocal babble and the noise of chair-legs scraping on wooden floors. Students poured out of seminar rooms and lecture theatres, swarming on the landings, cascading down the staircases, swinging their rucksacks and briefcases, chattering and calling out to each other, releasing all the pent-up energy and frustration and boredom of the past hour, or perhaps, who knows, the awe and excitement of an inspiring educational experience. They carried me along like a river in spate, indifferent to my presence, oblivious of my identity. I floated on their tide like a piece of academic wreckage, until they spilled and spread out over the ground-floor lobby as far as the revolving door, which expelled me into the damp November air. The sun was already low in the western sky, sinking in an orange haze of pollution behind the Mech.Eng. block and silhouetting the workmen mending the leaky roof of our prize-winning Education building. I feel a fit of the third person coming on.

It struck him as he walked across the campus towards the main gate that if he had carried on at the University until the usual retirement age of sixty-five this would have been the first term of his last academic year. He wondered nowadays, with increasing frequency, if he had done the right thing, taking early retirement four years ago. At the time it had seemed a very attractive proposition. He was finding teaching increasingly difficult because of his deafness – not just in seminars, but when giving lectures too, because he believed in interactive lecturing. It had always seemed to him that the typical humanities lecture – an uninterrupted discourse of about fifty minutes duration, often read from the page with lowered eyes in a dull monotone – was the most ineffective teaching method ever devised. There was some excuse for it before the invention of printing, but even the ancient Greeks used a dialogic form of oral instruction. Experiments had demonstrated that the average attention span for receiving continuous speech from one speaker is twenty minutes and that it diminishes the more closely the discourse resembles written prose, with its greater density of information and reduced redundancy. It was necessary therefore to break up the flow of information, to pause and recap and reinforce – and he didn't mean by this the tedious practice, especially dear to management consultants, of projecting a summary of one's lecture on to a screen and reading it aloud, as if the auditors were unable to read it for themselves. Q&A was the way to do it. He encouraged students to raise their hands in the middle of his lectures if they didn't understand something, and he would ask them questions himself occasionally to keep them on their toes, but the method depended on his being able to hear them, so he used it less and less as time went on. In seminars he was aware that he was talking far too much himself because it was easier than straining to hear what the students were saying. Meetings became stressful too, for the same reason, and there seemed to be more and more of them in the 1990s – Departmental meetings, Faculty boards, Senate meetings, and subcommittees and working parties attached to all of those – as the bureaucratic octopus tightened its tentacles on academic life. More and more he found himself struggling to pick up the gist of an argument, falling silent, afraid to intervene in case he had got the wrong end of the stick, eventually giving up altogether and falling into a bored reverie – unless of course he was chairing the meeting himself. Then he would sometimes catch the ghost of a smile on someone's lips or an exchange of amused glances across the table and realise that he had misunderstood something or made an inapposite remark, and some friendly colleague or the Departmental secretary would tactfully rescue him.

So when he was offered early retirement it seemed too good an opportunity to miss: a full pension straight away, and freedom to do his own research untrammelled by the duties of teaching and administration. It came about because of one of the periodic organisational upheavals to which the University's senior management had become addicted. It had been decided that the Linguistics department, of which he was Head, was too small to be cost-effective as an independent unit, and that it should be merged with English. Staff in Linguistics were offered the alternative options of transferring to another department if they could find one that was willing to have them, or severance on enhanced terms, or early retirement if they were old enough to qualify. His colleagues in Linguistics were up in arms about the proposal, claiming variously that it was a covert way for the University to shed staff, or a cunning plot devised by English to boost their submission to the next Research Assessment Exercise. But he told them resistance was useless. He recognised the logic of the proposal, because several people on the Language side of the English department did work very similar to that of himself and his colleagues. Personally he had no objection in principle to working in an English department. His own first degree had been in English Language and Literature, and although he had taken all the language options in the course, and switched to linguistics as a postgraduate, he had always made extensive use of literary texts in his teaching and research, and he still read poetry for pleasure, which couldn't be said for many people, including some who taught courses on it. There was however a certain loss of prestige and independence entailed in the plan which made the prospect uninviting. Though he was finding the responsibilities of being the head of his department increasingly irksome, he was not sure he would relish being just one professor among several in English. As a newcomer he would be obliged to be cooperative and accommodating about what he taught, so probably wouldn't be able to give his third-year seminar course on literary stylistics because that was the speciality of Butterworth, the youngish professor who was the rising star of the English Language sub-department. Putting all these considerations together the conclusion seemed obvious that early retirement would be the best option for himself, and accordingly he took it.

At first it was very enjoyable, like a long sabbatical, but after eighteen months or so his freedom from routine tasks and duties began to pall. He missed the calendar of the academic year which had given his life a shape for such a long time, its passage marked by reassuringly predictable events: the arrival of excited and expectant freshers every autumn; the Department Christmas party with its traditional sketches by students mimicking the mannerisms and favourite jargon of members of staff; the reading week in the spring term when they took the second year to a residential conference centre in the Lake District; the examiners' meetings in the summer term when, sitting round a long table heaped with marked scripts and extended essays, they calculated and classified the Finals results like gods dispensing rewards and punishments to mortals; and finally the degree congregation itself, processing to organ music in the Assembly Hall, listening to the University Orator fulsomely summarise the achievements of honorary graduands, shaking hands afterwards with proud parents and their begowned children, sipping fruit punch under the marquee erected on the Round Lawn, after which all dispersed to a well-earned long vacation. He missed the rhythm of the academic year as a peasant might miss differences between the seasons if they were suddenly withdrawn; and he found he missed too the structure of the academic week, the full diary of teaching assignments, postgraduate supervisions, essay marking, committee meetings, interviews, and deadlines for this and that required report, tasks he used to grumble about but the completion of which, however trivial and ephemeral they were, gave a kind of low-level satisfaction, and ensured that one never, ever, had to confront the question: *what shall I do with myself today?* In retirement, he confronted it every morning as soon as he woke.

There was his research, of course: he had envisaged that that was how he would mainly fill his days in retirement. But to his dismay he soon found that he had no real appetite to pursue it. He still found linguistics a fascinating subject – how could one ever lose interest in it? As he used to tell the first-year students in his introductory lecture of welcome, 'Language is what makes us human, what distinguishes us from animals on the one hand and machines on the other, what makes us self-conscious beings, capable of art, science, the whole of civilisation. It is the key to understanding everything.' His own field was, broadly speaking, discourse: language above the level of the sentence, language in use, *langue* approached via *parole* rather than the other way round. It was probably the most fertile and productive area of the discipline in recent times: historical philology was out of fashion and structural and transformational linguistics had lost their allure since people had come to realise the futility of trying to reduce the living and always changing phenomenon of language to a set of rules illustrated by contextless model sentences often invented for the purpose. 'Every utterance or written sentence *always* has a context, is always in some sense referring to something already said and inviting a response, is always designed to *do* something to somebody, a reader or a listener. Studying this phenomenon is sometimes called pragmatics, sometimes stylistics. Computers enable us to do it with unprecedented rigour, analysing digitised databases of actual speech and writing – generating a whole new sub-discipline, corpus linguistics. A comprehensive term for all this work is discourse analysis. We live in discourse as fish live in water. Systems of law consist of discourse. Diplomacy consists of discourse. The beliefs of the great world religions consist of discourse. And in a world of increasing literacy and multiplying media of verbal communication – radio, television, the Internet, advertising, packaging, as well as books, magazines and newspapers – discourse has come more and more to dominate even the non-verbal aspects of our lives. We *eat* discourse (mouthwatering menu-language, for instance, like "flame-roasted peppers drizzled with truffle oil") we *drink* discourse ("hints of tobacco, vanilla, chocolate and ripe berries in this feisty Australian Shiraz"); we *look* at discourse (those minimalist paintings and cryptic installations in galleries that depend entirely on curators' and critics' descriptions of them for their existence as art); we even have sex by enacting the discourses of erotic fiction and sex manuals. To understand culture and society you have to be able to analyse their discourses.' (Thus Professor Bates, giving his introductory pep talk to the first year, throwing in a reference to sex to capture the attention of even the most bored and sceptical student, the one with indifferent A-level grades who had really wanted to do Media Studies, which was oversubscribed, so had switched to Linguistics at the clearing stage of admissions.)

He had not lost faith in the value of discourse analysis, and he still had original ideas for doing it from time to time, but the thought of putting them into a form acceptable to the academic profession, of obtaining data, or setting up an experiment, and reading all the relevant literature, and writing an article with footnotes and references acknowledging the work of other scholars in the same field, and then sending it off to the editors of jour-nals, and waiting weeks for them to have it refereed, and then emending it in the light of the referees' comments, and then sending it back and correcting the proofs and waiting months for it to appear in the journal – just thinking of all the effort that would be required to complete such a project generated a kind of proleptic mental fatigue so overwhelming that he invariably abandoned it before he had properly begun. An article of this kind would probably be read by only a few hundred people, if you were lucky, which was incentive enough if you cared what they thought of it, if it enhanced your standing in your peer group and contributed usefully to your Department's RAE rating (as Head of Linguistics he had felt obliged to give a lead in this respect); but once you retired, the professional incentive melted away. Needless to say there was no economic incentive: academic journals did not pay their contributors, and even if you were for-tunate enough to have the article reprinted in a book the permis-sion fees were modest. There had been a time when he made a little extra money as a consultant, acting as an expert witness in cases that involved linguistic evidence – interpreting covertly recorded conversations, determining the authorship or authentic-ity of documents, and suchlike – and he had enjoyed this work as well as profited from it. But since a humiliating experience in court in the first year of his retirement, when he had difficulty hearing the questions put to him by his own side's barrister in a thick Scottish accent, and the opposing QC seized the opportun-ity to question his competence to give an opinion on a recorded telephone conversation which was at the heart of the case – since that occasion, which still made him twitch and grimace when he recalled it, he had received very few offers of such work, and those he had declined for fear of repeating the experience. Apart from his pension, the only income he received was from the steadily declining royalties of a textbook, which he privately referred to as *Discourse Analysis for Dummies*, first published some twenty-five years ago.

It was fortunate therefore that Winifred's business began to be profitable at just about the time that he retired. A tax-free bond linked to the FTSE-100 index which her first husband had purchased in her name in some fit of generosity or remorse, or perhaps as a tax reduction device, matured and yielded a large lump sum which she used to start up an interior design and soft furnishings business with her Health Club friend Jakki, who had a diploma in textiles from Manchester Polytechnic, and some experience of spreadsheets and computerised accounting from working in the office of her husband's Japanese car franchise before she divorced him (obtaining a generous settlement which provided her stake in the business). Winifred's qualifications for the enterprise were more nebulous: one half of a Combined Honours degree in Art History, and an amateur enthusiasm for decorating and furnishing her own home, but in due course she showed an aptitude for retail trade that surprised Desmond. It was an opportune time to discover it. In the Nineties the northern city which had seemed so dour and drab to him and Maisie when they first came to it, and whose native citizens traditionally prided themselves on their frugality and thrift, was overtaken by the global craze for consumption. Shops with internationally famous names opened branches there, and new malls sprang up to accommodate them along with the national chain stores – rather too many malls all at once, in fact. Fred and Jakki were able to lease a spacious unit in the city centre at a very reasonable rent from developers desperately anxious to fill the space (nothing looks less inviting to punters than a row of vacant shops). It was on the ground floor, so that anybody who entered the Rialto mall from the street, enticed by gleaming vistas of stainless steel, ceramic tile and plate glass, or by the soothing murmur of muzak and tinkling water features, had to pass the frontage of *Décor* (as it was called – Jakki's suggestion of 'Swish Style' fortunately having been discarded) on their way to the escalators which wafted them to the higher levels of the building. In spite of this location, however, *Décor* struggled to break even for two or three years, until a sought-after and very expensive hairdresser moved his operation into the mall on the first floor. His clientele – women from the affluent outer suburbs or green-belt villages, with time to spare and money to spend on beautifying themselves and their homes – were just the right kind of customers for *Décor*. Winifred and Jakki specialised in quality imported fabrics for curtains, blinds, cushions, bedspreads, etc., but they also displayed works of art by local artists – paintings, prints, ceramics, jewellery and small sculptures – which were available for purchase. If these sold the shop took forty per cent, and if they didn't they contributed eye-catching decor to *Décor* for free. The posh suburban women would pause to glance with interest into the shop as they passed its front window on their way to have their hair done, and drop in on·their way back to browse among the fabrics and *objets d'art*. Winifred and Jakki installed a small but perfectly formed Italian coffee machine to serve them with complimentary espressos and lattes, after which they invariably purchased something, if it was only a piece of chic costume jewellery or a unique handmade greetings card. The business prospered. *Décor* was featured in the local paper in a gushing article, illustrated with flattering colour photographs of its smiling proprietors. They were able to employ a young woman just out of art college to help look after the shop and came to an arrangement with a reliable self-employed handy-man called Ron to provide a measuring and fitting service for their clients. The cutting and stitching of the soft furnishings was con-tracted out to a women's cooperative of seamstresses made redundant by the decline of the city's clothing industry. They did excellent work.

While he was still employed himself Desmond was amused and pleased by his wife's success in her late entrepreneurial career. If there was a slight decline in domestic comforts as a result of her busy life – more prepared food from the supermarket for dinner, an occasional shortage of clean socks and laundered shirts – that was a small price to pay for the satisfaction she obviously derived from it, and his own social life was enlivened by contact with new people and places through association with her. Winifred had presence and confidence, bred in the bone and polished by private education, which had been suppressed by her unhappy first marriage but now revived in her mature years. She became by tacit consent the senior partner in the business, although she and Jakki had invested equal amounts in it, by virtue of her maturer years and social poise: and in due course she became something of a figure in the local community, invited to sit on boards and committees connected with the arts, which in turn generated invitations to private views, first nights, charity concerts, festival openings, and parties and receptions connected with these events, in which Desmond was naturally included. Sometimes he encountered the Vice Chancellor or other senior figures in the University hierarchy on such occasions and observed that they regarded him with a new respect. The VC began to address him by his first name, and to ask after his 'good lady' when encountered on campus. They were invited to the occasional private dinner party at the VC's residence.

His retirement, however, put the whole phenomenon in a different and less agreeable perspective, and shifted the balance of their marriage. His career was over while Winifred's was steaming ahead, and she now brought considerably more money into the household than he did. Her days were brimming with activity while he struggled to fill his own with routine tasks like shopping, or other errands undertaken more for exercise than need. When he accompanied her to this or that social event he sometimes felt like a royal consort escorting a female monarch, walking a pace or two behind her with his hands joined behind his back, a vague unfocused smile on his face. The social events themselves had become more of an ordeal than a pleasure because of the deterioration of his hearing, and there were times when he thought of refusing to go to them any longer, but when he contemplated the consequences of such a decision the prospect filled him with a kind of terror: more empty hours to fill, sitting alone at home, with a book or the telly. So he clung on grimly to the social-cultural merry-go-round, simulating an interest and enthusiasm he did not really feel.

It's the sitting alone I dread, not the book and the telly in themselves. Print and television are the only media that I can still truly enjoy – print for obvious reasons, and television because of subtitles and headphones. Going to the theatre, for instance, is fraught with difficulties. Most theatres have infrared systems with headsets available, but they vary a lot in efficiency and even when they work the voices have a thin, distant timbre, as if you are listening to the performance through a telephone on stage that has been left off the hook. It's usually preferable to sit in the front row and rely on your own hearing aid, but then you risk getting a crick in your neck from holding your chin up at an angle of forty-five degrees for two or three hours, and being sprayed with the actors' spittle in scenes of high emotion. Also Fred reasonably complains that they always seem to be over-acting when you are sitting that close, so we rarely do. If the dialogue has a lot of unfamiliar dialect or regional accents then it doesn't matter where you sit or what kind of hearing aid you use: you'll miss most of the consonants as usual, and the vowels will all be unfamiliar, so you might as well be listening to Hungarian. Theatre-in-the-round is equally hopeless. I never did see the point of making actors turn their backs on a substantial section of the audience while they're speaking, even when my hearing was good, but now it's like listening to a play through a door which keeps opening and shutting. But the most exasperating thing about going to the theatre, even if the play is in standard English and performed on a proscenium stage, is missing the jokes. I'll be following the dialogue perfectly well and then suddenly one of the characters says something which makes the audience roar with laughter, but I missed it. The reason being that lines are only funny when they are unexpected as well as relevant, so I can't anticipate them or infer what was said from the context. This can happen repeatedly all through a play, and is incredibly frustrating: comprehensible but banal exchanges of speech are punctuated by apparently witty and amusing lines which I don't hear. Sometimes after such an evening I buy the playtext and read it to discover what I missed, thus experiencing the work in two different forms, once as theatre of the absurd and again as well-made play. Occasionally I read the text in advance of going to the theatre: then I get all the jokes, but of course they aren't funny any more, because I'm expecting them.

Going to the cinema is no less frustrating, except for foreign films which have subtitles; but there are not many of those which you can't wait to see, and most will turn up on television eventually. The films which Fred wants to see because everybody is talking about them are nearly all British or American, and I reckon that I miss between fifty and eighty per cent of the dialogue in most of them, because the characters have regional accents (Glaswegian is worst), or the actors drawl and mumble in Method style, or the music and other background noise on the soundtrack overwhelm the words, or a combination of all those things. When we saw *Brokeback Mountain,* for instance, I completely missed the significance of the scene at the end when the cowboy finds his old shirt in the closet of his dead buddy's bedroom, because I didn't catch the word 'shirt' in his line when they came down from the mountain much earlier in the story and he said he must have left it behind. In fact the other guy had taken it surreptitiously as a sentimental memento of their homosexual idyll on the mountain, as the cowboy realises in the wordless scene when, visiting the bereaved parents, he discovers his shirt in the closet. Fred had to explain all this to me in the car on the way home. She often has to explain such things to me on the way home from the theatre or cinema. It's got to a point where I am reluctant to offer any opinion at all on what we have just seen in case I reveal some ludicrous and humiliating misunderstanding of a basic element of the plot.

I discovered recently that there are occasional performances in local cinemas of new feature films with subtitles for the hearing-impaired, listed on the Internet, but they are put on at very antisocial times, like eleven o'clock on a weekday morning, when Fred is either unable or unwilling to keep me company. I went to see a subtitled Woody Allen movie at such an hour, in an almost deserted multiplex on the outskirts of the city, sitting in the middle of a huge auditorium all on my own, and have not repeated the experiment. An empty cinema has a depressing effect on the viewer: better to wait and see the movie on TV.

Television is the saviour of the deaf. How did they ever manage without it? Most networked programmes, including old films, have subtitles which you can access through Teletext; even live transmissions, like news bulletins, have subtitles, though if you have any hearing at all it's distracting because the text runs a few seconds behind the speech and often contains grotesque mistakes (like the weather forecast for 'the aisle of man' last night). Alternatively you can use headphones, either wired or infrared, which are far more effective than the headsets they lend you at the theatre, and have an independent volume control which means you can turn up the sound without deafening other people watching with you, or watch on your own with the loudspeakers mute. Not that this arrangement is without its social disadvantages. If your partner should wish to share a comment on the programme with you, or to convey some other message, she must wave her hand to attract your attention, and then you must take off the headset and insert your hearing aid to receive the message, and then remove the hearing aid before donning the headphones again. When this procedure is required very frequently both parties are likely to become irritable.

For programmes I'm really interested in I prefer to use both headphones *and* subtitles, on the belt-and-braces principle, because I still miss occasional words and phrases through the 'phones, and the subtitles don't always reproduce the speech with total accuracy. Sometimes the subtitles abbreviate the dialogue so as not to lag behind or take up too much space on the screen. I have noticed a curious and interesting phenomenon in this connection: when I watch using both headphones and subtitles together I hear spoken words and phrases which are *missing* from the subtitles, which I'm sure I would not have heard using the headphones alone. Presumably my brain is continuously checking the two channels of communication against each other and, when they don't match, the word or phrase missing from the subtitle is foregrounded and somehow becomes more audible in consequence. It might be worth writing up for a psycholinguistics journal if I could be bothered. But I can't.

4

4th November. This seems to be turning into some kind of journal, or notes for an autobiography, or perhaps just occupational therapy.

I went to London to see Dad yesterday, a duty visit which I make every four weeks or so. If I describe this one in some detail it will serve as a record of most of the others, since the routine seldom varies. It was a long exhausting day. While Mum was alive I often stayed the night with them when academic business took me to London, and I kept up this practice for a few years after she died, but now when I make these trips to see Dad I prefer to return the same day. I leave home early in the morning – with my Senior Citizens railcard I can get a Saver ticket even at peak hours – so as to get to Brickley in time to take Dad out to lunch, then I spend the afternoon with him and leave after tea to catch an evening train back home. He always says, 'Why don't you stay the night, son?' and I always say, 'No, I can't, Dad, I'm too busy.' And he says, 'I thought you were retired,' and I say, 'I'm still doing research,' and he nods, acquiescent if a little disappointed. Though he argues the toss with me on every other subject, my professional life is a mystery to him which he treats with respectful deference. He never comments on or asks about the inscribed publications I have sent him over the years, but they have an honoured place in the glass-fronted bookcase in the front room, and I have overheard him boasting to total strangers encountered in shops or on buses about his son the professor. So the invocation of my 'research' is always a winning card to play when the question of staying overnight comes up. The fact is that I shrink from sleeping in the sagging, lumpy and always slightly damp bed in the back bedroom which was my room as a boy, and sharing the cheerless bathroom and smelly toilet (the lino-tiled floor reeks of pee because Dad's aim is not as good as it used to be), and making my breakfast in the cramped kitchenette where everything is covered with a film of grease – the chairs, table, plates, cutlery, cups and saucers, toaster, saucepans, work surfaces, everything – from the daily precipitation of molecules of burned cooking fat. The house has never looked really clean since Mum died thirteen years ago, but it's gone steeply downhill since Irena, Dad's Polish home help, got sick and retired, because he won't have anyone else. The local council tried sending replacements, but he suspected them all of trying to steal his 'things' and the money he's got hidden under the floorboards in various places, and told them not to come back, so eventually the council stopped sending them and he won't let me find him somebody privately even though I said I'd pay for it.

The best part of the day was the journey to London. My train was on time, I found a seat in the Quiet Coach, removed my hearing aid, and settled down with the *Guardian* and a new biography of Hardy. Whether and when to wear your hearing aid on a journey by public transport, if you're travelling alone and don't have to make conversation with anybody, is a complex question. Obviously you need to wear it to buy your ticket and hear possible change-of-platform announcements at the station, but it's tempting to take it out once you're on the train, though you will then not be able to hear information delivered over the PA system by the train manager, such as why it has been stationary beside a field for ten minutes, or possibly more important messages, such as a signal failure which has halted all trains travelling in and out of King's Cross for an indefinite period; and you may have confused exchanges with the catering staff when they come round with the refreshment trolley, about milk and sugar in your tea or the contents of sandwiches. Of course I could leave the hearing aid in place but switched off until needed, in which case the earpieces would act like earplugs, but if they're not serving their real purpose I find I become acutely aware of and irritated by the intrusive presence of these little plastic pellets lodged in my head, a sensation I can't stand for very long before plucking them out. So usually I remove my hearing aid as soon I've found a seat and the train moves out of the station. The only advantage of being deaf is that one is, as it were, naturally insulated from a lot of irritating or unpleasant environmental noise (which becomes even more irritating and unpleasant when amplified by a hearing aid) and one might as well make the most of it. Removing the hearing aid on the train is like a magical instant upgrade from Standard to First Class: the metallic rattle and grind of the wheels on the track is reduced to a faint rhythmical clickety-click and the voices of your fellow passengers are muted to a soothing murmur.

Only mobile phones retain their power to annoy even the hearing-impaired traveller, both by their ringtones and by the peculiarly irritating staccato rhythm that characterises one side of an indistinctly overheard telephone conversation, which is why I always try to get a seat in the Quiet Coach where these devices are prohibited. But it's surprising how many people either ignore or don't see the notices to this effect, and proceed to make and receive calls while seated right under a window sticker saying, *'Quiet Coach. Please refrain from using mobile phones'*, and it often falls to me to point this out to offenders since most of my fellow passengers cravenly restrict themselves to disapproving looks, to which the mobile-phone user, mentally focused on his or her distant interlocutor, is of course oblivious. I don't welcome this task, since it disturbs the tranquillity which I hoped to achieve by removing my hearing aid; in fact I sometimes replace it in order to be equipped if necessary for an argument. A certain amount of adrenalin has to flood the system in order to act, and to decide how and when – do you intervene as soon as the phone is in use, or wait till the call is finished, or interrupt in the middle if it seems to be going on for an inordinately long time? I now have a sentence prepared for these occasions, *'Excuse me, but did you know this is a Quiet Coach?'* uttered in a polite and confidential tone, with a finger pointing helpfully to the window sticker, but the responses from the addressees vary considerably. Some, usually women, simper and smile and nod, and extend a placatory hand, as if admitting they are at fault but craving indulgence, while blithely continuing their telephonic conversation; others, evidently genuinely unaware that they are in a Quiet Coach, and indeed unable to get their heads round the very concept of a Quiet Coach, a place where a man's inalienable right to have loud private conversations in public might be forfeited, stare at you with incomprehension until the truth sinks in, and then say something uncomplimentary about you to their interlocutor, and sulkily terminate the call or take themselves off to the next carriage with an air of persecution. One man, who was drunk, threatened to punch my fucking nose through my fucking face and out the other fucking side. Fortunately he fell asleep before attempting this rearrangement of my features.

Yesterday's journey however was uneventful, and I was sorry to exchange the relative tranquillity of the Quiet Coach for the bustle and clamour of King's Cross, where we arrived only a few minutes late. I descended into the bowels of the Tube and took the Northern City Line to London Bridge, and then a half-empty commuter train down to Brickley, a journey through Graffitiland. There are graffiti inside the train, gouged into the carriage windows with glass cutters, or scrawled on the laminated melamine panelling with coloured marker pens, and spray-painted graffiti outside – on the stations you pass through, on rolling stock inert in sidings, on buildings overlooking the railway, on walls and bridges and staircases and the doors of lock-up garages, on every inch of available surface. The riot of lettering adds a bit of colour, I suppose, to this drab segment of south-east London, but linguistically it always seems to me somewhat impoverished – mostly the names or pseudonyms of the artists, seldom a witty epigram or sharp political comment. When was the last time I laughed at a graffito? Years ago I spotted one which still makes me smile when I think of it: under a sign, 'Bill Posters Will Be Prosecuted' some wag had written, '*Bill Posters is innocent*'. Nothing as amusing greeted my eye as I made my way over the footbridge at Brickley Station. Just names, obscenities and acclamations mostly to do with football teams.

Brickley is one of the older London suburbs, first developed about a hundred years ago, with streets of squat identical terraced cottages on the flat bits, and larger terraced houses and tall detached and semi-detached villas on the hilly bits. These properties, built of the old yellowish London brick with stone and stucco decoration, much modernised, converted, divided and extended, still dominate the district, interspersed with more recent post-WW2 redbrick developments – low-profile blocks of flats and tiny terraced town houses for first-time buyers. But Lime Avenue, where I was born and where Dad still lives, doesn't belong to either of these architectural periods. It's a gently curving street of small inter-war semis squeezed in on rising ground between a main road and the railway, and it leads nowhere except to the main road at each end. The houses on the railway side have back gardens which abut on to an unusually high and wide embankment, with trees and bushes and grassy hollows; the kids who lived there in my childhood had access to this illegal adventure playground which I envied. Our house, number 49, like all the houses on the other side of the street, has a small back garden raised up artificially on landfill contained by a high concrete wall. A main road runs beneath our rear fence, and the tops of the buses that pass are just visible from the first floor, though you can always hear them in the garden. The street's name derives from the lime trees which in my childhood were placed at staggered intervals along the pavement on each side, and have since been removed and replaced by rowans, after a campaign by car-owners who objected to the sticky gum dropping from the lime trees on to the bodywork of their vehicles. The houses are separated by narrow side alleys and have no garages or carports, so the street is lined with cars parked nose to tail on both sides. When I was a kid we used to play football and cricket in the road, pausing and stepping aside to let the occasional car or van pass, but it would be impossible now. Whenever I go back to Brickley and turn into Lime Avenue from the main road I experience a mental lurch of memory, and I am a short-trousered schoolboy again, coming home in the late afternoon, socks round my ankles, shoes scuffed from playground football, looking forward to another game with my mates before being called in for tea and homework. It always seemed to me a nice street to come home to, and it still looks smarter and more inviting than the drab older terraces that surround it. The houses are covered in pebble-dash, with timber features painted in a variety of contrasting colours, and neat little front gardens with shrubs and flower pots and crazy-paving, though number 49 is looking a bit sad these days: the privet hedge needs cutting, the wooden gate is rotting along the bottom, and the short concrete path to the front door is fissured and uneven, with weeds growing in the cracks. Dad still insists on doing the basic maintenance himself, which means that it mostly doesn't get done, or not done very well. Ten years ago, when he was recovering from an operation, he grudgingly agreed to let me pay somebody to repaint the house, but I dare not suggest having it done again in case he gets his ladders out and tries to do it himself.

I rang the doorbell, and then when that had no effect, used the door knocker, banging hard four times. Dad is hard of hearing – not as deaf as I am, but as he won't use a hearing aid he is, for practical purposes, just as deaf as me, indeed rather more so. Five years ago, after a long and exhausting series of arguments, I finally persuaded him to be tested and fitted with an NHS hearing aid, but he complained that it was uncomfortable and fiddly, and the batteries kept packing up, and it whistled. He soon stopped wearing it. Living alone, he didn't have much incentive to persevere. He listens to the television through headphones since the neighbours on the other side of the party wall complained of the volume coming through the speakers, and he has a telephone with a specially loud ring and a flashing light. But he often misses

46

calls by tradesmen because he doesn't hear the knocker, and if he hadn't been expecting me I might have waited a long time for him to open the front door. The first sign that he was about to do so was that a curtain behind the round frosted-glass window in the door was drawn aside. This is a thick felt full-length curtain which he rigged up himself to keep the draughts out and the warmth in during the winter months. He keeps most of the other curtains in the house drawn or partially drawn for the same reason, adding a sepulchral gloom to the general seediness of the interior. The door opened. An elderly man dressed like a tramp smiled at me.

'Hallo, son,' he said. 'You made it, then.' He stood aside to admit me, then poked his head out of the door to look suspiciously up and down the road, as if he feared I might have been tailed by criminals bent on armed robbery, before shutting it and drawing the curtain. 'How was the journey?' he said, as I took off my overcoat and hung it on the coat rack by the door.

'All right. The train was on time for once,' I said.

'What?' This word occurs very frequently in our dialogues.

'The train was on time,' I shouted.

'There's no need to shout,' he said, and led me along the passage into what we always called the dining room, presumably the estate agent's designation, though it was and still is the living room, and a very small one, about thirteen feet square, I would guess. It's at the back of the house, next to the kitchenette. The front room or 'lounge' is a little bigger, but was rarely occupied in my childhood except on high days and holidays, especially in winter because of the bother of lighting a second fire. The dining room did, it is true, contain the table where we ate most of our meals, and a sideboard, but it also contained two easy chairs and a bureau desk and a radiogram and in due course a television, and it was there that we mainly lived as a family. In those days Dad used the front room to practise on the saxophone and clarinet. He was scrupulous about doing an hour's practice every day, in the late morning, to keep his fingering supple and accurate, playing over and over again what sounded to me like fragmentary scales and phrases with no continuous melody. It was maddening to listen to and I wonder if that wasn't one reason why I never seriously tried to learn an instrument myself when I was young – there seemed to be no pleasure in it. It was a revelation when I first heard him on the bandstand, playing a proper solo on the tenor sax. Later I got interested in jazz through listening to his records and had fantasies of playing the trumpet like Harry James or Dizzy Gillespie but I was on an academic track at school by then, aimed towards university with loads of homework, and not sufficiently motivated to give up any of my meagre spare time to music lessons, so I never learned to play an instrument, and now that I have plenty of time to spare it's too late because hearing impairment has taken most of the pleasure out of music for me.

For Dad too, I think. He doesn't play any more of course, he sold his instruments some years ago – his teeth have gone and he has arthritis in his fingers – and he doesn't listen to music as much as he used to. The turntable and the cassette player of his music centre are broken and he won't replace it or have it mended. When I offered to buy him a new system with a CD player last Christmas he flew into one of his irrational fits of temper: 'Are you mad? What would I want with a CD player? You think I want to waste my money buying a lot of CDs, and they cost a fortune, a complete take-on if you ask me, when I've got a marvellous set of records like those?' (Making a sweeping gesture towards the shelf that holds his modest collection of LPs.) I said, all right, I would get him a hi-fi with a turntable, and he said, 'Where would I put it? I don't have room for any more clobber,' and I said you can put it where the music centre is now, and he said, 'What? You mean get rid of my music centre? I paid a hundred quid for that.' And I said, but it doesn't work, Dad, and he said, 'The radio works,' though in fact he never uses that radio, because he can't turn up the volume loud enough without annoying the neighbours. He has one in the kitchen which he plays so loud it rattles the crockery, and a smaller portable which he listens to in the dining room or in bed through a pair of lightweight earphones, mostly to talk radio. He might try Classic FM occasionally but gone are the days when he would sit down and listen to a whole symphony or concerto by one of his favourite composers, Elgar, Rachmaninov, Delius – late Romantic stuff, no Mozart or Beethoven for him ('can't stand the bloody Germans, too heavy') – recording it on to a cassette for future use, an economy which gave him great satisfaction. Modern jazz no longer seems to interest him, though he does like nostalgic radio programmes about the big swing bands of the Forties, Benny Goodman, Glenn Miller, Tommy Dorsey. Electric guitar-based rock and pop music he despises, needless to say, and always has done since it put an end to the dance-band business, though he made an exception of the Beatles. They were real musicians, he would say. 'Clever tunes and songs you can understand, with proper rhymes.' 'Eleanor Rigby' was his favourite.

'So how are you?' I said when we were seated in the two easy chairs each side of the hearth, where one bar of an electric fire was switched on. Although I forced him to let me pay for central heating to be installed at the time of Mum's last illness he has never taken to it; he keeps the radiators turned off in the house most of the time for economy's sake, and uses an electric fire in the dining room because he doesn't really feel warm unless he can see an orange glow and feel his shins getting scorched as he used to with a coal fire.

'What?' he said. I'm sure he heard me perfectly well, but like most deaf people he's got in the habit of saying 'what?' automatically to every conversational gambit – I notice myself doing it sometimes.

'How have you been?' I said, more loudly.

He grimaced. 'Not too good. Never get a proper night's sleep these days.'

'You should get a new mattress,' I said. This was a familiar topic, and the conversation took a well-trodden path, which went something like this, with much repetition and shouting:

'There's nothing wrong with my mattress.'

'I'll pay for it, Dad.'

'It's not a question of paying for it. I've got plenty of money.'

'You would sleep much better on a firm mattress.'

'It's nothing to do with the mattress. It's because of my . . . how's your father. What d'you call it?' He glanced down at his groin.

'Prostate.'

'That's it. I was up four times last night.'

'Have you been to the doctor about it?'

'Old Simmonds? Oh yes. He says there's an operation you can have. I said no thanks very much.'

'Well, I don't blame you, Dad.' I essayed a joke: 'I believe it can affect your sex life.' But he didn't hear and I didn't feel like repeating it.

'He gave me some tablets,' he said. 'I suppose they're sort of astringent. You know, to shrink the . . . whatsit. They don't seem to make much difference.' He shook his head gloomily. Then as usual he found a thought with which to cheer himself up: 'Mind you, I can't grumble. Eric for instance, he had it the other way.' Eric was a second cousin who died several years ago. 'He couldn't go at all. They had to rush him to hospital. Put a thing up his . . .' He mimed the insertion of a catheter with a wincing expression. Then after a pause, he said mildly: 'No, I'll get a new mattress one day. There's no hurry.'

I could no longer restrain myself from commenting on his clothes. 'I hope you're going to change before we go out.'

'Of course I'm going to change!' he said crossly. 'You don't think I'd go out in these, do you?' In truth I didn't, but it irritates me when he dresses like a down-and-out at home, perhaps because there's such a clear family resemblance between us. It's as if he's presenting to me a mocking effigy of myself. We're both tall, bony, with high, stooped shoulders, and lined, long-jawed faces, so looking at him dressed like a guy on Bonfire Night is like seeing myself in dire straits twenty-odd years from now. He was wearing a pair of filthy high-waisted trousers, made of checked tweed so thick, and so stiff with dirt and stains of various kinds, that I imagined he stood them upright in the corner of his bedroom when he took them off, a soiled beige cardigan with holes in the sleeves at each elbow, and a frayed plaid shirt with the top two buttons missing, revealing his scrawny Adam's apple and a crescent of yellowish undervest. With the possible exception of the undervest these clothes were not, I knew, worn-out items that he had long had in his possession, but fairly recent acquisitions scavenged from charity shops and jumble sales. On his feet he wore a pair of shabby carpet slippers trodden down at the heel.

'Well, I wonder why you wear them at all,' I said. 'Anybody would think you haven't got any decent clothes.' I knew that upstairs he had two wardrobes full of respectable clothes in good condition.

'What's the point of my dressing up when I'm indoors?' he said indignantly. 'I don't see anybody here from one day's end to another.'

This was a covert appeal for pity, and not without effect, but I felt obliged to continue on the offensive. 'You knew you were going to see *me* this morning,' I said.

'That's different,' he said. 'Anyway, I've been doing jobs.'

'What kind of jobs?'

'Cleaning the stove.'

'How are you getting on with it?'

The electric cooker is a new acquisition, though not a new appliance. I had offered to buy him a new one but typically he insisted on getting a reconditioned cooker from a shop up the road, the kind that has white goods displayed outside on the pavement with handpainted placards boasting bargain prices. It was certainly cheap, but there was no manual with it, and I wasn't able to get him one since the manufacturers have discontinued the model, so he has been struggling to master the controls ever since. The operation of the oven in particular has been a problem, sometimes resulting in the food being burned and sometimes not cooked at all.

'Not bad,' he said, with a shifty sort of grin. 'I've nearly got it beat.' Since he can blame nobody but himself for the purchase of this unsuitable cooker he has personified it as a cunning adversary which has somehow intruded itself into his house and against which he must pit his wits. 'But just when I think I've got it sorted it comes up with another little wrinkle,' he said. 'It turns out that the grill doesn't work if you close the flap.'

'No, with the flap closed it becomes a second oven,' I said. 'I told you that, Dad.'

'It's no use telling me things at my age, you have to write them down,' he said.

'All right, I'll write down a few basic instructions for you,' I said. 'Why don't you go and get changed?'

While he was upstairs I went into the kitchen to make a few notes about the cooker. It was in an appalling state, like the whole room, coated with grease, inside and out, which he had made a few ineffectual attempts to scrape off. There were circular scorch marks on the Formica work surface next to it, left by saucepans that must have been nearly red hot when he put them down, and a great plume of soot was imprinted on the wall above the hotplates where a pan of cooking fat had obviously caught fire. I opened the fridge and found it full of bits of food, cooked and uncooked, wrapped in greaseproof paper and tin foil, the more unwholesome of which I disposed of in the dustbin outside the back door. An awful feeling of hopelessness and helplessness enveloped me. It is obvious that Dad can't go on living on his own indefinitely, that sooner or later he is going to either set fire to himself or poison himself. But he will never leave the house willingly – and, in any case, where would he go?

When he came downstairs he was transformed, wearing a heather-coloured Harris tweed jacket, grey worsted trousers and a clean striped shirt with a tie. There was a food stain on the lapel of the jacket, but, I told myself, you can't have everything. On his feet were a pair of polished brown brogues. His thin grey hair was combed back neatly from his forehead. 'Very nice,' I said approvingly, scraping the congealed food off the jacket with my fingernail on the pretext of feeling the cloth.

'You can't get material like that now,' he said. 'Cost me five quid in Burtons. That was a lot of money then.'

'Where d'you want to have lunch?' I said.

'The usual,' he said.

'You wouldn't like a change?'

'No,' he said.

The usual is the cafeteria in the local Sainsbury's supermarket. Suggesting a change was just a token gesture: I've given up trying to persuade him to go elsewhere. Most of the restaurants in the neighbourhood are Indian or Chinese which he 'wouldn't touch with a bargepole'. I managed to lure him into an Italian trattoria once but the prices on the menu shocked him, and he claimed to dislike the taste of garlic and olive oil in the food. He looked sour and unhappy throughout the meal and I didn't repeat the experiment. Pubs he regards as places for drinking beer, which he has given up because he believes it exacerbates his prostate condition, not somewhere to go for a hot dinner, which he wouldn't enjoy anyway, surrounded by people enviably quaffing pints. So by a process of elimination we have ended up going regularly to Sainsbury's.

'OK, I'll ring up and reserve a table,' I said, but that was another quip he didn't hear and I didn't repeat.

'What?'

'I'll ring for a minicab.'

There was a time when he would have bitterly opposed this extravagance, but of late he has grudgingly allowed me to pay for a cab on the outward journey on the understanding that we return by bus. As usual he said, 'Have a glass of sherry first?' and as usual I accepted. I don't like his cheap syrupy sweet sherry, but the Sainsbury's cafeteria is not licensed and I need a shot of alcohol to get me through the lunch. When we'd had the sherry I called the local minicab office and they said it would be five minutes, at which point Dad decided, typically, that he had to go to the loo again before he went out. I took the opportunity to sneak a second glass of sherry, in fact a small tumbler of the stuff, while he was upstairs but, as I feared, the minicab honked to announce its arrival outside the house before he had got his hat and coat on. Then he couldn't find his keys to lock up the house. The minicab honked impatiently again. I looked out and saw that it was blocking the narrow channel between the rows of parked cars and was holding up the progress of another vehicle. I went out and asked the driver to go round the block and come back in two minutes. He muttered something I didn't catch and drove off at speed. I was by no means confident we would see him again. I went back into the hall, where Dad was frantically going through the pockets of various coats and jackets hanging in the hall. 'Don't you have a hook in the kitchen where you keep them?' I said.

'They're not there.'

I went into the kitchen and found the keys on the hook. 'Here you are,' I said, giving them to him.

His face lit up with relief. 'Thank Gawd for that. Where were they?'

'On the hook in the kitchen. Come on, let's go.'

The cab driver was back, scowling from the window of his beaten-up red Honda, and I hurried Dad into the back of the car. We took off with a screech of tyres, rolling and sliding on the slippery vinyl seat.

'I could swear I looked at that hook and they weren't there,' Dad said.

'Never mind, Dad,' I said.

'Did I turn off the electric fire?' he wondered.

'Yes, yes,' I said, though I couldn't remember whether he had or not. I couldn't face telling the driver to go back. And if the house burned down, I reflected darkly, that might solve the problem of how to get Dad out of it.

It's a big new Sainsbury's built on a brownfield site near the railway line. The cafeteria is clean and brightly lit, cordoned off from

54

the long loaded aisles of the shop on one side, and overlooking a vast car park on the other. The food, I have to admit, is not bad, and extraordinarily good value. You bag a numbered Formica-topped table and line up with a tray, taking your cold items from the cabinets on the counter and ordering your hot dishes when you pay. One of the cheerful motherly women who mostly staff the place brings them to your table after an interval which depends on how busy they are. On the wall behind the counter are glossy coloured photographs of the dishes on offer which Dad stares at for some time before taking his place in the queue: this is his big treat and he is anxious not to waste it by making a bad choice. He usually has steak and kidney pie with two veg or fish and chips, with apple pie and custard for pudding. The bill for the whole meal for the two of us probably comes to less than the price of one starter at the Savoy Grill.

We must look an odd couple to the other customers, a mixture of students from the local sixth-form college, young mothers with babies and toddlers, local shop assistants taking their lunch break, and the chronically unemployed. It's a multiracial work-ing-class area, and people dress casually in the grungy modern style: layers of synthetic clothing emblazoned with trademarks, and trainers of baroque design with thick sculpted soles. Per-versely I regretted having criticised Dad's ragged attire earlier in the morning, thus goading him into a sartorial counter-attack. I am a rather formal dresser myself, never at ease with the fashion-able open-neck look, and always wear a tie with a jacket or the navy-blue blazer I was wearing yesterday. I felt we were both con-spicuously over-dressed for the venue; as if we had set out to go to the Savoy Grill but found we didn't have enough money, so set-tled for Sainsbury's instead.

Dad ate his meal quickly and greedily, then sat back with a sigh of satisfaction. Over a cup of tea he began to reminisce. Like all deaf people he finds it easier to talk than to listen, and I was happy to let him. Having heard all his stories many times before I don't have to pay much attention in order to follow and respond appropriately. Something, probably the drizzle that had started to fall outside, darkening the tarmac of the car park, had reminded him of coming back from India at the end of the war to be demobbed, after a nine-month tour of duty in a small Air Force band. He has polished the phrasing of the story in the course of many repetitions. 'We docked at Southampton, and took a train to London. It was raining, but we didn't mind. It was lovely soft English rain, and the country looked so green! We hadn't seen any green for months. Only dust. "Dust, spit and spiders, that's India," as Arthur Lane used to say. "If the Indians want it back, they're welcome to it." The green of the fields and the trees, coming up through Hampshire, was incredible, like water to a man dying of thirst. It was as if we were trying to drink England. We couldn't get enough of it. We hung out of the windows as the train went along, getting soaked with the rain, not caring. And Arthur Lane – trust Arthur – he opened the door of our carriage – you know, the trains had separate compartments in those days, with doors – he pushed the door wide open and sat on the floor with his feet hanging out over the wheels, just staring at the fields, saying "Unbelievable, un-bloody-believable".' Dad chuckled at the memory. Arthur Lane was the drummer in the band Dad had spent most of the war with, and figured in many of his anecdotes, admired for his dry wit and independent spirit. I never met this legendary character in the flesh but have seen a snapshot of him and Dad in baggy khaki shorts, grinning and squinting into the glare of the Indian sun, Dad tall and thin with his hand on the shoulder of the squat and rotund Arthur.

Then the smile faded from Dad's face and he sighed and shook his head. 'Poor old Arthur,' he said. 'Dead now. Dead years ago. Did I tell you?'

'No,' I lied.

'Yeah. Cancer.' He lowered his voice as he pronounced the dread word, and mimed drawing on a cigarette. 'Lungs. Always was a heavy smoker, Arthur. Even when he was playing the drums, he'd have a fag on.'

'Did you keep in touch with him after the war?' I said, like a comedian's feed.

'We used to see each other in Archer Street,' he said, naming the drab little street behind Piccadilly Circus where dance musicians used to congregate on Monday afternoons to fix up gigs, settle debts and exchange gossip, before discotheques took away their livelihood. 'But when Archer Street died out, I lost touch with him. I heard he'd packed in the music business and got a day job, like so many. Then one day I thought I'd give him a ring, see how he was getting on. I don't know why. Thinking of the old days I suppose, I just wanted to hear the sound of his voice again. His wife answered the blower. I never met her, but I recognised her voice. I said, "This is Harry Bates, is Arthur there?" And there was a long silence. I thought at first I'd been cut off. And then she said, "Arthur died eight years ago." Well, you could have knocked me down with a feather. Arthur dead all that time, and I had no idea. He was younger than me, too.' He pursed his lips and shook his head again. 'There aren't many blokes I knew in the business who are still around now.'

'No. You're a survivor, Dad.'

'Well, I looked after myself, see? Gave up fags when I developed that cough – you remember? And I was never a drinker, not what you'd call a drinker. A glass of beer yes, but no spirits.' He mimed holding a glass of liquor between finger and thumb and raising it to his lips. 'Spirits was the death of many a good musician. When a customer in a club or the gaffer at a Jewish wedding treated the band to a round of drinks most of the boys would order double whiskies, but I always had just a half of bitter. You can get a taste for whisky.' He added severely: 'I hope *you* don't drink whisky.'

'Very rarely,' I said. 'Wine is my tipple, as you know.'

'Yes, well, I don't mind a glass of sweet white wine now and again, but not that sour red stuff you like.'

'Don't worry, Dad, I'll get in some Liebfraumilch for you at Christmas.'

57

He looked at me with a rheumy eye. 'Am I coming to you for Christmas, then?'

'Of course you're coming. You can't spend Christmas all on your own.' In fact nothing would please me more than not having Dad to stay at Christmas. Christmas is bad enough without the extra stress of looking after him and trying to smooth the inevitable friction between him and Fred and Fred's mother, but the guilt at leaving him all alone in London for the duration of the holiday would be even worse.

'I'm not sure I'm up to the journey,' he said.

'I'll fetch you in the car, as usual,' I said.

'But I need to pee practically every half an hour,' he said.

'There are plenty of drive-ins all the way up the M1,' I said. 'And we'll have a bottle in the car for emergencies.'

'What?'

I looked around to check there was nobody seated near us. Fortunately the lunchtime rush was over, and most of the other tables were unoccupied. 'You can have a bottle in the car,' I said in a louder voice.

'Oh, very nice,' he said bitterly. 'Supposing we're stuck in a traffic jam and all the people in the other cars are looking at me through the windows?'

'Then you can do it under a blanket,' I said irritably. 'Anyway, you're not as bad as you make out. You haven't needed to go since we came in here.'

'*Now* I do,' he said, getting to his feet. 'That tea's gone right through me.' It's the kind of remark that sets Fred's teeth on edge, and Fred's mother's teeth even more.

When we had both been to the Gents we went round the shelves picking up some groceries for Dad. Although he knew I would pay at the checkout he insisted on buying the cheapest products – so cheap that many of them have no brand names on them at all: cans of baked beans with a plain white label stating baldly in black type 'Baked Beans', or loaves of sliced white bread with 'Economy White Loaf' printed on the plain plastic wrapper.

They even had bottles of 'German Liebfraumilch', with no other information on the label about its provenance, for under two pounds. When we got outside, with a couple of full carrier bags, the drizzle had turned into a steady downpour, which I made the excuse to grab a black cab that was just delivering a passenger, bundling Dad into the back seat before he had a chance to protest. He kept his eye on the meter throughout the journey, commenting incredulously every time the digits moved forward, and averted his eyes when I paid the driver as if it was a transaction too shameful to witness.

Back at the house, Dad covered his eyes with a silk handkerchief and fell asleep in his armchair in front of the electric fire. I dozed off myself for a while, but I woke first and did not rouse him. In truth, the longer I can perform my filial duty of keeping him company without having to make conversation, the happier I am. He was slumped in his chair, with his head back and his mouth open, as if gasping for air. He is, indeed, a survivor. When the war broke out he had the wit to volunteer for service in the Air Force as a musician instead of waiting to be called up and drafted into some probably more dangerous and certainly less congenial occupation. On East Anglian airfields he paraded in marching bands at the funerals of young airmen killed in training accidents, and in the evenings played at dances and ENSA concerts for the entertainment of heroes returned from bombing missions over Germany, who had a one-in-two chance of not returning in the future. He was posted to the Shetlands, possibly the safest place in the British Isles at the time, and sent me, his three-year-old son, cartoon-style sketches of himself fishing and playing golf watched by puzzled sheep. In the last year of the war his band was sent to India, another combat-free zone. He always travelled by train and boat, turning down the offer of a lift home from Bombay in a military plane although it would have meant a much quicker demob, and completed six years' service in the Royal Air Force without ever going up in an airplane, a form of transport he regarded, not without reason, as inherently dangerous. Nor has he ever been up in one in peacetime, though he has sat inside several parked on the ground, impersonating passengers in TV airline commercials. He is a man of great resilience and resourcefulness, who overcame a disadvantaged background and adjusted deftly to changing circumstances. A natural but largely untutored violinist as a youth, he left school at fourteen to work as an office boy, was turned on by jazz, a kind of music not hospitable to the violin (Stéphane Grappelli excepted), taught himself to play the saxophone and clarinet, supplemented his office-job earnings by playing in dance bands in the evenings, went professional, played in nightclubs, orchestra pits, radio big bands, sang ballads on the air in a sweet high tenor voice that suited the taste of the Thirties, came back from the war to find crooners were all the rage, blew the dust off his violin when Mantovani made the instrument popular again, played palm-court background music for banquets and wedding receptions, learned to play reels for hunt balls, and had a regular job with a quartet of his own in a West End nightclub for several years. When the club closed and he tried to get back into doing gigs he found they were few and far between, so acquired an Equity card and an agent to find him work as a TV and film extra in the daytime. He still catches glimpses of himself on television occasionally in repeats of very old sitcoms and rings me up to ask if I saw him, and I always pretend that I did.

He has also been a man with many other interests – serially. At different periods of his life he always had some hobby or recreation which consumed all his spare time and energy until he would suddenly lose interest in it and let it lapse, sometimes returning to it years later. For a long period it was golf – a convenient recreation for a man who worked in the evenings and was free in the weekday afternoons when municipal courses are uncrowded – but try as he might, practising for hours and studying golf manuals, he could never get his handicap down into single figures, and eventually his knees began to trouble him and he gave up the game. Then it was sea angling, taking day trips to

Brighton to fish off the West Pier until it burned down, a disaster that upset him deeply and seemed to crush his enthusiasm for the pastime. Then it was collecting antiques, trawling through the local second-hand stores and flea markets for promising-looking small objects (there was no room in the house for large ones) and poring over library books in an effort to date and value them. Then it was dealing in stocks and shares. Then it was calligraphy. Then it was oil painting. He invariably taught himself these various skills from library books and magazines, or cadged advice and information from more experienced practitioners. The idea of, for instance, joining a painting class was anathema to him. He was an instinctive autodidact. Perhaps for this reason he never really excelled either as a musician or in any of his leisure activities, but I take my hat off to his professional versatility and the range of his enthusiasms, beside which my own life seems dull and narrowly specialised.

All the more poignant, then, is it to contemplate him now, stripped of all these life-enhancing interests. He has only one hobby these days: saving money, observing prices, economising on food, clothing and household bills. It's no use asking him what he is saving the money for, or pointing out that if he drew more deeply on his assets he would be very unlikely to exhaust them, and that in such a contingency I would provide whatever funds were necessary. Indeed he is apt to take such comments as unfeeling hints that he hasn't got much longer to live – which is of course, in actuarial terms, true, but not what I mean to convey. One of the reasons I selfishly let him drowse on in his armchair was the consciousness that we hadn't yet touched on this sensitive area, and the less time there was available to do so before I had to leave, the better. I knew that the drawers of the bureau desk behind my back were stuffed with a disordered collection of old bills and bank statements, tax forms and share certificates and National Savings certificates, chequebook stubs and paying-in books and building society passbooks and Premium Bond counterfoils and God knows what else, and that when he woke up he would almost certainly want my advice on some item plucked from this financial midden. Sure enough, when he awoke of his own accord, and had revived himself with a cup of tea, he went over to the desk and pulled out some correspondence to do with National Savings.

'This woman up north keeps pestering me to buy more Savings Certificates,' he said. 'What's the matter with her?'

'I don't suppose she signed them personally,' I said. 'They're computer-generated.' I glanced at the papers, which were form letters bearing the printed signature of the Commercial Officer of the National Savings headquarters in Durham. 'You've got several certificates that have expired. They want to know if you want to cash them in or buy new certificates.'

'Can't I just leave them there?' he said.

'Well, you can, but they'll earn less interest than new ones.'

'But if I buy new ones I'll have to wait another five years for them to . . . whatd'youcallit . . .'

'To mature, yes.'

We silently contemplated the possibility that he might not live long enough to enjoy the accumulated interest on his loan to the government.

'I think I'll leave them where they are,' he said.

'Why don't you cash them in and treat yourself to something.'

'What?' he said, meaning, for once, not *What did you say?* but *What sort of thing?*

'I don't know . . . Hire a limousine to take you to Brighton.'

'Don't be so bloody ridiculous,' he said.

'You're always complaining you miss the sea. You could fish off the marina.'

'I tried that for a while. It's nothing like the old West Pier. You have to walk for miles to find a place to cast. Then it's miles back to find a lav.'

He obviously felt this was a knock-down argument against my frivolous suggestion, and I did not contest it.

'There must be something you would like to do,' I said.

'No, there isn't,' he said dourly. 'I'm past doing things. If I can get through the night without getting up more than three times, if I can do a decent job in the lavatory after breakfast, if I can make my dinner without burning anything, if there's something worth watching on the telly . . . that's as much as I can hope for. That's a good day.'

I could think of nothing cheering to say to this.

'Take my advice, son,' he said. 'Don't get old.'

'But I *am* old, Dad,' I said.

'Not what I call old.'

'I'm retired. I'm on a pension. I have a Senior Citizens railcard and a bus pass. I always have to get up in the night at least once. And I'm deaf.'

A faint grin lightened his countenance. 'Yes, you are a bit Mutt and Jeff, aren't you?' he said. 'I've noticed. I wonder where you get that from? At your age I had perfect hearing.'

Having asserted this superiority over me, his mood improved. 'What would you like for your tea?' he said. 'We could have those baked beans with a bit of bacon.'

I looked at my watch. 'I'll have to be going soon,' I said.

'Why don't you stay the night? The bed in your room is made up.'

'No thanks, Dad. I've a lot on tomorrow.' Lie.

'Well, have a bite to eat first.'

I said I would if he would let me cook it and show him how the grill on the cooker worked.

'No need, I've got it taped now,' he said.

But I insisted, to ensure that the meal was edible, and grumblingly he acquiesced.

I left the house at about six. He watched me putting on my overcoat in the cramped hall under the low-wattage bulb, and pulled back the felt curtain over the front door to let me out. We shook hands, his musician's fingers cool and soft in mine. 'Well, goodbye Dad,' I said. 'Take care of yourself.'

''Bye son, thanks for coming.' He gave me a smile that was

almost tender, and stood at the open door until I passed through the front gate. I raised my arm in a final salute, and set off for the station with a guiltily light heart. Duty done.

5

5th November. The responsibility for Dad's welfare weighs heavily on me because there is no one to share it with. I am the only child of parents who themselves had no siblings. Dad and I have practically no relations with whom we are in contact, and none at all living in London. He has two elderly female cousins on his mother's side, living in retirement in Devon and Suffolk respectively, with whom we exchange Christmas cards, and that's about it. My own children visit their grandfather very occasionally, but they both live at some distance from London and have busy lives of their own. And he has almost no friends. Those he had in the music business are either dead, or he has lost touch with them; and he never had what one would call a social life. Work was his social life, as I knew from the rare glimpses I had of him doing it: swapping jokes on the stand between sets, chatting to customers in a nightclub, always laughing, smiling, shaking hands, because that's what's expected of a dance musician, as he explained to me once. 'The punters are out to enjoy themselves and they like you to look as if you're enjoying yourself too, even if you're feeling miserable.' So in the hours when he wasn't working he didn't want any social life, he just wanted to play golf or fish or pursue one of his other hobbies. He was at work in the hours when ordinary folk were enjoying their leisure, and if he happened to be at home in the evening it was because he hadn't got a gig or a regular job, so he wouldn't be in the mood for spending money on going out. Even on Sundays he was often playing at a Jewish wedding or bar mitzvah. The main victim of this lifestyle was my mother, who had little social life, and an unglamorous working life for about twenty-five years as an underpaid clerk in the office of a local builder's merchant. She had some friends in the street, but since she died most of them have died too, or moved away, and Dad is only on nodding terms with most of his neighbours, apart from the Barkers in the adjoining semi – a railway clerk, now retired, and his wife, who have been there for some thirty years, and whom he trusts without liking. Occupying the house on the other side of the alley fence is a Sikh family with whom he has a relationship that is politely distant on both sides. In effect, he is all alone in Lime Avenue, and I am probably the only person who crosses the threshold of the house these days apart from the doctor and the man who reads the electricity meter. It's a lonely and vulnerable existence. What's to be done? I discussed this with Fred when I got back home the night before last.

It was just after ten-thirty when my taxi turned into the gravel drive of 9 Rectory Road. As I let myself in at the front door I was, as always on returning from these excursions, struck by the contrast between the meanly proportioned, dark and dingy semi from which I had come, and the tactfully modernised and beautifully maintained Regency house which is now my home, with its gleaming paintwork and stripped wooden floors, its high ceilings and elegantly curving staircase, its magnolia walls hung with vivid contemporary paintings and prints, its comfortable, discreetly modern furniture, deep pile carpets, and state-of-the-art curtains which move back and forth at the touch of a button. The air was warm, but smelled sweet.

Fred acquired ownership of the house as part of her divorce settlement, and made its improvement her chief hobby until, with the opening of *Décor*, it became an extension of work, a laboratory for new ideas and an advertisement to potential customers. When we married I was glad to sell the serviceable but rather boring modern four-bedroomed detached box in which Maisie and I brought up our children, and to move into Fred's house, the money I acquired in this way funding her ambitious improvements. Its three floors provided enough bedrooms for our combined children, two of mine, who were in any case at or about to go to university by then, and three of hers. Nowadays the house is extravagantly large for just the two of us, but Fred likes to throw big parties, and to host inclusive family gatherings at Christmas and similar occasions. Besides, she insists, living space is her luxury: some people like fast cars, or yachts, or second homes in the Dordogne, but she prefers to spend her money on space she can enjoy every day.

I hung up my coat in the hall, and called out 'Fred!' to announce my return, and found her, as I expected, in the drawing room. The lights were restfully subdued, the gas-fired artificial coals in the grate glowed and flickered welcomingly. Fred reclined on the sofa with her feet up, watching *Newsnight* on television, and I caught a glimpse of soldiers in battledress patrolling a dusty Middle Eastern street before she quenched the picture with the remote. I went over to the sofa and she tilted her face to receive a kiss.

'Carry on watching if you want to,' I said.

'No, darling, it's too depressing. Another suicide bomb in Baghdad.'

I sank down in an armchair, and took off my shoes. Fred said something I didn't catch, I presumed about the news, something about a mine. 'How could you commit suicide with a mine?' I asked. I saw from her expression that this was wrong. 'Hang on,' I said, and fumbled in my pocket for my hearing aid, which I had taken out in the train. As I inserted the earpieces I discovered that one of them was already switched on. 'What did you say?'

'I said you're whining, darling. Or you were.'

'I must have forgotten to turn one of these things off. Either that or it turned itself on somehow. I suspect them of doing that occasionally.'

'So how was your Awayday?' Her tone was sympathetic, but the micro-humiliation of the whining hearing aid, reminder of my infirmity, lingered like the irritation of an insect bite, and diminished the pleasure of my homecoming. *Deaf, where is thy sting?* Answer: everywhere. Perhaps for that reason I painted a darker picture of Dad's situation than I might otherwise have done. I described the state of the house, especially the cooker and the fridge.

'He can't go on living on his own much longer,' I concluded.

Fred looked serious. 'Well, darling, I don't like to sound hard or unfeeling, but I have to say it: he can't live with us.'

'I know.'

'I just couldn't cope with it. Christmas, and a few other times a year I can manage, but not having him here permanently.'

The truth is that neither could I, but I am grateful that Fred is prepared to take upon herself the odium of this decision. 'He wouldn't want to anyway,' I said. This is true. Dad has never felt at ease in Fred's house. The big rooms and high ceilings intimidate him; they make him afraid of draughts and frighten him with visions of huge energy bills. He actually suggested to Fred once, in all seriousness, that she should divide the drawing room with a big felt curtain suspended from the ceiling to create a sitting area near the fireplace; I think the motorised rails for her velvet window curtains gave him the idea. He honestly feels more comfortable in his frowsty little nest crowded with furniture, where three or four steps will take you from the door to the furthest corner of the room, than he does in this splendidly proportioned and luxuriously appointed salon.

'But what shall we do with him?' I asked.

'You'll have to look for a care home of some kind.'

'You mean here?'

'Would he move up here?' Fred asked doubtfully.

'He won't move anywhere willingly,' I said. 'But it would make sense. We could keep an eye on him more easily, have him round for meals occasionally.'

'*You* could, darling, he's your father,' Fred said. 'Of course he'll always be very welcome here, but you'll have to entertain him. You know how busy I am.'

I contemplated this prospect for a few minutes, Dad popping in every day for a chat, or rather grumble, and didn't much care for it. On the other hand I am wearying of the regular pilgrimage to London to see him, and visiting him in a care home there, supposing I could find one, wouldn't be any less of a fag.

'I suppose I could see what's available,' I said, 'and get him to look at some places while he's up here at Christmas. I've no idea what they cost, have you?'

'Anything decent is expensive,' said Fred. 'But if he sells his house that should cover it for a few years.'

I tried to imagine persuading Dad to accept this arrangement, living extravagantly off his diminishing capital, and failed.

'And after a few years?'

'If necessary we could take care of it.' Clearly she didn't think it would be necessary. 'Speaking of Christmas,' she said, 'I want to have a big party here on Boxing Day, for friends and neighbours and clients. Buffet lunch and drinks.'

I pictured the pleasant, peaceful room full of people grinning and sweating and Lombard-reflexing away for all they are worth, and groaned inwardly. 'Won't that be a lot of work for you, after Christmas dinner the day before?' I asked, seeking an acceptable objection.

'We'll have it catered. Jakki knows an Asian company who don't mind working over Christmas. She says they do delicious Thai curries and salads. People will be glad of a change from turkey and mince pies.'

'Dad won't,' I said.

'Well then, he can have a cold turkey leg all to himself in his bedroom,' Fred said crisply, 'and as many mince pies as he can eat.' I sensed that it would suit her very well if he were to choose this option.

Fred offered to get me something to eat, but I had bought a sandwich on the train and was not hungry. I poured myself a substantial whisky nightcap – a kind of rebellious Oedipal act, perhaps, prompted by Dad's homily on the subject, for it is not a regular habit of mine – and took it upstairs to sip in the bath before going to bed. I lolled in the steam and the warm water, leaching out the stress and fatigue of the day, then put on a pair of clean pyjamas and got into bed. I usually read a bit of poetry before I go to sleep. I keep my favourite poets on the bedside table – Hardy, Betjeman, Larkin – and dip into them at random. I was reading 'Beeny Cliff' when Fred came in to the bedroom:

O the opal and the sapphire of that wandering western sea,
And the woman riding high above with bright hair flapping free –
The woman whom I loved so, and who loyally loved me.

Glancing up covertly from my book from time to time I watched Fred getting ready for bed, undressing, going in and out of her bathroom, putting on her nightgown, and was rewarded with a glimpse of her generously curved but firm bottom and the profile of a shapely bare breast. The bottom is her own work, but the breast owes something to the surgeon's art. A few years ago she had a breast-reduction operation. At the time I was against it on health and safety grounds (given all the infections rampant in hospitals these days only a life-threatening illness would persuade me to have an operation), and the sight of her bandages and stitches initially made me queasy, but I had to admit that the final result, when everything had invisibly healed, was stunning. At about the same time she joined the Health Club and began serious exercising, taking courses in yoga, clocking up miles on running machines and stretching herself out like a medieval martyr on racks attached to weights and pulleys, sculpting her matronly torso into an alluring hour-glass shape. This wasn't done for my benefit, but as part of a general personal make-over accompanying her new career, which included dieting, hair-colouring and the substitution of contact lenses for spectacles. It all had its effect on me nevertheless, provoking an unexpected onset of what Betjeman called 'late flowering lust', adulterous in his case, uxorious in mine. As I sneaked glances at Fred's routine and entirely uncoquettish preparations for bed I felt a stirring in the loins, and had to resist the temptation to slide my hand under her nightdress as she got between the sheets and turned on her side, knowing that in my tired and slightly tipsy state I would not be able to pursue any amorous overture to a satisfactory conclusion. I settled instead for a comfortable cuddle, fitting my body spoonwise to the curve of her bottom and putting an arm round her waist, a waist that didn't exist five or six years ago. I chanted 'Beeny Cliff' silently to myself and fell asleep somewhere in the last stanza:

> What if still in chasmal beauty looms that wild weird western shore,
> The woman is now – elsewhere – whom the rambling pony bore,
> And nor knows nor cares for Beeny, and will laugh there nevermore.

I woke at three-thirty, probably because the effect of the alcohol had worn off, went for a pee, and tossed and turned for some time afterwards, unable to get back to sleep. I tried cuddling up to Fred again, but she shrugged me off, not with any conscious irritation, I believe – it was probably just a reflex action in her sleep – but the withdrawal of her warm body left me feeling rejected and vulnerable. My thoughts picked up from where they had left off when I fell asleep: sex with Fred, or rather not-sex with Fred, and Hardy's elegy for his first wife, which led me into uncomfortable memories of Maisie.

I try not to think of Maisie too much. The last years of her life were so awful, not just for her, but for all of us. From the moment she told me she had found a lump under her armpit I knew with terrible certainty how it would end, but not how long it would take: the endless hospital appointments, the stuffy crowded waiting rooms, the anxious consultations, the operations and chemotherapy and radiotherapy, the brief periods of respite and hope, the unspeakable depression and despair when the next scans showed they had been delusory, the gradual mutation of the house into a hospice, first with the installation of a stair-lift, and then, when even that became too much for her to manage, the conversion of the lounge into a sick room with an en suite bathroom extension, and a Macmillan nurse calling daily. Maisie was determined to die at home. She got her wish, it was all we could do for her in the end, but it took its toll of me and the children. I think one of the reasons I'm so bitter about my deafness is that having got through all that, survived that, and then found new happiness with Fred, I somehow thought I had suffered my fair share of misfortune, paid my dues as the Americans say, and that life would be plain sailing from then on. But of course that isn't how it works, not at all.

The only way he survived the strain of that time was through work, devoting every hour that wasn't taken up with caring for Maisie and the children to his teaching and research. In the early stages of her illness they made love to comfort each other, but as Maisie's condition worsened it became painful for her and difficult for him, and they stopped by tacit mutual consent. Maisie raised the subject once in a touching but embarrassing way, about six months before she died, saying she would understand if he needed what she called 'solace' from another woman, as long as she didn't know about it, and none of her friends did. He assured her quite sincerely that he felt no such need. She told her sister that he was 'a saint', but he vehemently repudiated the compliment when it was relayed to him. He claimed no virtue for his continence. He simply felt numbed by the misery of the situation. The idea of entering into an emotional relationship with another woman while Maisie was dying by inches was unthinkable, and he was not the kind of man to resort to prostitutes or massage parlours.

After Maisie's death, that is to say after about a year had passed and he had got over the immediate sense of grief and loss, mingled with relief that her suffering was over, and his own burden lifted, he became conscious that he was a free man again, and that he was being observed with an interest that was sometimes kindly and sometimes prurient – as if his circle of acquaintance were conspiring to help him find another partner, or secretly placing bets on who it would be. He was aware, too, that Anne and Richard, both then teenagers, and fiercely loyal to the memory of their mother, reacted with extreme suspicion whenever he was out late in the evening, or mentioned some female colleague approvingly in conversation. This, he found, had an inhibiting effect on his relations with the unattached women he met, fearing that any effort to be pleasant on his part might be misinterpreted – and probably it had the same effect on them. Then Winifred Holt came into his life, initially as a student taking a Combined Honours degree in Art History and Linguistics.

It was an unusual combination, since there were not many connections between the two subjects in content or methodology. In fact the only one he could think of, as he told her in her first tutorial (the Department still had a tutorial system in those days) was Jakobson's application of his famous metaphor/metonymy distinction to Surrealism and Cubism. She cheerfully admitted that there was no rationale for her combination of subjects, she just happened to be interested in each of them for different reasons. She had always loved going to art galleries and looking at pictures, and as the mother of young children she was fascinated by the ease with which they acquired language and wanted to learn more about it. In truth she never had any natural aptitude for linguistics, but she made the best of her limited ability and, with only a little help from himself, scored a straight A in Art History for an extended essay on the difference between Surrealism and Cubism. He had always taken a mild interest in visual art, and it developed further through his association with Winifred.

She was a 'mature student' in her late thirties, and looked rather more mature than that. She was tall, big-boned and heavy-breasted, and her wavy dark brown hair was already flecked with grey. She wore gold-rimmed reading glasses which, when they were not perched on the bridge of her nose, reposed on her impressive bosom, suspended from her neck by a thin gold chain. In other ways too she stood out from the student crowd when she arrived in the Department. She was posh – obviously, inescapably, unignorably posh. Her speech was posh, her manners were posh, and her clothes were posh in a curiously old-fashioned way: twin-sets and tweed skirts and leather court shoes. She had the idea when she started the course that you ought to present yourself to professors and lecturers as you would to your doctor or solicitor. The young women students in her first year seminar groups, in their monogrammed tee-shirts, denim miniskirts, striped tights and Doc Martens, stared at her in disbelief, or rolled their eyes at each other as she asked a perfectly formed question in her cut-glass accent. In due course she adopted a more casual style of dress, and blended in better with the habitat, but she could never disguise her accent.

It wasn't until her second year that he became her tutor (he was a Senior Lecturer at that time). The Department's system in those privileged days was a weekly tutorial group of two or three students to discuss an essay or other assignment, and the staff also kept office hours when their tutees were free to drop in for advice and counselling. Winifred availed herself of this facility with some frequency, perhaps because she had no close friend among her fellow students, and he soon learned the outline of her life story, which she shaded in with more intimate detail as their relationship ripened. She belonged to an English Catholic family who could trace their descent back to the Norman period and had kept the faith through the penal days of the Reformation – there was a Jesuit martyr somewhere in the record. Her grandmother had been the daughter of a Viscount, but there was no significant wealth or property in the immediate family. Winifred's father was in the consular service, and she had been brought up in various foreign countries and at an English convent boarding school, insulated from the youth culture of the 1960s. She had not distinguished herself academically and there was no family tradition of sending girls to university, so instead she spent six months at a finishing school in Geneva, followed by a secretarial course at a commercial college in London, in the expectation that she wouldn't have to earn her living for very long before acquiring a husband. A favourite aunt took Winifred under her wing, as her parents were abroad, and introduced her to eligible Catholic young men, one of whom was an investment adviser called

Andrew Holt, Downside and Oxford, with whom, as she said, 'I imagined I was in love, when really I just wanted to have sex with him, and since I believed then that the only way you could have sex was in marriage, I married him.' They had their first child, Marcia, within the year, followed fairly rapidly by Giles and Ben. 'Catholics and birth control, you know,' she said, grimacing. 'But after Ben, I went on the pill. And then we came here.' Andrew's firm was expanding, and he was offered a promotion if he moved to one of the new branches they were opening in the north of England. They looked for a house near the University because it was convenient for travel to the city centre and not too expensive in those days, before the big property boom: an area of more or less shabby older houses, mostly big Victorian villas built of the grey local stone for the city's merchants and manufacturers, many of them converted into flats popular with students. The Rectory Road house, with its classic proportions and stucco facade, was more attractive than most of its neighbours, but was dilapidated when they bought it and they couldn't afford to have it done up properly. Winifred struggled to look after her three young children in a cold damp home with antiquated wiring that was always failing and a husband who was at work all day and late into the evenings. 'Only he wasn't just working, he was also having an affair with a colleague.' They tried marriage guidance and patched things up, but soon Andrew strayed again and Winifred finally divorced him. She got the house and some maintenance from the settlement, and supplemented her income for a time by taking in postgraduate lodgers. Talking to them gave her a sense of what she had missed by not going to university, so when the children were settled at school she applied for admission as a mature student, a procedure that waived certain matriculation requirements. 'So here I am – and loving it.'

They had to be very discreet in managing their relationship until they were sure they wanted to make it public, and it involved a good deal of subterfuge at first, which intensified the excitement and gratification of the affair. For him it was like coming back to life again after being encased in ice in a state of suspended animation. He would never forget the ecstasy of their first weekend away together, at a country house hotel, under cover of alibis ingeniously contrived to deceive both sets of children. He was nervous about having sex again after such a long interval, but Winifred made it easy. She had – and continued to have – an uncomplicated attitude to sex, regarding it, he sometimes thought, as a healthy and exhilarating kind of exercise, comparable to horse-riding or body-surfing. She enjoyed it, but she could do without it for long periods without feeling greatly deprived. 'How lovely,' she sighed after they made love for the first time. 'I'd forgotten how nice it is.' Maisie in contrast had become anxious if they didn't make love regularly, fearing his affection was cooling, but she was sexually timid, perhaps the effect of her Scottish Presbyterian background. The early years of their marriage had been a time when respectable married couples everywhere were eagerly learning how to enhance the joy of sex from the manual of that name and similar sources, and Maisie gamely attempted some of the postural variations he proposed; but he could see that her heart wasn't in it and after a while they reverted to more conventional conjugal embraces. She had an unconquerable aversion to oral sex in any form. It was therefore a delightful surprise when on their third time in bed together Winifred treated his penis as if it were a particularly delicious stick of seaside rock. 'Do you like that?' she said, lifting her tousled head. 'Very much,' he said. 'Andrew taught me how to,' she said, 'but he wouldn't reciprocate, the rotter.' 'I will,' he said.

It was on that weekend that she mentioned that her nickname at boarding school was 'Fred', and he adopted it as a kind of code name in notes and diary entries for the duration of their clandestine affair. He had never much liked the names Winifred or Winnie, and it became his pet name for her. They waited till their various children had done whatever exams they were doing that summer before breaking it to them that they were getting married. By that time the children had guessed that their parents were seriously involved and accepted the union with resignation and in some cases approval. They were less pleased about sharing a home, but in due course their departures to various colleges and careers solved the problem. He and Winifred were married quietly in the long vacation and she resumed her studies the following term. After discussion with the Dean it was agreed that to avoid any suspicion of favouritism Winifred should not take any course with him in her third year, and that he would withdraw from the Finals examiners' meeting when her degree result was under discussion. She got a 2.1, which wasn't as commonplace as it later became, did a part-time MA over two years in late nineteenth-century Art History, and started a desultory PhD on Art Nouveau and the Viennese Secession, which she abandoned when *Décor* began to consume her time and energies.

They were married in a registry office because Fred was still married to Andrew in the eyes of the Catholic Church. This didn't bother her at the time, though it upset her parents. She had pretty well lost her faith as a result of the turmoil of her first marriage, blaming the indoctrination of her upbringing and education for her impetuous and ill-considered choice of a spouse and for the stress of having too many babies in too short a time. They agreed not to try having any children of their own: it would have been risky at her age – she was thirty-eight when they married – and they felt they had already brought enough children into the world. The early years of their marriage were therefore like a prolonged and passionate honeymoon, in which they rediscovered erotic pleasure without the distractions and interruptions of caring for babies and infants that had followed their first nuptials. The diagnosis of high-frequency deafness cast a faint shadow over his happiness, but their mutual enjoyment of sex was not much affected, the sounds which accompany it being mostly non-verbal and low frequency in wavelength.

Inevitably, with the passing of years, his vigour began to decline, Fred grew stout and less seductive, and like most couples they settled into a more sedate routine of love-making which he assumed would gradually taper off into a serenely chaste old age for both of them. But Winifred acquired her rejuvenating new career and new look, while he grew older and deafer and subject to occasional erectile dysfunction. He had not thought anything of the eight-year age gap between them when they married, but it began to prey on his mind. They were not quite January and May – more like March and April; but that small difference seemed more significant as he grew older, especially as Fred actually began to look younger. She was always understanding and good-humoured if intercourse petered out, as one might say, without a climax. There were, as she observed, other ways of giving and receiving sexual pleasure, and she was up for most of them, but to him they were only foreplay. He tried Viagra on the advice of his GP, which had the desired effect, but it caused an allergic reaction and he had to give it up. So he relied on very careful planning for sex these days, involving abstinence from alcohol beforehand, an invigorating shower rather than a soak in a hot bath, and fine-tuning of the heating and lighting in the bedroom, before proposing an early retirement to bed. But these preparations did not always work. Sex had become an object of anxious rather than pleasurable anticipation, and his peace of mind was not helped by the daily penetration of his computer firewall by spam advertising Viagra, Cialis, and quack herbal remedies promising enhanced virility. 'Impress your girl with prolonged hardness, plentiful explosions and increased duration. Boost your manhood to astonishing levels . . . Everything a real man would ever need . . . Hello my friend! You have a unique chance to forget this distress forever . . . Extra-Time is the unmatched comprehensive non-hormonal solution . . . Did she ever tell you your size is insufficient? No? Maybe she was just being polite? Just imagine your new happy life with more size, more adoration from females and more self-assurance. Come in here . . .'

It occurs to me that if this were a novel anyone reading it would probably think: 'Ah-hah, poor old Desmond obviously hasn't realised that Winifred has a lover, and all the slimming and cosmetic surgery was for *his* benefit, and that with the connivance of Jakki she regularly slips away from the shop for afternoons of adultery, while keeping the old man happy at home with an occasional blow-job.' But I'm quite sure that isn't the case. Putting aside my intuitive trust in her fidelity, the beautifying process more or less coincided with Fred's return to religious observance, a development I deplore on intellectual grounds but which I feel is some kind of guarantee that I am not being cuckolded. It seemed to start when Marcia got married, with a nuptial mass, and Fred couldn't go to Communion along with her mother and other members of her family without, as she said 'giving scandal'. Before that she used to go to Mass occasionally on her own when she felt the urge, especially when we were on holiday in Catholic countries, but I assumed it was just a wistfully nostalgic self-indulgence. After Marcia's wedding, however, she began to brood on her marital status and decided to apply for a Church annulment of her marriage to Andrew, on the grounds that they were both too emotionally and psychologically immature at the time to understand what marriage entailed. It seemed to me that the same might be said of at least fifty per cent of people who marry young, including Maisie and myself, but I didn't say so, because I could see that restoring her good standing in the Church mattered a great deal to Fred. The process took a long time, entailing interviews by clerics with her mother and siblings to confirm that she had been emotionally and psychologically immature at the time of her marriage. The family of course was happy to cooperate. Andrew, remarried and no longer a practising Catholic, was initially reluctant to admit to his youthful immaturity, but he agreed for the sake of maintaining good relations with his children by Fred, and eventually the annulment was granted. I wondered how the children really felt about it, and questioned Fred on this point. Didn't the annulment make them illegitimate? She said no, legitimacy was a civil legal concept. As far as the law was concerned she and Andrew were truly married and their offspring legitimate, but in the eyes of God they hadn't been married even though they thought they were, and everybody else including the priest who married them thought they were, because a fundamental requirement for a valid marriage had not been met. I teased her a little: 'So really Andrew didn't commit adultery when he had it off with those other women, because he wasn't really married?' 'Of course he committed adultery,' Fred said testily. 'That's why I divorced him. Don't be silly darling.' 'Adultery in the eyes of the law, perhaps, but what about in the eyes of God?' I said. 'Him too,' Fred said, with a steely look in her eyes. I didn't argue the point any further. It seemed obvious to me that the annulment process, which has recently become much more liberal and accessible than in the past, when only people rich and powerful enough to pull strings in the Vatican could get one, is a device for getting round the Catholic Church's historic opposition to divorce without appearing to contradict it, but since the effect is humane I wasn't going to make an issue of it. I even agreed to go through a form of marriage service at Fred's parish church – a quiet, private ceremony, with only Marcia and her husband present as witnesses – though I felt a bit foolish making the vows we had inserted into our registry office wedding all over again. 'Do you feel any different?' I asked Fred afterwards. 'Yes, of course, darling,' she said. 'You mean, you didn't really feel we were married before?' I said. 'No, of course not – I mean, yes, of course I did. It's just that now I feel . . . right. At peace.'

I was baptised in the C of E but didn't have a religious upbringing. Mum taught me to say my prayers at bedtime when I was a child, and took me to church at Christmas and Easter, but that was about it; Dad claimed – and still does occasionally – to believe in God, but never set foot in a church except for weddings and funerals. I attended a grammar school which went in for religious assemblies and encouraged pupils on the arts side to take Scripture at GCE O-level, and most of what I know about Christianity derives from that education and studying English literature, especially Milton and James Joyce, at university. I envy religious people their belief and at the same time I resent it. Surveys have shown that they have a much better chance of being happy than those whose belief systems are totally secular – and you can understand why. Everyone's life contains some sadness, suffering and disappointment, and they are much easier to accept if you believe there's another life to come in which the imperfections and injustices of this one will be made good; it also makes the business of dying itself a much less depressing prospect. That's why I envy religious believers. There are of course no firm foundations for their belief, but you're not allowed to point this out without seeming rude, aggressive and disrespectful – without in fact seeming to attack their right to be happy. That's why I resent religious belief, even among my nearest and dearest – indeed especially among my nearest and dearest, since with them the impossibility of discussing religion dispassionately is most apparent. Fred goes off every Sunday morning to Mass, leaving me behind with the Sunday papers, and comes back ninety minutes later looking virtuously pleased with herself. I might ask her what the sermon was like, and she will say something vague in reply – frankly I doubt whether she listens to it attentively – but I wouldn't dream of asking her if, for example, she received Communion with unreserved assent to the doctrine of transubstantiation. I don't think Fred's faith ever had a strong intellectual basis. It was an effect of upbringing and education and family tradition. The storms of sexuality and an unhappy marriage in early adulthood blew her away from the Catholic faith, and when those subsided she returned to its safe haven. From the few occasions when I have accompanied her to Mass for family reasons I would say it's pure ritual for her, a ritual of reassurance. She sits and stands and kneels and sings the hymns and murmurs the responses in a kind of trance, happy to be connected to a general ambience of transcendental faith and hope without needing to enquire closely into the rational basis of it all. And who am I to say she is deluding herself, left alone in the house with my doubts and my deafness and the shallow excitable chatter of the Sunday newspapers?

*

Marcia and family came round to lunch today, as they often do on a Sunday. Of all our children Fred's Marcia lives the closest, indeed only a couple of miles away, so we see more of them than of the others. I'm always pleased to see Dauphin Daniel and his older sister Helena – 'Lena' as she's familiarly known. Marcia and her husband Peter I get along with up to a point, but I have a feeling that as a teenager Marcia was the most resistant of Fred's children to the idea of her mother marrying me – an older man, her teacher, a non-Catholic, with kids of his own – and that she has never quite overcome her early resentment of our union. Indeed, as Fred blossomed and became successful in business, while I shrank into retirement and succumbed to deafness, I suspect I appeared to Marcia more and more as a redundant appendage to the family, an unfortunate liability. As she is the dominant partner in their marriage Peter takes his cues from her and is guarded in his attitude to me. When I hinted as much to Fred one day, she said, 'Nonsense, Marcia has a great respect for you, and if Peter seems a little "guarded" as you say, it's because he thinks you must be silently criticising his English all the time because you're a Professor of Linguistics.' I laughed at that, because modern linguistics is almost excessively non-prescriptive, but I suppose there might be some truth in it. Peter is from a working-class background, speaks with a perceptible local accent and uses the occasional dialect word. He studied accountancy at what was then the Poly and works in industry, so he is culturally a little undernourished and a bit in awe of the family he has married into. I tried to put him at ease next time I saw him by attacking Lynne Truss's bestselling book on the apostrophe, but only succeeded in upsetting him – it turned out he is a devout believer in Truss and uses her book as a kind of bible. Oh well . . . They're an admirable couple in many ways, both with demanding careers, but dedicated to the welfare of their children, making quality time for them in the evenings and at weekends, never as far as I can tell having any quality time to themselves, and I wish I could love them more. That's no problem with the children, who are beautiful and charming, and at that interesting age when they begin to acquire language with astonishing rapidity, and sometimes make expressive mistakes, if I could only hear them. Today when I complimented Lena on her pretty dress, and she replied that her Mummy had bought it at Marks & Spencer, everybody laughed except me. When I looked puzzled, Fred explained that she had said, 'Mummy bought it at Marks and Spensive.' Then I laughed on my own.

6

7th November. I got up this morning before Fred and was having my breakfast when she came into the kitchen in her dressing gown. She said 'Good morning, darling,' and then, going over to the stove, said something else which I didn't catch because I wasn't wearing my hearing aid; I took it out last night in the family bathroom, which is my bathroom when there are no family or other guests in the house, before going to bed, and it was still there. I said 'What?' and she repeated the utterance, but I still didn't get it. She was opening and shutting drawers and cupboards as she spoke, which didn't help. 'Sorry,' I said, 'I haven't got my hearing aid in – it's upstairs.' She turned to face me and said more loudly what sounded like 'long stick'. I said, 'What do you want a long stick for?' My mind was already considering the possibilities – to recover something that had rolled under the bed? Or fallen down the back of a chest of drawers? She came closer and said, 'Saucepan. Long-stick saucepan.' 'What's a long-stick saucepan?' I said. 'You mean a long-handled saucepan?' She raised her eyes to the heavens in despair, and went back to the stove. I thought about it for a minute or two, and then the penny dropped. 'Oh, you mean *non-stick* saucepan! It's in the top right-hand cupboard.' But I was too late: she was already making her porridge in a stainless steel saucepan which would be much more trouble to clean afterwards. And it was my fault for putting the non-stick one away yesterday in the wrong place.

Fred sat down at the kitchen table, propped up the *Guardian* tabloid section against the marmalade jar, and began to read with silent concentration. I had intended to mention casually over breakfast that I would be meeting Alex this afternoon. I had a little speech prepared: '*Yes, d'you remember the young woman I was talking to at the ARC show last week? The blonde one? It was so noisy that I literally didn't hear a word she said, but it seems she's doing research of some kind, with a linguistics angle I presume, because apparently I agreed to give her some advice about it. She phoned to complain because I hadn't turned up for our appointment, though I haven't the faintest memory of making one. Embarrassing really. I more or less had to agree to meet her . . .'* But because of the contretemps over the non-stick saucepan it seemed an unpropitious moment to make this announcement, and I let it pass. I will have to tell Fred about the meeting after it has happened, when it will be far more difficult to explain.

'My mother's deafness is very trifling you see – just nothing at all. By only raising my voice, and saying anything two or three times over, she is sure to hear; but then she is used to my voice,' says Miss Bates in *Emma.* How subtly Jane Austen hints at the politely disguised frustration and irritation of the company at having to bear the repetition of every banal remark in louder and louder tones for the benefit of old Mrs Bates. I must be in a worse state than my fictional namesake, because I'm used to Fred's voice, but I still can't hear what she's saying without a hearing aid.

Is there anything to be said in favour of deafness? Any saving grace? Any enhancement of the other senses? I don't think so – not in my case anyway. Maybe in Goya's. I read a book about Goya which said it was his deafness that made him into a major artist. Until he was in his mid-forties he was a competent but conventional painter of no great originality; then he contracted some mysterious paralytic illness which deprived him of sight, speech and hearing for several weeks. When he recovered he was stone deaf, and remained so for the rest of his life. All his greatest work belongs to the deaf period of his life: the Caprices, the Disasters of War, the Proverbs, the Black Paintings. All the dark, nightmarish ones. This critic said it was as if his deafness had lifted a veil: when he looked at human behaviour undistracted by the babble of speech he saw it for what it was, violent, malicious, cynical and mad, like a dumb-show in a lunatic asylum. I saw the Black Paintings some years ago, when I was in Madrid on a British Council lecture tour, and went back to the Prado twice for another look. Goya painted them as murals for his house in the country – the local people called it La Quinta del Sordo, the House of the Deaf Man – slapping the paint straight on to the plaster, but later they were lifted off the walls and transferred on to canvas. Now they're in the Prado, *Saturn Devouring His Children*, *The Witches' Sabbath*, *Fight With Clubs* and the rest, predominantly black in pigment as well as subject matter. But the one that always has the most spectators lingering in front of it, intrigued and puzzled, is lighter in colour tone than the others. It's known as the *Dog Overwhelmed By Sand* (none of these titles was Goya's). It might be a modern Abstract Expressionist painting, composed of three great planes of predominantly brownish colour, two vertical and one horizontal, if it wasn't for the head of a little black dog at the bottom of the picture, painted almost in cartoon style, buried up to its neck in what might be sand, looking upwards pathetically and apprehensively at a descending mass of more of the same stuff. There are lots of theories about what the picture means, like the End of the Enlightenment, or the Advent of Modernity, but I know what it means to me: it's an image of deafness, deafness pictured as an imminent, inevitable, inexorable suffocation.

Did Goya, I wonder, think he owed his greatness as an artist to his deafness? Was he grateful for the illness which deprived him of his hearing? Somehow I doubt it. But it must have crossed his mind that he was fortunate to have lost that sense rather than sight. In practical terms deafness is no handicap at all to a painter, in fact it could even be an advantage, an aid to concentration – not having to make conversation with your sitters for instance. Whereas for a musician it's the worst thing that could happen to you. Beethoven is the great example. I read a book about him too, Thayer's *Life* – I have a kind of morbid interest in the great deafies of the past. I was surprised to discover how young he was when he became deaf, only twenty-eight. He caught a chill which

86

developed into a serious illness, not quite as severe as Goya's, but it left him with impaired hearing, hair-cell damage probably, which steadily worsened for the rest of his life. When he first became aware of it, he was chiefly known as a virtuoso musician and conductor, careers that were obviously impossible to pursue with hearing loss, and that was why from then onwards he concentrated exclusively on composing. So I suppose you could argue that deafness was responsible for his greatness as an artist too, like Goya's, but Beethoven certainly didn't look at it in that way, as a blessing in disguise. He was distraught when he realised he was losing his hearing, searched frantically for cures (none of which worked of course), and was afflicted with spells of deep depression, cursing his Maker and sometimes contemplating suicide. He swore to secrecy those of his friends in whom he confided his plight, fearing that he would lose all professional credibility if it became widely known. And for a long time he was surprisingly successful in concealing it, partly by avoiding society, and partly by feigning absent-mindedness when he failed to hear something said to him. But as all deafies know, these strategies have a certain cost: they make the subject seem withdrawn, unsociable, curmudgeonly. Six years after he began to go deaf, when he had given up hope of a cure, Beethoven wrote a letter, addressed to his two brothers, but in a way to everybody who knew him, evidently designed to be read after his death, explaining the 'secret cause' of his off-putting temperament and manner. It's known as the Heiligenstadt Testament, because he wrote it in a little village of that name outside Vienna to which he had withdrawn for six months of solitary rest on the advice of his doctor. I copied it from Thayer, and have it on file. It begins like this:

Oh you men who think or say that I am malevolent, stubborn or misanthropic, how greatly do you wrong me. You do not know the secret cause which makes me seem that way to you . . . It was impossible for me to say, to people, 'Speak louder, shout, for I am deaf.' Ah, how could I possibly admit to an infirmity in the <u>one sense</u> which ought to be more perfect in me than in others, a sense which

I once possessed in the highest perfection, a perfection such as few in my profession enjoy . . . Oh, I cannot do it, therefore forgive me when you see me draw back when I would gladly have mingled with you. My misfortune is doubly painful to me because I am bound to be misunderstood; for me there can be no relaxation with my fellow-men, no refined conversations, no mutual exchange of ideas, I must live alone like someone who has been banished.

It's a very poignant document, an outpouring of suppressed emotion, a cry wrung from the heart. Sometimes, he says, he would yield to the desire for companionship.

But what a humiliation for me when someone standing next to me heard a flute in the distance and <u>I heard nothing</u>, or someone heard a <u>shepherd singing</u> and again <u>I heard nothing</u>. Such incidents drove me almost to despair, a little more of that and I would have ended my life – it was only my art that held me back. Ah, it seemed to me impossible to leave the world until I had brought forth all that I felt was within me.

The references to the flute and the shepherd remind me of Philip Larkin, unable to hear the larks singing in the sky when he was walking with Monica Jones in the Shetlands. They also evoke the Pastoral Symphony, which Beethoven composed six years later, a supreme musical evocation of sounds that he himself hadn't heard for more than a decade. Nor could he hear the music itself when it was performed. I suppose he heard something – but what? A faint distorted version of the score, like a concert heard on a cheap portable radio with a fading battery? Or was he able, by watching the musicians, to re-create in his imagination the full richness of symphonic sound, and hear it inside his head like a modern iPod user? I fear the former is more likely.

What comfort can I draw from these case histories? Not much. Both men happened to be geniuses and found some kind of compensation for their affliction in their art. I'm neither a genius nor an artist. I suppose a linguist who can't hear what people are saying is more like a deaf musician than a deaf painter, so I can identify more readily with Beethoven than with Goya. But I can't claim that only my work on discourse analysis has held me back from despair these last twenty years, or that I feel it impossible to leave the world until I have given it my last thoughts on, say, topic-drift and skip-connecting in casual conversation, which I could still do using transcripts of recorded speech. In fact I *have* given the world my last thoughts on those and similar subjects, some time ago. So what will I have to live for, when social and sexual intercourse are effectively at an end too? Let us not enquire further into that question.

7

8th November. I met Alex Loom yesterday, as arranged. That's her surname, Loom: it was written beside the bell push for flat 36 outside the entrance to Wharfside Court, the apartment block where she lives. An unusual name, easy to remember, and because it was written down I know I've got it right. I'm not so confident about anything else that I gathered in the course of the afternoon, because much of what she told me was surprising and she tends to drop her voice at crucial points in her utterances so that I was never quite sure whether I had understood her correctly. What follows is a tidied up, disambiguated and not altogether reliable record of our conversation.

Like so many industrial cities, ours has collaborated with British Waterways on refurbishing its canals in recent years, to make them attractive and accessible as a leisure amenity: smartening up the towpaths, painting the locks, erecting signposts and lamp standards of retro design, encouraging people to walk, jog and cycle on the paths. There has also been a lot of new property development alongside the canal that zigzags through the city centre in the form of apartments, aimed at the buy-to-rent market. Alex's flat is in one of the cheaper-looking buildings, a four-storey block in a style Fred calls Lego Postmodern, bright red brick with green plastic features pasted on, overlooking a kind of backwater at the end of which an unsightly scum of half-submerged non-biodegradable garbage has accumulated. It took me quite a while to find it, since the address Alex had given me isn't in my dog-eared *A-to-Z*. I drove through an area of vacant lots, derelict warehouses and small workshops until I reached the car park behind Wharfside Court. I was surprised by how quiet the place seemed: the traffic of the city centre only half a mile away was just a murmur, and there was nobody about. It was the middle of the afternoon, when most residents would be at work, but the near-silence seemed eerie in the middle of this city of over half a million people; indeed the city itself looked unfamiliar seen from this angle, all its landmarks – the Castle Keep, the Town Hall campanile, the ziggurat Hilton – rearranged, as if it had been turned inside out. It was a cold, clear afternoon, with good visibility. The sun was low, casting long, sharp shadows over the deserted towpaths, like one of Chirico's spellbound paintings.

The unnatural quiet, I suddenly realised, was enhanced by the fact that I wasn't wearing my hearing aid. I prefer to drive without it when I'm on my own because it makes my four-year-old Ford Focus seem as noiseless as a Mercedes. Having inserted the little plastic hearing machines in my ears I pressed the bell for flat 36, and heard Alex's voice through the crackling of the entryphone: 'Hi. It's on the third floor, I'm afraid you'll have to walk up, the elevator's out of order.' I ascended three flights of raw, dusty, untreated concrete stairs, and she was waiting at the open door of her flat when, a little out of breath, I arrived. She was wearing black trousers and a black V-neck sweater, with little make-up, except around her eyes, accentuating their intense blue. It's like the blue of the Microsoft desktop, luminous but opaque. 'The elevator is out of order most of the time,' she said with an apologetic smile. 'I keep calling the management company but nothing happens. Come in.'

It's a small flat: one bedroom, bathroom with loo, and a kitchenette off the living room. She took my overcoat and hung it up in the tiny hall, then ushered me into the living room. It is not much bigger than Dad's, but lighter and brighter. A laptop was open on a table, its abstract screen-saver pattern restlessly dissolving and re-forming, and there was a shelf unit against one wall holding books, box files and ring-binders. The other walls were decorated with modern reproductions and posters – I recognised a Munch painting of a thin naked adolescent girl sitting on a bed. Two upright chairs, a small sofa, an easy chair, a coffee table, a white two-drawer filing cabinet, a radio/CD player and a small flat-screen TV completed the furniture, most of which looked as if it had come quite recently from Ikea. She smiled and spread her hands. '*Chez moi*,' she said.

I went across to the window, which faced a similar apartment building across the canal backwater. 'Nice view,' I said politely. 'Have you lived here long?'

'Not very long,' she said.

'Did you buy it?'

'Lord, no!' She laughed. 'I rent – but it's quite cheap. The owners are pretty desperate, there's a lot on the market. Most of the apartments in this block are unoccupied.'

'Doesn't that make you feel rather lonely?'

'No, I like it. It's very quiet. Good for writing up my research.'

'Research into what?' I asked.

'Let me make a pot of tea first. Earl Grey or Assam? Or herbal?'

I chose Assam, and she went into the little kitchenette, which opened off the living room without a dividing door. I sat down in the easy chair, but I did not feel at ease. It crossed my mind for some reason that nobody knew I was here. She said something in which I seemed to hear the word 'suicide'. I jumped to my feet and took a step towards the kitchenette. 'I beg your pardon?' I said.

She came out of the kitchenette with the tea things on a tray. 'Suicide notes,' she said, putting the tray down on the coffee table. As she stooped over the table the neckline of her sweater gaped and I glimpsed the shadowy division of her breasts, as I had at the gallery. 'That's my PhD topic. A stylistic analysis of suicide notes.'

I was about to ask how she got interested in the subject, but stopped myself in case I would be trespassing on sensitive personal territory. She noticed my hesitation, and laughed. 'I can see you're wondering why I chose such a morbid subject. Everybody does. I was dating this clinical psychologist at Columbia a while back and he was doing a content-analysis of suicide notes for purposes of risk assessment, comparing notes by successful and unsuccessful suicide-attempters. He'd acquired a small corpus and I thought it would be interesting to analyse them stylistically, you know? Like, are they a genre? Do people under such extreme stress fall back on rhetorical formulae? Or does their desperation make them transcend the normal limits of their expressive skills?'

'How can you tell,' I said, 'without getting hold of other writings by these unfortunate people?'

'You can't, of course, except from internal evidence – every now and then you get a sentence that rises expressively way above the rest of the discourse. But that's only one aspect of my dissertation.'

I asked her where she was doing the PhD, and was surprised to learn that she is a postgraduate student in our English Department, being supervised by Colin Butterworth.

'Why in England, rather than America?' I asked. 'You *are* American, I take it?' Her accent was not strongly marked by any drawl or twang, but it was unmistakable.

'Right. When Bush was re-elected I felt I just had to get out of the country. I'd been working for the Kerry campaign for months and I was *so* depressed . . .'

'You were a volunteer?' I asked.

'No, I was paid. I'd been thinking of working in government actually, but I decided to go back to school, try for an academic career. I like England, I spent some time here when I was a kid – my dad had a job at the Embassy in London. And doing a PhD here costs a whole lot less than in the States. I didn't realise when I applied that's because they don't teach you anything.' She laughed as I showed my surprise at this judgement. 'I mean there are no courses, no exams, just the dissertation, which you're expected to do on your own, with an occasional meeting with your supervisor.'

'Surely there's a research seminar of some kind?' I said.

'You mean where people get to talk about what they're working on, and everyone else is terribly polite and supportive and asks easy questions? Yeah, we have that,' she said drily. 'Fortunately I like working on my own. The system suits me fine, or it would do if the supervisions were any good.'

'You don't get on with Professor Butterworth?' I asked. I

began to understand why she had not wanted to meet me on the campus.

'That's an understatement,' she said. 'I read an article by him about the effect of email on epistolary style which made me think he would be a good person to work with, that's why I applied to come here, but he's really been no help at all.'

'He probably just doesn't have enough time,' I said. 'He's probably too busy attending meetings, and preparing budgets, and making staff assessments, and doing all the other things that professors have to do nowadays instead of thinking.'

'Maybe, but he's not very smart either,' Alex said.

I could not suppress a faint smile of complicity in this judgement. I have always thought Butterworth's reputation is somewhat inflated, owing more to his instinct for trendy subjects, and his popularity with the media as a pundit on contemporary linguistic usage, than to original scholarship. But I was disconcerted by her next remark.

'That's why I want you to supervise me.' She said that she had been reading a lot of my work lately and been very impressed by it. 'I'd read some things before, of course, way back, when I was doing my Master's at Columbia, but when I found out you actually taught here till recently, I was really excited . . . I've read everything by you in the Library. I think you're just the adviser I need.'

'But I'm retired,' I pointed out.

'Yeah,' she said. 'But I've heard that some retired faculty go on supervising graduate students.'

'Those would be students they were supervising before they retired,' I explained. 'They're just seeing them through to the completion of their dissertations. But one can't take on new students after full retirement.'

'Can't one?' she said, with a little pouting smile. 'Can't he make a special arrangement?'

'I'm afraid not,' I said. 'Putting aside the question of whether I were willing –'

'Are you, in principle?' she interposed.

'Putting that aside, it would be incredibly insulting to Professor Butterworth if I were hauled out of retirement to take over one of his research students. He would never agree to it. And the University would never wear it. It's just not on, I'm afraid.'

I was glad to have this well-founded reason for declining her request, because otherwise I might have been a little bit tempted by it. The idea of getting involved in some research again, applying my knowledge and expertise to this rather bizarre but undoubtedly interesting topic, and meeting this obviously intelligent and articulate and, let us be honest, very personable young woman on a regular basis to discuss it, was not unattractive. But experience has taught me that postgraduate supervision can be a complex and worrying business: you easily find yourself becoming somehow responsible for the student's achievement, self-esteem, destiny, and it goes on for years. It was a good thing that I didn't even have to weigh up the pros and cons in this case before saying no.

'Oh. I'm very disappointed,' she said disconsolately.

'I'm sorry,' I said. I drained a cup of tea that had gone cold, and glanced at my watch. 'Perhaps I should be going.'

'Oh, no, please don't go,' she said. 'Have some more tea.' She refilled my cup.

'Tell me a bit more about your research,' I said. 'Where do you get your raw data from?'

'Oh, there are anthologies. And the Internet is useful. I'll show you.' She got up and took down a large lever-arch file from the shelves. 'This is my corpus to date. It's all on my hard disk, of course, but I keep this as a kind of scrap book to browse through occasionally.'

The file was heavy on my knees, and metaphorically heavy with human suffering. I leafed through photocopies of suicide notes, some from printed sources, some reproductions of typed and handwritten originals. I can only remember a few of the sentences and phrases which Alex had marked and annotated in a minuscule, almost illegible script. *'I'm tired of life so I've killed myself. This shitty family just takes advantage of you'* . . . *'The gas is making a noise, it's hissing fear into me'* . . . *'I don't have any choice in the matter. To make everything better I have to die'* . . . *'The man lying beside me is just an unfortunate coincidence . . .'* This last was by a woman who had evidently picked up an unlucky stranger and had sex with him before turning on the gas while he was asleep. I looked up to find Alex regarding me intently.

'Interesting reading, isn't it?' she said.

'Fascinating – but uncomfortable. Don't you get depressed working with this material day after day?'

She shrugged. 'Do pathologists get depressed doing post-mortems day after day?'

'I suppose you've done some statistical searches on your data?'

'Yeah – know what the most commonly recurring non-grammatical word is?'

'Kill? Die?'

'Love.'

'Hmm. And the collocations?'

'Oh, no surprises there: names, pronouns, some negatives. *I love you, Mom. I love you Dad, I love you Jack, you never really loved me, Mum and Dad never loved me, nobody loves me . . .'*

I read a few more of the letters – it's customary to refer to sui-cide 'notes', but many of them were full-length letters – and com-mented that there seemed to be often some ambiguity about the addressee. 'Ostensibly they're addressed to a relative or partner, but sometimes they contain information well known to both par-ties, so it's as if they're also addressed to the world at large.'

'Right, and sometimes they'll throw in something addressed to God as well. As if they want to cover all the bases with their last words,' she said. 'You obviously have a feel for this topic. Are you sure you won't supervise me?'

'Quite sure,' I said. 'How far are you into the project?'

'Well, I started it in the States some time ago, and dropped out. I registered here in the spring and started over.'

'I don't recall seeing you on campus.'

'No, but I've seen you. Somebody pointed you out to me in the Library. That's how I recognised you at the ARC reception.'

'Ah,' I said. I had thought that conversation was a chance encounter, but evidently not.

'I don't go into the University much, except to the Library. I prefer to work at home. And I have to do other kinds of work to pay the rent.'

'What kinds?'

'Casual stuff. Waitress, barmaid. I was hoping to get some teaching in the English Department, but nothing doing.'

'No, we rarely use postgraduates for teaching, as they do in the States,' I said.

Then she giggled and said something in a throwaway fashion, in which I caught only the word 'panty-sniffer'. As she elaborated I gathered that a girl she had worked with for a time in a bar had told her about a man who paid for panties that had been worn and not laundered. You sent them through the post, sealed in a freezer bag, once a week, and three days later back came a cheque. You never met him. It was easy money. 'The easiest money I ever heard of,' she said. But having missed the introduction to the story I couldn't tell whether Alex herself had actually become involved in this trade, or was just reporting her friend's experience. So I was reduced to nodding and smiling and murmuring phatically, taking my cues from Alex's tone and expression, and maintaining an attitude of urbane unshockable amusement, until I asked a careless question, 'Does he tell you what style of lingerie he prefers?' which implied that it had at least crossed my mind that Alex herself might be subsidising her doctoral research in this way.

She gaped at me for a moment and laughed. 'Professor Bates! You don't imagine *I* mail my panties to this guy?'

I blushed deeply – I don't often blush but I did then – and said, 'No, no, of course not.'

'I believe you did!' she said archly. She didn't seem to be offended.

'I said "you" in the sense of "one",' I said pedantically.

'Well, I don't say one might not be tempted if she were really broke,' Alex said lightly.

'I wonder why American English uses "one" in that way?' I said, desperate to change the subject. 'Just once at the beginning of a sentence, then shifting to the appropriate personal pronoun, *he* or *she*. Whereas we would say *"One might not be tempted if one were really broke."*' I realised that my example had returned us to the subject of my faux pas.

'I really don't know,' she said, smiling at my embarrassment. She took advantage of it to press me again about her research, asking me if I wouldn't read her stuff and give her some advice, informally and confidentially. Anxious to make my departure, I said I would think about it. She gave me a card with her mobile telephone number on it – she doesn't have a landline. I tried to think of some way of discouraging her from phoning me at home that wouldn't sound either rude or conspiratorial, and failed.

Driving back to the house I decided that I must tell Fred about my meeting with Alex before she found out as the result of another phone call. But to tell the whole story as it happened from the beginning – the request I had agreed to at the ARC private view without hearing a word of it, Alex's phone call after I didn't show up, the arrangement to meet in her flat, and then the meeting itself – seemed so lengthy and complicated a narrative as to beg the question why I hadn't mentioned any of it to Fred before. So I prepared a condensed account implying, without explicitly stating, that it all happened this afternoon at the University: *'You remember that blonde woman I was talking to at the ARC the other night, and couldn't hear a word she was saying? Well I met her again this afternoon and it turns out she's a postgraduate in the English Department, an American doing a PhD under Butterworth, on suicide notes of all things. We had a cup of tea. She wanted to pick my brains – dropped a fairly heavy hint that she'd prefer me as a supervisor in fact. I told her that was out of the question, of course. But I might give her a bit of help unofficially. It's an intriguing topic . . .'*

98

I delivered this speech, or something like it, over dinner this evening, and Fred seemed to receive it without suspicion, or indeed much interest. She was preoccupied with a problem about some expensive Italian curtaining fabric which had been delivered to *Décor* this morning. It turned out to have a flaw in the weave which ran right through the roll, and so would have to be sent back, but the suppliers didn't have any more in stock, so it would have to be manufactured again from scratch in Milan, which would take several weeks, and the client had been promised the curtains for Christmas. 'It's just possible we could still do it, but it will be touch and go,' she said. 'Is it a very noticeable flaw?' I asked. 'No,' she said. 'Well, then,' I said, 'perhaps the customer would accept the material with a discount.' 'She might,' Fred said. 'But it would niggle at her for as long as the curtains hung in her front room. She would never draw them without being reminded of it. She would always be wondering whether other people noticed, and having to stop herself from telling them. She would always associate us with something less than perfection. I can't accept that.' 'So what will you do?' 'We'll go for it,' she said with a grin. 'We'll get that material in time if I have to fly to Milan myself to fetch it.' A strong-minded woman, my wife.

Alex Loom is an intriguing person, but a bit of an enigma. Even her name is a puzzle. I couldn't find 'Loom' in the *Penguin Dictionary of Surnames*. It might be one of those American mutations of an immigrant name. German or Scandinavian perhaps – she has Nordic, ice-maiden looks. Out of idle curiosity I looked up the noun *loom* in the OED and it has had an extraordinary variety of meanings, some now obsolete, as well as the familiar one of an apparatus for weaving: for instance, an implement or tool, a spider's web, an open vessel, a boat, the part of an oar between the handle and the blade, a variety of diving birds in northern seas, a glow in the sky caused by reflection of light from a lighthouse, a mirage over water or ice, a bundle of parallel insulated electric wires, and most bizarrely, a penis. The citation for that one is '*And large was his odd lome the lenthe of a yerde*', from a fifteenth-century alliterative romance coincidentally called *Alexander*. (I presume her full name is Alexandra Loom.) It would make a good slogan for one of those Internet sex-aid ads: '*You too can have a lome the lenthe of a yerde.*' The word has fewer meanings as a verb: to appear indistinctly, to come into view in an enlarged and indefinite form, freq. threateningly; of a ship or the sea, to move slowly up and down.

In spite of the embarrassing conclusion to my visit, I don't regret making it. It's a long time since I did something that wasn't part of my predictable daily routine – even the canalside location was a part of the city I've never seen before. And Alex's thesis topic is undoubtedly interesting. I think I might give her some unofficial help with it – the idea of covertly supplementing, even subverting, Butterworth's supervision is rather seductive. I can imagine him being startled when she comes up with some bright idea that she actually owes to me . . . it makes me smile just to think of it.

8

9th November. There was a strange sequel to my visit to Alex Loom. I was getting ready this afternoon to go to the bank and the post office in our local high street, and decided to wear my overcoat. I hadn't worn it since Tuesday, because yesterday the weather was mild and wet, but today was chilly again. As I was buttoning up the coat and checking my appearance in the hall I noticed a slight bulge over my chest, as if there was a bunched-up handkerchief or small scarf in the inside breast pocket of the overcoat. I slid my hand into the pocket and, like an involuntary conjurer, drew out a pair of women's knickers. I held them out, extended between my index fingers and thumbs, and stared at them. They were made of white cotton, with a narrow lace trim. I realised instantly how they had got into my pocket: I had used Alex's toilet before I made my departure – the cups of tea having exerted an uncomfortable pressure on my bladder – and she must have taken the opportunity to stuff a pair of her knickers – or 'panties' as she would call them – into my overcoat as some kind of postscript to our conversation. But what was the import of it?

They were not unworn, but they were freshly laundered – I did not have to sniff them to ascertain that, for they were spotless and the material was soft and springy to the touch. I peered inside the waistband and found a faded Bloomingdale's label attached, confirmation that they belonged to Alex – not that I could think of any other suspect who might have played this trick in the last forty-eight hours. It occurred to me that I might easily have pulled them out of my pocket in the presence of Fred. If for instance I had worn the overcoat instead of my raincoat yesterday evening, when we went to a press night at the Playhouse, I might have done so here in the hall as we were going out, or in the foyer of the theatre as I was checking my coat into the cloakroom, surrounded by curious and amused spectators. 'What on earth . . . ?' I imagined myself saying, drawing the folded panties from my inside pocket and holding them out, gaping at them as people laughed and nudged each other and Fred looked astonished and then furious. In either scenario she would have demanded an explanation, and what could I have given, without revealing my visit to Alex's flat and making it look a much more guilty action than it was? I was seized with a spasm of anger at Alex's reckless behaviour.

I looked at myself in the hall mirror, a gaunt, grey-haired man in a formal dark overcoat holding up a pair of white knickers, like a detective with a piece of incriminating evidence, and wondered what to do with them. To put them out with the garbage was my first thought, but there have been occasions in the past when Fred lost her keys or a piece of jewellery and made a meticulous search of our garbage bins, laying out their contents on sheets of newspaper in the back yard, and fate might decide that she should do so again before our next refuse collection. I thought of burning them, but we don't have any solid fuel fires indoors, and if I did it outdoors, on the barbecue say, there was always a chance that I would be observed by a neighbour, turning over the charred panties with a pair of tongs. I thought of cutting them up with scissors into small pieces and flushing them down the lavatory; but the plumbing in this old house is not its strongest point, and what would happen if the soil pipe got blocked and Dyno-Rod retrieved a sodden ball of cotton fragments, one bearing a Bloomingdale's label? These scenarios got more and more bizarre and paranoid as I ruminated. In the end I put the cause of all this agitation in a jiffy bag addressed to Alex at Wharfside Court, and enclosed a postcard with a curt message: 'I believe this undergarment is yours. I don't understand why it came to be in the inside pocket of my overcoat, but it was a very foolish action which could have caused me acute embarrassment. In the circumstances I cannot undertake to give you any assistance or advice concerning your research. D. B.' I mailed the package at the post office on my way to the bank. I sent it first class, wanting her to feel the force of my displeasure as soon as possible.

10th November. Alex Loom phoned me this morning, having just received the package. Fortunately Fred had already left home to go to the shop.

'I'm sorry,' she said abruptly, without giving her name, as soon as I answered the phone. 'I'm very very sorry. It was a stupid thing to do.'

'Yes, it was,' I said coldly. She murmured something which I didn't catch. I turned up the volume on my phone and said 'What?'

'It was just a joke.'

'Well I'm afraid I didn't find it funny.'

'They were clean panties.' (This said as if pleading mitigation.)

'I know they were clean,' I said, unnecessarily. In the pause that followed I could sense her inference that I had examined them closely. 'That's beside the point. It could have been highly embarrassing if I had pulled them out of my pocket in front of . . . in front of other people.' There was a faint sound on the line which might have been a stifled snigger.

'You mean, like your wife?'

'Precisely.'

'I didn't think of that,' she said. 'I was sure you would find them before you got home.'

'Well, I didn't.'

'Look I'm really sorry. I promise not to do it again.'

'There won't be another opportunity for you to do it again,' I said.

'Oh, you don't really mean that stuff about not helping me with my research?' she protested.

'I'm afraid I do,' I said. 'Goodbye.' And I put the phone down.

It rang again almost immediately. 'Please don't do this to me,' she said. 'Let's start over. Let's pretend the panties never happened. I need your help with my dissertation. You promised.'

'I only promised to think about it.'

'But you're interested, aren't you? In the topic? I could tell.'

I was thinking to myself that I must propose to Fred at the earliest opportunity that we change our telephone number and go ex-directory, and wondering what excuse to give, when I realised that there was an easier solution.

'All right,' I said. 'I'll think about it. But on one condition.'

'What's that?' she asked.

'That you promise never to call me at home again.'

There was a brief silence at the other end of the line, and then she said, 'OK. It's a deal.'

Afterwards I realised that I had tacitly agreed to help her, since otherwise I would have no sanction against further phone calls. Or as the speech act theorists say, my utterance would lose its perlocutionary effectiveness.

What kind of a speech act is a suicide note? It depends of course on what classification system you're using. In the classic Austin scheme there are three possible types of speech act entailed in any utterance, spoken or written: the locutionary (which is to say what you say, the propositional meaning), the illocutionary (which is the effect the utterance is intended to have on others) and the perlocutionary (which is the effect it actually has). But there are lots of further distinctions and subcategories, and alternative typologies like Searle's commissive, declarative, directive, expressive and representative, indirect speech acts and on. Most utterances have both locutionary meaning and illocutionary force. The hazy area is the line between the illocutionary and the perlocutionary. Is the perlocutionary properly speaking a linguistic act at all? Austin gives the example of a man who says 'Shoot her!' (a rather odd example to invent, when you think about it, a symptom of male chauvinism and misogyny among Oxford dons perhaps). *Locution*: He said to me 'Shoot her' meaning by 'shoot' shoot and by 'her' her. *Illocution*: he urged (or advised, ordered, etc.) me to shoot her. *Perlocution*: he persuaded me to shoot her.

The interesting level is the illocutionary: even in this example you can see how the same words can have quite different illocutionary force in different contexts. A little exercise I used to give first-year students was to imagine such contexts. 'He ordered me to shoot her', for instance, might describe an SS officer's command to a guard in a concentration camp. 'He advised me to shoot her' needs a little more imagination, there's such a moral gap between the cool finite verb and the brutal infinitive; some Mafia godfather perhaps, speaking to a member of his family whose wife has been unfaithful to him. (On further reflection, only beta minus for that one: normally both the weapon and the target must be present for 'shoot' to be felicitous.)

What about a suicide note that consisted entirely of the words, 'I intend to shoot myself'? *Locution*: he stated his intention to shoot himself, meaning by 'intend' intend, by 'shoot' shoot and by 'myself' himself. *Illocution*: there are several possibilities here. He could be explaining, to those who would find him dead, that he shot himself deliberately, not accidentally, or that he was not shot by another person. He could be expressing the despair which had driven him to this extreme step. He could be making his family and friends feel bad about not having realised he might kill himself, and not having prevented it. Without more context there's no way of knowing. As to the perlocutionary effect, I suppose that would depend on whether or not he actually committed suicide. Or would it? You don't need to say or write the words, 'I intend to shoot myself' in order to have the effect of shooting yourself. You don't *perform* suicide in words as, say, you perform marriage. The perlocutionary level of a suicide note is inseparable from the illocutionary level – its intended effect on those who read it. But that will probably be affected by whether you succeed or not.

In practice suicide notes, even short ones, are never as stark and simple as my example. I've been looking at some on the Internet, and they are bundles of speech acts with many different kinds of illocutionary force. For instance:

Why did he do this to me? He said he loved me. How could he go out with her and not care how I feel. I can not handle this on top of GCSEs and Mum's problem. The coursework is getting to much for me to copy with. I'm going to fail my exams. I wish I could just die, then I wouldn't be a problem to anyone.

Mum's drinking is getting worse I can not handle it. She hides the bottles and is furious if I find them and Gary is useless he just sticks up for her because he drinks himself. I'm so confused all we do is fight. Whenever I'm at home it is always fighting. I want out of all of it. Please make it all stop. Take the confusion away.

I'm all a lone, nobody cares whether I live or die. All I ever do is cause problems for everyone. How can I get him back. He doesn't know how much he means to me and my life. I don't have a life without him.

Mum and Gary have left me here on my own. Can't they see how bad I am. Don't they care. Please God do something for me and make this my time to go. I am no good at school and I'm so ugly nobody wants to care for me. I'm so stupid to think that he could've cared for me.

It goes on like this for another ten paragraphs, swinging between complaint, accusation, self-condemnation, self-pity, pleading, anger, fear and despair, addressed sometimes to her family, sometimes indirectly to the boyfriend who jilted her, sometimes to God, sometimes to herself, in sentences that switch from declarative to interrogative to imperative. I thought about Alex Loom's hypothesis that suicidal despair might raise the level of the subject's normal expressive skills and I couldn't see any evidence of it here. But if you give the document a literary reading the context gives the naïve style a poignant effectiveness – even her mistakes acquire a kind of eloquence. *'I'm all a lone'* might be Gerard Manley Hopkins. Her inability to *'copy with'* her classes is like a Freudian slip revealing her recourse to plagiarism. The loose punctuation conveys the urgency of her distress and the confusion of her mind with a stream-of-consciousness effect, and as the letter goes on the present tense creates a powerful narrative momentum: *'I keep thinking about the pills in the cabinet but I'm scared.'* The letter ends:

I'm so cold, please do something. I can't stand this empty feeling that I'm having. My head is horrible. Stop the pounding it hurts so much. I have no control over anything in my life. I'm breaking into pieces.

Somebody do something.

If it were a short story one would say that the three-word final paragraph was masterly in its simplicity. But this of course was not at all how the letter would have been read by those to whom it was primarily addressed, or those who found it; and to respond to it aesthetically, analysing it like a literary text, seems a somewhat callous procedure, indifferent to the human pain it describes. It was a relief to discover from a footnote that in this particular case the writer survived the overdose and 'moved forward with her life'. The letter is in fact posted on a suicide prevention website.

12th November. I phoned Dad, as I always do on a Sunday evening, at about six o'clock. Because he is expecting the call he answers promptly. I bought him a new phone recently, with big number pads like an educational toy and a volume control which he keeps permanently in the 'Maximum' position. I had a new socket for it fitted in the dining room. Before that, when the telephone was in the hall, it could ring for five minutes before he heard it. Tonight he must have been sitting beside the phone because he picks it up and bellows 'Hallo' after only one ring.

At first he sounds in a reasonably good mood. He managed to cook a small lamb joint for his lunch without burning or setting fire to anything, and is feeling pleased with himself. 'I think I've got that stove beaten now,' he says. 'And the joint will last me for a good few days.' But it's not long before he's complaining of not sleeping well and having to get up four or five times in the night. We have our mattress conversation again. 'You should get a new mattress, Dad. An orthopaedic one.' 'A what one?' 'A firm one.' 'What's the point of wasting money on a new mattress at my age?' 'I'll pay for it, Dad.' 'I don't want you wasting your money either.' The mention of money has the unfortunate effect of reminding him of recent correspondence with the Inland Revenue. 'This bloke up in Scotland keeps writing to me about income tax. What's Scotland got to do with me?'

'I expect the administration of your tax has been moved up there,' I say. 'You know, to create jobs.'

'Jobs! I bet it's creating a nice little job for somebody, writing me letters, sending me forms to fill in.'

'What do they say, Dad?'

As far as I can gather, the Inland Revenue are saying he is entitled to a refund of tax deducted at source on some building society accounts he has and asking him to fill in a form to that end, but he suspects a plot to defraud him is being hatched on the western seaboard of Scotland. 'Put all the correspondence in an envelope and send it to me,' I say. 'I'll try and sort it out.'

'No, it might go astray in the post. You can look at it next time you're down. A thieving lot the postmen are round here. And there's another thing. I've found some share certificates in British Leyland. What shall I do with 'em? Sell 'em?'

'I think it's too late Dad. British Leyland disappeared years ago.'

'Bloody hell! Just my luck!'

'How many shares did you have?'

'Twenty-five. At five bob each.'

'Well, you haven't lost much.'

'They might've increased in value.'

I assure him that they didn't. He then raises more financial worries, and I say, as I have said before, that if he would give me power of attorney I would sort everything out to his best advantage, but he immediately becomes suspicious and hostile. 'You'll be telling me to make a will, next,' he says sarcastically.

'Well, I do think you should make a will,' I say. He knows this, of course: it is another conversation we have from time to time.

'There's no need,' he says angrily. 'You're going to get everything I have. You know that. You're my only, whatd'youcall it. Next of kin. There's no need to pay some solicitor to make a fancy will.'

'All right, Dad, have it your own way,' I sigh. It will cause me some inconvenience when he dies intestate, but it would be unkind to pressure him further: I know he shrinks superstitiously from making a will, as if he feels it would be signing his own death warrant. I chat aimlessly for a while about the weather and television programmes until he has calmed down enough for me to end the call.

Then I call Anne. She's in the sixth month of pregnancy and says she's feeling fine, just a spot of backache, and cock-a-hoop because their bathroom is finished. She works for Derby social services, and lives in a village outside the city with her partner Jim. He's an amiable if unconventional fellow who makes a living by buying old properties, doing them up while living in them, and then selling them at a profit, and buying another one, so they always seem to live in a state of semi-chaos, with only half their living space habitable. 'I hope you're not going to be moving house again in the near future,' I said.

'No, I've made Jim promise we'll stay in this one for a while,' she said. 'Until the baby's at least two.'

'That's good,' I said. I confirm that she will be coming to us for Christmas dinner and staying overnight. 'Fred is having a big party on Boxing Day,' I tell her.

'Oh, aren't you having it too, Dad?' she says. She is always hinting that Fred rules the roost here.

'Well, I suppose I am,' I say. 'But needless to say it's Fred's idea.'

'Will Granddad be there at Christmas?'

'Of course.'

'And Rick?'

'I don't know about your brother. He's been invited.'

My son Richard is a scientist at Cambridge, low-temperature physics is his field. I understand hardly anything he says about it, and even less about Richard. He seems to me to have been in a low-temperature state ever since his mother died. He's single and as far as I know celibate, lives in rooms in his college, has a passion for wine and baroque music and low-temperature physics, not much else. Sometimes I wonder if he might be gay but I don't really think so. Would I mind if he were? Probably. I try calling him, but the answerphone is on. I expect he's listening to a Handel opera on his state-of-the-art hi-fi, and doesn't want to be interrupted. I have to say that he seems quite contented with his life, though to others it seems lacking in joy.

9

16th November. Alex Loom kept her promise not to phone me, but two days later I got an email from her saying: 'When are we going to meet to discuss my research?' I emailed back: 'I don't know. As a matter of interest, how did you get my email address?' She replied: 'I figured you probably use the University network and have the same form of address as all the other faculty.' She was right of course. Retired academic staff are allowed to go on using the University network, which gives you access to the Library catalogue and saves paying a commercial service provider for email. She added: 'So when are we going to meet?' I wrote: 'I don't see the point of meeting unless there is something to discuss. Can you send me a chapter?' She emailed me a copy of her dissertation proposal, all very general and abstract. I emailed back: 'I need to see something more specific, like a chapter.' She replied: 'Nothing I've written so far is fit to show you.' I replied: 'Well then I'll wait.' Since then, silence.

I find myself checking my email more frequently than usual to see if she has responded and feeling slightly disappointed when I see from my inbox that she hasn't. Her unusual topic seems to have reawakened my appetite for research. I went into the University library today and browsed in the stacks dedicated to linguistics, looking in indexes for references to suicide notes. I didn't find anything, but I borrowed a couple of books on document analysis which I thought might be relevant. I was shocked to find one of them had several passages marked with a turquoise highlighter pen, not just in the margins but with parallel strokes drawn right through the lines of text from left to right. I pointed out the vandalism at the issue desk. 'It seems to me extraordinary that anyone educated enough to have access to a university library should do this to a book,' I said. The librarian grimaced and shrugged. He explained that since students could now check out books themselves on a computer terminal and return them through something like a laundry chute in the entrance hall, there was no way of keeping tabs on how the books were being treated. 'But you must have a record of all the borrowers of a given book on your computer,' I said. 'Can't you call them all in, one by one, and question them? The vandals might not confess, but they wouldn't do it again.' He looked at me as if he thought I was unhinged. Well, perhaps I am a bit, on this subject. To me the treatment of books is a test of civilised behaviour. I admit to making light pencil marks in the margins of a library book occasionally, but I erase them scrupulously as I go through the pages writing up my notes. It enrages me to encounter passages in library books that have been heavily underlined, usually with the aid of a ruler, by a previous borrower evidently under the delusion that this procedure will somehow engrave the words on his or her cerebral cortex, and the offence is of course vastly increased if the writing instrument is a ballpen rather than a pencil. The application of a felt-tip highlighter is a new and particularly flagrant kind of abuse, disfiguring the text with stripes of lurid colour, completely indifferent to the distracting effect on subsequent readers.

The episode threw me into a what-is-the-world-coming-to mood, a state I am increasingly prone to these days, prompted by phenomena like *Big Brother*, four-letter words in the *Guardian*, vibrating penis rings on sale in Boots, binge-drinkers puking in the city centre on Saturday nights, and chemotherapy for cats and dogs. Somehow it is easier to focus one's anger and despair on these comparatively trivial offences to reason and decency than on the larger threats to civilisation like Islamic terrorism, Israel/Palestine, Iraq, AIDS, the energy crisis and global warming, which seem to be beyond anyone's ability to control. I don't think I have ever felt so pessimistic about the future of the human race, even at the height of the Cold War, as I do now, because there are so many possible ways civilisation could come to a cata-strophic end, and quite soon. Not in my lifetime probably, but conceivably in the lifetime of Anne's unborn child.

17th November. I had a curious encounter with Colin Butterworth yesterday evening. I went to the new Theology professor's Inaug-ural Lecture, more for the sake of a glass or three of wine at the reception afterwards (the Deputy Dean who is responsible for buying the SCR wine has a good palate) than out of interest in 'The Problem of Petitionary Prayer', but there is a decent loop system in the main Humanities lecture theatre, so if it turned out to be interesting I could be sure of hearing it. I went on my own because Fred had a meeting, the board of a charity she's involved in, though she wouldn't have gone anyway, she said, 'Because I know what a hotbed of atheism that theology department is.' A slight exaggeration, but it's true that academic theologians these days tend to be a rather sceptical lot, and profess something called Religious Studies rather than Christianity or any other faith. This chap certainly adopted an attitude of amused detachment from his subject. 'Petitionary prayer is asking God to do something,' he explained. 'When you petition on behalf of others it's called intercessionary prayer. Roman Catholics have a special form of that which consists of asking the Blessed Virgin or the saints to intercede for *you*, forwarding your request to God.' The audience tittered, as they were meant to do. There were, he said, several problems with the idea of petitionary prayer. One was that it usu-ally didn't work. Another was that in many cases if it worked for you it negated somebody else's petition – as when two warring nations or two rugby teams prayed to the same God for victory. But the biggest problem of all was the idea of a supreme being who intervened in human history to reward some petitioners and deny others manifestly no less deserving. What was surprising was that religious people were so resourceful in rationalising and reconciling themselves to these disappointments and contradic-tions that they persisted in petitionary prayer. At this point I recalled the suicide note on the Internet, *'Please God do something for me and make this my time to go . . .'* and I wondered if the writer, when she came round from her overdose, was grateful or disappointed that her prayer had not been answered, and in the reverie this provoked I lost the gist of the lecture and never discovered if there was a solution to the problem of petitionary prayer.

The reception in the Senior Common Room afterwards was the usual ordeal by Lombard Reflex. There were several fellow sufferers among the elderly guests whom these occasions tend to attract, and I had some exchanges along the familiar lines of *'Terribly noisy in here'* – *'What?'* – *'I said it's terribly noisy in here'* – *'Sorry, can't hear you, it's so damned noisy in here . . .'* Then Sylvia Cooper, wife of the former Head of History, engaged me in one of those conversations in which your interlocutor says something that sounds like a quotation from a Dadaist poem, or one of Chomsky's impossible sentences, and you say 'What?' or 'I beg your pardon?' and they repeat their words, which make a banal sense the second time round.

'The pastime of the dance went to pot,' Sylvia Cooper seemed to say, 'so we spent most of the time in our shit, the cows' in-laws finding they stuttered.'

'What?' I said.

'I said, the last time we went to France it was so hot we spent most of the time in our gîte, cowering indoors behind the shutters.'

'Oh, hot, was it?' I said. 'That must have been the summer of 2003.'

'Yes, we seared our arses on bits of plate, but soiled my cubism, I'm afraid.'

'I'm sorry?'

'We were near Carcasonne. A pretty place, but spoiled by tourism, I'm afraid.'

'Ah, yes, it's the same everywhere these days,' I said sagely.

'But I do mend sherry. Crap and sargasso pained there, you know. There's a lovely little mum of modern tart.'

'Sherry?' I said hesitantly.

'Céret, it's a little town in the foothills of the Pyrenees,' said Mrs Cooper with a certain impatience. 'Braque and Picasso painted there. I recommend it.'

'Oh yes, I've been there,' I said hastily. 'It has a rather nice art gallery.'

'The mum of modern tart.'

'Quite so,' I said. I looked at my glass. 'I seem to need a refill. Can I get you one?'

To my relief, she declined. Having obtained my refill I moved to the fringes of the throng where I was able to hear the people who came up to me reasonably well. I caught sight of Butterworth and his wife on the other side of the room, chatting to the inaugural lecturer and no doubt lavishing the usual insincere compliments on his performance. Butterworth – tall, athletic, tanned, with a mop of glossy dark curly hair worn long over the collar of his silky black suit – looks the more youthful and handsome of the pair, though I suppose they are both in their early forties. Mrs Butterworth is or used to be a nurse, I remember being told, and was wearing a rather severe uniform-like pinafore dress. She stood in an erect posture and studied the theologian attentively as if she were observing his symptoms and might at any moment whip a thermometer out of her starched blouse and pop it into his mouth. Butterworth's eyes in contrast were flicking around all the time looking for the next person it would be in his interest to speak to. For a moment his glance met mine but quickly moved on: we were never closely acquainted, and as a retired former colleague I would have nothing to contribute to the furtherance of his career. Then the VC, who had introduced the lecturer, as is the custom at inaugurals, came up to me and asked me how my good lady was and what we had thought of the new play at the Playhouse, having spotted Fred and me at the press night. I hadn't been able to hear most of it, but managed to bluff my way through the conversation plausibly. Out of the corner of my eye I saw Butterworth weaving his way through the crowd towards us as fast as he could manage with a glass of wine in his hand. He greeted me by my first name as if I was his oldest friend and then turned his attention to the VC, who was however almost immediately taken off by the Dean to meet someone else. 'So how are you enjoying retirement?' Butterworth said, looking disappointedly at the VC's retreating back. People still ask me this at parties, as if I retired four months rather than four years ago. 'Very much,' I said, not wishing to give him the satisfaction of knowing the truth. 'How are things with you?' 'Frantically busy,' he said. 'You've no idea how much paperwork we have to deal with these days. You got out at the right time.' This is another thing former colleagues tend to say to me at parties, darkly implying some equivalence between early retirement and generals being helicoptered out of besieged cities or rats leaving sinking ships. He went on to list all the assessment exercises he was involved in, and all the committees he sat on, and all the grant applications he had to make, and all the articles he had to referee, and all the postgraduate students he had to supervise. 'Yes,' I said, as he paused for breath. 'I met one of them the other day.' He focused his gaze on me for the first time since the VC had left us together. 'Oh? Who was that?' 'Alex Loom,' I said.

He gave me a look which I can best describe as wary. 'How did you meet her?' he said. I told him it was at a private view at the ARC gallery, without mentioning our subsequent contacts. 'She told me about her research,' I said (which was true, though I hadn't heard a word on that occasion). 'It's an intriguing subject.' 'Yes,' he said. 'If a little morbid,' I added. 'Yes,' he said. I had never known him so sparing in speech. 'Getting on well with it, is she?' I asked innocently. 'It's early days,' he said. 'She's still assembling a corpus. She needs more British letters for a balanced sample. Most of the available stuff is American.' As he talked about the methodological problems he relaxed a little and recovered some of his normal fluency. I pretended to know less than I do about Alex to try and draw him out. Why had she come to England to do research, I asked. 'She wanted to work with me,' he said, as if the answer was obvious. 'And I suppose it's cheaper than in the States,' I said.

'Yes,' he said, reverting to monosyllabic mode. 'Where did she do her first degree?' I asked. 'I forget,' he said. 'Some liberal arts college in New England, and then a Master's at Cornell.' 'Oh, I thought she said Columbia,' I said. He looked at me warily again. 'Perhaps it was. I really don't know a lot about her. She doesn't come into the University much. Works on her own, keeps to herself, doesn't mix with the other graduate students.' 'An enigma,' I said smilingly. 'You could say that,' he said, looking past me across the room. 'My wife is signalling to me, I think she wants to go home. Excuse me.' He moved away.

He was so obviously reluctant to say anything about Alex which might reveal that his golden touch as a supervisor is failing with her that I wonder whether she hasn't in fact already dropped a hint that she would like me to take her on in his stead. I watched him go over to his wife and say something which seemed to surprise her, and shortly afterwards they left the party.

I felt pleased with myself for having discomposed the normally smooth and self-satisfied Butterworth, and consequently drank rather too many glasses of the SCR Beaujolais. I left my car in the campus car park and walked home, arriving there in a still somewhat inebriated state, which turned into an amorous state when I discovered Fred in her bathroom having a soak in the big claw-footed bathtub, looking like a rosy Bonnard nude, her blunt nipples just breaking the surface of the water, her pubic hair moving like seaweed beneath it. I undressed and got in behind her, and soaped her fine new breasts as she lay back with her head on my shoulder, and told her about the lecture and the people I had spoken to (except Butterworth) and she told me about her meeting. Afterwards we went to bed, both naked and I with a quite promising erection, but I fell asleep in middle of our first embrace, so abruptly that I wasn't aware of feeling drowsy before I passed out. I woke in the small hours, cold because I had no pyjamas on, with Fred sleeping soundly beside me, swathed in one of her all-enveloping winter nightdresses. She made a dry comment at breakfast this morning, about my having had too much to drink the night before, but did not complain about my falling prematurely asleep, which was sporting of her.

18th November. In my inbox this morning: *The longest most intense orgasms of your life – Rock hard erections – Erections like steel – Ejaculate like a porn star – Multiple orgasms – Cum again and again – SPUR-M is The Newest and The Safest Way of Pharmacy – 100% Natural and No Side Effects – World Wide shipping within 24 hours.* I don't understand how most of these spam messages reach me because they don't have the correct surname in the addressee box, only the correct initials, like 'D. S. Jones', 'D. S. Ford', 'D. S. Bellwether' and, my favourite, 'D. S. Human'. Today's was addressed to 'D. S. Limp'.

19th November. A slightly deranged outpouring from Dad when I phoned him today, complaining that he hasn't had any Premium Bond wins for six months. He holds several thousand pounds' worth. I'm pretty sure he would obtain a better return from a good building society account, but he gets much more fun out of Premium Bonds. It always gives him a kick when a warrant for fifty pounds turns up in the post, sometimes two at once, but apparently he has been going through a barren period. 'Six months! What a liberty!' I explain to him what he seems to have forgotten, that it is a lottery, and there is no guarantee how often you will win a prize, or indeed that you will ever win a prize, only that you never lose your stake. 'It's done by a computer program designed to produce random numbers.' 'You mean Ernie?' he said. 'I know all about that. But you don't think those blokes up in . . . wherever it is, up north somewhere, Blackpool, d'you think they can't make the computer pick whatever numbers they like?' 'Why would they do that?' I said. 'They're not allowed to hold Premium Bonds themselves.' 'No, but what about their relatives? Their mates?' 'Dad, if the system was corrupt I think it would have been discovered by now.' 'I'm not saying they feed their family's numbers into the machine, they're too fly to do that. But they can favour certain areas.' 'Areas?' He had lost me for a moment. 'Yes, areas, areas,' he said impatiently. 'The places where the bonds were bought. They know which numbers come from where. They can reduce the odds for people they know. I bet you more people win prizes in Blackpool than anywhere else in the country.' There was a kind of crazy logic to his speculations, and I was impressed by the amount of thought he had given to the subject. 'I don't think so, Dad,' I said. 'Well, I do, and I'm going to write and complain,' he said. 'OK, Dad,' I said. It is something to keep his brain exercised, I suppose.

I have started to collect brochures of care homes in our section of the city, getting addresses from the Yellow Pages and the Social Services. A depressing task. I shall have to make a shortlist and look at them myself before Dad comes up for Christmas. I haven't dared to broach the subject with him on the phone. Perhaps I will next time I go down to London – there will be one more day-trip before then. Not only will he strenuously resist the idea of leaving his house – the idea of moving to what he calls, with a kind of intonational shiver, 'the North' will make it doubly upsetting. His England is London and the south-east: the great metropolis, the seaside towns of the south coast with their piers and promenades, and a nice bit of country in between, nothing wilder than the South Downs. His wartime postings to East Anglia and the Shetlands he saw as exile, almost to another country. When he comes to stay with us he finds everything beyond our leafy suburban street strange and rather threatening: the different colour of the buses, the broad 'A's and cryptic contractions of the local dialect, the grids of grimy terraced houses surrounding huge carcasses of abandoned mills waiting for demolition or conversion. The surrounding country, much admired for its sweeping moors, rushing rivers and picturesque ruined abbeys, holds no charms for him. Show him a fine panorama of peaks and valleys and his comment is likely to be, 'Nowhere to get a cup of tea round here, is there?'

20th November. I had an email from Alex Loom today: 'Still working on that chapter, but here's something to amuse you while you're waiting.' She gave the address of a website called *The Suicide Note: A Writer's Guide*. I've read it through several times, and I'm completely unable to make up my mind about it. Is it a serious document, or a sick joke? Or a cunning device to put off potential suicides? It certainly exerts a horrible fascination.

The first thing you must decide is what method to use. Are you going to type your note on a typewriter or a computer? Or are you going to write it out by hand? A handwritten note is more personal, and will therefore have a greater emotional effect on your readers. But if you compose it on a computer you will be able to read it through and edit it. After all, this is the last thing you will ever say, it is your final statement to your family, friends, and the world. It may be read out in the coroner's court, and quoted in the media. It may even end up in an anthology of suicide notes! So you want to make it as clear and unambiguous as you can. You might consider composing your note on a computer and then copying out the final draft by hand to give it that personal touch. But don't make the note too polished. Switch off your computer's spellchecker and grammarchecker. A few mistakes in your letter will give it an effect of urgency and authenticity.

I felt the cold touch of the uncanny as I read that last sentence: it was as if the writer had hacked into my journal entry of a few days ago and stolen my observation about the effective artlessness of that girl's suicide note.

Give yourself plenty of time to write your note. Don't leave it till the last minute, when the pills or whatever are already doing their work. You may panic and forget all the things you meant to say. You may lose consciousness before you have finished the note. It's best to start writing a day or two before you actually kill yourself. Sleep on it, and read it through the next morning, like professional writers do. You will see all kinds of ways to improve it.

Here I began to wonder if the author of this document was sadistically teasing the poor desperate creatures who might have lighted on his website while searching the Internet for sympathy and succour under 'Suicide', or whether by treating the whole business in such a cool matter-of-fact way he was aiming to shock them into understanding the finality of death and perhaps rejecting it as a solution to their problems. Or was it simply a tasteless parody of writer's manuals?

It's best to write your letter in the first person. Referring to yourself in the third person will seem affected and insincere. Avoid literary quotations for the same reason. Write in your own voice, using vocabulary that comes naturally to you. Don't search a dictionary or thesaurus for a more impressive-sounding word than the one you first thought of. At the same time, avoid clichés like 'I can't take any more', 'My life is not worth living', 'I want to end it all' etc. They have been used so many times before that they have lost all their expressive effect, and your readers will become bored and lose interest.

The author of the 'guide' had obviously studied a lot of suicide notes, and was familiar with some of their characteristic strategies and pitfalls.

You may express a wish for the kind of funeral you would like, but don't make it too extravagant (e.g., kilted bagpipers playing a lament over your grave) or your relatives will resent the trouble and expense you put them to . . . Don't give instructions or reminders to your partner like, 'Remember your raincoat is at the dry cleaner's and will be ready for collection on Thursday.' You may think this makes you sound like a thoughtful, unselfish person, but your partner will see it as a ploy to make them feel bad, and others will think you were stupid to be thinking about such trivial matters instead of concentrating on the business at hand . . . Make sure you leave your note in a prominent place where it is sure to be found, otherwise you will have wasted your time writing it; but don't mail it, in case you take longer to kill yourself than you planned, in which case you might be prevented.

Alex evidently thought the document was a joke, something to 'amuse' myself with, and I have to admit that I laughed aloud in places, but in a slightly guilty way, appalled that humour could be wrung from such a subject. And who was doing the wringing?

22nd November. We went to a private view yesterday evening at the Old Wool Mill, one of many buildings in this city which have changed their function in the last decade or so. There are warehouses which have turned into nightclubs, banks into restaurants, and factories into arts centres, as the traditional manufacturing on which this city was built, mainly steel and wool products, gives way to the postmodern economy of information, recreation and style consumption. There is a feverish public appetite, relentlessly encouraged by the media, for new styles in fashion, food, home decor, electronic gadgets, everything. Artists, who have been committed to 'making it new' since the advent of Modernism, but at their own pace, now find themselves overtaken by the rate of change in popular culture, and struggle to find ways of making marks on paper and canvas, or assembling three-dimensional objects in space, which no one has thought of before. The exhibition at the Old Wool Mill is called 'Mis-takes' and is a collection of photographs, photocopies, faxes, and other images which for one reason or another suffered a malfunction in the reprographic process and thus produced new, unexpected and allegedly interesting artefacts. There were photographs which had been over-exposed by opening the camera body before the film had been rewound, photographic images either intentionally or accidentally superimposed on each other because the film spool was not advanced, unidentifiable images produced on a digital camera by randomly altering the default settings, palimpsests produced by printing out five-page fax messages on a single sheet of paper, and photocopies of pages in books which had been spoiled because the machine jammed, or the book was twisted as the platen moved across, producing wave-like swirls of distorted text, stark shadows and white spaces. One exhibit was a blank sheet of A4 taken from a copier whose operator had omitted to insert a document to be copied. It was entitled *Oh*, and was on sale for £150 (£100 unframed). According to the catalogue, the artist, by introducing or accepting 'mistakes' in the reprographic process, was interrogating the accepted opposition between 'original' and 'reproduced' works of art, and the necessity of accuracy, uniformity and repeatability in the application of technology to artistic creation, thus carrying forward to a new level the debate initiated by Walter Benjamin in his essay 'The Work of Art in the Age of Mechanical Reproduction'. Nothing could illustrate better my thesis that much contemporary art is supported by an immense scaffolding of discourse without which it would simply collapse and be indistinguishable from rubbish. I was saying as much to Fred in the midst of a crowd of chattering, wine-sipping private viewers when she raised her finger to her lips, which I took to be an indication that someone who would not take kindly to this remark was nearby, probably the artist, which indeed proved to be the case. When you're deaf, as well as not being able to hear what other people are saying, you don't realise how loudly you are speaking yourself.

Fred's partner Jakki was at the exhibition with *her* partner, i.e. new boyfriend. 'Boyfriend' seems too youthful a designation for Lionel, a stocky, balding, middle-aged accountant, but heaven knows he looks young enough beside myself, light on his feet and spry as a ballroom-dancing champion, able to waltz through the party throng with four glasses of wine in his paws without spilling a drop. Jakki is also younger than Fred, in her late forties I would guess, a sharp-featured brunette with a trim figure and good legs, which she makes the most of by favouring short skirts. She has a wide, perpetually mobile mouth and fortunately very good teeth, which she bares in brilliant smiles that range from the ingratiating to the lascivious depending on her mood or the circumstances. She has a loud voice and a Lancashire accent which reminds me of comediennes on the radio in my childhood, though she has little sense of humour. In every personal respect Jakki seems antithetical to Fred, but they get on surprisingly well.

It had been agreed that the four of us would have supper after the private view at a new Italian restaurant in the city centre Jakki had heard about, called the Paradiso. As soon as we passed through the door I knew that Inferno would have been a more appropriate name as far as I was concerned. The walls were clad in marble, the floors were covered with ceramic tiles, the tables were glass-topped and the chairs made of hard wood: sounds ricocheted off these surfaces like machine-gun fire. The place was full of diners and the air resounded with the roar of their conversation, the shouts of orders passed by the waiters to the open kitchen, the clash of crockery and cutlery and glassware as dishes were served and removed, and several other contributory noises which I couldn't actually distinguish and only learned about later from my companions, like air-conditioning and, ludicrously, 'background' music. Even they – my companions – found the cacophony a challenge to conversation, and were reduced to bending forward over the table with their noses almost touching in order to communicate. But communicate they did, whereas after a few attempts I gave up with a helpless shrug, and occupied myself solely with the food, which was quite good, if slow to appear, and with the wine, of which I drank more than my fair share. I was tempted to remove my hearing aid since it was serving no purpose except to amplify the circumambient din, but I remembered that Evelyn Waugh used to signal his boredom with people sitting next to him at dinner parties by laying aside his ear trumpet, and publicly taking the little plastic prostheses out of one's ears might convey the same message.

We had entered the restaurant at the peak of the evening's business, and by the time we finished our main courses the noise had diminished to a point where I could rejoin the conversation, which Lionel steered to the topic of my disability. This is not something I usually welcome, however sympathetic and well-intentioned the instigator may be. I get tired of explaining that even the highest-tech hearing aids cannot restore my brain's ability to screen out the sounds I don't want to hear from those I do want to hear, and that my hearing impairment is not the kind that can be rectified by implants, but an incurable condition that will gradually get worse, 'the only uncertainty,' as I concluded on this occasion, 'being whether I shall be totally deaf before I'm totally dead, or vice versa.'

Lionel said: 'Have you tried learning to lip-read?' I had to admit that it had never occurred to me – I associate lip-reading exclusively with the profoundly deaf, especially people in public life, and think of it as an almost miraculous skill which must have been acquired over many years from childhood onwards. 'I had a client once, a lady, who got deaf in later life like you, and she used to go to lip-reading classes,' said Lionel. 'She said they were a lot of help.' 'What a brilliant idea, darling!' said Fred, squeezing my hand and beaming gratefully at Lionel. 'Well, I suppose I do lip-read to some extent, unconsciously,' I said. 'I mean, I can always hear what Fred is saying much better when I'm looking at her face to face.' 'Yes, but that's not the same, Des,' Jakki said. (I have never invited her to call me 'Des', but she does anyway. She also calls Lionel 'Lie', but he doesn't seem to mind.) 'It's not the same as *learning* to do it.' Her rubbery lower lip protruded as she pronounced the participle, and it crossed my mind that watching Jakki's lip movements might be more distracting than helpful. Fred asked where the class was held, and Lionel said he would find out. Unfortunately the old lady in question had died a couple of years ago but he was still in touch with her son. It was definitely somewhere local. 'That sounds marvellous, I don't know why we didn't think of it before,' Fred said. 'Lie is a fund of information,' Jakki said smugly. 'Well, it's certainly a thought,' I said cautiously. 'I'll have to look into it.'

'You might have sounded a bit more enthusiastic, darling,' Fred said to me as she was driving us home.

'Well, I need to know more about this class, what's entailed, who's running it,' I said. 'I'm not sure I like the idea anyway. It's a bit late in the day to go back to sitting in a classroom.'

'Maybe you could have private lessons,' Fred said.

'Yes, maybe,' I said. 'But that would be expensive.'

'Expensive! My God! If it worked, it would be worth a hundred pounds a lesson. More.'

She spoke with such feeling that she omitted to interject her customary 'darling'. I was a little affronted and said nothing. 'You took practically no part in the conversation this evening until Lionel dragged you into it,' Fred continued. 'I know it was very noisy in there, but it sometimes seems to me that you've almost given up *wanting* to hear what other people are saying – deafness is a convenient excuse to switch off and follow your own train of thought.' 'Nonsense,' I said. 'It's the bane of my life.' 'Well, then, why don't you see if lip-reading would help?'

I was cornered. I did not relish the thought of being a student again, and had little confidence in my ability to learn lip-reading at my time of life, but I realised I would have to give it a try or be accused of selfish indifference to the impact of my infirmity on Fred and others. And I wonder uncomfortably whether there isn't some truth in what she says. Could there be a Deaf Instinct, analogous to Freud's Death Instinct? An unconscious longing for torpor, silence and solitude underlying and contradicting the normal human desire for companionship and intercourse? Am I half in love with easeful deaf?

This afternoon Alex Loom at last emailed me a specimen chapter. A short one, but quite promising. It's about paragraph breaks in suicide notes. She makes a distinction between 'depressive' and 'reactive' suicides, the former being triggered by subjective feelings of disappointment, failure, frustration etc., and the latter triggered by objective circumstances, like terminal illness, bankruptcy, public disgrace etc., her theory being that short paragraphs are more frequent in the former type of suicide note than the latter (this assertion itself needs more statistical evidence) because there is less of a cohesive flow to the writer's thoughts; rather, the depressive note is composed in a series of what she calls 'emotive spurts', which may have no connection with each other and even be mutually contradictory, as the writer reviews the reasons for her suicidal impulse and the impact of her action on others. (The feminine pronoun is used throughout in generalising statements.) The examples she gives confirm my own impression from what I have seen that there is a high frequency of one-sentence paragraphs in suicide notes. For instance, '*Somebody do something.*'

I emailed some cautiously positive comments, and she shot back a fulsome thank-you and a request to meet again at her flat to discuss the chapter in more detail. I can't see any easy way to decline, nor can I think of a better venue: if we were seen conferring at the University or in some public place like the ARC gallery it might start speculation and gossip, and I obviously can't invite her here. Her flat has the advantage of complete privacy. The question is how to tell Fred in a way which will not reveal that I have been less than candid about my previous contact with Alex.

23rd November. Lionel discovered the email address of Bethany Brooks, the lip-reading teacher, and passed it to Jakki, who passed it to Fred, who brought it home and gave it to me. So I had to carry out my promise to 'look into' the matter, and an exchange of emails followed. First I asked Bethany Brooks if she gave private lessons, and she said she didn't, because she runs classes all over the region and doesn't have time to give individual lessons, but that anyway really it was better to learn lip-reading in a group. She holds a weekly class at an adult education centre not far from us and she said I was welcome to join. 'In fact we could do with more men in the class,' she wrote, which I did not find reassuring. To my surprise it is entirely free, 'apart from a small charge for tea and coffee', being supported by a charity for the deaf and hearing-impaired. The class meets every Thursday morning from 10.30 to 12.30. I suggested, hopefully, that as a beginner perhaps I should wait until the start of a new course, rather than attempt to join an ongoing one, but she told me that there was no need, because there was no real beginning or end to the course, and most of the participants had been coming for years. 'It's not like learning a new language,' she wrote. 'It's more a matter of developing habits of observation. Identifying what's easy and what's difficult. Learning how to anticipate problems and get round them. The more practice you have the better.'

'That sounds sensible,' Fred said when I reported this message. In spite of my misgivings I couldn't disagree, or think of any good reason not to join the class next week.

24th November. I've just come back from a very disturbing visit to Alex Loom. She is either totally irresponsible or mentally unbalanced, or perhaps both, and I deeply regret that I ever got involved with her.

I mentioned to Fred at breakfast, as casually as I could manage, that I was meeting Alex at the University this afternoon to give her some tips about her research, though in fact I had agreed to go to her apartment again. My plan was to tell Fred this evening that Alex had phoned later in the morning and asked me to come to her flat instead of the University because she had to be at home to receive a delivery. Fred might raise an eyebrow at my willingness to put myself out for a postgraduate's convenience, but I could think of ways to get round that, saying for instance that I had always been curious to see the inside of one of those new canalside developments. Then I could describe the flat to Fred as if I had seen it today for the first time, and there would be no need for further subterfuge about my relationship with Alex in the future. Now I desperately wish that it had no future. If only I had heard what she was saying when we first met it would never have started. Deaf and the maiden, a dangerous combination.

I parked my car as before, and made my way to the front of her apartment block under a raised umbrella. It was a still, grey day, with a fine drizzle falling from the low cloud cover, sinking imperceptibly into the canal and covering the pavement with a shiny slick. I held the umbrella low to conceal my face. I could not shake off the feeling that there was something transgressive about this expedition and I did not wish to be recognised, remote as the possibility was. Moisture dripped from the plastic trim on the eaves of Wharfside Court, and the backwater on which it is situated seemed even more hushed and deserted than before. There was slightly more half-submerged garbage at the dead end than on my previous visit. Checking that my hearing aid was in place I rang the bell for flat 36 to announce my arrival, and Alex's voice responded: 'You're in luck. They fixed the elevator. Come on up.'

She was standing at the open door of her apartment to greet me as the doors of the lift opened on the third-floor landing, dressed in black trousers and top as before. I noted with reflex attention that her sweater had a high turtle neck, so there would be no glimpses of cleavage on this occasion, though to compensate the cotton jersey clung revealingly to the contours of her breasts. She smiled with her perfect American teeth. 'Hi. Give me your umbrella and I'll put it in the bath to dry off. What a day!' While she was attending to the umbrella I hung up my raincoat on a hook in the little hall, and wondered whether to make some joke about hoping not to find any foreign objects in it when I got home, but decided that it was best to pretend, as Alex herself had requested, that 'the panties never happened'.

I went into the living room, taking my document case with me, and sat down in the easy chair. Alex quickly followed, and sat down on the sofa. 'Thanks *so* much for coming!' she said. 'And for reading my stuff. I really appreciate it.'

'I only have a few comments,' I said, taking her chapter out of the document case. 'And you do understand this is all off the record and unofficial?'

'Of course. What did you think of the Writer's Guide, by the way?'

'I thought it was very clever.' She gave a pleased smile. 'But I couldn't work out the intention behind it,' I added.

'Oh, I was just having a little fun,' she said.

It took me a moment to draw the inference. 'You mean, *you* wrote it?'

'Sure,' she said. 'I thought you would guess. You didn't think I was smart enough?'

'No, not at all, but . . . why?'

She flicked back her curtain of silky pale blonde hair. 'Oh, you know, when you spend day after day reading suicide notes you get a little impatient with the writers, their self-pity, their bad grammar, their sheer stupidity. I suppose I was letting off a little steam.'

I asked her what effect she thought reading it would have on someone who was really thinking of committing suicide.

'I think it might have a good effect,' she said. 'I think they would say to themselves, "Who is this asshole making fun of my tragic despair?" And then they would get so mad at me perhaps they wouldn't kill themselves after all. You know, like in movies, when the cop says to the guy sitting on the parapet of the skyscraper, "OK, go ahead, if you're going to jump, jump, but don't keep me waiting, I go off duty in fifteen minutes," and the guy is so mad he takes a swing at the cop and the cop drags him to safety.'

'Supposing they're not sophisticated readers,' I said. 'Suppose they take the whole thing entirely seriously?'

'Then they deserve to die,' she said flippantly. 'No, I mean, I can't believe anybody would read my Guide and actually follow its advice, can you?'

'I'm not sure,' I said. 'Literary history is full of examples of misunderstood irony.'

She frowned slightly. 'I get the feeling that you disapprove.'

'Well, to be frank,' I said, 'I don't feel that suicide is a suitable subject for parody.'

'Oh . . .' She looked uncomfortable.

'But then I'm an old man with old-fashioned views,' I said to let her off the hook.

'I wouldn't describe you as old,' she said with a shade of coquetry. 'Mature, yes, but not old. Shall I make us some tea?'

I suggested we should discuss her chapter first. She fetched her own printout from the white filing cabinet, and pulled the sofa round so that she sat facing me, with pencil poised. It felt like a tutorial situation, and I believed she intended this effect, defining roles for us to play, master and pupil, creating the illusion that there was a contractual bond between us. I warned myself to be very careful, as I went through the chapter developing the notes I had scribbled in the margins of my copy and she listened attentively, making rapid notes of her own, nodding and murmuring, 'Yes, absolutely, you're right, that's brilliant, etc. etc.' I knew I was being groomed, but I didn't enjoy the flattery any the less for that. I realised I had been missing for the last few years the gratification of impressing minds less well stocked than my own, and the pleasure was enhanced by the fact that I was doing most of the talking and Alex most of the listening, so that for twenty minutes or so I quite forgot my hearing disability. The perfect quiet of the flat, as noiseless as a recording studio, helped.

'Well, that was really terrific, thanks so much,' she said when I had finished. 'What should I do next?'

I laughed at the transparency of this gambit. 'I can't tell you that! I'm not your supervisor.'

She pulled a face. 'No, alas. I can tell you, Desmond – may I call you Desmond? "Professor Bates" sounds so stiff.'

'If you like,' I said, hesitantly.

'Well, Desmond, I can tell you this discussion we've just had has been more useful than all my supervisions with Colin put together.'

'It's nice of you to say so,' I said, noting the familiar ease with which she referred to 'Colin'. 'But the amount of help I can give you is strictly limited.'

'What are the limits, then?' she said, with a smile.

'Well, I can't keep coming here, for one thing.'

'Why not?'

'My wife might get suspicious,' I said lightly.

'Does she know you're here?' Alex asked.

'Oh yes,' I said, but I couldn't meet her unblinking blue gaze as I said it, and I suspect she knew I was lying. 'But if it became a habit she might reasonably wonder why I was giving so much unpaid assistance to a good-looking young postgraduate student.'

She looked troubled. 'I'm afraid I can't afford to pay you right now, but –'

'No, no, I didn't mean that,' I protested.

'But if I get a teaching job in the Department –' she went on.

'For heaven's sake, I don't want you to pay me for anything,' I said in a fluster. 'No. That's not what I meant at all. It's just that Fred . . .' My sentence trailed away. She had a knack of wrong-footing me in conversation, and now I had forgotten precisely what I *did* mean.

'Fred?'

'My wife. It's short for Winifred.'

She threw back her head and laughed. She almost chortled. 'You call her Fred? And she doesn't mind?'

'I don't think so,' I said feebly.

'What does Fred do?' she asked.

'She doesn't mind me calling her Fred, but she doesn't like other people doing so,' I said.

'Sorry. What does Winifred – Mrs Bates – do? Or is she just a faculty wife?'

'Far from it. She and a partner have a shop-cum-gallery in the city centre.' I told her something about *Décor*.

'It sounds fascinating, I must go there. I need some drapes for these windows.' She gestured at the rain-smeared windows, which were fitted with venetian blinds but lacked curtains.

'I wouldn't bother,' I said. 'Their prices are very steep.'

'You don't have to worry,' she said. 'I wouldn't be indiscreet.'

I could think of nothing to say that wouldn't say too much.

'I'll go make some tea,' she said, getting to her feet. 'Assam, right?'

While she was in the kitchenette I stood up to stretch my legs and wandered over to look at the contents of the bookshelves. As I passed the table which served as her desk my glance fell on a turquoise felt-tip highlighter lying in a small tray with a number of pens and pencils.

As I sit at my desk, writing this in the Anglepoise lamp's cone of light, I still feel the shock of that observation, and the mental turmoil into which it plunged me. I pretended to carry out my intention of examining the books on the bookshelves, but I did not take in the titles inscribed on their spines. I told myself it was just a coincidence, that turquoise highlighters were ubiquitous, and I must not jump to conclusions, but some instinct told me that this was the murder weapon, covered with fingerprints and dripping with blood. Then my eye was caught by a familiar paperback on one of the shelves, *Analysing Discourse: An Introduction*, by Desmond Bates. I took it down and opened it. Alex's name was written inside the front cover in small, neat handwriting: '*Alex Loom*'. I flipped through the book. On many pages passages of the text had been highlighted in turquoise. Hearing the tinkle of tea things being placed on a tray I hastily replaced the book on the shelf, and returned to my seat.

Though I tried to remain calm, Alex obviously noticed some change in my demeanour when she came back into the room. 'You're looking very serious,' she said, as she poured the tea. 'Is there something about my chapter you've been holding back?'

'Not about the chapter, no,' I said. 'I was wondering if you know a book called *Document Analysis*, by a chap called Liverwright.'

'Read it!' she said triumphantly.

'Have you got it here?'

'No, it was a library copy. Much too expensive to buy, and anyway I didn't get a lot out of it.'

'The University library?' I asked.

At this point she picked up the inquisitorial tone of my questions and paused for a second before replying. 'Yes. Why d'you ask?'

'Well, I happened to borrow the library's copy myself the other day, and I found that it had been defaced by some previous reader. It was covered in marks made with a turquoise highlighter.'

'Really?' She didn't blush or show any other sign of guilt. Her bright blue eyes met mine without wavering. 'It was unmarked when I borrowed it.'

'Then perhaps you marked it,' I said.

She laughed, but it was a forced laugh. 'What makes you think that?'

'I noticed a turquoise highlighter on your table.'

She laughed again. 'They're quite common, Mr Holmes,' she said.

'And I just had a look at your copy of my book on discourse analysis, which is marked in the same way.' She dropped her eyes and said nothing. 'Of course you're perfectly entitled to mark your own books in any way you like,' I went on. 'But doing that to a library book is sheer vandalism.'

'I forgot it was a library book,' she said. 'I was working late, very tired, going from one book to another, some mine, some library copies . . .'

'You don't expect me to believe that,' I said.

'It's true. I didn't do it maliciously. Anyway, is it such a big deal? It's not as if I ripped the pages out of the book. It's still readable.'

'It's the principle of the thing,' I said, getting to my feet.

'Oh, don't go!' she said urgently, getting up too, and looking as if she might at any moment fall to her knees. 'Don't go while you're angry with me.'

'I'm not angry,' I said. 'I'm embarrassed.'

'Tell me what to do. I'll do anything you say. I'll buy a new copy for the library.'

'That would be a good idea, certainly. But how many other books have you vandalised?'

'None!' she said. 'Trust me.'

'I'm afraid I could never trust someone who would make irre-movable marks in a library book,' I said.

'Oh, for heaven's sake, Desmond!' she said with a pouting smile, trying a change of tack. 'Just listen to yourself. *"Irremovable marks in a library book* . . ." Lighten up!'

But I was not to be teased out of my anger. 'And after that fool-ishness with your underwear the other day . . . I've had enough,' I said. 'I'm leaving now, and I won't be coming back. Or giving you any more advice about your research.' I picked up my document case and closed it, leaving the copy of her chapter on the coffee table.

'Oh no!' she wailed.

'Oh yes,' I said, and walked out of the room. Behind my back I heard her say 'Stupid! Stupid! *Stupid!*' I think she was addressing herself. I grabbed my coat from the hook in the lobby, and left the flat. As I pulled the front door shut behind me I heard a sound as if she had flung the tea tray and its contents across the room. I took the stairs rather than wait for the lift. A fine drizzle was still falling outside, and I realised I had forgotten my umbrella, but I did not go back for it.

25th November. I didn't imagine Alex would accept the severance of relations between us without an attempt at reconciliation. I thought she might offer to return my umbrella, and make that the pretext for another meeting. Instead I got this email from her this morning:

Dear Desmond,

You're right to be angry, it was a despicable thing to do, a stupid, lazy, selfish, moronic thing, and I deserve to be punished for it. I want you to punish me. Come to my apartment at the same time on the same day next week. If you can't make it, email me your free afternoons and I'll choose one. Come to Wharfside Court, and at exactly three o'clock ring my bell three times. I won't answer on the intercom, but I'll open the entrance door – you'll hear the buzzer. You'll find the door of my apartment unlatched: just push and it will open. Close it behind you and release the latch, so it locks. Don't call out. Say nothing. Hang up your coat in the lobby. Go into the living room. The blinds will be down and it will be in semi-darkness. Don't switch on the main light. There will be a table lamp with a red bulb switched on. You'll see me bent over the table, with my head on a cushion. I'll be naked from the waist down. Say nothing. Come up behind me and position yourself to spank my butt. Take off your jacket and roll up your shirtsleeve if you like.

Don't try to fuck me. This is NOT an invitation to fuck me, but to
punish me. Use just the flat of your hand, no stick or other implement,
but hit me as hard as you like, as many times as you like. If I cry out, if
I sob into the cushion, don't stop. Get the anger out of your system.
When you've had enough, when you feel purged, just leave, silently, as
you came. Pull the door of the apartment shut behind you, and leave
the building.

The next time we meet we will say nothing about what has passed,
or about the library book. The file will have been closed. We can carry
on as if nothing had happened. This is good.

Alex

I must have read this through half a dozen times and every time I
had an erection. I have no intention of keeping the proposed
appointment, but I can't get the Sadean scenario out of my mind.
It is so easy to picture myself approaching the apartment building, as if in a film, checking my watch, pressing the bell push for
flat 36 three times at precisely three o'clock, hearing the buzz and
click as the lock on the entry door is released, ascending to the
third floor, stealthily entering the apartment, closing the door
behind me, taking off my coat in the almost dark hall, lit only by
a dim red glow from the living room. When I enter the room it is
exactly as she described: the blinds are down, the room illumin-
ated by a red lamp in one corner, and there she is, bent across the
table, her head turned sideways on a cushion, away from me so
that I cannot see her face, wearing a black top on the upper half
of her body, but naked from the waist down, except for a pair of
shiny black high-heeled shoes (a detail my imagination added),
her rosy buttocks exposed. I take off my jacket, roll up my right
shirtsleeve, then with the fingers of two hands adjust the angle of
her hips and lightly caress the curve of her buttocks, like a dog
fancier steadying his trembling thoroughbred for display. I draw
back my arm and then swing it forward, bringing my open palm
smack into contact with her bottom. The sound and the sensation of my flesh against her flesh explodes in my head. I hear her

gasp. I let my hand rest for a second where it landed before withdrawing it and smacking her again, and again, and again, pausing deliberately between each smack, favouring one cheek, then the other, in alternation, each time letting my stinging hand rest a little longer where it landed . . .

I have never had such a fantasy before. How did this woman intuit that somewhere in my psyche it was lurking, unsuspected, only waiting to be released?

26th November. Yesterday evening Fred came home from the shop a little late but in a good mood, having had a Happy Hour drink with Jakki to celebrate the sale of a quite expensive painting that afternoon. Over the chicken casserole I had prepared for us, and another glass of wine, she told me, with giggles, Jakki's confidential account of her sex life with Lionel. Apparently they have erotic theme nights from time to time, dreamed up by him. For instance an Indian Night with incense burning in the bedroom, a raga on the tape-recorder, and the illustrated Kama Sutra open for reference on the bedside table. Or a Japanese Night: sexual congress on a floor mat with cushions, dressed in yukatas, with little cups of sake to hand for refreshment. Or Italian sex, with Amoretti sweetmeats to nibble, Asti Spumante to drink, and Puccini arias as background music. We amused ourselves with thinking up additional themes that would test their imagination and/or stamina: Eskimo Night, Roman Orgy Night, D. H. Lawrence Night . . . Though we mocked them it was not without a tinge of envy on my part, and, I sensed, on Fred's too. 'Oh well, good luck to them,' she said, pouring herself another glass of wine. 'They obviously enjoy it, and why not?' 'Would you like to try something of the sort?' I ventured. 'We're too old for high jinks of that kind, darling,' she said, generously including herself in the same age bracket as myself. 'Besides, to enjoy that type of thing you have to take it absolutely seriously, and I'm afraid I would burst out laughing at the absurdity of it.' 'True, laughter is the enemy of the erotic,' I said, a little sadly. 'But we could have a

138

little old-fashioned sex tonight, if you feel like it,' she said. 'OK,' I said, corking the wine bottle.

Later, in the bedroom, as we came naked from our respective bathrooms and embraced, she said: 'If you *did* have a theme night what would it be?' I said: 'Spanking Night.' She drew back her head and stared. '*Darling!* What an idea! Who would spank whom?' 'I would like to spank you,' I said, 'but I suppose we could take turns, if you fancy it.' She laughed almost hysterically. 'You want to take me over your knee? Wouldn't I be a bit heavy?' I looked round the room. 'You could clear the top of your dressing table and bend over that.' She gave me quite a hard slap on the bottom, and I yelped, '*Ow!*' 'You see?' she said. 'You wouldn't really like it.' 'You took me by surprise,' I said, 'but the effect is actually quite stimulating. Look.' Grinning, she gave me another, harder slap. I retaliated. Struggling and laughing, we collapsed on to the bed. Later, not laughing, I did to Fred what Alex had forbidden me to do to her, closing my eyes and imagining myself in that red-lit room. It was the best sex we have had for a long time.

II

28th November. I went to London yesterday to see Dad. Those last three words are redundant. Why else do I go to London now? Gone are the days when I would travel down on business, expenses paid, to attend a committee meeting or examine a PhD, or to meet a publisher, paying my own fare but getting a bibulous free lunch, with time to spare afterwards to catch a film, see an exhibition, or browse in the Charing Cross Road bookshops before taking the train back home. Nowadays, burrowing underground at King's Cross, hurtling through the dark wormholes of the Tube, and surfacing again beneath the girdered vault of London Bridge station, I don't even *see* the West End. The last time I saw it in fact was on July 7th last year when I arrived in London in mid-morning to find the terminus seething with bewildered travellers and the whole city paralysed by what was at first reported as a massive power failure of the Underground, and later as four coordinated bomb attacks. All public transport was suspended. There was no way of either getting across London to see Dad or returning home. I queued for half an hour for a public phone – for once I wished I possessed a mobile, though people who had them were complaining bitterly to each other that the system was overloaded and that they couldn't get a connection – and having called both Dad and Fred to assure them I was safe, I went for a long walk in an eerily quiet central London.

There were plenty of pedestrians about, especially in the afternoon as offices and shops closed and their employees began their long treks home on foot to far-flung suburbs, but the roads were empty of traffic, apart from the occasional police car or ambulance racing by with lights flashing and sirens redundantly wailing. At that stage nobody knew the extent or nature of the explosions, but there was a general assumption that they were the work of Al Qaeda or some similar group and that the long-awaited sequel to New York's 9/11 had finally come to London. There was no panic but a stoical, phlegmatic, Blitz-like mood on the streets. An angry, red-faced drunk in a filthy raincoat shouted 'Fucking Arabs!' in Leicester Square, but nobody took much notice of him. In John Lewis, the last department store to stay open on Oxford Street, I bought a silver rollerball pen for Fred's birthday on the almost deserted ground floor with the exclusive assistance of three sales staff. One mentioned that she had been up to the sports department and bought a pair of trainers in which to walk home to her flat in Chiswick. It stuck in my mind as an eminently sensible, pragmatic reaction to the emergency.

All the theatres and big cinemas closed down in the course of the day but the Curzon Soho was open and I passed a couple of hours agreeably there watching an Argentine film, *Bombón: El Perro*, an engaging art-house comedy set in Patagonia, perfect escapist entertainment for the occasion, and subtitled to boot. I found an Italian trattoria in Dean Street defiantly open for business where I had a decent early supper, and walked back up Tottenham Court Road and along the Euston Road to King's Cross, where a skeleton mainline service had resumed. I was leg-weary but curiously content. It had been a kind of unexpected holiday, a reprieve from the tedious duty of visiting Dad, but most of all I had enjoyed the unaccustomed urban quiet. Paradoxically, being deaf doesn't make quietness any less attractive, but rather the reverse. Aural experience is made up of quiet, sounds and noise. Quiet is neutral, the stand-by state. Sounds are meaningful, they carry information or they give aesthetic pleasure. Noise is meaningless and ugly. Being deaf converts so much sound into noise that you would rather have quiet – hence the pleasure of walking those traffic-free streets. Terror had temporarily pedestrianised the whole of central London.

Later, as the full horror of the bombings was reported – the terrific force of explosions in the packed, tunnel-trapped rush-hour trains, the darkness, the smoke, the screams, the panic, the severed limbs – my reaction seemed in retrospect frivolous and self-indulgent. For some months, like many others, I avoided using the Tube in London, taking expensive cabs instead; but after a while, again like many others, I returned to it. Irrational, really: the more time that passes without serious incident, the more likely it is that there will be another one, since the underlying causes, Islamist fanaticism, alienated British Muslims, the provocations of Palestine/Israel, Iraq, etc., remain. How can the Tube system ever be made secure? The suicide bomber will always get through. So you place your trust in the enormous odds against being in the wrong carriage of the wrong train at the wrong time. I read recently about a victim of the bomb on the Piccadilly Line train on the 7th of July, who happened to be reading her own account, just published in a magazine, of how she had been raped and nearly murdered in July 2002, exactly three years earlier, when Germaine Lindsay, aka Abdullah Shaheed Jamal, blew himself to bits in the same carriage and scarred her for life. What are the odds against that happening, I wonder?

I am late getting to Lime Avenue, but it doesn't matter because Dad has forgotten I am coming. I have to bang the door-knocker for about five minutes before he opens it, keeping the door on the chain. He stares at me through the gap.

'What are you doing here?'

'I've come to see you, Dad. We arranged it last Sunday, on the phone.'

'Oh yes,' he says quickly, trying to conceal his memory lapse. He shuts the door to remove the chain and opens it wide. 'Well, come in, then,' he says tetchily, as if I have been keeping him waiting. He looks more like a down-and-out than ever, his dirt-encrusted tubular tweed trousers drooping on one side where a button securing his braces has come off, and he hasn't shaved. He leads me into the living room. There is an ominous heap of papers on the open flap of the bureau. 'I've been looking for those savings certificates, but I can't seem to find them.'

'Well, I'm not surprised,' I say. 'Why don't you use that filing system I gave you?' More than a year ago I gave him a cardboard box file with divided compartments labelled 'Bills', 'Bank', 'Savings Certificates', etc., but it stands unused on the floor in a corner of the room, empty apart from a few fliers offering discounts on double glazing and garden furniture.

'I couldn't get on with it,' he says, closing the flap of the bureau and sending a small avalanche of papers sliding into its interior, his preferred filing system. 'Will you have a cup of coffee?'

'I'll make it myself.'

'Yes, make it yourself, I don't know how much to put in.' He means how much of his instant coffee, an economy brand called 'Instant Coffee', best taken black with a little sugar. He follows me into the kitchen, which is in a dispiriting state of dirt and disorder. 'Will you have a cup?' I ask, searching for one that isn't cracked or chipped or covered in grease.

'No thanks, coffee goes right through me.'

'The usual place for lunch?'

He looks worried. 'Well I've got a bit of cold scrag of lamb left from the weekend, but it's not enough for two.'

'No, do you want to go to Sainsbury's for lunch?' I say, raising my voice. His face lights up with relief, and he bares his false teeth in a smile. 'Yeah, that would be nice.'

'Well, go and have a shave and get changed.' While he is upstairs I put on a very dirty floral apron that is hanging behind the door, and a pair of yellow rubber gloves, and try to clean up the kitchen a bit, beginning with a stack of soiled dishes on the draining board which I realise belatedly have already been washed up, but not so that you would notice. Then I tackle the work surfaces with a scrubbing brush and some cleaning fluid I find under the sink. I notice a new burn mark next to the stove. I don't hear Dad coming down the stairs.

'Have you seen my brown suede shoes, dear?' he says from the kitchen doorway, behind my back. I turn round, startled by this mode of address, and see his expression change from enquiry to surprise and then disappointment. He is shaven and fully dressed apart from his feet, which are in thick woollen socks. 'I thought you were Norma,' he says. 'In that apron. And the gloves.'

'Sorry, Dad,' I say. 'I didn't mean to . . .'

'You haven't seen her, have you?'

'Mum?' He nods. 'Mum's dead, Dad,' I say gently. 'She died thirteen years ago.'

'Did she? Yes, of course she did. Course she did . . . But I hear her, you know, moving about upstairs when I'm down here. I hear the floorboards creaking. And when I'm upstairs I hear her in the kitchen, washing up.' He doesn't appear to regard these experiences as unusual or disturbing – on the contrary, they seem to have relieved his loneliness. I am moved as well as worried by his account.

We take a minicab down to Sainsbury's. We both have fish and chips with peas in the cafeteria, and when he has finished his pudding, apple pie and ice cream, and seems to be in a good mood, I float the idea of his moving into a residential care home somewhere near us. Immediately the corners of his mouth turn down and he shakes his head emphatically. 'No, son. Thanks, but no thanks.'

I take out of my pocket a brochure for the most attractive-looking of the homes I have contacted in the last week or so and show it to him, pointing out the pictures of bright, well-furnished bed-sitting rooms with en suite bathrooms, the comfortable lounge, and the dining room with separate tables. 'You have your main meals cooked for you, but there's a little hotplate and kettle in the room so you can make your own breakfast and snacks.'

'How much is all that going to cost?'

'Never mind that now,' I say. 'You could afford it, and if necessary, I'll make up the difference.'

He looks at the brochure as if trying and failing to imagine himself inhabiting the place it pictured. 'No, son, it wouldn't suit me. I like my own home. I know where everything is . . .'

'You don't, Dad,' I say, rather unkindly. 'You don't know where your savings certificates are, or your suede shoes. You can't find anything when you need it.'

'That's because I've got such a lot of gear. What would I do with all my things in a poky little place like that?' He prods a picture of a bed-sitting room in the brochure.

'Well, you'd have to get rid of most of them, obviously.'

'You mean – chuck 'em away?' he says indignantly.

'Sell them, give them to charity, whatever you like. You could take a few bits of furniture that you're attached to.'

'Oh, thanks very much!'

I pause for a moment, thinking that I am handling the conversation badly, getting drawn into trivial side issues and antagonising the old man at the same time. 'I'm worried about you, Dad,' I say. 'You might have an accident one day.'

'What kind of accident?' he demands.

'You've had some accidents in the kitchen lately, haven't you? Things burning, I mean.' His sulky silence is a confession of guilt. 'You're not as fit as you used to be. You might fall down the stairs.'

'How did you know about that?' he says.

I pounce: 'You mean you *have* fallen down the stairs? When?'

He looks away shiftily. 'The other day. It was dark. I thought I was at the bottom, but there was one more step.'

'That's because you won't keep the light on in the hall,' I say. 'It's a false economy.'

'I didn't hurt myself, just a bit of a bruise on my hip.'

'You could've hurt yourself badly. Suppose you'd broken your hip – you wouldn't have been able to get to the phone.'

'Are you trying to frighten me?' he whimpers. 'It's as bad as watching *Casualty*, listening to you.' He has an aversion to hospital soaps. I remember him saying once, 'The people who watch *Casualty* must want their flesh crept.'

'I'm only trying to be realistic, Dad,' I say. 'You're getting to the point where you can't look after yourself safely any more.

Now's the time to move into sheltered accommodation, before it's too late. All I ask is that you have a look at this place, when you come up to stay with us at Christmas.'

He shook his head again. 'Well, I'll look, son, to please you. But I'm not moving anywhere. I wouldn't know what to do with myself up north.'

'It's not that far north, Dad.'

'It's all the same to me. I can't understand people in your shops when they speak to me. I don't know the bus routes. I wouldn't be able to go to Greenwich in the summer and watch the big ships on the river at high tide. And she wouldn't come there.' He pushes the brochure across the tabletop towards me. I don't need to ask whom he meant by 'she'.

'All right, Dad,' I say with a sigh. 'We'll drop the subject for now. But think about it.'

When we get up to leave a middle-aged woman at a nearby table smiles at me sympathetically, and as we pass she says, 'They can be very stubborn at that age, can't they?' I notice people at other tables looking at us with interest and amusement, and realise that Dad and I have been talking at the tops of our voices. Leaving the cafeteria feels like walking off a stage.

30th November. I had my first lip-reading class today. The experience evoked dim memories of my first day at primary school, which I joined halfway through the school year because of illness: there was the same sense of being a new boy, uncertain and self-conscious, in a group that was already bonded and familiar with the routine. As Bethany Brooks had intimated in advance, most of the participants, about fifteen of them in all, have been coming regularly for years. They are mostly women, middle-aged or elderly. Bethany herself, known as 'Beth', is a buxom, motherly lady of about fifty, I would say, with fluffy white hair, and a round, rosy-cheeked face, who looks like a farmer's wife in a child's reading book. She introduced me to the group as 'Desmond', and they all smiled and nodded. Everyone is addressed by their first names. 'Desmond is a retired teacher,' she said. That was how I had described myself in our correspondence, not wishing to pull rank as a Professor of Linguistics. It was a wise move.

We sit on stacking chairs in an arc around Beth, who faces us with a whiteboard at her side, and the apparatus of a portable loop system (the wire runs along the floor under the chairs and one has to be careful not to trip over it). All the participants – it seems somehow incongruous to call them students – wear hearing aids of various kinds, and some are very deaf indeed. When I tried the loop facility on mine I found it was much too loud, and managed perfectly well without it. Beth's basic teaching method is to say something silently in lip-speech and if members of the class look puzzled, she writes the problematical words on the whiteboard. Then she repeats the statement with voice. Her own speech is extremely clear but with one or two slightly distorted vowel-sounds that one associates with the profoundly deaf. She told me in the tea break that she lost her hearing completely at the age of nine as the result of a virus infection. She also told me that thirty per cent of English is not lip-readable, a statistic which makes it all the more remarkable how well people like herself cope with their disability, but removed any illusions about lip-reading being a magic bullet for my condition.

It was not only the sense of being a new boy that reminded me of primary school. Beth evidently tries to make the class interesting by enhancing the participants' general knowledge and testing their wits, as well as improving their lip-reading skills. So she tells us little stories or relates interesting facts about some subject, which she presumably finds in newspapers or magazines or encyclopaedias, alternating lip-speech with voiced speech, sentence by sentence, and then sets us related exercises in a quiz format, which we have to complete in pairs, lip-speaking to each other. This week she began with a brief history of the origin of Thanksgiving Day in America, which was celebrated last week. Her own lip-speaking, as one would expect, is relatively easy to read. She forms the words with lips, teeth and tongue carefully and deliberately, but not artificially, and if you don't get the sentence the first time, you have a second or third chance, because she repeats it three times to different segments of the arc of students. I have to admit that I learned some things about the *Mayflower* pilgrims that I hadn't known before, or had forgotten, for instance that there were only 102 of them, and that forty-six died in the first winter, which wasn't entirely surprising since they landed on the north-east coast of America on December 26th, 1620. I just stopped myself from putting up my hand and asking why they hadn't started their colony in the summer, reflecting that Beth might be irritated at having her demonstration of lip-speaking interrupted by an irrelevant question, or embarrassed by not knowing the answer. In the first year the local Indians helped the Pilgrims with growing crops and hunting and ninety-one of them attended the harvest feast of 1621, which was the origin of the modern Thanksgiving. I didn't know, or I had forgotten, about the friendly Indians. Later Beth handed round a typewritten quiz about the Pilgrim Fathers, which we had to complete in pairs, collaborating in lip-speech with the person we were sitting next to. *In which century was the first Thanksgiving Day? In which year did the Pilgrim Fathers go to America? Where did they sail from? What was the name of their ship?* And so on. I was paired with a nice but rather timid middle-aged lady called Marjorie who was quite content to let me suggest all the answers and confined herself to nodding agreement and writing them down on the form. Still, she seemed to be able to read my lips. Then Beth went round the circle asking individuals to tell the group in lip-speech the answers they had come up with. Some are better at it than others. Some, perhaps out of shyness, barely move their lips at all. But there was no difficulty in lip-reading them since you could guess what they were going to say. The same was true of a game we played, a kind of simplified 'Twenty Questions'. Each person was given a card with the name of something round on it, say, an orange, and a list of questions to ask other people about their round objects: *Is it big? Is it small? Is it soft? Is it heavy? Can I touch it? Can I eat it?* etc. I created some consternation by asking a question not on the list, *Is it manufactured?* There was much hilarity when the resulting puzzlement was cleared up. The atmosphere of the class is very good-humoured and supportive. There is a lot of laughter, of a totally innocent kind. At the beginning of another little talk Beth wrote on the board, *'An Enormous P –'*, and nobody sniggered or even smiled. The subject turned out to be a giant pumpkin which someone had grown on their allotment. After the talk Beth handed out pictures of it taken from a magazine which we passed round from hand to hand. The analogy with the infants' class seemed complete when each of us had to think of a nursery rhyme and recite it in lip-speech to the group. I started *'Ride a cock horse to Banbury Cross / To see a fine lady upon a fine horse,'* and then my mind went blank and I couldn't remember how it went on. More hilarity, as they competed to remind me: *'With rings on her fingers and bells on her toes / She shall have music wherever she goes.'* Of course! What a dunce I was. There were two things which were interesting about this exercise: one that the poetic rhythm helped to make people's lip-speaking more decipherable, and secondly that even if you failed with the opening lines you would recognise the rhyme sooner or later, because it was familiar. The first point is not much use in ordinary conversation, and the second merely illustrates a general rule that the more predictable a message is, the easier it will be to receive it in an incomplete form.

Fred quizzed me eagerly about the class when she got home that evening. I made her laugh with my description of the proceedings, especially my failure with the nursery rhyme, but she looked disappointed when I said I thought the exercises were of limited usefulness because they were loaded in favour of the addressee. 'You are going on with it, though?' she said. 'Oh, I'll carry on for a while,' I said. 'I'll give it a chance.' 'Good,' she said. 'That's the spirit, darling.' The fact is that in a curious way I quite enjoyed being back in the infants' class.

*

1st December. Today was the day Alex had appointed for her 'punishment'. I became increasingly nervous as the hour of three o'clock approached. I was alone in the house, and paced restlessly from room to room, glancing at the clocks in each of them. I had decided that the best response to her bizarre proposal was to ignore it, but now that seemed like a mistake. She had asked me to reply only if I wanted to change the day, so she might easily have interpreted my silence as agreement. I imagined her preparing the flat, closing the blinds in the living room, setting up the red table lamp in the corner, then stripping her lower limbs and bending over the table with her face resting on a cushion, waiting for my ring on the entryphone – no, I revised the scenario, she wouldn't bend over the table until she had heard my ring and admitted me to the building, but she would be naked from the waist down, ready to take up her position at the table at once. So now she might be pacing anxiously like me, but half-naked, or sitting on the sofa with her bare knees together, like the adolescent nude in the Munch picture, waiting, wondering if I would come. Perhaps she would go to the window, prise the louvres of the blind apart, and peer down to see if I was coming along the towpath. How long would she wait after the hour of three before she realised I wasn't coming, and got fully dressed again? How foolish would she feel? How angry? What would she do next?

At about four-thirty the phone on my desk rang. I jumped, and picked it up without first putting in my hearing aid. It was Alex, of course.

'You didn't come,' she said.

'No,' I said.

'A pity. It would have been good for both of us.' She didn't sound as if she was phoning from her flat, but from a public place: there was a good deal of noise, including music, in the background.

'I thought you agreed not to phone me at home again,' I said.

'Well, that was on condition you helped me with my dissertation,' she said. 'Anyway your wife isn't at home right now.'

'How do you know?' I said.

'Because I'm looking at her.'

I was seized with a sick sensation of bewilderment and dread. 'What do you mean?'

She laughed. 'I'm looking at her through the window . . .' Her voice faded and my hearing was not good enough to pick up the following words.

'What? What?' I said, scrabbling frantically for my hearing-aid pouch. 'I can't hear you.' I stuffed a hearing instrument into my right ear, and her voice became just about audible.

'I guess the signal is not too good in this place,' she said.

'Where are you?' I said. But I had already guessed.

'I'm in the Rialto shopping mall, outside *Décor*,' she said. 'It's a nice shop. I can see your wife inside, showing a customer some beautiful cushions. She's the tall one in the corduroy pants suit, right? Not the brunette with the short skirt.'

'What is this all about?' I said stonily.

'It's about your folding umbrella,' she said. 'You left it in my flat last week.'

'I know,' I said. 'It's an old one, of no consequence.'

'Well, I happen to have it with me. I thought I would take the opportunity to return it.' I was silent for a moment. 'Are you there?' Alex said. 'Did you hear that? I thought I'd go into the shop and introduce myself to your wife and say, "Your husband left this in my apartment last week, would you give it to him?"'

'Please don't do that, Alex,' I said.

'Why not? She knew you were there that day, didn't she?'

'No, she didn't,' I said.

'Ah, then I have you in my power,' she said, with a giggle.

'What is it you want?' I said.

'I want to continue our discussions. I find them very useful.'

I thought for a moment. 'All right – but not in your flat,' I said. To my relief she accepted this condition, and I arranged to meet her in a café I know on the other side of the city. 'Bring the umbrella,' I said, before terminating the call.

2nd December. Fred has taken to giving me an occasional smack on the bottom when I'm not expecting it, but if she was hoping to reawaken the passion of the other night, she has been disappointed. I am far too preoccupied with the problem of how to disentangle myself from Alex's coils to have any appetite for sex. In fact I can hardly suppress an oath of protest when I receive one of these tokens of affection, Fred's idea of a playful pat being fairly robust. Indeed I wonder whether she isn't in fact relieving her own frustration by this means. These last couple of days, since that phone call from the Rialto mall, I have been particularly abstracted and more than usually inattentive to what Fred says to me, and she gets understandably exasperated. 'Have you got your hearing aid in, darling?' she keeps saying, and when I say yes she raises her eyes heavenwards in mute appeal.

Again and again I resolve to confess the whole story of my involvement with Alex, but again and again my nerve fails me. Why? It's not as if I have been unfaithful to Fred – I haven't touched the girl, or even flirted with her. It must be because I'm afraid of looking silly. That's it. I have been silly. I have let an unscrupulous young woman twist me round the little finger of her flattery. To confess that would make me look smaller in Fred's eyes, further weaken my status in our marriage. But there is more to it. I know that, if I confess, I must confess everything, otherwise I won't achieve real peace of mind, that blissful state which Fred claimed she achieved when she became a practising Catholic again and went to confession after a gap of some twenty-five years, a feeling she said was 'like being spiritually laundered, like having your soul washed, rinsed, spun dry, starched and ironed. Or no – more like being washed in a waterfall and spread out to dry on a sweet-smelling bush in the sunshine.' But to achieve anything like that enviable state I would have to confess everything, including Alex's invitation to 'punish' her. 'And did you?' Fred would ask, and 'Of course not,' I would say. But she would know that I had desired to do so. I had committed spanking in my heart. That too is silly, but also shaming. And worse still, she would realise that I had sought to act out my fantasy on her.

12

4th December. Christmas, how I hate it. Not only it, but the thought of it, which is forced into one's consciousness earlier and earlier every year. For weeks a whole aisle of Sainsbury's has been dedicated to Christmas decorations, Christmas wrapping paper, Christmas crackers, Christmas napkins, plaster Santas, plastic reindeer, and gifts of hideous design and doubtful utility, mostly manufactured in non-Christian China. Now the newspapers and their glossy magazine supplements are so full of ideas for presents, parties, punch, and leering advice to men about buying lingerie for their womenfolk, that you can hardly find anything worth reading. Illumination addicts compete to festoon the facades and front gardens of their suburban houses with the most elaborate displays of blinking coloured lights and animated Christmas icons, causing collisions of rubber-necking motorists. Restaurants offer special Christmas menus throughout December, as if one plate of turkey with all the trimmings per year wasn't quite enough. Even the sex-aid emails strike a seasonal note: one received this morning was illustrated with a drawing of a blonde bimbo wearing only stockings and high-heeled boots, her arms and legs wrapped round a snowman, and the caption: *'Our Cialis made him hot in fifteen minutes!'* Unsafe sex for a snowman, surely?

What can explain this blight of creeping Christmas? When I was a child Christmas Day and Boxing Day were holidays and then life went back to normal, but now Christmas extends seamlessly into the New Year, an even more pointless festivity, so the whole country is effectively paralysed for at least ten days, stupefied by too much drink, dyspeptic from too much food, broke from expenditure on useless gifts, bored and irritable from being cooped up at home with tiresome relatives and fractious children, and square-eyed from watching old films on television. It is the very worst time of the year to have an extended enforced holiday, when the weather is at its most dismal and the hours of daylight are most restricted. Scrooge is my hero – the unregenerate Scrooge of Part One of *A Christmas Carol*, that is. 'Bah, humbug!' How right he was. What a pity he had a change of heart.

I feel a bit better for having got that out of my system. Fred is a true Christmas devotee and gets annoyed if I moan about it. Of course it has a genuine religious significance for her, but it's also good for business, so now she embraces it with both arms. Then she likes bringing the family, or families, together, and the fact that we invariably get on each other's nerves after a few hours doesn't seem to bother her, or rather it does bother her but she has a knack of deleting the unpleasantness from her memory well before the next Christmas comes round.

7th December. I couldn't get away from Christmas even at the lip-reading class. This afternoon Beth handed out questions on a piece of paper which we had to ask each other and answer without voice: *Have you started your Christmas shopping? Do you get up early on Christmas morning? Do you visit family and friends at Christmas? What present would you like to receive this Christmas? Do you have a turkey for Christmas dinner?* etc. Then she read without voice a magazine article about the biggest Christmas pudding in the world, and handed round pictures of this gross and repulsive object. In the tea break Marjorie reminded us that we should put our names down on a list if we wanted to join the Christmas lunch party at the end of term. She left the list on a table and I carefully avoided going anywhere near it.

Fortunately it wasn't all Christmas. We had an exercise in small groups involving homophenes – the deafie's equivalent to homophones, words which look alike on the lips but have a different meaning, like *mark, park* and *bark,* or *white, right* and *quite, rewire* and *require.* We had to make up sentences using one of these words and lip-speak them to the group. I made up a sentence using all the words in two sets, '*Quite right, the white room requires rewiring,*' which of course nobody could lip-read, and there was much protesting laughter when they gave up and I said it with voice. I was justly punished for showing off in this fashion by the next exercise, a quiz, to be completed in pairs, called Animal Crackers, which was a list of words with letters missing which themselves spelled out the name of an animal. Thus the solution to *Ball - - - ing* was *Ballbearing*, *Bl - - t - -* was *Blotter*, and *Pu- i - -* was *pumice*. It reminded me of puzzles in the comics which I read as a very young child, but I found the exercise surprisingly difficult, while Gladys, the elderly lady I was paired with, was an absolute wizard at it, and guessed nearly all of them before I did. She told me she is eighty-six.

It is too early to tell how far these classes will improve my ability to use lip-reading in real conversations, and I doubt whether it could ever help me much in situations where there is a low level of redundancy and predictability in the flow of information. Nevertheless I find the class a soothing and refreshing interlude in the week, a welcome suspension of the troubled introspection for which retirement gives so much scope, and a distraction from the anxieties of my personal life at the moment. Above all, it is wonderfully relaxing to be in a social environment where you don't have to feel in the least foolish or worried or apologetic about being deaf.

8th December. I met Alex today as arranged, at Pam's Pantry, a café near the main campus of our second university, the former Poly. There used to be a second-hand bookshop next door, in which I browsed occasionally before the Internet made it redundant. The café is a stripped-pine and home-made carrot cake type of place, busy in the lunch hour, but quiet in mid-afternoon, and it doesn't have any piped music. I haven't been there for a long time and didn't recognise the bored-looking young woman behind the counter. I arrived early, got myself a cup of tea, and sat down at the back of the room with a view of the door. There weren't many other customers: a couple holding hands and a whispered conversation, and a few solitary young people who looked like students reading text messages on their phones or listening to their iPods. When Alex came in she did not look round or catch my eye, but went straight to the counter and ordered a coffee – a latte, I deduced from the server's movements at the coffee machine. This took some little time, during which Alex kept her back turned to me. She was dressed in black as usual, a shiny black quilted nylon coat over black trousers and boots, with a long red knitted scarf wound round her neck, trapping her pale blonde hair. Then, with the cup and saucer in one hand, and a capacious handbag in the other, she went through an elaborate mime of looking around, hesitating about where to sit, then catching sight of me, and giving a surprised smile of recognition before coming over to say, in a loud voice, 'Hi! May I join you?' The other occupants of the café, who had taken no notice of either of us till this moment, looked up. I realised she was teasing me by this unnecessary and in fact counterproductive pretence that we had met by chance. She unwound her scarf, shrugged off her coat and sat down opposite me. She took my folding umbrella out of her bag and laid it on the seat of an unoccupied chair beside our table. 'Don't pick it up now,' she said, in a lower voice, as I made a move to do so. 'When we're through, I'll go out first and leave it there. You stay for a few minutes and then just casually pick it up when you leave.'

'You've been reading too many spy stories,' I said.

She smiled in acknowledgement of the source of this bit of business, and stirred her latte. 'Have you forgiven me, Desmond? For the library book and all?'

'It's not for me to forgive,' I said. 'It's for the Librarian.'

'You want me to go and confess to the Librarian? Then they'll banish me from the Library! Probably from the University. Probably from the country! I'll be forcibly repatriated, like an asylum seeker caught shoplifting.' There was a mischievous gleam in her bright blue eyes.

'What is it you want from me, Alex?' I said. I was tiring of this badinage.

'Right now, it's a suicide note.'

I asked what she meant. She said there had been a psychology research experiment years ago, in America, mixing up genuine suicide notes with what were called 'pseudicide' notes composed by friends and family of the research team, and asking a class of graduate students to distinguish the genuine ones from the fakes. 'They scored a surprisingly high success rate. It turned out to be a useful way of identifying the stylistic features of real suicide notes. I want to repeat the same experiment, so I'm asking everybody I know, which isn't an awful lot of people here in England.'

'You want me to write a suicide note –'

'Yeah, make it as realistic as you can.'

'I wouldn't dream of it,' I said.

'Why not?'

I hesitated. I recalled as she spoke that there was a murder case some years ago in which a man had tricked his wife into writing a suicide note and then killed her. I could hardly cite this as a reason for refusing to cooperate, and I didn't seriously suspect her of any murderous intention, but I was sure it would be extremely unwise to put such a potentially compromising document into her irresponsible hands. I quickly invented another reason to decline: 'For the same reason I wouldn't use that website where you enter all your personal details and a computer program calculates the day you will die.'

She looked taken aback. 'You mean, you're afraid it might come true?'

'Something like that.'

'Have you been tempted to commit suicide, then? Why?' She had dropped the tone of badinage. Her blue eyes were intently focused on me, waiting for my answer.

'I'm gradually losing my hearing,' I said. 'There's no cure. Eventually I'll be stone deaf. It's very depressing.'

'Gee, yeah, I can imagine but . . .'

'But what?'

'I never came across a case where somebody killed themselves because of deafness,' she said.

'Beethoven came near,' I said.

'But he didn't.'

'No. He still had all that marvellous music inside him which he wanted to get down on paper. I don't have any marvellous music inside me. I don't have any marvellous anything.' I was almost persuaded by my own story, moved by the pathos of my imagined plight. Alex anyway was convinced.

'Hey,' she said, putting her hand over mine on the table. 'Sure you do.' Her fingers were cool and soft, like Dad's. I was startled, but did not remove my hand. She wore a sapphire ring on her middle finger which seemed to reflect her eyes. 'You have a lot of knowledge, Desmond, which you can share with people like me,' she said, in a lighter tone, withdrawing her hand.

We talked for a while about my past research – or rather I talked. She was charming and receptive, and I have to admit that I enjoyed her company, forgetting the embarrassment and worry she had caused me in the past few weeks. I bought her another cup of coffee and myself another tea, with two portions of carrot cake. But when I glanced at my watch and said I had to be going she reverted to the mood of her entrance, and said with a conspiratorial smirk, 'I'll leave first. Don't forget your umbrella,' reviving the memory of her email prescribing her 'punishment', and its sequel. Neither of us had mentioned that episode, and it was as if by not registering my disapproval I had acquired some virtual complicity in it. I smiled feebly and stayed obediently in my seat as she gathered up her bag and her scarf and did up her coat. 'Thanks for the coffee and cake,' she said. 'And if you change your mind about the suicide note –'

'I won't,' I said.

'Well . . . I'll be in touch.'

About what, I wondered. I had come to the café with the intention of bringing our relationship to an end once and for all, and failed again. I watched her make her way between the tables to the door, and to my dismay she paused briefly to greet a young man sitting on his own with a laptop open on the table, who looked up as she passed. Absorbed in our conversation, I hadn't noticed him come into the café. After Alex had gone out he glanced across at me, and I stared him down. I wondered if he had been observing us, and whether he had entered the café in time to see Alex cover my hand with hers.

Tonight, after writing up our meeting, I began idly drafting a pseudicide note – not with any intention of offering it to Alex, but as a stylistic exercise. It was addressed to Fred of course, but just deciding on the form of address was difficult. Fred or Winifred? Dearest or Darling? In the end I decided on Dearest Winifred, the intimacy of the epithet balancing the formality of the full first name, which seemed more appropriate to the occasion than 'Fred'. Imagining what had brought me to the point of preferring extinction to the continuation of consciousness was easier, for I had already thought of it in conversation with Alex: a drastic acceleration of hearing loss, leading to almost total deafness. Everything I suffered now – frustration, humiliation, isolation – multiplied exponentially. Barely able to hear *anything*. At cross purposes in every conversational exchange. In the home a silent, withdrawn, unresponsive companion at the best of times; a surly, self-pitying misery at the worst. A damper on every party, a dud at every dinner table. A grandfather unable to communicate with his growing grandchildren, in the presence of whose blank looks and idiotic misunderstandings they must strive to stifle their giggles. It's not a life worth living, I would tell Winifred – *My deafness is a drag on you and the rest of the family, and an inescapable, irremediable grief to me. So I'm going to put an end to it. Please don't feel bad about it, my darling, it's not your fault, and you mustn't blame yourself; no one could have been more kind and understanding. But everyone's patience has its limits, and I have reached mine.* But as I drafted the note its insincerity showed in every word, even in punctuation marks (did anyone ever use a semicolon in a suicide note?). I don't really believe Fred would show such saintly forbearance as it implied, nor would I expect her to. And depressing as the state I had conjured up for myself might be, it wouldn't be utterly unbearable. There would still be some pleasures left, and no pain. I could have written a convincing note based on the premise of a painful terminal illness, but just thinking of it stirred up distressing memories of Maisie. I abandoned the exercise.

Perhaps it's true that nobody ever committed suicide on account of deafness. Beethoven came pretty close, but, as Alex said, he didn't. You could say that the Heiligenstadt Testament was *instead* of a suicide note, designed to be found after he died by natural causes, but having just the same motives as a suicide note: to reveal the depth of his despair to his family and friends, to explain why he seemed outwardly such a grouchy unsociable bastard, and make them feel bad for not realising how wretched he had been. Maybe that's why I started writing this journal; maybe that's what it is, a testament. The Rectory Road Testament.

9th December. Dad phoned this morning, cock-a-hoop because he has won three £50 prizes in Premium Bonds, received this morning, only two weeks after sending off his letter of complaint about not winning anything for six months. 'You see? I told you!' he crowed.

'Dad,' I said, 'you don't seriously think your letter made them give you a prize?'

'*Three* prizes! 'Course it did! I got 'em rattled. They said to themselves, this Harry Bates is no fool. He's going to cause trouble if we're not careful. Let's bung him a few quid and keep him quiet.'

I was about to argue that it was just a coincidence, but then I thought: why deprive him of his moment of triumph? 'Well, congratulations, Dad. You did well.'

'I did, didn't I? No thanks to you – you didn't want me to write that letter, remember.'

'I must admit I didn't expect it would have such a magical effect,' I said. 'But I'm not sure it will work again.'

'Well, we'll see, won't we? Maybe somebody up there in Blackpool will make it his business to keep me happy in future, so I don't have to send them another letter.'

'Well, I hope so, Dad,' I said. 'What are you going to spend the prize money on?'

'What?' I repeated the question. 'Oh, well, I don't know,' he said, the euphoria quickly leaking away from his voice. 'I don't know that I want to spend it on anything. I'll put it in the bank for a rainy day.'

'Well, I won't suggest you get a new mattress –'

'Good.'

My reason was that if he moved into a care home in the near future a bed would probably be provided, or we might seize the opportunity to buy him a new one, but I didn't think it would be politic to explain this. To change the subject, I told him I had started going to a lip-reading class.

'A what class?'

After several repetitions and explanations of the term I got him to understand.

'Oh. Well, I suppose that might be useful to someone with your problem, son,' he said.

12th December. A disturbing encounter with Colin Butterworth in the University today. I had been in the Library, browsing in the periodical room, and he was ascending the steps of the building as I came out. He was actually bounding up them – he always gives the impression of being in a hurry – but came to a halt as he saw me, and waited for me to descend. There was a strong wind blowing, ruffling his dark curly locks, which in daylight are visibly flecked with grey. He wore a suede leather jacket and an open-necked shirt. 'Hallo, Desmond,' he said. 'How are you?'

'All right,' I said, wondering what this was about. Usually we do no more than nod to each other when we meet.

'Have you got a moment?'

I said I had, and he suggested we go to his office, postponing his visit to the Library. 'It can wait,' he said. On the way to his office he made conversation about the University's position in a recently published league table of applications per student place, in which English had apparently done well, but that was obviously not what he wanted to talk to me about. I had an intuition that it would be about Alex, and I was not wrong. When he had closed the door of his office behind us, he gestured me to an upright armchair and sat down behind his desk in a hi-tech tilting swivel chair which is not standard University issue.

'You know Alex Loom,' he said.

'I've met her, yes,' I said. 'As I mentioned the other day.'

'More than once, I believe,' he said.

'Yes,' I said, wondering if he knew about our meeting in Pam's Pantry, for I could not imagine Alex telling him about our meetings in her flat. 'Why do you ask?'

Although he was in the inquisitor's seat, he seemed ill at ease, unconfident, and swung his chair to look away, out of the window, at the dark grey clouds scudding across the sky. 'You may think it's none of my business. I certainly don't want to intrude . . .'

He lowered his voice and I didn't catch what he was saying. 'I'm afraid I'm rather hard of hearing,' I said. 'I didn't quite –'

He swung his chair back to face me. 'Sorry! I said . . . well, in a word, I would advise you not to get involved with her.'

'I've only met her a few times,' I said, 'to discuss her research project, at her request. I made it quite clear that I could only help her very informally, in no way encroaching on your role as her supervisor.'

'You didn't think of consulting me about that?' he said, with a hint of complaint now.

It was a perfectly legitimate point, and I groped a little for a satisfactory reply. 'Well, I didn't think of it – I *don't* think of it – as an ongoing arrangement. I thought it would be a one-off conversation. But she's rather persistent.'

'She's a menace,' he said. 'Has she said anything to you about me?'

'No,' I said unhesitatingly.

'Well, if she does, disregard it. She's seriously disturbed in my opinion, a classic schizoid type.'

'Why do you say that?' I said.

'Haven't you noticed anything odd, not to say bizarre, in her behaviour?'

Remembering the panties in my coat pocket, the vandalised library book and the invitation to spank her, I could only produce an unconvincing, 'Not particularly.'

'You probably haven't known her long enough,' Butterworth said. 'She has violent mood swings. She'll do something quite outrageous and then beg for forgiveness.'

'What kind of thing?' I asked.

'Oh . . . stupid things . . .' He obviously didn't want to specify them. 'But potentially embarrassing.'

'Perhaps she should get some help,' I said. 'The University Counselling Service . . .'

'I've hinted that she might do that, but she laughs and denies that there's anything wrong with her. Then she says she's through with therapy, and you discover she's had years of it in America . . .'

'She seems quite bright,' I said.

'She's clever, but not as clever as she thinks she is, or would like others to think. She has a chronic problem about producing anything for assessment, in case it doesn't match her own self-estimate.'

I thought it would be tactless to mention that she had shown me a passable chapter of her thesis, so I said: 'She posted something on the Internet which shows considerable wit and intelligence, whatever one thinks of the ethics of it.'

'You mean that Writer's Guide to suicide notes? Yes, I've seen that, she directed my attention to it. I very much doubt whether she wrote it.'

This suggestion surprised me, but I immediately saw how plausible it was. I felt a strange disappointment. 'Why do you say that?' I asked.

'It's an anonymous document – anybody could claim authorship.'

'Why would she do so?'

'To impress. You were impressed, obviously.'

I couldn't deny it. I also remembered Alex frowning when I aired my doubts about the possible effects of the piece, and saying, '*I get the feeling you disapprove.*' Perhaps she was wondering whether she would rise or fall in my estimation by confessing that she hadn't written it. 'Well, you may be right, I suppose,' I said. 'There's no way of knowing.'

'There's internal evidence,' he said. 'The lexis of the piece is more English than American.' He allowed himself a little moment of professional one-upmanship. 'I'm surprised you didn't notice that.'

'Well, she was educated for a time in England,' I said, piqued into defending myself. 'It can have a permanent effect on a person's writing style.'

'True,' he conceded. 'But she really is completely untrustworthy. The only piece of written work I've managed to get out of her turned out to be largely cribbed from another source.'

'What was it about?' I asked, with a sinking feeling.

'Oh, paragraph breaks in suicide notes. Two types, related to the subjects' motivation. There was a brief footnote acknowledging the other article, in a psychology journal, but when I chased it up and read it, I found that almost everything she said was derived from it. It turned out that the author of the article was a former boyfriend. She said he wouldn't mind – seemed to think that put her in the clear as regards plagiarism.'

'I see,' I said. I felt like a foolish dupe, and I suppose I must have looked it.

There was a tap on the door. Butterworth glanced at his watch. 'I've got a supervision,' he said. 'Look, Desmond . . .' He leaned forward in his chair and spoke earnestly. 'This girl is trouble, and I rue the day I ever took her on. I don't need to tell you the pressure we're under to take on eligible postgrads from abroad for their fees, and as you can probably imagine she gave a very plausible performance when I interviewed her, and her references looked OK. But it's my belief that she's not capable of completing a PhD, as much for psychological as intellectual reasons. My advice to you is not to get involved with her, or you'll find yourself writing her thesis for her. And don't trust a word she says.'

I thanked him for his advice and took my leave. Loitering in the corridor outside was the young man with the laptop who had been in the café.

I must find some way of severing relations with Alex without inviting retaliatory mischief. But how?

13th December. Something happened yesterday evening which in some ways made the Alex problem more manageable, and in other ways less so. Fred and I went to the press night for the Playhouse's Christmas show, *Peter Pan.* It was nicely staged, with meticulous period detail, but had a black Peter Pan. The young actor playing the role was actually rather good, but I found his exotic appearance in the middle-class Edwardian milieu, which would certainly have excited comment from the Darling children, but which the text did not permit them to notice, a constant distraction. I might accept the socio-political case for colour-blind casting, as I believe they call it, if its proponents would admit that it often carries a certain aesthetic price, but they won't. I was arguing about this with Fred in the foyer during the interval – she sits on the Friends of the Playhouse committee and was taking a contrary view – when to my dismay I saw Alex approaching us, with a smile of recognition on her face. She was wearing the same red silk blouse as when I first met her, but with a swift, almost imperceptible movement of her hand she did up the lower of the two buttons at her throat as she drew near.

'Hallo, Professor Bates,' she said.

I think I performed fairly well the part of an elderly, slightly absent-minded professor, mildly pleased to meet a presentable slight acquaintance in these circumstances and introduce her to his wife if he could only remember her name. 'Oh, hallo!' I said. 'Fred, this is, er . . .'

'Alex,' she said, helpfully, playing her part, and shaking Fred's extended hand.

'Yes, Alex Loom, she's a postgraduate at the University, in the English Department, I think I told you about her research project –'

'I've seen you before somewhere,' Fred said to Alex. 'I know – at the ARC – you were talking to Desmond at a party, their last opening.'

'Yes,' I interposed. 'You asked me afterwards who she was and I had no idea because I hadn't heard a thing she said.' I smiled rue-fully to show this was a joke against myself. 'But we met subsequently in quieter circumstances.'

'Desmond is hard of hearing,' Fred explained.

'Oh dear,' Alex said sympathetically. 'How do you manage in the theatre? It must be difficult.'

'It is. But I use this thing,' I said, taking the wishbone-shaped headset out of my jacket pocket and brandishing it in the air. 'I've discovered the optimum place to sit in this auditorium for using it. And I do know this play pretty well.'

'So do I, I love it,' Alex said.

'What do you think of the Peter Pan?' Fred asked her.

'I think he's brilliant. Such a bold bit of casting. It gives a whole new dimension to his outsider-character.'

How did she know that was the right answer to impress Fred? Or was she quite sincere? With Alex, how could one possibly know? The roar of conversation in the foyer had now reached a decibel level that ruled out any further part in the conversation for me, but I could see the two women were getting on well together. When the bell rang for us to return to our seats, Fred shook Alex's hand again and I heard her say: 'Drop in any time, we're open from nine-thirty to six, seven on Thursdays.'

'Thanks so much, I will,' Alex said, with her most winsome smile.

'What a nice young woman,' Fred said, as we made our way back to our seats in the front stalls. 'I told her about *Décor*, and she was very interested. She needs some curtains for her flat.'

'She couldn't possibly afford anything in your shop,' I said, irritably and injudiciously.

'How would you know?' Fred retorted, but without any tone of suspicion. 'She may have rich American parents.'

I was going to say that Alex was paying her own fees, but decided not to reveal this much knowledge of her circumstances.

'You told me about her PhD topic, but I forget what it was,' Fred said as we took our seats. 'Something rather odd . . .'

'A stylistic study of suicide notes.'

'That's right. What a depressing subject to choose. You would never have guessed to look at her. Do you think she has a personal interest in it?'

'I don't know,' I said, as the lights went down for the second half. 'I don't know much about her.'

I paid little attention to the rest of the play because I was thinking about the implications of this meeting. I was relieved to have established in Fred's mind the idea of an entirely innocent acquaintance between myself and Alex. On the other hand the likelihood of their getting together again, without me, is full of alarming possibilities.

Dad has been on the phone a lot lately, asking about what Christmas presents to get for members of the family. I try to persuade him that nobody expects him to give presents, but he brushes this suggestion aside, claiming that he would feel embarrassed if people gave him presents and he didn't give them any in return. It's a reasonable point and highlights the unreasonableness of the whole present-giving ritual. I try to suggest some cheap, simple token presents for him to give, but he forgets what they were and rings me up to ask again. In the end I say with some exasperation, why don't you give everybody the same thing – a small box of After Eights, say? 'Don't be daft,' he says. 'Imagine everybody opening my presents and finding the same thing inside. I'd be a laughing stock.' 'Well, buy them all different kinds of chocolates, then.' To my relief he accepts this suggestion. 'But not for Daniel and Lena,' I remember to add. 'Marcia doesn't like them eating sweets.' 'Who are they?' he asks. 'Marcia is Fred's daughter. Daniel and Lena are her children.' 'Gawd,' he said, 'I hadn't reckoned with them. I'd better write down their names.' 'No, no, don't bother! You don't have to give them anything,' I say, but it is too late. 'What about you, son? I can't give you a box of After Eights.' 'Of course you can,' I say. 'I love them. I can't get enough of them. When we have any, Fred eats them all.' This of course is a total fiction, but it does the trick.

We discuss the logistics of his visit. I will drive down to London on the day before Christmas Eve to pick him up, and take him back to Lime Avenue two days after Boxing Day. 'It would help if you are all packed and ready when I arrive,' I say. 'I'll have to drain the tank that morning,' he says. 'It takes time.' 'Why?' I say. 'Well if the weather turns cold the pipes might freeze,' he says. 'Leave the central heating on, then they won't,' I say. '*What?*' he exclaims. 'Leave it on when I'm not here?' We have a long argument about this at the end of which I threaten not to come and fetch him if he won't agree to leave the central heating on while he's away. Reluctantly he agrees. Whether he'll keep his word is another matter.

I've been to see two more residential care homes for the elderly in our part of the city. The cost is finely calibrated to the degree of comfort offered, like air fares. At the lowest end of the scale you get a stale smell of cooking in the dining room, and of pungent air-freshener in the lounge, fumed oak furniture and faded floral wallpaper in the bedrooms; at the top end air-conditioning and sleek modular furniture and tasteful decor. But there is the same rather melancholy atmosphere in all of them, of lonely old people waiting stoically for death, deepened rather than relieved by the tinselly Christmas decorations in the common rooms. One can imagine them all carefully chewing their Christmas dinners in a couple of weeks' time, wearing paper hats on their grey or bald heads, and pulling crackers if they have the strength. Well, at least Dad will be able to join us for Christmas dinner if he can be persuaded to move into such a place. The most promising is the one whose brochure I showed him last time I was in London, Blydale House it's called, a purpose-built place, so the ambience is light and modern and comfortable. It's a couple of miles from us, but on a bus route that passes the end of Rectory Road. Expensive, but not impossibly so. I have made an appointment to take him there on the day after Boxing Day.

14th December. The last lip-reading class of the year today. We had more exercises and talks to do with Christmas. Ordering Christmas dinner at a restaurant. The origin of Father Christmas. The history of mistletoe. The biggest Christmas cracker in the world. At the end of the class they all went off to have their turkey and trimmings at a local restaurant. I had not signed up for the lunch on the pretext of another engagement, but felt a little guilty about this fib as we split up, wishing each other a Happy Christmas. Beth announced the dates of the next term in the New Year, and a guest speaker. It seems that there really is a deafies' equivalent to guide dogs for the blind. Not specially trained parrots; they're called hearing dogs, and we are to have a talk about them in January.

Beth brings to the class magazines published by the RNID and similar organisations and leaves them on the table for people to borrow or read in the coffee break. An article called 'Researching a cure for deafness', about the experimental use of stem cells to regrow hair cells, caught my eye. Sadly the programme won't produce any results for ten years and then will need another five years of clinical trials, so is unlikely to be of much use to me. But it was an interesting article, which began by stating that there are nine million people who are deaf or hard of hearing in this country. I had not thought deaf had undone so many. And the writer used a chilling phrase to describe traumatic hair-cell loss: '*exposure to damaging drugs or noises causes these hair cells to die with a kind of suicide program. They basically commit suicide in your ear.*' Is it possible, after all, that that rock band at Fillmore West provoked mass suicide in my inner ears? If I could remember the group's name I might sue them, but no doubt the statute of limitations would apply. They're probably all deaf themselves by now, anyway. I hope so. The good news is that the anti-oxidants in red wine may help prevent hair-cell loss.

15th December. Fred came home yesterday evening and reported that Alex had been in the shop and ordered some curtains. 'I gave her a discount – I thought it was only fair since we'll have a sale in January – not that we'll be putting that particular fabric in the sale. She has excellent taste. Her comments on the art we've got in the shop at the moment were all spot on.' Fred was obviously taken with this new acquaintance. 'I think I'll invite her to our Boxing Day party,' she said, to my dismay. 'Is that a good idea?' I said. 'Why not, darling?' I couldn't think of a reason that I could give to Fred. 'The poor girl will be lonely, all alone at Christmas, thousands of miles from home,' she went on. 'I'll send her an invitation. I've got her address on the order form for the curtains. She has a flat in one of those new canalside developments.' 'Does she?' I said, in a tone as uninterested as I could make it. The thought of Alex gaining entrance to this house, mingling with the guests at our party, ingratiating herself with members of the family, meeting Dad, who would be impressed by her blonde good looks and no doubt regale her with his wartime reminiscences of playing at dances on American airbases, is deeply unsettling.

18th December. I woke up this morning with a tickle in the back of my throat which presaged the onset of a sore-throat cold. Sure enough, by lunchtime it hurt to swallow: all I need in the run-up to Christmas. And there was a letter for Fred in this morning's post with Alex's name and address on the back of the envelope, which I didn't doubt was an acceptance of the invitation. I put it on top of a small pile of other mail for her on the hall table, and glanced at it apprehensively every time I went up and down the stairs. When Fred came in she brought her letters into the kitchen, as she usually does, to open them at the table over a cup of tea or a drink, according to the hour or her inclination, and I was there, waiting for her. 'Tea or drink?' She asked for a glass of white wine, being in good humour because the faulty Italian fabric which had caused a minor crisis some weeks ago had been replaced in time to make up the client's curtains for Christmas and Ron was going to fit them tomorrow. I turned my back on her to get a bottle of Aligote out of the fridge, and she said something I didn't catch. When I turned round she had a letter-card in her hand.

'What?' I said.

'Alex Loom is going back to the States.'

'For good?' I said. A vain hope had leaped from my brain to my lips – in an instant I anticipated the bliss of Alex being suddenly, miraculously removed from my life.

'No, of course not, darling,' said Fred. 'Just for Christmas. Why would she order curtains if she was going home for good?'

'Oh, I'd forgotten that,' I said lamely.

'Anyway, she hasn't finished her PhD, has she?'

'No. I thought perhaps she had decided to pack it in. She's not very satisfied with the supervision she's getting from Butterworth.'

'Well then, you must give her what help you can, darling,' Fred said. 'You have plenty of spare time.'

'Oh, thanks very much,' I said. There was more irony in my remark than Fred was aware of. Now I have her permission to meet Alex as often as I like – when it's the last thing I want.

'She says she's very sorry to miss the party,' Fred continued, scanning the letter-card, 'but her father sent her the money for a flight home for Christmas, so of course she has to go.'

'Well, God knows there are enough people coming to this party already,' I said, disguising my emotions behind a familiar grouchy mask. If it is not the miraculous reprieve I dreamed of for an instant, it is at least a relief to know that Alex will not be around to contribute to the stresses of Christmas.

13

22nd December. I have spent the last two days in bed, trying to get over my cold before I have to make the journey to London to pick up Dad – the bed in the guest room, to avoid infecting Fred or disturbing her at night with my coughing and spitting. It was also a way of going to ground, avoiding contact with Alex or anybody else. I hunkered down under the duvet with Radio Four on earphones for company and a Trollope novel for comfort reading.

Today I felt better and ready to resume normal life. I had a look at my email this morning, expecting to find a lot of messages from Alex, but there was just one, saying she was sorry to miss the party and looked forward to seeing me again in the New Year. There were a lot of seasonal ads for Viagra – *'Give her a present she'll really appreciate!' 'Get a power charge for the Christmas break!'* I wonder what they will come up with for the next big holiday – *'Rise Again this Easter'*? And there was a computer-generated message from the University library recalling Liverwright's book on document analysis. I wondered idly if Alex was going to borrow it again and try to remove the turquoise marks with some chemical solution.

23rd December. The epic journey is over. Operation Fetch Dad is accomplished – not without difficulty. Many times today I wondered if it would have been more sensible to do it by train, but whenever I have considered this option in recent years it seems to entail so many possibilities of things going wrong that I decide against it. The trains just before Christmas are crowded, so I would have to reserve seats, and book a minicab from Brickley at a time which, allowing for possible traffic jams in central London, would get us to King's Cross in good time to catch the appointed train, but not so early that we would be hanging about in the station for ages waiting to board it. Then even if this leg of the journey worked to perfection there was always the possibility that the train would not be ready for boarding when we got to King's Cross because it had been late in arriving, or had been cancelled, in which case our seat reservations would be invalid, and we would have to join a Gadarene rush for unreserved seats on the next train. All in all, it seemed preferable to take my chances on the road. I knew it would be slow, I knew there would be traffic jams, but once I had got Dad in the car and his luggage in the boot I wouldn't have to worry about getting anywhere at any particular time, and I could be confident that sooner or later we would get to Rectory Road.

I left home in the winter dark at 6.30 a.m., with only a cup of tea inside me, whizzed through the nearly empty city centre and was soon cruising down the M1 in light traffic, with Radio Four turned up to a volume which nobody with normal hearing could have borne. The road bulletins were making worrying remarks about fog in the south, delays at airports, etc., but I made good progress as far as a service station near Leicester, where I stopped for breakfast. After that the traffic and the atmosphere gradually thickened and I didn't get to the end of the M1 until just before ten. From there it was a slow drive across a misty London, its streets congested with Christmas shoppers frantically stocking up with food and drink as if for an expected siege, and I didn't reach Lime Avenue until gone eleven. Dad was waiting for me in the darkened house, the curtains drawn in every room, wearing his overcoat and cap, with his bags packed and his walking stick in his hand. He looked as if he had been ready for hours. We shouted at each other for a few minutes. 'Where have you been?' he demanded. 'I told you I'd get here at about half-ten,' I said. 'I thought you said half-past nine,' he said. 'How could I get here by half-past nine without getting up in the middle of the night?' I said irritably. 'It's a long way.' 'Too bloody long, if you ask me,' he said. 'What did you have to go and move up north for?' 'The job was there, Dad,' I said, as I have said many times.

I go through a check list with him: 'Have you cancelled the milk?' 'Yes.' 'Have you cancelled the newspapers?' 'Yes.' 'Have you left the central heating on?' A sullen 'Yes'. He has in fact turned most of the radiators off, but I calculate that the hot water circulating through the system will serve. 'Have you told the Barkers?' 'What?' he says. 'Have you told the Barkers, next door,' I repeat, thinking he hasn't heard me. 'Told them what?' he says. 'Told them you're going away.' 'Why should I, none of their business,' he says. 'Don't you give them a set of keys when you go away?' I ask. I know he doesn't, I'm just pretending I don't to relieve my irritation. ''Course not!' he says indignantly. 'I don't want them coming into my house nosing around while I'm away.' 'I should think they'd have better things to do at Christmas,' I sneer. We are getting off to a bad start.

Before we leave I knock on the front door of the adjoining semi. The Barkers are not the most charismatic couple in the world but I rely on their goodwill to keep an eye on Dad and to phone me if they have any cause for concern. Mrs Barker opens the door. 'Oh hallo!' she says in a high-pitched whine, and giggles. It is a nervous giggle which punctuates all her speech. 'How's your Dad?' The bulky shape of Mr Barker looms in the hall behind her, in shirtsleeves and braces, a cordless power drill held like a weapon in his hand. I tell them that I'm taking Dad to spend Christmas with us ('Oh, that'll be nice for him, won't it?' – giggle), and that I'd be grateful if they would keep an eye on the house. 'There's a leaking gutter on the side of the roof that needs attention,' says Mr Barker. 'Is there? Thanks for telling me,' I say. 'I'll get it seen to after he comes back.' The Barkers' house is in immaculate condition, its upkeep being Mr Barker's chief occupation in retirement, and I know that the relatively scruffy appearance of Dad's is a sore point. 'Well, we'd better get going,' I say. 'Have a nice Christmas.' 'Yes, same to you!' Mrs Barker giggles. Her spouse returns to whatever DIY operation I interrupted, but so barren of incident is Mrs Barker's life that she stands at the door hugging herself against the cold, and watches as I escort

Dad out of the house and settle him in the front seat of the car. She simpers and waves to us as we drive away.

The traffic in central London was even worse on the way back, and we had to stop at the first service station on the M1 for a late lunch, with the larger part of the journey still before us. The fog slowed the traffic, there were frequent hold-ups on the motorway, and I began to see that we wouldn't reach home until well into the evening. Dad was garrulous at first, advising me on the route across London (*'Don't go through Camberwell and Victoria whatever you do, it's the land of a thousand traffic lights'*), criticising other motorists' driving (*'Did you see that idiot? Not even a signal! Diabolical!'*), asking me to convert the price of petrol by the litre displayed at the garages we pass into gallons (*'What, four quid a gallon? You must be joking!'*), recalling epic car journeys to play at hunt balls in remote rural venues: *'Hills? You've never seen hills like they have in Wales. The whole country is hills. There was the time Archie Silver – he was a bass player – dead now – he had five of us in his old Wolseley – all the instruments in a trailer – going down this hill like the side of a mountain and the brakes failed . . .'* Surprisingly, he didn't seem worried by the fog. I think he attributed it to the cataract in his left eye. After lunch he fell asleep and I drove on in blessed silence. But when he woke up he wanted to pee. I had just passed a service station, and the next one was at least thirty minutes away. 'Did you put that bottle in the car?' he said, groping under his seat. 'What bottle?' I said, with a sinking feeling. I had forgotten all about my suggestion weeks ago that he should have a bottle with him for such an emergency. 'The milk bottle, in a brown paper bag, in the hall by the front door. I told you to put it under my seat, when you took out my things.' 'I didn't hear you, Dad,' I said. I had driven to London without wearing my hearing aid and didn't insert it until several minutes after my arrival, during which time he must have mentioned the bottle. Or possibly he mentioned the bottle later, when I was wearing my hearing aid, but in a low voice because he was embarrassed, or when I had my back turned to him, or when my mind was on something else and I wasn't paying attention to him. 'Oh, well done, son,' he said bitterly. I felt bad.

'I could stop on the hard shoulder,' I said. 'You're not supposed to, but if it's an emergency . . .' 'Where would I go, then?' he demanded. 'Climb over a barbed-wire fence into a field, in the dark?' 'No, of course not. You could pee up against the back wheel of the car, like a cab driver – they're allowed to by law, you know.' He ignored this attempt to lighten the tone of the conversation. 'What, with all these cars picking me out in their headlights? No thanks.' In fact, I was glad he didn't want to stop because it would have been dangerous: it was getting dark and visibility was poor. 'What will you do, then?' 'I'll hang on till the next place,' he said grimly.

He really did very well. It was only as we were crossing the car park to get to the brightly lit complex of shops and cafés that he couldn't control his bladder any longer. 'Oh Jesus Christ!' he said, doubling up and clutching his groin. 'I'm sopping wet.' 'All right, Dad. Don't worry,' I said. 'Don't *worry*!' he exclaimed. 'What am I going to do? Sit in the car in a pair of stinking wet trousers for the rest of the journey?' I quickly conceived a plan. 'We'll go to the Gents. You go in a cubicle and take your trousers off, give them to me under the door and stay there while I go back to the car and get another pair of trousers from your case – you did bring another pair, didn't you? Good. Then I'll push them under the door, and you can change into them. All right?'

So that's what we did. It worked well enough, except that I forgot to bring a pair of dry underpants as well as trousers from the car. I asked him if he wanted me to go back and fetch a pair. 'Well, you don't expect me to sit in that car for Gawd knows how long in trousers without pants, do you?' he demanded through the cubicle door. 'They're pure wool you know, these trousers. They'll chafe if I don't have pants.' This conversation, which had to be conducted at high volume and with much repetition through the door of the WC, gave considerable entertainment to other patrons of the Gents. So back I went to the car to rummage in his case for a pair of his droopy trunk-style underpants, and returned to the Gents with them. While he was changing I rinsed out the wet pants in a handbasin and dried them under a hot-air hand dryer. I received some curious looks as I performed this task, but I was beyond shame or embarrassment by this time, or perhaps it would be truer to say that I accepted it as a just punishment for being remiss over the bottle.

It's been a long, draining day, the only compensation being that Dad duty got me out of some Christmas duties. Marcia helped Fred with the big Christmas shopping mission to Sainsbury's in the morning, a chore I always detest: the gridlock of overloaded trolleys in the aisles, the long slow-moving queues at the checkouts, everybody behaving more like looters than shoppers, scrabbling for the best produce (last Christmas I actually saw a woman pinch the last box of organic mushrooms in the store from somebody else's trolley while their back was turned). I was very glad to be spared all that. And I didn't have to meet Fred's mother, who came up from her retirement flat in Cheltenham by train, at the station – Fred did so herself, Jakki having generously volunteered to man, or woman, the shop, since she has no family to cater for.

When Dad and I arrived home at about seven Fred was decorating the big Christmas tree in the lounge, watched and advised by her mother, who was seated in an upright armchair by the fire in the Britannia pose she favours: back straight, head up, knees slightly apart under her full skirt, holding the *Daily Telegraph* she had brought with her like a shield. There was already a small heap of wrapped presents under the tree. The little crib with carved olive-wood Nativity figures bought in Bethlehem and presented by Fred's parents years ago was in place on the bookshelves. Carol music filtered from the discreetly placed speakers. It was a pleasant scene, almost as if staged to make an impression. I have to admit that Fred does Christmas very well. But almost at once there was a little friction between us: she asked me if I would help her drape the coloured lights around the tree, and I said I was too tired and couldn't it wait till tomorrow, so with an impatient sigh she did it herself while I got myself and Dad a drink, and the lights didn't come on, and Fred got irritable, and in the end I had to lay the flex out on the floor and check that all the fragile little bulbs were screwed tightly into their sockets before I found the culprit which was breaking the circuit. I hope this is not a foretaste of contretemps to come. The trouble is that as soon as there is the slightest disagreement between Fred and me, our respective parents instinctively line up behind their offspring, and so the friction factor is squared. Dad urged me to finish my drink before attending to the lights and Fred's mother mentioned that her late husband always used to regard the Christmas tree lights as his special responsibility. Mr Fairfax died five years ago.

Mrs Cecilia Magdalene Fairfax, to give her name in full, is a tall vigorous seventy-seven-year-old widow with an enormous bust which gives me some idea of how Fred might look at the same age if she hadn't had her breast-reduction operation (she never told her mother about this, pretending that she had 'dieted'). Cecilia has absolutely nothing in common with Dad and some-times looks at him with a kind of horrified distaste, like a lady of the manor who finds that the under-gardener has unaccountably been invited into her drawing room by a member of the family and cannot therefore be ejected. He for his part regards her as a 'stiff old bird' whom it is his duty to cheer up with quips and anecdotes. He calls her 'Celia'. When she corrected him once, he said 'Cecilia' was one syllable too many for an old man with false teeth. 'So I call you "Celia" for short. You don't mind, do you?' She replied frostily, 'If you must. But of course they are two quite different names. Cecilia was a virgin martyr of the Early Church. Celia was an ordinary Roman name, a pagan name.' I think she would really prefer if he called her 'Mrs Fairfax'. She invariably addresses him as 'Mr Bates', in spite of repeated invitations to call him 'Harry'.

*

24th December. The house is filling up. Giles, Fred's second child, and his wife Nicola arrived this afternoon, with their infant son, Basil, aged nine months, having driven up this afternoon from Hertfordshire in their black BMW 4x4, a huge high vehicle recently acquired in exchange for a Porsche to provide maximum protection for their precious offspring. It has almost opaque tinted windows to foil potential kidnappers, and a sticker on the rear window, *'Baby On Board'*, appealing to the consciences of drivers who might be intent on ramming them from behind. Of Fred's three children Giles is the most prosperous. Andrew paid for him to attend Downside, and after university he followed his father's footsteps into the City and a job in a merchant bank. Today he wears the expression of a man who has just been given a very satisfactory Christmas bonus and can barely restrain himself from telling you how much it was. Nicola is a commercial lawyer, but has decided to take four years out of her career to have two babies – the figures are specified precisely, like a balance sheet. One feels sure the babies will balance too, a boy and a girl. She is good-looking in a featureless sort of way, nicely dressed, pleasantly spoken and rather dull.

Fred's youngest son, Ben, and his girlfriend Maxine arrived in the middle of the evening, later than expected, delayed not so much by the fog as by a festive lunchtime party at the premises of the TV production company he works for, 'after which we had to chill out for a few hours in case we got nicked on the motorway'. I have always found Ben the most likeable of Fred's children: a cheerful, relaxed, extrovert young man who declined his father's offer to send him to Downside like his brother and opted for a local state school. He works in some capacity on one of those television programmes about buying and selling or swapping or renovating or redecorating houses to which British viewers seem to be addicted, there are so many of them on every channel. He describes the genre dismissively as 'property porn', but says it's a good way to learn the ropes of documentary-making. Maxine, his partner for the past two years, is a TV make-up artist, pretty, leggy and friendly, with an estuary accent and hardly an idea in her head that isn't connected with TV, fashion and cosmetics. She makes Ben take her to trashy horror films because she wants to see the make-up. The unspoken consensus of Fred's family is that she is rather common, and Cecilia is painfully divided between a fear that Ben will marry her and a moral disapproval of cohabitation. But Maxine gets on well with Dad, who is rather smitten with her, and has bought her his biggest box of chocolates.

Fred, her mother, Giles, Ben and Maxine have gone off to Midnight Mass (pronounced 'maass' by the Fairfax family) which begins at ten-thirty with a carol service. Ben is not a practising Catholic, Giles only a nominal one, and Maxine doesn't practise anything except make-up, but they accompany Fred and her mother in a spirit of seasonal solidarity. In the past I have sometimes gone with them, since it is just about the only religious service I positively enjoy, the carol singing bit anyway, but I didn't like to leave Nicola, who has retired to bed with her baby, responsible for Dad. He has in fact gone to bed too, but last night I found him wandering about on the landing in his pyjamas looking for the bathroom in a dazed and confused state, with an enamel jug in his hand which I had given him to pee in if he was taken short, having somehow got it into his head that he had to empty the jug immediately in the bathroom, due no doubt to the antihistamine tablets which his doctor gives him as sleeping pills – they are safe but fuddle his old brain. I didn't think Nicola would know what to do if she ran into him on the landing in similar circumstances.

Tomorrow morning Anne and Jim are driving up from Derbyshire, and Richard from Cambridge, in good time for Christmas dinner, which is really a late lunch. Marcia and Peter and their two children will join us, so it will be a big party. Richard's presence is a bit of a last-minute surprise. He phoned up this morning to say he'd like to join us, but would have to drive back to Cambridge the same evening. I shall try to persuade him to stay the night. There is too much fog about on the roads – worst of all in the Thames Valley, apparently. Heathrow is immobilised, flights

cancelled, travellers sleeping in the terminals. Trains are consequently overcrowded and roads jammed. This mass multi-
directional migration in midwinter is insane. All our bedrooms
are spoken for, but I can rig up a camp bed for Richard in my
study. I haven't seen him for months.

25th December. Another Christmas Day is nearly over. It's ten past
eleven. Richard declined with thanks my offer to make up a bed for
him here in my study, and has driven off back to Cambridge, so I
am able to make some notes on the day before going to bed myself.
A lot of people have already retired, exhausted by hours of compulsory festivity and each other's company: Fred (who has certainly earned a long rest) led the retreat at ten, accompanied by her
mother, followed by Giles and Nicola (who said they were woken
up by their teething baby last night), and Anne, who needed no
excuse, for she looks heavily pregnant – hard to believe that the
birth is still two months away. Marcia and Peter went home with
their offspring hours ago. At ten-thirty Ben, Maxine and Jim settled
down to watch a classic Hollywood film noir on the television.
Dad, who slept – and snored – in the drawing room for some time
after lunch, with a newspaper over his head, was inconveniently
perky this evening. The film was not to his taste, and after a few
critical remarks about the depressing effect of the black-and-white
photography and the melodramatic style of the acting, designed to
persuade the others to switch over to something lighter and
brighter, which failed to have the desired effect, he turned his attention to me and began a rambling series of anecdotes about his life
as a dance musician. The amount of cigarette smoking going on in
the film revived memories of Arthur Lane's addiction, his trick of
pinching out fag ends between his foot-operated cymbals and the
famous occasion when he set fire to his bass drum while the band
was playing 'Smoke Gets in Your Eyes'. 'And did I ever tell you
about Sammy Black's wig? A lovely trombonist Sammy was, but he
wore a terrible wig . . .' If Maxine had not been otherwise occupied, she might have been an interested auditor, but I had heard all

the stories before, several times. I was desperate for some peace and quiet, longing to prise the hearing aids, which I had been wearing all day, out of my hot, sweaty earholes, and to enjoy a spell of silence. So after about a quarter of an hour I pretended that I was going to go to bed, which persuaded Dad that he should go too, and having seen him to his room I bade him goodnight and slunk back downstairs to my study.

Went the day well? It could have been worse, I suppose, but it didn't pass without some squalls and squabbles, conflicts and complaints. Dad woke early, came downstairs to make himself a cup of tea, and set off the burglar alarm. I had gone to bed and to sleep before the others came back from Midnight Mass, and Fred set the alarm on the assumption that I had reminded Dad about it, whereas I thought we had agreed not to set the alarm with a houseful of guests and to rely on locking and bolting the external doors – a misunderstanding no doubt caused by my hearing problem. I didn't hear the alarm go off for the same reason, and was woken from an early-morning doze by Fred's elbow in my ribs and a grunted command to do something. I found Dad at the bottom of the stairs, in his dressing gown and slippers, with a hand cupped to his ear and a puzzled expression on his face. 'Hallo, son,' he said. 'Can you hear a funny noise?'

I de-activated the alarm, and phoned the security company to tell them it was a false one. 'Have a nice day,' said the man who took my call, when he had taken down the details. 'Well, it hasn't been an auspicious start,' I said. He laughed uncertainly. I don't think he was sure what 'auspicious' meant. I expect he was feeling sorry for himself at being on duty on Christmas Day, but I imagined him sitting all alone in a quiet, warm office, with a book and a portable radio to hand, and only the occasional telephone call to disturb his peace, and I envied him.

I made Dad some tea in the kitchen and gave him a digestive biscuit with it. 'Ain't you having breakfast, then?' he said, inspecting the biscuit with a disappointed expression. 'It's too early,' I said. He looked at the clock on the wall. 'Blimey! A quarter to six!

Is that all it is?' He hadn't got his teeth in so he dipped the biscuit in the tea before mumbling it between his gums. 'I'm going back to bed,' I said. 'What will you do?' 'I suppose I could take half a pill,' he said. 'Get another couple of hours' kip.' I encouraged him in this plan, and escorted him upstairs. I crept into our bedroom and into bed. Fred muttered something which I didn't hear but assumed was an accusing question about the alarm and Dad. 'Don't let's talk about it now,' I said, snuggling up to her, not from any tender or amorous impulse but simply for animal warmth. I find it's the best way to get off to sleep again when I wake early. It worked, but it didn't seem very long before she got up herself and went downstairs to prepare the turkey and put it in the oven. It's an enormous bird, and she believes in slow cooking.

As the morning passed the smell of the roasting turkey filled the kitchen and seeped out into the dining room and front hall and could be faintly sniffed even in my study. 'Mmm! What a delicious smell,' the newly arriving members of the family party exclaimed as they took off their coats and shed their burdens of wrapped presents, though personally I find it falls only just short of faintly nauseous on the olfactory scale. Still, the morning was all right, on the whole. Dad slept till gone nine, which meant I was able to read yesterday's paper over my breakfast before I had to make his and sit with him while he ate it in his dressing gown, and there was just time to get him upstairs and out of sight to wash and dress before people started to arrive. Anne and Jim were the first. I was glad to see that she looked well. Jim looked as he always looks, genial but detached, slightly spaced out, though he assured me once that he never smokes grass before lunch. Although he was only a child in the Sixties, he looks and acts like a fossilised relic of that era, wearing his hair shoulder length, dressing always in denim, and sporting one of those long straggly moustaches that were popular on the West Coast during the Summer of Love. Cecilia can hardly bring herself to look at him without flinching. He and Anne have been together for eight years now. I must admit that he wouldn't have been my first choice as a partner for my daughter, and I sometimes feel he is living off her rather than supporting her, but she seems happy with the relationship, so I keep my doubts to myself.

I took Anne into my study and asked her how she was. 'Fine, just a bit of backache,' she said.

'And the baby?'

'Kicking. He's fine.'

'How do you know it's a he?'

'I had a scan. I knew you'd be pleased.' She could tell by my expression.

'Well, you know . . . My first grandchild. Perhaps the only one. Not much sign of Richard producing any progeny . . . and I don't suppose you'll risk having another at your age, will you?'

'Well, we'll see how this one goes,' she said.

She looked very like her mother at that moment, when Maisie was carrying Anne herself, except that Maisie used to wear tent-like smocks, whereas Anne follows the modern fashion for flaunting her swollen belly, sheathed in a tight-fitting top above matching trousers. The fluffy ginger hair, the round face, the hesitant smile, and the two vertical worry lines in the middle of the forehead, were just the same. It was always said that Anne took after her mother, whereas Richard was more like me.

'And how are you, Dad?' she said.

'Oh, all right. Getting deafer and deafer.'

'You seem to be managing all right.'

'It's quiet in here.'

'And what about Rick? Is he coming today?'

'Yes, he's coming.' The doorbell chimed at that moment. 'That might be him,' I said.

But it was Marcia and Peter and their children. It's a cliché, of course, that children are an essential ingredient of any celebration of Christmas, but like most clichés it is true. Adults, even sour and cynical ones like me, can at least for a while see Christmas through their innocent eyes and recover some sense of the wonder and excitement we experienced ourselves long ago. Lena entered the house with a beatific smile on her face which shone like a reflected sunbeam on everything and everybody that she encountered, while Christmas had made Daniel more solemn and dignified than ever, though there was a visionary gleam in his eye. 'So what did Father Christmas bring you, Dauphin Daniel?' I asked him, crouching down to bring myself to his level. 'Father Christmas bringed Daniel an icicle,' he said. 'An icicle? That doesn't sound like much of a present,' I said. 'A *tricycle*, Desmond,' Marcia said, and everybody around us laughed. One thing we deafies can do at a party is give people a few laughs with our mistakes, and I did not begrudge them this one. Daniel, however, didn't laugh, but turned his wide eyes on the grinning grown-up faces with a puzzled and faintly disapproving air. 'And it's "brought", not "bringed", Daniel,' his mother added. 'Father Christmas *brought* you a tricycle.' Being a teacher (though of maths not English), Marcia thinks it her duty to correct her children at every opportunity. Of course Daniel's mistake was perfectly logical and shows that he has already mastered the way to form the past tense of regular English verbs. You've got to grasp the rules before you learn the exceptions.

There was a discussion, which almost turned into an argument, about whether presents should be exchanged before or after lunch, and in the end a compromise was reached whereby each person should open one present immediately (to assuage the impatience of little Lena in particular) and the rest would be opened after lunch, when Fred and others engaged in the preparation of the meal would be more at leisure. Then it was time for drinks – champagne and Buck's fizz, Giles having brought a case of Bollinger as a house-gift (an index of the size of his Christmas bonus) – which put everybody in a good mood, as the first drink of the day usually does.

Richard arrived at this juncture, somehow managing to get into the house without ringing the bell, and sidling into the drawing room so unobtrusively that I didn't notice him until Fred pointed him out to me. He was standing just inside the door, examining a painting on the wall like a guest at a party who didn't know anybody. I beckoned him over to the sideboard where I was dispensing the drinks. 'Richard! Happy Christmas!' I said, pouring him a glass of champagne. 'Same to you, Dad,' he said. He held the glass critically up to the light, sniffed the exploding bubbles, sipped and nodded approvingly. 'Nice temperature,' he said. 'I've brought you a couple of bottles of Savigny-les-Beaune, *premier cru*,' he went on. 'They're in the hall. I shouldn't open them at lunch – they won't be appreciated.' He was dressed exactly as I used to dress forty years ago, in a tweed sports jacket and grey flannels, a discreetly checked shirt and a plain dark tie. He was the only man in the room wearing a tie – even I was wearing an open-necked sports shirt, and a rather dashing suede waistcoat that Fred gave me last Christmas, in honour of the occasion. I noticed his hair was getting thin – something he must inherit from Maisie's father, who was already quite bald at our wedding. 'So how are you?' I said. 'Fine, fine.' 'How is low-temperature physics?' He smiled. 'Interesting,' he said. He tried to explain it to me once. The object apparently is to get the temperature of substances down to a point as near as possible to absolute zero, which makes particles behave in odd and interesting ways. I remember him saying: *'You have to identify the energy within a given substance and then devise a way of removing it.'* It seemed to me a strange and obsessive sort of quest, a kind of reverse alchemy. We chatted for a while about his drive up. Little Lena tugged my sleeve. 'Grandma says will you check the table,' she said. I went into the dining room where Fred and I had constructed an irregularly shaped surface around which thirteen adults and two children could be seated by joining our extended dining table to a card table, and covering them with overlapping cloths. I checked the glasses and the cutlery, and opened some bottles of wine to breathe.

There were rather too many women endeavouring to help Fred in the kitchen, with conflicting views about how the ingredients of the meal should be cooked and served, and several of them were slightly tipsy from the champagne, so that some dishes were overdone and some underdone and I was instructed to start carving the turkey before all the vegetables were ready, and Fred had forgotten, or I forgot (there was disagreement about whose responsibility this had been) to warm the dinner plates in the device we have for this purpose. By the time people were seated there was some danger that the main course would be tepid rather than hot, so I suggested that they should start eating as soon as they were served, but Cecilia asked plaintively if we weren't going to say grace first, so we had to stop serving ourselves and adopt suitable expressions and postures, while Cecilia closed her eyes and joined her hands and intoned a grace – all except Dad, who had not noticed her intervention and carried on cutting up his dinner. This happens every year: we forget that Cecilia likes to say grace before Christmas lunch, and she deliberately doesn't remind us until the last minute so that she can make everybody feel chastened or edified or otherwise put in their place.

'I think it's a great shame that grace before meals seems to be dying out even among practising Catholics,' Cecilia declared, as she unfolded her napkin and prepared to eat her dinner. 'My late husband used to say grace before every meal even if there were only the two of us at table.' I looked at Jim and winked. We had a bet last Christmas predicting how many times during the day Cecilia would use the phrase 'my late husband' (it was nine, and I won). The grace gave the food a further opportunity to cool, a fact to which Dad tactlessly adverted by asking if his portion could be warmed up a bit in a frying pan and volunteering to carry out this operation himself. His table manners are an inexhaustible source of amusement, irritation or embarrassment, according to one's point of view. He doesn't feel that a dinner plate is equipped for its function unless it has a generous smear of mustard and a small hill of salt on the rim, irrespective of the ingredients of the meal, and it is no use telling him that mustard doesn't go with turkey or that too much salt is bad for you (though we do, every year). Nor is it any use handing him a salt mill – either he twists it the wrong way, causing it to come apart and scatter crystals of sea salt all over the table, or he labours with increasing impatience to grind out enough minute fragments to make a perceptible heap on the edge of his plate. Fred was so irritated by this procedure on one occasion that she provided him with a half-kilo plastic container of Saxo salt beside his plate at the next meal, but so far from taking the hint, or any offence, he thanked her for the thought. I had remembered to place an old-fashioned cruet with a salt cellar and a pot of prepared mustard within his reach at table today, but forgot that he would also require a slab of white bread, spurning the warm ciabatta rolls provided as being too crusty for his false teeth and contaminated by bits of indigestible olive, and I felt obliged to fetch a slice of white loaf from the kitchen in spite of Fred's injunction that I should stop fussing and sit down.

And so the day proceeded on its predictable course, through the Christmas pudding and mince pies, the pulling of crackers, the donning of paper hats, the reading out of atrocious riddles (rendered still more atrocious when they had to be repeated in a louder voice for my benefit), and the exchanging of presents, leaving the lounge awash with torn wrapping paper. 'History repeats itself once as tragedy and the second time as farce, but Christmas repeats itself as surfeit,' I remarked, looking round the drawing room at people in various attitudes of torpor, inebriation, indigestion and boredom, clutching new books they would never read, gadgets they would never use, and items of clothing they would never wear. 'Speak for yourself, darling,' Fred said sharply. '*We* enjoy it, anyway. Don't we Lena?' She gave her grandchild, who was sitting on her knee, a hug. 'Yes, grandma,' Lena said obediently. 'Granddad's an Eeyore,' said Fred. 'Yes, you're an Eeyore!' cried Lena delightedly. Fred has been reading *Winnie-the-Pooh* to her when baby-sitting. Well, perhaps I am. After all, Eeyore was deaf too. It comes into the story about his birthday party. When Piglet wishes him 'Many happy returns of the day', Eeyore asks him to say it again.

Balancing on three legs, he began to bring his fourth leg very cautiously up to his ear. 'I did this yesterday,' he explained, as he fell down for the third time. 'It's quite easy. It's so I can hear better . . . There, that's done it. Now then, what were you saying?' He pushed his ear forward with his hoof.

Deafness is always comic.

I had a surprising conversation with Richard before he left. All through the day he had been as politely inscrutable as ever, fending off all enquiries, however subtle or oblique, about his private life. Then just as he was leaving – when he was actually outside the house, and I was walking him to his car, which he'd had to park in the road – we had the most intimate conversation, brief as it was, that we have had in years. We were talking about Anne's pregnancy, and I said, 'She looks just like your mother when she was expecting you.'

His response seemed a non sequitur: 'I suppose that's why you hate Christmas, is it?'

'What d'you mean?' I said.

'It reminds you of Mum's death.'

'Maybe,' I said. 'Though I was never a great Christmas enthusiast.'

Maisie died a week after Christmas Day. I cooked Christmas dinner with the help of the children and we ate it sitting round her bed. She managed to swallow a little herself. We all tried hard to be cheerful, but it was not a very festive meal. 'It's almost my last memory of her,' Richard said. 'Sitting round her bed, with our plates on our knees. Anne and I went off on that skiing holiday just after.'

'Yes, I remember,' I said. I had arranged it with some friends, the Ryders, who were taking their teenage children to Austria, thinking the kids deserved a break from the sickroom atmosphere of the house.

'I didn't want to go,' Richard said. 'I had a feeling that Mum was going to die very soon.'

'You didn't say so,' I said, surprised at this revelation.

'No, I didn't want to explain. I didn't like to say the words.'

We had reached his parked car. He pressed his key ring and the car's lights blinked and the driver's door obediently clicked open. 'There was no reason to think the end would come so quickly,' I said. 'We thought you and Anne needed a break.'

'I know,' he said. 'But I've always regretted that I wasn't there when Mum died. When Mrs Ryder told us, at the chalet, after you phoned her, when we came in from skiing, Anne burst into tears and howled, and I thought: "I mustn't do that. It's all right for Anne to do it, but I mustn't cry, not now, not in front of other people." The result was I never did cry over Mum's death. I tried to later, but I couldn't. Then I felt bad about that.'

'I'm sorry, son,' I said.

'It wasn't your fault, Dad. You meant well.'

He smiled sadly and extended his hand. I shook it. It was a moment when we should have hugged each other, but it is not in our lexicon of body language. The most we could manage was a stronger, longer handshake than usual.

'Bye, Dad,' he said, getting into his car.

'Goodbye, and thanks for coming.'

He shut the car door and lowered the window. 'I'm sorry I can't stay for the party tomorrow.'

'Oh, God – you don't know how lucky you are!' I said.

Our emotional moment was over. He laughed, and drove away with a wave of his hand.

14

The tall, bespectacled, grey-haired man in the rather dashing mustard yellow suede waistcoat, talking animatedly to a bemused-looking middle-aged woman standing near the Christmas tree in the crowded drawing room, has had, he is aware, quite enough to drink at this halfway stage of the party, but cannot stop himself from taking an occasional quick sip from his glass of red wine, quick enough to prevent the lady from interjecting more than a couple of words before he resumes his monologue. Her name is Mrs Norfolk, a fact he established several minutes ago by getting her to write it down for him, and he is engaged in explaining to her why the famous line in Noël Coward's *Private Lives*, 'Very flat, Norfolk', is funny.

'You remember that Elyot tells his ex-wife Amanda that he met his new wife Sybil at a house party in Norfolk, and Amanda says, *"Very flat, Norfolk"*, and everybody in the audience laughs. It never fails. But if she'd said, *"Norfolk is very flat"*, which would be the most logical way to convey the information, it wouldn't be funny at all. Amanda has given a rhetorical spin to this banal statement of fact by inverting the normal subject-predicate word order, and omitting the finite verb, transforming *"Norfolk is very flat"* into *"Very flat, Norfolk"*. This foregrounds the word *"flat"* both positionally and intonationally. The intonation of *"Norfolk is very flat"* is almost completely level, whereas when I say, *"Very flat, Norfolk"*, my voice rises and falls in pitch, peaking on *"flat"*. And there's a slight pause, a kind of caesura, after *"Very flat"*, which creates a tiny moment of suspense for the audience. What, we wonder, will this portentously foregrounded adjectival phrase, *"Very flat"*, qualify? The answer is a bathos: *"Norfolk"*. And that's one reason why the line is funny – as if in spite of Amanda's efforts to make her remark seem interesting and original, she is defeated by its semantic content. It remains irretrievably, irredeemably, "flat". Like Norfolk.'

He snatches a gulp of wine. Mrs Norfolk gapes at him, then seems about to speak. Hastily he prevents her. 'But there's a double-take effect, because we immediately see another possibility, which is also funny – that "flat Norfolk" is a metonym for boring country-house parties where one meets boring women like Sybil. When, a few lines later, Amanda complains of Elyot's disrespectful remarks about her new husband, Victor, and says, *"At least I have good taste enough to refrain from making cheap gibes at Sybil"*, he retorts accusingly, *"You said Norfolk was flat."* And she replies, *"That was no reflection on her unless she made it flatter."* Either she is being disingenuous, and pretending she didn't mean that when she said *"Very flat, Norfolk"*, or – another amusing possibility – Elyot has admitted that he finds Sybil "flat", i.e., boring, by wrongly accusing Amanda of implying it. In any case, if Elyot had met her somewhere else, in Wales for instance, and Amanda's line was, *"Very hilly, Wales"*, it wouldn't be funny at all. *"Wales is very hilly"*, *"Very hilly, Wales"* – there's no difference in effect, because there is no pun concealed in *"hilly"*, no metaphorical and referential equivalence, as there is in *"flat"* . . .'

His wife comes up to them, glares at himself, smiles sweetly at Mrs Norfolk, says something to her and bears her off to the dining room, where he infers, from the aromas of lemon grass, coconut, cardamom and other spices percolating into the drawing room, the buffet lunch is beginning to be served. It would probably be a good idea for him to follow them, and get something to eat to soak up all the wine he has drunk, but by now there will, he knows, be a queue and it would not be polite for the host to jump it. So instead he goes to his study where he has secreted one of the bottles of Savigny-les-Beaune given to him by his son the previous day, and refills his glass. The visual memory of the glare from his wife troubles him slightly. It belongs to a series of frowns and disapproving glances and remarks hissed into his ear (which conveyed as much sense to him as air escaping from a tyre valve) received in the past hour, which he suspects are messages that in her opinion he is either drinking too much or talking too much – probably both. But then the two things are connected: without alcoholic fuel injection he wouldn't be able to keep up such a steady stream of discourse with such a variety of people. It seems to him that he is doing very well in extremely difficult circumstances.

About twenty minutes before the first guests were due to arrive that morning both of his hearing aid batteries died almost simultaneously, a most unusual occurrence. He was aware that one of them had packed up when he had difficulty understanding something Jakki was saying to him in the kitchen (she had arrived early with a couple of white-aproned Asian caterers bearing stainless steel containers of fragrant curry and rice for the buffet lunch) and before he could find an opportunity, in the bustle of party preparation, to replace it, the other earpiece went dead. Going to the drawer in his study where he keeps all the accessories for his hearing aid he discovered that, contrary to his confident expectation, it contained no spare batteries. Or, to be more precise, there *were* spare batteries in the drawer, but they were the wrong size for his hearing aid. These tiny discs vary slightly in thickness and diameter according to the type of device they are designed to fit, but the little carousel bubble packs they come in are identical apart from the numerical codes printed on them. He is accustomed to buying six packs at a time, scooping them off the display rack in the chemist's shop; and when he last made such a purchase he must have omitted to check that all the packs were of the type he required and failed to notice that some careless shop assistant had hung two different types of battery on the same rail, so that while believing he had put thirty-six spare batteries in his drawer, enough to last him well into the New Year, he had in fact deposited only eighteen that were any use to him, the last two of which have just expired.

What to do? It is Boxing Day, there are no shops open in the neighbourhood, and while it is possible that a pharmacy will be open this morning somewhere in the city centre he could well miss the first hour of Fred's party looking for it, and he has already had a couple of glasses of wine to fortify himself against the imminent social ordeal, so is not sure that it would be prudent for him to drive anyway, and although he could send some other member of his extended family on this errand it is more than likely that the pharmacy, if it exists, will have closed before it is located, since they open for only a few hours in the morning on Christmas Day and Boxing Day, and even if still open they will quite possibly refuse to sell batteries because on bank holidays their service is restricted to dispensing medicines. His brain reviews these possible actions and the objections to them with lightning speed, as he stares dismayed at the three packs of useless batteries in the palm of his hand. He drops them into the waste-paper basket. There really is no alternative but to try and get through the party without a hearing aid.

When you can't hear what people are saying you have two options: you can either keep quiet and nod and murmur and smile, pretending that you are hearing what your interlocutor is saying, throwing in the odd word of agreement, but always in danger of getting the wrong end of the stick, with potentially embarrassing consequences; or alternatively, you can seize the initiative, ignore the normal rules of conversational turn-taking, and talk non-stop on a subject of your own choosing without letting the other person get a word in edgeways, so that the problem of hearing and understanding what they are saying doesn't arise. The latter course is the one he has followed for the past hour or so.

It was necessary to find topics on which he could expatiate at length and without having to pause for thought. The method he used was to draw on certain ideas he had long nourished without ever having an opportunity to air them, or which he had thought of only after the opportunity had passed, products of *l'esprit de l'escalier*, and then to introduce as soon as possible into any conversational encounter whichever of these topics seemed most appropriate. The first guest to whom he applied this strategy was a left-wing playwright whose agit-prop play about the miners' strike he had seen several years ago at the Playhouse Studio theatre. He had been unable to follow much of the dialogue, which was spoken in thick Geordie dialect, but the sympathies of the play were not in doubt and further confirmed when the entire cast joined in singing 'The Red Flag' in the final scene. He took great satisfaction in explaining to the author of this work why the miners' strike had failed – for a reason unaccountably overlooked by all the numerous commentators on the subject, including the playwright himself. It was not because of the determination of the Thatcher government to break the power of the unions, though that was real enough, but because the strike attracted no public support, apart from the affected mining communities, militant trade unionists, and the left-wing intelligentsia who supported all strikes on principle. It attracted no wide support because the British people as a whole had been culturally conditioned to regard mining as the most inhumane and oppressive type of industrial wage slavery, and felt secretly guilty about depending for their energy requirements on men who laboured for most of the hours of daylight in dark, narrow, claustrophobic tunnels miles underground, hacking and cutting at seams of coal, sweating, choking and covered in black grime. The literature they had read which described mines and mining, from school history books about the early industrial revolution, with horrifying illustrations of pregnant women pulling coal trucks along low-roofed tunnels on their hands and knees, to Zola's *Germinal*, Lawrence's *Sons and Lovers*, Orwell's *The Road to Wigan Pier*, and periodic newspaper reports of fatal mining accidents and disasters, all enforced the same message, that mining was a cruelly oppressive kind of work without which the world would be a better and more civilised place. And although it was understandable that the miners themselves and their families wanted to keep their jobs and feared unemployment, nevertheless this seemed a relatively small-scale and transient problem which could be solved by benevolent social policy (retraining, generous redundancy terms, etc.), rather than by keeping uneconomic mines going merely to provide dangerous, dirty and dehumanising employment for miners. The miners' strike failed because most of the public felt, either consciously or unconsciously, that if changes in economic conditions and energy supply-and-demand meant that Britain no longer needed most of its coal-mines, it was a matter for rejoicing rather than protest. The playwright, who had beamed with pleasure at the first mention of his play, grew more and more restive as he listened to this lecture, opening his mouth several times in a vain attempt to speak and interrupt its flow, but when he himself could think of nothing more to add he said what a pleasure it had been discussing the man's play and excused himself on the grounds of having to see to the wine.

Seeing to the wine meant going to his study for a top-up of the Savigny, after which he re-entered the throng in the drawing room again and was greeted by a woman in a purple sleeveless trouser suit whose name he had forgotten but who, he recalled, worked in advertising. 'How are you?' he said. 'What kind of a Christmas Day did you have?' and she said something in reply which he couldn't hear, during which time he racked his brain for a conversational topic. Advertising, advertising . . . ah yes, he knew what to talk about.

'You know when you see an advertisement and you don't really understand it – well *you* probably don't have that experience – but it happens quite often to me. I see an advertisement on a hoarding, and either I don't understand what it's selling or I don't understand what it's saying, and the more ubiquitous the advert is, the more it puzzles you and the more difficult it becomes to admit to anyone that you don't actually understand it. You think to yourself that there must be some simple explanation which is so obvious that you would look a fool by asking for it. On the other hand you wonder if everybody else isn't just pretending to understand it, or overlooking some contradiction or anomaly in the ad that only you have perceived. But in due course the advertising campaign comes to an end, the posters disappear, and there is no longer any opportunity to casually ask someone what they think the ad means, and you have to go through the rest of your life with this unresolved enigma. For instance, I never understood – and this is the first time I have ever admitted it to anyone – I've never understood that famous Wonderbra advertisement, the one with the blonde girl in her underwear saying, "Hallo boys!" – she's either saying it or thinking it, it's not entirely clear which – you know the one I mean?' The woman nods in a rather curt fashion and the social smile she has been wearing fades from her features to be replaced by something very like a frown. He wonders belatedly whether this is really a suitable subject to explore with a female guest he hardly knows, and who, it now strikes him, has a rather prominent bosom under her purple tunic, but it is too late to change course now, so he carries on: 'Well I could never work out who or what she is addressing. Who or what are the "boys"? Is it a literal reference or a metaphorical expression? If you examine the picture closely you see that she is looking down, at such a steep angle that you can't actually see her eyes at all, just the lids, which have a lot of mascara on them. She is either looking down and admiring her breasts, newly shaped and uplifted by the Wonderbra, with delighted surprise, in which case "boys" is metaphorical – but would a woman address her own breasts as "boys"? It seems unnatural – surely she would personify them as female? She would say, "Hallo girls!" Alternatively she is addressing actual boys, and we are to assume that she is looking down at some young men who are below her, out of the frame of the picture. But where are they – where would this scene be taking place? Is there a knock on her door, perhaps, and she opens it in her underwear, liberated young woman that she is, looks down and sees these boys who have been irresistibly attracted by her wonderful bust, and have prostrated themselves at her feet? It seems improbable. And in that case they are in the worst possible position to view and appreciate her bust. They can't see her cleavage from where they are lying. You see the problem? I tried googling the phrase, but for once it didn't shed much light. There was a book of patriotic First World War poems by Ella Wheeler Wilcox called *Hello, Boys!* which doesn't seem very relevant, and apparently in competitive gymnastics the phrase "Hallo Boys" is colloquially applied to a particular move by male gymnasts when they spread their legs while performing a handstand, presumably because it reveals the shape of their testicles under their tights, which rather supports my point about personification, but doesn't explain what *"boys"* means in the Wonderbra ad . . .'

It occurred to him that his addressee, who was showing signs of impatience, might know the answer to the puzzle and be about to give it to him, in which case he would have to pretend to understand it, but fortunately her attention was distracted by the sight of some other guest, evidently a dear friend, whom she turned to greet and kiss on both cheeks, bringing their conversation to a convenient end.

After that he expounded to a musicologist from the University a theory he had long entertained that it had been of enormous advantage to song writers of American popular music that so many American place names, because of their Spanish or native Indian origins, were anapaestic, the stress falling on the third syllable, like Cali*for*nia, Indi*an*a, Massa*chu*setts, Caro*li*na, San Fran*cis*co, or iambic, like Chi*ca*go, At*lan*ta, Mis*sou*ri, words which were easily set to syncopated music, whereas English place names were typically dactylic, like *Bir*mingham and *Man*chester or trochaic, like *Brigh*ton and *Leic*ester, inherently unmusical. To illustrate the point he crooned, '*When you go to Birmingham, Be sure to wear a flower in your hair*', and in a creditable imitation of Frank Sinatra, '*Leicester, Leicester, that toddling town, Leicester, Leicester, I'll show you around*'. Amused heads turned around the room. The musicologist, who had seemed disposed to challenge his argument, seemed impressed, and was certainly silenced, by this demonstration.

Altogether he feels he is doing pretty well in finding topics on which he can expatiate that are appropriate to the guests he encounters. His disquisition on 'Very flat, Norfolk' was, he has to admit to himself, as he tops up his wine glass in the quiet refuge of his study, a little forced, prompted only by the name of his interlocutor, but he hopes she found the brilliance of his explication an adequate compensation. At that moment his wife comes into the room, shuts the door behind her, and says something. 'What?' he says. She speaks again, louder, and more deliberately, and he reads her lips without difficulty.

'What. Do. You. Think. You're. Doing?'

Fred was angry. Very angry. She got even angrier when I answered her question by saying I was topping up my wine glass from one of the bottles Richard had given me for Christmas. She launched into a tirade in which I could only distinguish occasional phrases: 'too much to drink . . . insulting my guests . . . you and your father . . . wrecking my party . . .' I held up my hands placatingly.

'It's no use, Fred, I can't hear what you're saying.'

She stopped ranting and said something I took to be a question about my hearing aid.

'Both batteries packed up at the same time, just before the party started. I didn't tell you – I thought you had enough on your plate.'

She said something in which I lip-read the phrase 'spare batteries'.

'I thought I had some, but I haven't. The ones I've got in my drawer are the wrong size.'

She rolled her eyes and raised them to the ceiling.

'I bought them by mistake. It's easily done.'

She said something like: 'Which drawer is it?'

'That one,' I said, indicating the top drawer of the steel multi-drawer unit where I keep my hearing-aid accessories. A small knot of unease was already forming in my gut. The shock of finding the wrong type of batteries in the place where I had such a confident expectation of finding the right type had perhaps prevented me from making a thorough search of the drawer.

Fred pulled out the drawer and emptied its contents on to the surface of my desk in a single movement. She rifled through a heap of leaflets, instruction manuals, pouches, boxes and purses belonging to past generations of hearing aids, some containing little brushes and widgets and impregnated cloths for their cleaning and maintenance, old broken NHS behind-the-ear aids with bits of plastic tubing sticking out of them, dead, discarded batteries of various sizes, and picked out of this debris a carousel bubble pack which enclosed four empty circular concave spaces and two batteries. She handed them to me with a question which ended with the words, 'right size?' They were 312ZA batteries, with their little brown plastic tabs in place and intact.

'Yes,' I said.

She waited and watched with silent contempt as I fitted the batteries into my hearing instruments, inserted the latter in my ears and confirmed that they were working. Then she denounced my boorish behaviour in detail. I had drunk too much wine, and talked too loudly – talked at, rather than to, whoever was unfortunate enough to engage me in conversation, without pausing for breath or allowing them to say a word themselves, on topics which were either of no interest to them or positively upsetting. It appeared that the lady in the purple trouser suit was not in advertising at all, but the headmistress of Lena's primary school, who had had a mastectomy and wore a prosthetic brassiere, so she had not appreciated my playful deconstruction of the Wonderbra ad; while Mrs Norfolk, one of *Décor*'s most valued customers, who was in the process of ordering curtains for every room in a recently acquired second home, had clearly been baffled and faintly insulted by my manic analysis of the negative connotations of her name; and the left-wing playwright, who sat on the governing board of the Playhouse, and whom Fred had invited to parties and dinner parties on numerous occasions without ever persuading him to come until today, had been talking to his girlfriend in a corner, with his back turned to the rest of the company, ever since I spoke to him. And what did I mean by singing in the drawing room? It was bad enough to have my father singing in the kitchen, after being caught peeing in the front garden.

'What was that again?' I said. 'About Dad?'

I didn't put the full story together until some hours later, from various witnesses and Dad himself. He had declined to take Fred's hints yesterday that he should feel free to absent himself from the party, a noisy, crowded gathering of people mostly unknown to him, as she presented it, eating foreign food which he probably wouldn't like, so he might prefer to have a plate of cold turkey and pickles in his own room, with a portable television for company which he could turn up as loud as he liked without disturbing anybody. Instead he took a great deal of time over his morning toilet, dressed himself in his best clothes – Harris tweed sports jacket, sharply creased worsted trousers, a clean shirt and a tie with only a small and inconspicuous gravy stain – came downstairs about half an hour before the party was due to start, and announced that he was going for a walk. This was just before my hearing aid packed up. I asked him where he was thinking of going. He said to our local high street. I reminded him that all the shops would be closed, but he thought he might find a newsagent open where he could buy a lottery ticket, and anyway he needed a breath of air. I thought he couldn't come to any harm on such an excursion, so let him go, and asked Anne and Jim if they would look after him when he came back, if I were otherwise occupied, and see that he got something to eat and drink. I have to admit that after that I forgot all about him in the stress of my hearing-aid crisis, and the false euphoria of the conversational feats with which I sought to conceal it.

It seems that in the course of his walk he went into a pub for a half-pint of draught bitter – something he hasn't done in London for years. Some atavistic memory of Christmases long ago, perhaps before he was married, when all the men of the family would go for a drink as soon as the pubs opened on Boxing Day, and then go on to watch a football match, may have prompted this unwonted indulgence, and the knowledge that there would be only wine and fizzy canned lager to drink at the party may have contributed to it. Anyway he enjoyed his half-pint and imprudently ordered another one. On the way home the pressure on his bladder became acute. As he approached our house he doubted whether he would be able to make it to the front door without wetting himself, and was certain that if by any chance the downstairs loo were occupied when he got inside he would be quite incapable of mounting the stairs to the first-floor bathroom. So with some presence of mind he pushed his way into the thick laurel bushes beside our front gate and relieved himself against the inside of the boundary wall. A late-arriving guest noticed him and reported, as he was taking off his coat, that a vagrant appeared to be committing a nuisance in the shrubbery. Cecilia, overhearing this, summoned Fred and recommended calling the police, but Anne said, 'It's probably Granddad taken short,' and sent Jim out to bring him in, which he did. They took Dad into the kitchen, sat him down at the kitchen table and, not knowing that he had already imbibed a pint of beer, gave him a large glass of sweet white wine and persuaded him to taste the Thai curry, which to his own surprise he pronounced very tasty and ate with appetite. Ben and Maxine relieved Anne and Jim in chatting to him, and Ben poured him another glass of wine. Dad began to get into the party mood and invited Maxine to sit on his knee, which she sportingly did for a while until he said his leg was going numb. He told them about his career as a dance-band musician before the war, and about the one and only recording he had made as a singer, 'The Night, the Stars and the Music', with the band of Arthur Roseberry, who composed the words and music; and when Maxine said she'd love to hear it, he sang it to her. It's what is known in the business as a ballad, and the tune was imprinted on my memory from many playings of the old 78 vinyl disc on the radiogram at home, which Dad later transferred on to an audio cassette. He gave me a copy which I have somewhere. 'The night, the stars and the music / The magic of the something something . . .' Apparently he stood up and sang two choruses without missing a word or a beat, got a round of applause from the people in the kitchen, sat down, farted loudly because of the curry, looked over his shoulder and called out 'Taxi!' (which made Ben laugh so much he choked on his lager), said he thought he'd better go and lie down for a bit, tried to walk out of the kitchen unassisted, stumbled over the threshold, recovered his balance by throwing his arms round Cecilia who entered the kitchen at that moment with a tray full of dirty glasses, causing her to tip them on to the tiled floor, and had to be helped upstairs to his room by Jim and Ben. 'I don't blame *him*,' Fred said. 'He's an old man. I blame you. He was your responsibility.'

'I'm sorry,' I said. 'I didn't know anything about it.' I had distinguished none of the various sounds associated with this episode in the general muffled background noise of the party.

There was a knock on the door of my study and Marcia put her head round it. 'Mother, the Jessops are going. Do you want to say goodbye?'

'Already?' Fred exclaimed. She turned fiercely on me. 'You see? You've driven people away, you and your father between you.' She swept out of the room past Marcia, who shot me a hostile look and hurried after her. I followed at a slower pace.

Actually the Jessops had double-booked themselves and apologised profusely for leaving early. Most of the other guests were enjoying their puddings and showed no sign of wanting to leave, and most had had enough to drink not to be worried by a bit of falling down and broken glass in the kitchen. But Fred had an idea of how a party should be conducted, with elegance and decorum, and between us Dad and I had wrecked this one in her eyes. When she had said goodbye to the Jessops she went back into the drawing room, and from the hall, where I skulked dejectedly, I saw her chatting and smiling serenely, but I had no doubt that inwardly she was still seething and that I would be in her bad books for some considerable time.

The doorbell chimed. Who the hell could that be coming to the party at this hour, I wondered. 'I'll get it,' I called out to anyone who might be listening, and went to open the front door. Alex Loom was standing in the porch, in her shiny black quilted coat and a red knitted pixie hat, holding a bunch of cut flowers wrapped in cellophane.

'Hi!' she said, with a smile. 'I guess you're surprised to see me.'

'I thought you were supposed to be in America,' I said.

'That was the plan,' she said. 'But Heathrow was socked in. After waiting two days for my flight, I gave up. Can I come in? I *was* invited.'

'The party's nearly over,' I said stupidly, as if I hoped this would make her go away.

'Who is it, darling?' said Fred from behind my back. The 'darling', I knew, was purely for appearance's sake, and implied no melting of her resentment. 'Oh, it's you, Alex!' she cried. 'Let the poor girl in, for goodness' sake. Come in! Come in! What on earth are you doing here? I thought you were going home for Christmas.'

Alex explained that her flight had been delayed several times and eventually cancelled, and as she couldn't get on another one that would have enabled her to get home in time for Christmas, she gave up, caught an airport-link bus, just about the only public transport running, and got back to her flat late on Christmas Day. 'So I thought you wouldn't mind if I took up your party invitation after all,' she said.

'Of course not – we're delighted to see you, aren't we, darling?' I responded to Fred's question with a forced grin and nod. 'But why so late?' she asked Alex.

'I wanted to get some flowers, but it proved harder than I'd figured,' Alex said, handing the bunch to Fred. 'I'm not used to the English Boxing Day, with everything shut. I got a taxi to drive me around and we finally found a flower stall outside a cemetery.'

'Well, you really shouldn't have taken the trouble, but thank you so much, they're lovely,' said Fred.

'What cemetery was that?' I asked.

'I've no idea,' Alex said with a smile.

'Stop asking Alex silly questions, darling, and take her coat.' Fred thrust the slippery black nylon coat into my arms and led Alex off to the dining room, saying, 'Now come and have some lunch, there's still plenty left.'

I was pretty hungry myself, having eaten nothing but a few nuts and nibbles snatched between my conversation pieces, and after hanging up Alex's coat I followed them into the dining room. Alex, a glass of white wine in her hand, was already entertaining a little group of guests with tales of the horrors of Heathrow – queues snaking out of the terminals into the open air, people sleeping slumped over their luggage or prostrate on the floors, distraught parents with crying babies and children . . . We had seen it all on the TV news of course, but there is nothing like a personal report from the front line to bring home its horrors and fill one with profound gratitude at not having been there. Fred brought Alex a plate of steaming Thai chicken curry from the hostess trolley and stayed to listen. I foraged for myself.

I'm not sure I believe Alex's story about driving round the city looking for flowers. If she got them from a cemetery she is more likely to have pinched them from a grave in the churchyard at the end of Rectory Road than paid for them. I think she intended to be late. By being the last guest to arrive she could very naturally be the last one to leave. In fact she lingered long after everybody else except the family had gone, and made herself useful clearing up the dirty glasses and dishes and stacking them in the dishwasher. Fred invited her to stay on for a cup of tea and she accepted readily. By the end of the afternoon, to my dismay, she had made herself thoroughly at home, and was effortlessly addressing everybody by their first names. I had to admire her conversational resourcefulness. She could talk money to Giles and babies to Nicola, and property to Jim and Ben, and make-up to Maxine. She even managed to charm Ben without making Maxine jealous, and Marcia, who might have been more resistant, had gone home soon after lunch with Peter and the children. Of the family party only Anne, I thought, regarded Alex with faint suspicion.

Eventually she said she guessed it was time she was on her way, and asked if we could call a taxi. 'You don't want to spend any more money on taxis,' Fred said, 'and besides you could wait for ever on Boxing Day. Desmond will run you home, won't you, darling?' Before I could reply she added unsmilingly: 'Or are you too drunk?'

'I'm not at all drunk,' I said stiffly. It was in fact nearly three hours since I had had my last glass of Savigny-les-Beaune, and I felt quite sober, even if in breathalyser terms I probably wasn't. Ben said *he* certainly was over the limit, otherwise he would have been glad to oblige, and Giles had gone upstairs with Nicola to bath their baby, so to prevent Fred from offering herself I insisted on acting as Alex's chauffeur. With a stern, 'Well, if you're quite sure . . .' Fred acquiesced.

So I found myself alone with Alex. For someone who had just spent two days in an airport trying unsuccessfully to join her family for Christmas she seemed in remarkably good spirits. She chattered away in the car about how great the party had been and what a lovely family I had, remarks to which I made minimal responses. When I drew up in the car park behind Wharfside Court, she said: 'You haven't asked me how my research is going.'

'How is it going?'

'Very well. I've just made a very interesting discovery. In all the specimen suicide notes I've collected, the word "suicide" itself very rarely occurs. Less than two per cent. A few more talk about killing themselves. About half the writers refer to dying, or wanting to die, and the rest pussyfoot around the subject, imply what they're going to do by "saying goodbye", or "I won't be a burden to you any more", and so on. Or they use euphemisms like "catch the bus" – "CTB" for short. But almost none of them says they're committing suicide. What do you make of that?'

'It reminds me of a saying of Borges,' I said. '"In a riddle to which the answer is 'chess', the only forbidden word is *chess*."'

'That's great!' she said. 'I could use that. But what do you make of it?'

I thought for a moment. 'Perhaps "suicide" seems too impersonal, too detached, too forensic a word to convey the intensity of their emotions at the time, especially as you have to combine it with the very legalistic word "commit" to make it into a verb. You can't say, "I'm going to suicide," or "I'm going to suicide myself". "Suicide" is just a noun, and a learned, Latinate one. "Die" is a simple, basic verb which goes back to the Anglo-Saxon roots of English, and must have its equivalent in every known natural language. It almost defines the human condition, whereas "suicide" categorises the act as something marginal, deviant, aberrant. That may be part of the reason.'

'Hey – that's awesome! You're really good, Desmond. Can I use that?' As I hesitated, wondering whether to say, '*I'm sure you will anyway,*' she added: 'With an acknowledgement, of course.'

'Actually, I'd rather you didn't acknowledge any help from me,' I said.

'OK, if that's the way you want it,' she said cheerfully.

Once again I felt that in trying to suppress any suggestion of an agreement between us I had somehow affirmed its continuation.

'Will you come up for a coffee?' she said.

'No,' I said.

'Well then – thanks for the ride. And the party.' She leaned over from the passenger seat and kissed me on the cheek. I felt her hand on my thigh. 'Sure you won't come up?' she breathed into my ear.

'No thanks,' I said. She slipped quickly out of the car, and I watched her cross the car park in her long shiny black coat, wondering what might have happened if I had accepted her invitation. As she reached the corner of the building she turned, waved, and disappeared from my view.

15

27th December. Dad was not on the best of form this morning. He had slept badly, claiming that he had to get up five times last night 'for the Usual', while 'the Other' was troubling him in a different way. 'I think it had a binding effect on me, that curry,' he confided to Cecilia over morning coffee. We were sitting round the kitchen table, because Fred had been cleaning spots of wine and curry from the carpets in the other rooms and nobody was to walk on them until the damp patches were dry. They were marked with squares of kitchen roll like a minefield. 'You'd think it would be the opposite, wouldn't you?' Dad said.

'I'm sure I don't know, Mr Bates,' said Cecilia, ostentatiously wiping her lips with a napkin, as a vain hint Dad should do the same: he had acquired a moustache of white foam from the cappuccino Fred had made him.

'Dad, your mouth,' I said, miming the required operation.

'What? Oh, right. Nice cup of coffee, Winifred, but the bubbles get up my nose.' He drew out of his trouser pocket a large, wrinkled, none-too-clean cotton handkerchief, wiped his mouth and blew his nose noisily. 'I need a drop of liquid paraffin,' he said. 'Have you got any?'

'Isn't paraffin always liquid?' Fred asked. 'I think we've got some in the greenhouse.'

'What? You mean pink paraffin for stoves? Gawd, that would be the finish of me. No dear, I mean the liquid paraffin you get from the chemist's. Best remedy for constipation there is.'

'Oh,' said Fred.

'We'll get some when we go out this afternoon, Dad,' I said in an effort to steer him away from the topic.

'Why, where are we going?'

'To look at Blydale House. You remember – I showed you the brochure in London, the last time we had lunch.'

A look of sulky displeasure came over his face. 'I'm not moving into one of those places,' he said.

'You promised to look at it,' I said. 'I've made an appointment at three o'clock.'

We argued for a while. To give Fred and her mother their due, they supported me in pressing on him the advantages of moving into Blydale House or something like it, though I'm sure that neither of them viewed the prospect of his being a near neighbour and frequent visitor to our home with any enthusiasm. 'All right, I'll look,' he said, in the end. 'But it's a waste of time.'

He accompanied me and the Warden of Blydale House on a tour of the building with an air of silent, sardonic detachment, walking a pace or two behind us, leaving me to ask all the questions and hardly attending to Mrs Wilson's answers. She is a pleasant, middle-aged woman, obviously well used to handling recalcitrant old people. There isn't a vacant room in the place at present, but she had obtained permission from one of the residents for us to peep into his bed-sitting room while he was having his tea in the lounge. She unlocked the door for us. I stood at the threshold and called Dad, who was feigning interest in a water-colour on the corridor wall, to come and have a look. It was smaller than the photograph in the brochure had suggested, but clean and neat. There was a sofa bed with cushions, an armchair, a fitted wardrobe and chest of drawers, an occasional table with one upright chair, and a television in one corner.

'Cosy, isn't it?' I said.

Dad sniffed and said nothing.

Mrs Wilson pointed out the door to the en suite bathroom. 'Actually it has a walk-in shower, not a bath. And a toilet of course.'

'You mean there's no bath?' Dad said. It was the first detail that had stung him into speech.

'We think showers are safer,' Mrs Wilson said. 'There's a rail for you to hold on to, and a folding seat if you prefer to sit down.'

Dad shook his head. 'A shower's not the same as a bath,' he said. In old age he has reverted to the once-a-week bath night of his early life, an epic event which takes hours rather than minutes, generating huge amounts of steam and condensation in the bathroom.

'We do have one bathroom with a chair-lift,' Mrs Wilson said, 'though it's mainly for the use of people in wheelchairs.'

'I'm not a wheelchair case yet,' Dad said. Mrs Wilson smiled and said she could see that.

We viewed the communal dining room, where two women in blue overalls were laying the tables for the evening meal, and the lounge, where afternoon tea and biscuits were being dispensed from a trolley to the residents, sitting upright in high-backed armchairs. A few were chatting to each other. Most sat alone and silent, lost in – what? Thought? Memories? Worries? Or just lost? A flicker of interest lit up their eyes as we came into the room, then faded. We looked at a noticeboard on which the times of whist drives, bingo sessions and keep-fit classes were displayed.

'So what do you think of Blydale, Mr Bates?' Mrs Wilson asked him, when we returned to her office.

'I think it's a very nice place,' he said, and paused to let a pleased smile form on my lips before adding: 'for old people who haven't got a home of their own.'

'Oh, a lot of our residents had very nice homes before they came here,' she said. 'But we all get to a point where running a house is too much for us.'

'Yes, well I haven't got to that stage, yet,' he said, and turned to me. 'Can we go now, son?'

On our way out I apologised to Mrs Wilson for Dad's churlishness. 'Don't worry about it, old folk don't like to leave their own homes, it's natural,' she said. I asked her if I could put Dad's name on a waiting list. 'We don't have a waiting list as such,' she said. 'Get in touch again if he changes his mind. Vacancies occur fairly frequently.'

In a way I understood his resistance. Blydale House is a decent place, clean, bright and well run, but I couldn't look round that lounge without feeling a strong desire to be out of it, and the little bed-sitting room we peered into, though comfortably furnished, seemed more like a cell than a home. However, as I pointed out on the way back to Rectory Road (we stopped at a chemist's on the way to get liquid paraffin for him and batteries for me), living near us he wouldn't be trapped in the place all day, he could always hop on a bus and call in and see us.

'You'd soon get sick of that,' he said, with disconcerting candour.

He's right, of course. I feel a guilty relief that he doesn't want to move into Blydale House immediately. I could sense that Fred and Cecilia shared this feeling when I reported the upshot of our visit, but I'm afraid that all of us, having altruistically done our duty in urging him to move, now accused him of stubborn ingratitude for refusing to do so.

'You're only postponing the inevitable, Harry,' Fred told him. 'If you don't move into a home up here, you'll have to move into one in London.'

'I don't see why I've got to move at all,' Dad said sullenly.

'Because you can't cope, Dad,' I said. 'You're a danger to yourself in that house. You won't even wear a panic alarm.'

'What's a panic alarm?'

'You know what it is, I told you. A thing you wear round your neck.'

'Oh, that. I don't need that. I might press it by accident and have the police or the fire brigade breaking down my door in the middle of the night.'

'If you were in supervised accommodation, you wouldn't need to wear one, Mr Bates,' said Cecilia, who occupies a superior type of apartment for the elderly in Cheltenham. 'In the flat

214

where I live there's a button in every room which I can use to summon the Warden.'

Dad now shifted his defence to his favourite ground. 'Anyway, how much does that place cost?' he asked me.

'I don't remember off-hand,' I prevaricated. 'Quite a bit, but you could afford it, and if not we –'

'It's two hundred and seventy-five pounds a week, Harry,' Fred interpolated.

'*What?*' Dad exclaimed. 'How am I supposed to find that sort of money?'

'It's very simple. You sell your house,' Fred said. 'Given London property prices, it would fetch enough to keep you at Blydale for as long as . . .' Fred hesitated, and Dad completed the sentence for her.

'As long as I need it, you mean? Which wouldn't be very long, living up here, I can tell you. Then you would all inherit my money.'

'Oh, for heaven's sake, Harry!' Fred said. 'Don't be ridiculous.'

'I can assure you *I* have no designs on your money, Mr Bates,' said Cecilia. 'My late husband left me well provided for.'

'Yes, I bet he did,' Dad muttered darkly.

Afterwards, when we were on our own, I told Fred I thought she had been hard on Dad, frightening him with the cost of Blydale House.

'There's no point in beating about the bush,' she said. 'He's got to face the facts. If he's taken into a state care home they'll confiscate his house to pay for it.'

'You've really put him off the idea of moving up here now,' I said. 'But perhaps that's what you intended to do.'

It was a mean thing to say. Why did I say it? I don't know. Put it down to the curdled spirit of Christmas.

'I can't believe you could think that, let alone say it,' Fred said. 'I've always made your father welcome here, even if I do find the constant bulletins on the state of his bladder and his bowels rather trying. I know Mother does.'

215

'I think I'd better take him back to London tomorrow,' I said.

'All right, if you wish,' Fred said. 'But please don't pretend that I'm driving him away.'

When I suggested to Dad that it might be a good idea to take him back to London tomorrow, when the traffic on the M1 was likely to be fairly light, halfway between Christmas and New Year, he agreed without argument. 'Whatever you say, son. Whatever suits you.' There was an air of martyrdom about him for the rest of the day, as if he felt he was being victimised but was not going to complain. Perhaps he had picked up vibrations of the ill-feeling between me and Fred, and intuited that he was part of it. Altogether it was an edgy and uncomfortable evening. After dinner, which he ate in silence, he declined my offer to fix him up with my headphones so he could watch the TV without disturbing us (we all wanted to read), and instead chose to listen to his little transistor radio through an earpiece, reclining in an armchair with his eyes closed.

'Can't you stop him doing that?' Fred said to me irritably, looking up from her book.

'Doing what?' I said.

She sighed and raised her eyes to the ceiling. 'Oh of course, you can't hear it. Can *you* hear it, Mother?'

Cecilia, who was reading our *Guardian,* and comparing it prejudicially to the *Telegraph* from time to time, said, 'Hear what, dear?'

'God give me patience! Am I the only person in this house with normal hearing?' Fred exclaimed. 'There's a faint tinny sound leaking from that radio. It's driving me mad.'

'It's leaking from his ear, he's probably got the volume too high,' I said. 'I'll ask him to turn it down.'

'No, don't bother, I'm sure to go on hearing it,' she said. 'I'll read in bed. You can look after him and Mother until they're ready to go too.'

'I won't be long,' Cecilia said to her; and to me, after Fred had left the room: 'My late husband had very good hearing up

216

to the end of his life. Mine, I must admit, is not what it was.'

'But you do very well, considering your age,' I said. 'You don't know how lucky you are.'

'No, I haven't had to put up a prayer to St Francis de Sales yet,' she said with some complacency. 'You know he's the patron saint of deaf people?'

I confessed that I didn't. 'Was he deaf, then?' I asked.

'No, but he catechised a deaf man, so that he could receive Holy Communion. I suppose he invented some kind of sign language. If you were a Catholic, Desmond, you could pray to St Francis de Sales.' She said this with a slightly mischievous smile. She enjoys having the occasional dig at my godless state.

'To cure me?'

'It has been known. But of course it's not the saints who actually work miracles, you know. That's a common misunderstanding.'

'They pass your prayer to God, don't they?' I said, remembering the lecture on petitionary prayer.

'They *intercede* with God on your behalf,' Cecilia corrected me.

'Why go through them when you could pray directly to God?' I asked.

Cecilia pondered this question for a moment, as if it had never occurred to her before. 'Perhaps we feel a little shy about bringing our problems directly before God. It feels more comfortable doing it through a saint, or Our Lady.'

'It makes me think of heaven as being like a Renaissance court,' I said, 'with all the saints clustering round the throne of God like courtiers, with petitions in their hands.'

Cecilia smiled. 'There's nothing to stop you praying directly to God,' she said. 'Our Lord cured many deaf people when he was on this earth.'

'But they were stone deaf, weren't they – and dumb too, usually.'

'You remember your New Testament, then,' said Cecilia, with an approving nod.

'I can see that would be a pretty spectacular miracle, making the deaf hear and the dumb speak,' I said. 'But hearing impairment is a much less interesting disability. Hardly worth troubling a saint with, let alone the Lord.'

'You could always pray for patience to bear your cross,' Cecilia said.

'Fred just did that,' I said, 'but it didn't seem to work.' When Cecilia looked puzzled I explained: 'She said "*God give me patience!*" but she went to bed instead.'

'Ah, but it wasn't a real prayer,' Cecilia said. 'Winifred has never regarded patience as a virtue to be cultivated. She was born impatient – the shortest labour of my four.'

This was the most interesting conversation I had ever had with my mother-in-law. In the course of it Dad stirred, levered his long body upright, switched off his radio, and went out of the room without saying anything or glancing in my direction. I presumed he had gone to the toilet, but he didn't come back, and when I went looking for him I discovered he had gone to bed.

28th December. I took Dad home today. He was in a better mood this morning, having swallowed some of his liquid paraffin last night to good effect. 'We got a result,' he told me at breakfast, in a hoarse stage whisper which Cecilia pretended not to hear. He was all packed and ready to leave by ten o'clock. Fred, perhaps feeling a little guilty for being sharp with him yesterday, gave him a food parcel to take home: slices of turkey breast and ham, wedges of cheese, mince pies, apples and oranges, all wrapped separately. He thanked her warmly and kissed her on the cheek. 'Thanks for everything, my dear,' he said. 'Goodbye Celia,' he said, shaking Cecilia's hand. 'Goodbye, Mr Bates,' she said. 'Have a safe journey. And a happy New Year to you.' 'Yes, happy New Year, Harry,' Fred chimed in. He grimaced. 'Oh, well, I won't be sitting up for it, I can tell you. New Year means nothing to me now. A happy New Week is the most I hope for.'

'Yes,' he said reminiscently, as we drove away from the house,

'New Year's Eve used to be the one night of the year when everybody in Archer Street would have a gig, no matter if they were one-armed drummers or tone-deaf sax-players, and at double the usual money. You got booked up months ahead for New Year's Eve. Not any more.' And he went into a familiar riff on the decline of live dance music. On the motorway he fell silent, and I thought he had dozed off, but he suddenly surprised me by saying: 'What happened to that man who was at your house last night?'

'What man, Dad?' I asked.

'There was a man in the lounge last night, talking to Celia.'

'That was me, Dad. I was the only man in the lounge, apart from you.'

'No, it was another bloke. I didn't say goodnight to him because I'd forgotten his name. I wanted to apologise to him this morning, but he must have gone.'

This delusion worried me, but I did not press the point.

The journey was not too bad. I had taken the precaution of putting a wide-necked bistro-style wine decanter under the passenger seat for emergencies, but there was no need to use it. We stopped at three service centres on the way at carefully calculated intervals, and got back to Lime Avenue at about three in the afternoon, as the winter daylight was already fading. The house, with all its curtains drawn, seemed dark and cheerless inside, and I felt a spasm of compunction at delivering Dad back to this depressing habitat, even though it was his own choice. The only mitigating factor was that it felt reasonably warm. 'Gawd, I left the hall radiator on!' Dad said, putting his hand on it as we came in. 'I could swear I turned it off.' In fact he had – turning it on again was the last thing I did before leaving the house. But the kitchen with its greasy oilcloth and chipped Formica, and the dining room with its threadbare carpet and sagging chairs, reminded me of stage sets for early plays by Pinter. 'Wouldn't you rather be in that nice clean, bright place we saw yesterday?' I said. 'With somebody else cooking you a hot meal?' 'No,' he said. 'I'm glad to be home. And I've got all that lovely grub your wife gave me.' We'd bought some milk and bread at one of the motorway services shops, so he was indeed well supplied for the time being. I had a cup of tea with him, and took my leave.

I drove back with the radio on at high volume – Jazz FM in the London area, then Radio Four and Classic FM on the motorway – stopping once for a meal and a short nap in the car, and got back home at about nine-thirty. Fred came out of the drawing room when she heard me in the hall and said something. She didn't smile. I said, 'What? Just a minute,' and put in my hearing aid. She said: 'Your father's been on the phone several times. I don't know what he's on about, but he sounds upset.'

I went into my study and called Dad. He answered immediately, as if he was sitting next to the phone. 'Hallo, who's that?' he said in a loud angry tone.

'It's Desmond, Dad,' I said. 'What's the matter?'

'What's the matter? I want to know what's going on,' he said. 'I've been dumped here, all on my own. That bloke who drove me down here just buggered off without a word of goodbye.'

'That bloke was me, Dad,' I said. 'And I had a cup of tea with you before I left.'

'What d'you mean, it was you? I'm talking about the bloke who lives up north. He has a huge house with four lavs, and curtains that open and close on their own, like a cinema. And a posh wife, called Fred for some reason, and a horde of relatives. He drove me down here, and hardly said a word the whole way.'

'That's me, Dad,' I said. 'I live up north and I have a big house and a wife called Fred. It's short for Winifred. She gave you some turkey and ham to take home.'

'That's true,' he said after a pause. 'I've just had some for my tea.' His tone was troubled. 'So it was you.'

'Yes.'

'What's the matter with me then?'

'It's because you've been away for a few days, and now

you're back home, you're a little bit confused. It's nothing to worry about.'

But it is.

29th December. Cecilia left today. Fred and I took her to the station and put her on the train to Durham. She's gone to stay with her eldest son and his wife, who live there; she usually spends Christmas with us and New Year with them. So Fred and I are alone at last. I was looking forward to a quiet weekend, apart from a few hours of deafened socialising at a neighbour's New Year's Eve party which we always go to, arriving late and sloping off soon after the compulsory kissing and oldlangsyning, but Jakki and Lionel have invited us to join them at a place called Gladeworld. Apparently it's an up-market holiday camp in a forest, about sixty miles from here. They were planning to spend the New Year holiday there with Lionel's brother and his wife, but Lionel's brother is ill in bed with bronchitis and a temperature, so they had to drop out at the last moment, and Jakki asked Fred if we would like to come in their place. Fred relayed Jakki's description to me: 'You stay in little chalets scattered among the trees. She says they're very comfortable, and they've booked an executive chalet which is extra-luxurious. En suite bathrooms and so on. You can either cater for yourselves or eat at one of the restaurants. There's a heated indoor swimming pool under a huge plastic dome with artificial waves and rapids and palm trees, and a spa, and an indoor sports hall and so on. There are no cars: you leave your car in the car park and everybody rents bikes or walks.'

'It sounds ghastly,' I said.

'Well I think it sounds rather fun,' said Fred. 'It's enormously popular – Jakki says you have to book up months ahead. It's very nice of her and Lionel to think of asking us.'

'Would we be paying for ourselves?' I asked.

'Well of course we'd pay our share.'

I asked her how much, and she named a sum which I thought

rather steep. 'So really we'd be doing them a favour, or Lionel's brother a favour, rather than the other way round?' I said.

Fred dismissed this comment with a contemptuous toss of the head. 'You're always complaining about how you hate New Year's Eve, almost as much as you hate Christmas – well, here's your chance to get away for it, do something different,' she said. 'A little exercise, some fresh air, a lot of relaxation. It would do us both good.'

'Cooped up with Jakki and Lionel for three days?'

'Jakki is my friend, and Lionel is perfectly pleasant. And we don't have to do everything together all the time. And it's only two full days. And anyway,' Fred concluded, 'if you won't go, I'll go on my own.'

I could see I would have to give in, because I couldn't risk having a third row with Fred in the same week. I eased the way with a joke.

'How do you know they aren't planning one of their theme nights? Wife-Swapping Night, say. With car keys in a bowl and porn videos on the television.'

Fred hooted with laughter. 'Do you fancy Jakki, darling?'

'Absolutely not!'

'Nor I Lionel. Anyway, there wouldn't be many car keys to choose from. You might draw me.'

'Or Lionel,' I said.

She chuckled. 'You'll come, then?'

'I suppose I'd better,' I said, 'or they might propose a Troilism Night.'

'Good, I'll tell Jakki you agreed – but not why.' She went off in good humour to phone Jakki.

You might draw me. The phrase lingered suggestively in my mind, provoking the thought that Gladeworld could assist the healing of relations between us. We haven't made love since the spanking episode a few weeks ago. Much as I dislike vigorous exercise as a rule, and especially swimming in chlorinated indoor pools, I have to admit that you get a sense of relaxed well-being afterwards that is conducive to sex. And the certainty that Jakki and Lionel would be at it like monkeys in the next bedroom might have an aphrodisiac effect. Though I wouldn't of course admit it, I am quite looking forward to the weekend.

16
Deaf in the Afternoon

Gladeworld. What a strange phenomenon. Like a negative image of a place with properties, such as confinement and induced pain, that you would normally regard as being themselves negative, which has the curious effect of turning them into positives, or so it seems from the contented looks of the inhabitants. A benevolent concentration camp. A benign prison. A happy hell. It is a square mile or two in area, with a high chain-link fence topped with barbed wire around the circumference, and a single entrance like a military checkpoint, with a barrier that is raised and lowered as the internees arrive in their cars, have their documents scrutinised by uniformed security guards, and are admitted. Inside the compound, several thousand men, women and children live in one-storey huts, much smaller than the homes they have come from, cunningly distributed among the trees to produce an illusion of privacy. They wear a kind of prison uniform: track suits, shorts, trainers and, in the rain, kagools. They spend their days toiling up and down, backwards and forwards, on foot or on bicycles, along the macadamed roads and paths connecting their huts to various assembly points: for example, a supermarket where you shop, as you shop at home, but less conveniently, because the produce is inferior, and the prices are higher, and you must carry your heavy shopping bags back to your hut because cars are confined to the car park; for example, a large sports hall where, for an additional charge, not negligible, you can play under artificial light and in artificial air various sports (tennis, badminton, squash, racquet ball, billiards, snooker, table tennis, etc.), watched critically by a ring of fellow internees waiting for your allotted time to end and their own to begin; and, most exemplary of all, the Tropical Waterworld, a huge geodesic plastic dome enclosing, in a heated, humid atmosphere, a complex of swimming pools and water features of various shapes and sizes: labyrinthine channels and tunnels with powerful pump-driven currents, steeply angled chutes, spiralling tubular slides, and white-water rapids sculpted in fibreglass, which begin at the very top of the structure in the open air and descend with increasing force and speed, at first outside and then inside the wall of the dome, to end precipitously in a deep pool at the bottom. Although theoretically dedicated to swimming, the place is designed to prevent one from swimming more than a few strokes in any direction. The main pool is randomly shaped with no way of ascertaining which dimension is its length and which its breadth, so people swim in all directions and keep bumping into each other, and every now and again an invisible machine creates a heavy swell in which they cannot swim at all but only bob up and down like survivors of an air crash in the sea waiting for rescue, except that they shriek with pleasure rather than fear.

Change the soundtrack, substitute screams and howls for laughter and badinage, put a red filter on the lens to give a fiery glow to the spectacle, and you would think you were in some modern version of Dante's Inferno, or the hells depicted by medieval painters. These half-naked crowds tossed in the turbulent waves, or hurtling down the spiralling semi-transparent tubes at terrifying velocity, or tumbled arse over elbow through the rapids, choked with water, blinded by spume, spun round in whirlpools, dragged backwards by undertow, entangled with each other's limbs, bruised and battered by impact with the fibreglass walls, to be at last tipped into a boiling pit at the bottom, irresistibly recall those antique images of the damned, condemned to endless repetition of their punishment. For as soon as they splash down at the bottom of the rapids, or are spat out from the ends of the spiralling tubes, and clamber out of the water, drenched and dazed, the Gladeworlders obediently mount the stairs that wind upwards between the artificial rocks and join the long lines of people queuing at the upper levels for the tubular slides, or plunge into the steaming open-air pool that leads to the rapids, to endure the terror and the pain all over again.

Desmond expounded this analogy to Fred, Jakki and Lionel, at the end of their first full day. It was New Year's Eve and they had decided to cook their own dinner in their 'villa', as the two-bedroomed chalet was rather grandly called, because the only eating place inside Gladeworld which looked remotely promising was fully booked, and so, almost certainly, was every restaurant in the neighbourhood – 'even if the security guards at the entrance would let us out for a few hours,' Desmond had remarked, when the arrangements for the meal were under discussion. 'Of course they'd let us out,' said Jakki, whose sense of irony was not highly developed. 'Take no notice of him,' said Winifred. 'It's just his way.' In spite of this advice Jakki reacted with the same literal-minded antagonism to his metaphorical description of the Tropical Waterworld. 'Terror and pain?' she said, frowning at him. 'I don't know what you mean. You can see how much everybody is enjoying themselves.'

'It's a joke, love,' said Lionel. 'Desmond's only joking. Do you know,' he went on, 'this place has ninety-five per cent occupancy all year round? Ninety-five per cent. They must be doing something right.'

'Well, I think it's marvellous for families,' said Fred. 'I'm going to recommend it to Marcia and Peter. I'm sure the children would love it.'

'Of course you've got to be an active sort of person to get the best out of it,' said Jakki. She and Lionel had been out jogging before breakfast and cycling on their rented bikes in the woods before lunch; Desmond and Winifred had volunteered to do the shopping for dinner, and walking the mile or so from their chalet to the supermarket and back again, burdened with bulging plastic bags, had been quite enough strenuous exercise, as far as Desmond was concerned anyway. The afternoon had been designated a time for relaxation in the Tropical Waterworld. He thought he had never been in a less relaxing place in his life than

226

the Tropical Waterworld, beginning with its changing area, a slimy-floored maze of cubicles each with two doors, one leading to the pool and one to the entrance/exit, that locked and opened simultaneously by a simple mechanism which it took him twenty minutes to work out, and lined with lockers that on the insertion of a one-pound coin would allow the key to be turned and extracted, attached to a rubber band which you wore round your wrist or ankle. On returning to the changing area rather earlier than his companions, having left his glasses and hearing aid safe in the locker, he was unable to read the number imprinted on his rubber band, and when he asked passing bathers to read it for him he was unable to hear their replies, so eventually he handed his key to a small child who led him like a helpless imbecile to his locker and opened it for him.

In between these humiliations he limited his activities under the dome to swimming around slowly in circles, a few strokes at a time, in the main pool and in the heated open-air pond at the top, keeping well away from the weir that led to the rapids. Nevertheless, even that small amount of immersion and exertion had imparted an agreeable inner warmth, a kind of sensuous lassitude, to his limbs; and now, after a good dinner – coq au vin prepared by Winifred and baked apples stuffed with dates cooked by Jakki – and especially after a generous share of the two bottles of Pomerol which he had prudently brought with him from home, he felt relaxed enough to forget the irritations and frustrations of the day, and let his thoughts play idly over the amorous prospects for the night.

One of the two bedrooms was a double, and the other a twin. Jakki and Lionel, who had got inside the chalet first, had bagged the double. 'You don't mind, do you?' Jakki had said, adding with a little smirk, 'You can always push the singles together.' 'I don't think we'll bother,' Winifred had said, which was unpromising. On the other hand, that was yesterday evening, after a drive made tedious by a long hold-up on the motorway and all the effort of unloading the cars and driving them back to the car park and walking back to their chalet, which seemed to be as far from the car park as it was possible to be within the confines of the perimeter fence. He and Winifred were both weary, retired early, and slept soundly under their duvets in the separate beds. But tonight, he thought, Winifred might be disposed to intimacy. Her nervous system would also have been flooded with endorphins released by exercise, she too would be experiencing the same transient but agreeable sense of well-being as himself, and it seemed to him that when their eyes met occasionally across the dinner table hers had a soft and inviting glow, and her smile a genuine warmth.

It was unfortunate, therefore, that it happened to be New Year's Eve, so that when, after they had cleared the table and stacked the soiled dishes in the dishwasher (this appliance, Jakki emphasised, being a luxury exclusive to the executive villas, along with jacuzzi baths in the en suite bathrooms and a private sauna on the back porch), and had partaken of decaffeinated coffee or herbal tea, Desmond declared, with a covert wink at Winifred, that he felt pleasantly tired and ready for bed, Jakki and Lionel protested that this was out of the question, and insisted that they must all sit up and see the New Year in. And it was doubly unfortunate that Lionel had brought with him a bottle of single malt to, as he waggishly put it, 'get the right spirit into us'.

It was only half-past ten when Desmond's proposal was ruled out of order by Lionel and Jakki, a decision in which Winifred acquiesced (out of politeness, he suspected, rather than enthusiasm), and there was nothing to do until midnight except make desultory conversation and drink the single malt. Winifred did not like whisky, and Jakki's consumption of the liquor was modest, so between them the men had accounted for about two-thirds of the bottle by the time Lionel switched on the television. The floodlit face of Big Ben, with its hands at seven minutes to twelve, filled the screen, and the camera tracked the movement of the minute hand with occasional cutaways to noisy expectant crowds in Trafalgar Square and other public spaces around the country, until at last the familiar bass notes boomed out. The crowds in the streets chanted the numbers – 'one – two – three . . .' – as the chimes sounded, and on the stroke of twelve erupted in cheers and yells and promiscuous embracing. Fireworks exploded over the Thames. The four of them rose to their feet – the two men somewhat unsteadily – and wished their partners a Happy New Year. Lionel engaged Jakki in a long, snogging kiss, and Desmond attempted something similar with Winifred but she quickly terminated it and averted her face. 'Sorry darling, but you know I don't like the smell of whisky,' she said. 'Then come to bed and I'll kiss your other lips,' he murmured into her ear, causing her to blush crimson and push him away. Lionel and Jakki at last unglued themselves and exchanged New Year greetings with Winifred and Desmond. Lionel kissed Winifred respectfully on the cheek and Jakki kissed Desmond on the mouth, thrusting her tongue between his teeth and leaning back afterwards to laugh at his startled expression. 'Happy New Year, Des!' she said. 'You can go to bed now.'

Once inside their bedroom he tried to undress Winifred, starting with the zip at the back of her dress, but she shook off his hand. 'Stop, you'll break it.' 'What's the matter?' he said. 'Aren't you in the mood for love?' 'No, I'm not,' she said, stepping out of her dress and speaking in a low but emphatic voice which he could just about hear. 'And if I were, it wouldn't be any use because you've had far too much to drink.' 'We could have some foreplay and see what happens,' he wheedled, pressing up behind her and cupping his hands over her breasts. She removed his hands and turned on him. 'What did you mean by saying that in front of Jakki and Lionel?' she said angrily. 'Saying what?' 'About lips.' 'They didn't hear it.' 'They would have to be deaf if they didn't – as deaf as you.' 'Ah,' he said. 'Oh well, I don't think they would have been shocked. Jakki gave me a French kiss just now.' Winifred stared at him as if doubting his word. 'Did she? Then she obviously had too much to drink too.'

She carried on briskly preparing herself for bed, but he could tell that the information had piqued her a little, planted a tiny seed of resentment which might work in his favour. When he said he would push the single beds together she did not assent, but she did not demur, and retired to the bathroom while he carried out this operation – which was just as well, as he found it surprisingly difficult. The beds were of light construction, mounted on free-wheeling castors, and cannoned around the room disconcertingly when he gave one of them an over-enthusiastic push, and he almost suspected the other one of deliberately tripping him up at one point, but eventually he managed to line them up next to each other – in the middle of the room, where admittedly they looked a bit odd, more like a catafalque than a double bed, but the night table between them was screwed irremovably to the wall so there was no alternative. He covered the combined bed with the duvets to make it look more inviting, threw a red polo shirt over the bedside lamp to create a dim romantic glow, and turned off the other lights. From the bathroom he heard the sound of the shower running, which was an encouraging sign. He undressed and lay down on the bed in his underpants, waiting for Winifred to finish, so that he could nip into the bathroom and quickly hose down his own nether parts. He gazed at the ceiling in happy anticipation of the intimacies to come, and fell fast asleep.

He woke with a stiff neck, a throbbing head and a dry mouth, chilled from lying on top of, instead of under, his duvet, got up, and groped his way in the dark to the bathroom. The light, bouncing off the white tiles, made him wince when he switched it on, but showed by his wrist watch that the New Year was four and a quarter hours old. He peed, but did not flush the toilet, to avoid waking Winifred. He allowed a segment of light to escape the bathroom door and saw that she had pushed her bed back to meet the headboard, which was fastened, like the night table, to the wall. His own bed was still marooned in the middle of the room, its pillow on the floor, doubtless the reason for his stiff neck. There was no cup or glass in the bathroom and the stiff neck inhibited him from bending and twisting his head to drink from the tap. Anyway, mere water could not slake his burning thirst; there was a carton of orange juice in the refrigerator which might do so. He tiptoed out of the bedroom, closing the door carefully behind him, and made his way to the open-plan living room/kitchen. On the way he passed the door of Jakki's and Lionel's bedroom. He realised that he had fallen asleep with his hearing aid on, and, in his fuddled state, not yet thought of removing it, when he heard through the cheap hollow-core door muffled sounds of unmistakable import. Four-fifteen and they were still at it! What stamina. What insatiable lust. It was the final seal on his own sexual failure. He slunk back to his bedroom without going to the refrigerator to quench his thirst, afraid that he might be heard moving about by the lovers and suspected of voyeurism, or whatever its auditory equivalent might be called. He went into the bathroom, removed his hearing aid, and swallowed four Nurofen caplets, washing them down with water sucked from his cupped hands. He did not attempt to manoeuvre his bed back to the wall, but crawled immediately under the duvet and, clasping the pillow like a lifebuoy under his head, fell asleep again.

When he woke, at eight-thirty, he was alone in the bedroom. He put on his dressing gown and put in his hearing aid and went into the living room. Jakki and Lionel were having breakfast, dressed in what might have been nightwear or sportswear, it was hard to tell. 'Good morning, Des,' Jakki said. 'Sleep well?'

'Not too bad,' he said. 'Where's Fred?' He had a dreadful fear that she had left Gladeworld, taken their car, and gone home, leaving him to be ignominiously brought back to Rectory Road by Jakki and Lionel.

'She's gone for a cycle ride,' Jakki said. 'I lent her my bike.'

He sat down at the table, poured himself a tumbler of orange juice, and drank it in a single draught.

'You needed that,' Lionel commented redundantly. The morning sunlight gleaming on his bald crown hurt Desmond's eyes.

'I'm afraid you boys had too much to drink last night,' said

Jakki, pouring him a cup of coffee. 'Lionel fell asleep while I was brushing my teeth, and then he had the cheek to wake me up in the small hours and start molesting me.'

'Jakki!' Lionel protested weakly.

'Well, it's true . . . and Winifred says you created havoc with the beds before you passed out yourself, Des.'

'Did I? I don't have a very clear memory,' he said. He drank the coffee greedily. Things were not quite as bad as he had feared. His wife had not left him and Lionel had not after all performed a four-hour sexual marathon.

'We thought we'd go to the spa this morning,' said Jakki.

'Good way to get rid of a hangover,' said Lionel.

'You mean, drinking the water?' he asked.

'What would you want to do that for?' Jakki said, with a frown.

'He's pulling your leg, again, Jakki,' Lionel said. 'It's a really nice place, Des. Saunas, steam rooms, a warm-water outdoor pool . . . Pricey, but good value.'

'We've got our own sauna here,' he observed, 'which is free.' It was a small wooden structure, with room enough for perhaps two people, on the deck at the back of the chalet, which they had heated up yesterday to dry their swimming costumes and towels. Outside was a primitive douche in the form of a wooden tub filled with cold water, suspended from a beam and operated by a rope. 'That? That's nothing,' Lionel scoffed. 'The spa has three kinds of sauna, and four steam rooms with different themes. Roman, Japanese, Indian . . . '

'I can see how that might appeal,' he said.

'And you can have all kinds of massage and beauty treatments,' Jakki chimed in, oblivious to any innuendo.

Winifred came in at this point, rosy-cheeked and looking pleased with herself. 'I've had a lovely time,' she announced. 'It's years since I rode a bike. I'd forgotten how nice it is, if you don't have cars and lorries to contend with.'

'Where did you go?' he asked. He wasn't really interested, but it was a way of making her speak to him.

'Oh . . . round the boating lake, through the woods . . . It was idyllic. There weren't many people about.'

'I would have come with you if I'd been awake,' he said.

'Yes, well, you were sleeping rather soundly,' she said drily. 'Oh, and I passed the spa,' she said, turning to Jakki.

'We thought we might spend this morning there,' Jakki said.

'Super,' said Winifred.

When they were back in the privacy of their bedroom, and while they were restoring it to some kind of order, he apologised for the debacle of the night.

'You drink too much, Desmond,' she said. The 'Desmond' was an index of her displeasure. Even an acidly ironic 'darling' was better than 'Desmond'.

'It was Lionel's fault, producing that bottle of malt.'

'You didn't have to drink it. Anyway, it's not just last night, it's most nights. You're getting addicted.'

'Nonsense.'

'It's not nonsense.'

'All right, I'll prove it,' he said. 'I won't have a drop to drink today.'

She looked at him appraisingly. 'You know we're eating out tonight – at the *soi-disant* French restaurant?'

'Yes.'

'And you won't have any wine?'

'No.'

'Even if the food is not up to much?'

'Even if it's horrible. As I confidently expect.'

She laughed. 'Well, if you keep to your resolution, darling, I'll be amazed – but delighted.'

He was pleased with his strategy. His vow of abstinence had made a favourable impression on Winifred, and put her into a forgiving mood. A dry day would do him no harm – in fact, a world of good. Furthermore, if he succeeded in keeping his promise – and he was determined to do so – he would be in the best possible shape to claim as a reward the sexual intercourse he had forfeited the previous night.

The spa session contributed to his plan by being thoroughly enjoyable, if mildly absurd. It was a large, self-important establishment, staffed by immaculately manicured and coiffed ladies in white coats, architecturally eclectic (Greek temple crossed with Taj Mahal), its interior walls clad in a plausible imitation of marble, and its floors covered with non-slip ceramic tiles. There were fountains and footbaths and replicas of classical statuary in the central area, off which various themed saunas and steam rooms were situated. They sampled the Roman Laconium, the Tyrolean Sauna, the Turkish Hammam, the Indian Blossom Steam Room and the Japanese Salt Bath. They meditated in the Aqua Meditation Room and, wrapped in the towelling robes provided, trod the stepping stones of the Zen Garden in their bare feet. They cleansed and closed the pores of their sweating bodies under the multisensory showers which shot jets of icy water at them from all angles, choosing from a range of options, including tropical storm with thunder and lightning effects, and mint-flavoured mist. Then they floated languidly in the warm outdoor pool, which periodically became a giant jacuzzi, pummelling their muscles therapeutically with its forceful bubbles. Between these experiences they reclined in loungers and sipped water and read or simply relaxed. There was, he was told, piped music of a gentle inoffensive kind, but he of course could not hear it. The others went off for various massages – reiki for Winifred, shiatsu for Jakki and Swedish for Lionel – but he was happy to stay in the relaxation area with the novel he had brought with him. He found a cosy nook containing a kind of ottoman covered with a shaggy artificial hide, a seat such as Tamburlaine or Genghis Khan might have lolled on after victory on the battlefield. If Waterworld was a kind of benign hell, he mused, the spa was a very acceptable kitsch heaven.

They spent several hours there, ate lunch with voracious appetites in its café, and then went ten-pin bowling, '*where half the fun of the simple and repetitive game,'* he remembered some writer saying, *'lies in watching the machinery set up the pins and return the balls'*. Neither he nor Winifred had ever bowled before, but they acquitted themselves well – Winifred indeed showing real aptitude and achieving the highest score. Then they returned to the chalet at four in the afternoon for a cup of tea and a rest before going out to dine at Gladeworld's premier restaurant, which Desmond now referred to as *Soi Disant*. It was all going so well, when with a self-indulgent remark he turned the conversation, and events, in an ill-starred direction.

'The spa is fine in itself,' he said, when they were discussing its merits, 'but of course having to wear swimming costumes is a nonsense. You really need to be naked in a sauna or a steam room to get the full benefit.' 'You're right, Des,' said Lionel. 'It's not very comfortable sweating into a pair of trunks.' 'But then they'd have to segregate the sexes,' said Jakki, 'which wouldn't be much fun for couples like us.' 'I've been to a public sauna in Germany where everybody was naked, men and women together,' Desmond said, 'and nobody turned a hair.' 'Not even a pubic hair?' Lionel quipped. 'Is this another of your jokes, Des?' Jakki asked suspiciously. 'No, it's true,' he said. 'It was in Bremen. I was on a British Council lecture tour.' It pleased him to remind the company that he had once been a well-travelled, sophisticated citizen of the world. 'Well, we've got our own private sauna on the back porch,' said Lionel. 'What are you suggesting, Lie?' Jakki said, slapping him playfully. 'That we all prance about in the nude out there?' 'After dark, nobody would see you,' Lionel said. 'We could give it a go when we come back from the restaurant. Not all together – one couple at a time.' 'Bad idea,' said Desmond. 'You should never have a sauna straight after a meal.' 'Well, it's nearly dark now,' said Lionel. 'We've got time before we go out.' 'I've had quite enough hot air and cold water for today, thanks,' Winifred said. 'Count me out.' 'Yes, me too,' said Jakki, in womanly solidarity. 'You boys can, if you like.' 'What about it, Des?' said Lionel. It seemed wimpish to decline after having set himself up as an expert on saunas. 'All right,' he said. 'Are you sure it's a good idea, darling?' said Winifred. 'You might catch a chill.' There was a steely edge to this 'darling' which he pretended not to notice. 'Impossible, if you have a cold douche afterwards,' he said airily.

Jakki had already switched on the sauna to dry their swimming costumes, and Desmond turned up the thermostat before withdrawing to the bedroom to undress and wrap himself in a bath towel. When he came out Lionel was waiting for him by the glazed patio doors, similarly garbed. Winifred, who was washing up the tea things in the kitchen area, looked at him disapprovingly. 'I hope you don't regret this,' she said. 'We won't draw it out,' he assured her. It was dark outside, and the lights were on in the living room. 'Pull the curtains together behind us, otherwise we'll be lit up for the whole of Gladeworld to see us under the douche,' Lionel said to Jakki. 'And no peeping,' he added. 'As if we'd be bothered,' said Jakki. She came to the patio door as they went out. 'Brr, it's getting cold. Rather you than me,' she said, sliding the door shut, and drawing the curtains behind them. There was already a touch of frost in the air. He and Lionel went quickly into the sauna, which was not much bigger than a sentry box, and sat down on their folded towels on the raised bench, haunch to haunch. The sauna was dimly lit by a small bulb in one corner but not so dimly that he could avoid seeing how well endowed Lionel was. He sat with hands on his parted knees, his flaccid organ hanging down like a rubber cosh between his thighs, and began talking, something to do with computer software for accountancy. 'I'm afraid I can't follow, Lionel,' Desmond said. 'I haven't got my hearing aid in.' Lionel nodded and signalled his understanding. Perspiration ran like rivulets down his face and disappeared into a thicket of hair on his chest. 'This is the real thing, a lot hotter than the spa,' he shouted into Desmond's ear. Desmond, who was also sweating profusely, wondered if he had perhaps turned up the thermostat too high. After ten minutes or so, Lionel indicated that he had had enough, and went out into the night, fanning a breath of cold air into the sauna with the door. There was a pause of about ten seconds and then, even without his hearing aid, Desmond heard the splash of water hitting the deck followed a second or two later by a bellow from Lionel as he recovered his breath sufficiently to register the shock. Desmond waited several minutes to allow the tub to refill, and went out himself.

Lionel had gone back indoors and drawn the curtains behind him. The scene was washed by a chilly moonlight. To his right there was a grassy bank which led down to a stream and a pond from which ducks and waterfowl came marauding for food in the mornings, waddling boldly up to the patio door, and on the far side of the pond there was a dark mass of trees and shrubs. Nothing stirred there now, and the neighbouring chalets were screened from his sight. It was a curious sensation, standing naked and alone on the cold, wet boards, directly under the tub, grasping a thick hemp rope in one hand, knowing that one firm jerk would bring several gallons of freezing water down on your defenceless body. It wasn't like pressing a chromium-plated button in the spa's multisensory shower, but something much more existential and perverse. It was like committing suicide. The rope and the gibbet-like beam from which the tub was suspended combined to make the act resemble a self-administered hanging. His whole body seemed to cry out: *Don't!* But the longer he hesitated the more difficult it became to act. Already he could feel the inner fire stoked up in the core of his body by the sauna beginning to die down. If he didn't do it now, he would never do it, he would have to creep back indoors, still sticky with perspiration, to the jeers of his companions. Now. Now! One, two, three . . . HEAVE!

It was the weight as much as the temperature of the mass of water that shocked him first, as if a small glacier had shattered on his head, blinding his vision and making him stagger; then the cold enveloped him as if he had fallen through a hole in the Arctic ice, and he sucked it into his lungs and held it there, unable to expel it in the form of a cry for (it seemed) minutes; then, as the ability to breathe returned, he gasped, he yelled, he blasphemed, he hopped from one foot to another, he grabbed his towel and tried in vain to swaddle himself in its folds. Someone drew back the curtain inside the room, light flooded out across the deck, and Jakki's grinning face appeared behind the glass. He begged her to open the door and, barely preserving his modesty with the towel, stumbled over the lintel into the living room.

'My God!' he said. 'That was brutal.'

Jakki said something to him. Lionel, who had exchanged his towel for a bathrobe, and had a glass in one hand, held up the bottle of malt, which had a few amber inches left at the bottom, in the other, and said something which he assumed to be the offer of a drink. 'No thanks, I'm off the booze today,' he said. Winifred, who was reading a book, looked up and said something. 'I'll go and get my hearing aid,' he said. He went to the bedroom to insert the hearing aid, and put on a shirt and a pair of trousers while he was about it. He was pleased that Winifred had been present when he declined the whisky. He felt no need of it: already his whole body was beginning to glow and tingle with radiant warmth.

He went back into the living room. Jakki said something. Lionel said something. Winifred said something. He looked blankly at them. 'I think my batteries must have gone,' he said. 'Sorry, won't be a moment.' He went back to the bedroom. It was odd that both batteries had once again failed at the same time – perhaps he had bought a bad batch. He inserted new batteries in the hearing instruments and returned to the living room. Winifred said something. Lionel said something. Jakki said something. He still couldn't hear them. A terrible dread gripped him. He was deaf. Really deaf. Profoundly deaf. The trauma of the mass of cold water suddenly drenching his over-heated head must have had some catastrophic effect on the hair cells, or on the part of the cortex that was connected to them, cutting off all communication. He had a mental image of some part of his brain going dark, like a chamber or tunnel where suddenly all the lights go out, for ever. He saw his concern reflected in the anxious, enquiring faces of the others. Winifred said something which he was able to lip-read: '*What's the matter?*' 'I'm deaf,' he said. 'I mean, really deaf. I can't hear a thing any of you are saying. It must have been the douche.' She said something else which he could lip-read: '*I warned you.*'

It was four hours before his fears were relieved, four hours of panic and anxiety such as he hoped never to have to live through again: fiddling frantically with his hearing aid, cleaning it, trying yet more batteries, all to no avail, unable to hear the advice and comments of his wife and friends unless they wrote them down or mouthed the simplest sentences. Jakki suggested that he should go to Gladeworld's medical centre to which he responded caustically that he didn't think they would have an Ear, Nose and Throat specialist in residence, and Jakki said she was only trying to help. Lionel rang the main reception desk and they said that the medical centre would be open in the morning but was only staffed by a nursing sister. They thought it would be difficult to get a doctor to see Desmond on New Year's Day and suggested the Accident & Emergency department of the hospital in a small industrial town some twenty miles away. Winifred said, or rather wrote, that she didn't see the point but she would drive him there if he really thought it would do any good, and did so, in stony-faced silence, and drove around the empty streets for some time till she found the hospital, and sat with him for two and a half hours in a waiting room full of people injured or made ill by drugs and drink the night before who had been waiting there all day, until eventually they were seen by a tired young doctor who looked in his ears with a speculum, and wrote out a prescription and gave it to him, and said something. He looked to Winifred for help. She wrote down on her notepad: *He said: 'I think the pharmacy is still open, but if not, some warm olive oil will do.'*

He stared at the prescription. 'What is it?' he asked the doctor.

The doctor wrote something on a piece of paper and pushed it across the desk. He read: *It's stuff you put in infants' ears for glue ear.*

The heat of the sauna melted the wax in your ears and the sudden deluge of cold water solidified it into a perfect seal.

When they got back to the chalet at about ten-thirty, Jakki and Lionel said the meal at *Soi Disant* had been surprisingly good.

17

3rd January. There were a lot of abbreviated, unintelligible messages from Dad on the answerphone when we got back from Gladeworld yesterday. He didn't seem to understand that he was addressing an answering machine, or perhaps he had forgotten how to do so, and began speaking each time before my outgoing message was finished, so that his first sentence or two were not recorded and I could only hear a fragment of what he had said before he became irritably aware that no one was listening and rang off. '*. . . don't know what to do with them . . . Hallo? . . . are you there? . . . Hallo? . . . [beep] . . . apart from the old lady, I hear her moving about upstairs, I think it's her . . . Hallo? . . . Can you hear me? . . . [beep] . . . so what happened to the other house? . . . Do you know? . . . Have you gone dead again? . . . [beep] . . . with all these letters about the tax . . . you know what I mean . . . are you listening? . . . No. Gawdstrewth. [beep].*'

I called him. 'Hallo, Dad, we're back.'

'Where you been, then?'

'A place called Gladeworld.'

'Is that another old people's home?'

I laughed. 'No, a kind of holiday camp . . . We went with some friends. I told you we were going.'

'I've been trying to phone you all weekend. I think there's something wrong with your phone. I kept getting cut off.'

'It's an answerphone, Dad. You have to leave your message after the tone.'

'Oh . . . Well, I've got all these letters from this bloke, what's his name, Moynihan, Mogadon, something like that.'

'You mean about your tax?'

'Yeah. He's up in Scotland, you know, up on the left there, where all the islands are.'

'Cumbernauld. It's near Glasgow. Your tax office is there.'

'That's right. I've got all these letters from him.'

'I think you'll find they're old letters, Dad. It's about a tax rebate. I dealt with it for you. You should get your money in a few weeks' time.'

'Really? How much?'

'I don't know exactly. A few hundred pounds.'

'Cor, that's the best news I've had for a long time. Thanks, son.'

'What will you do with it?'

'Put it under the floorboards. Don't want the tax people to know about it.'

'Dad, it's *from* the tax people. It's a rebate. You don't have to pay tax on it.'

'Oh, well, that's even better.'

He rang off in good spirits, but about an hour later he phoned again.

'I want to ask you something,' he said. 'What happened to the other house?'

'What other house, Dad?'

'The house in Brickley.'

'That's where you are, Dad. You're in Brickley.'

'Am I? Are you sure?'

'You're in Lime Avenue, Brickley. The Barkers live next door.'

'That's true,' he said, after a pause. 'I saw her through the back garden fence this morning. So what happened to the other house?'

'What does it look like?' I said.

'It's joined up to all the other houses in the street. It has coloured windows in the front door.'

'That's the house in Dulwich you grew up in, Dad.' I remembered the windows from visits to my grandparents when I was a child – two narrow panes of glass, red and green, and the patches of colour they cast on the tiled floor of the hall when the sun shone through them in the afternoon.

'Oh, is it? When am I going there?'

'You're not going there. It belongs to someone else now, if it hasn't been demolished.'

'Oh . . . It's very quiet here. Apart from her moving about upstairs. I never see her though. Why's that?'

'Is it Mum you're talking about?'

'No, my mother's dead. Passed away years ago, in Dulwich.'

'Yes, that's right,' I said.

'You're getting mixed up, son,' he said.

I phoned Dad's GP, Dr Simmonds, and told him I was concerned. He's a man of few words, and those tend to be discouraging, but he's conscientious and efficient and he's been looking after Dad for some twenty-five years. He said he would visit him at home as soon as he could manage it, and call me back.

4th January. Dr Simmonds called today. 'Your father's mildly demented,' he said. 'I'll set up a mental health assessment, but it will take some time.'

'Is he capable of living on his own?'

'Just about,' Simmonds said.

'I wanted to move him into a care home up here,' I said. 'But he wouldn't hear of it.'

'No, well, his instinct is right,' Simmonds said, to my surprise.

'It was a very nice place.'

'I don't doubt it. But old people have a kind of mental map of their home which helps to tell them what to do and when to do it. Plonk them down in a strange place and they completely lose their bearings.'

'What happens if he gets worse?'

'Eventually he'd have to go into care. I'd have to section him if necessary.'

'God!' I had a vision of Dad being escorted out of his house by men in white coats, Mrs Barker watching from her front doorstep, and waving as the ambulance draws away.

'It may not come to that,' Simmonds said. 'It would improve

his present situation if he could have some help in the house. Social services would arrange it.'

'He won't let anyone in,' I said. 'Anyone he doesn't know. He's afraid they'll steal the money he's squirrelled away.'

Dr Simmonds chuckled drily. 'He's got a prostate problem too, of course. I made an appointment for him to come to the surgery for a check-up.'

As I expected, I got a call from Dad not long afterwards.

'Old Simmonds came round today,' he said.

'That was nice of him,' I said.

'I didn't ask him to. What's he after?'

'He's not after anything. He's your doctor. He's just seeing that you're all right.'

'I think he wants to get me into hospital for an operation.'

'No he doesn't, Dad.'

'He's given me an appointment, next Monday. I don't think I'll go.'

'You must, Dad. It's just for a check-up.'

'Yes, that's what he said. But I know how his mind works, him and his mates at the hospital. They want to experiment on me.'

I spent several minutes trying to persuade Dad that Dr Simmonds had absolutely no motive, professional or financial, for conspiring to force an already overstretched National Health Service to operate on him, at the end of which he said, 'You believe him, do you?'

'Yes, Dad,' I said.

'Then there's no hope for me on this earth,' he said dolefully. 'Harry Bates is all alone.'

I told him not to be silly. Then I offered to come down to London and escort him to the doctor's, but he reacted angrily: 'What d'you think I am – a child? I'm perfectly capable of going to the doctor's on my own.'

'Well, then, prove it,' I said. 'Go.'

'I'll see how I feel on Monday,' he grumbled. 'Anyway, how are you?'

'All right.'

'You don't sound very happy,' he said.

No, I'm not. With a demented dad and an alienated spouse I have no reason to be. Fred is still pissed off with me for ruining the Gladeworld excursion, which I have written up as a kind of short story, to try and exorcise the humiliation and embarrassment of the experience. I think she would be not speaking to me if it wasn't for the fact that when she does speak to me I don't hear what she's saying half the time. She couldn't wait to get back to work at *Décor*, where they're having a Sale. She leaves the house early in the morning, comes back late in the evening, cooks a perfunctory dinner, or I make one with pre-cooked chilled meals from Marks & Spencer's; she delivers a monologue about what happened in the shop, recounting verbatim what the stroppy customer said to Jakki and what Jakki said to the stroppy customer, and what she herself said to the stroppy customer to calm her down and what she said later to Jakki to calm *her* down, all so that she doesn't have to engage in a proper conversation with me, and then she has a bath and goes to bed early. I drink too much wine at dinner, fall asleep in front of the television, wake up feeling too alert to go to bed, and come in here to keep this record of my discontents up to date. The Christmas decorations, which must not be taken down and removed until Epiphany, provide an incongruous backdrop to my gloom as I pad around the silent house during the day, and the weather and the news do what they can to lower my spirits further. Blustery showers discourage going out, though temperatures are unusually high for the first week in January, in further confirmation of global warming. And Saddam Hussein has been hanged in a fashion that makes one of the worst tyrants of all time look dignified, courageous and abused. No, I am not happy.

I recalled an interesting observation about collocations of *happy* in a book on corpus linguistics I reviewed years ago, and after a short search I found it. In a small corpus of 1.5 million words the most frequent lexical collocates of *happy* in the three words occurring before and after it were *life* and *make*. Not surprising: we all desire a happy life, we all like things which make us happy. The next most common collocates were: *entirely, marriage, days, looked, memories, perfectly, sad, spent, felt, father, feel, home*. I am struck by how many of them are keywords in my own pursuit of happiness, or lack of it, especially the nouns: *marriage, memories, father, home*. Of the verbs, *feel* is obviously the verb most frequently combined with *happy*, counting *feel* and *felt* as one. Predictably the only adjective among the words, apart from *happy* itself, is its opposite, *sad*. It surprised me that the most common adverbs qualifying *happy* in the corpus were *entirely* and *perfectly*, rather than, say, 'fairly' or 'reasonably'. Are we ever entirely, perfectly happy? If so, it's not for very long. The most interesting word is *days*. Not *day*, but *days*. Larkin has a wonderful poem called 'Days', which also contains the word *happy*.

> What are days for?
> Days are where we live.
> They come, they wake us
> Time and time over.
> They are to be happy in:
> Where can we live but days?

The familiar, nostalgic collocation *happy days* doesn't actually occur in the poem, but it's inevitably evoked; it echoes in our heads as we read, and reminds us of the transience and deceptiveness of happiness. The days we live in always inevitably disappoint, by not being as happy as they were, or as we falsely believe they were, in 'the good old days', when 'those were the days'. But where can we live but days?

> Ah, solving that question
> Brings the priest and the doctor
> In their long coats
> Running over the fields

A footnote to the above: it occurred to me that negative particles might have been omitted from the analysis of collocations of *happy*, so I did a check on the small corpus I have on CD here at home, and sure enough, *entirely happy* is frequently preceded by *not* or some other negative word like *never*. But *perfectly* is usually unqualified. In fact the distribution is almost exactly equal: *not entirely happy* occurs about as often as *perfectly happy*, and *entirely happy* is as rare as *not perfectly happy*. I wonder why? Corpus linguistics is always throwing up interesting little puzzles like that. I looked up *deaf* a few years ago in the biggest corpus of written and spoken English available, about fifty million words, and the most common collocation, about ten per cent of the total, was *fall on deaf ears* (counting *fall* as a lemma, standing for all forms of the verb). Now it's no surprise that the main contribution of *deaf* to English discourse is as part of a proverbial phrase signifying stupid incomprehension or stubborn prejudice; what's puzzling is the verb *fall*, given that the human ear is positioned to receive sound waves from the side, not from above. And the enigma is not peculiar to English. A quick dictionary search revealed that German has *auf taube Ohren fallen*, French has *tomber dans l'oreille d'un sourd*, and Italian *cadere sugli orecchi sordi*. Subject there for another article that never got written.

5th January. I had an unexpected phone call today, from Simon Greensmith, a British Council chap I haven't been in touch with for years. He was a very friendly junior member of staff in the BC office in Madrid, who showed me round the city and took me to the best tapas bars, when I was on that lecture tour in Spain. Later he did a spell in the Council's Specialist Tours department in London, and was instrumental in sending me to several other foreign countries, for which I was grateful. He's now in a senior post in Warsaw, where he was calling from. After a New Year greeting and a few courtesy questions about how was I and did I have a good Christmas, he came to the point of his call. 'A bit of an emergency, Desmond. I'm hoping you will help us out.' He explained that a linguist at Lancaster, who had been due to do a short tour in Poland at the end of January, speaking about discourse analysis to staff and postgraduates in university English departments, had a nasty skiing accident a few days ago in the Haute-Savoie and was going to be in traction in hospital there for the next six weeks. Simon was asking if I would step into the breach. 'It's very short notice, I know,' he said, 'but it's your field and I'm sure you've got lots of lectures filed away that you could use. It's only ten days and three places, Warsaw, Lodz and Cracow. Cracow's lovely, by the way, if you haven't been there, European City of Culture and all that –'

'I've never been to Poland before,' I said.

'Well, then, all the more reason. It's a very interesting country. English language studies are booming – you'd be sure of good audiences. And it would be great to see you again.'

'The trouble is, Simon, I don't do this sort of thing any more. I'm too deaf.'

'Well, I know you have a bit of a problem, but we can work round that.'

'It's much worse than it was when we last met,' I said. 'I can do a lecture of course, but I can't hear questions.'

'You'll have a chairperson who will repeat them for you.'

'But the chairperson will be Polish and speak with a thick accent which I won't understand. The vowels will be distorted and I won't hear the consonants,' I said. 'Polish itself is pretty well all consonants, isn't it? Must be hell being a Pole with high-frequency deafness.'

Simon chuckled. 'The language *is* a bit of a beast to learn,' he said. 'But look, we'll have a break after the lectures and invite the audience to write their questions down and pass them up to you.'

He was very persistent, and in the end I agreed. The fact is I wanted to be persuaded. I wanted to go to Poland – anywhere, really, to get away from the dull routine of a house-husband, the worrying problems of a mildly demented father, and the dangerous attentions of an importunate, unscrupulous postgraduate groupie; anywhere where I would once again be respected, deferred to, entertained and looked after, with the decorum appropriate to a visiting scholar. Like a disabled cowboy moping in forced retirement, I jumped at the chance to get back in the saddle again for one last round-up. As Simon talked I already envisioned his smiling face at the airport terminal exit, with a dark-suited chauffeur beside him ready to carry my luggage to the waiting Council limousine; saw myself sipping a cocktail and receiving compliments at a post-lecture reception, dining sumptuously in an elegant, wood-panelled restaurant with white napery and shaded lamps, and being given a personal guided tour of some historic church or castle by a charming young female academic with impeccable English . . .

'Wonderful!' he exclaimed, when I said I would do it. 'I'll get on to London straight away. They'll send you a contract and the air tickets. I'll email the itinerary to you today, and we'll confer next week about what lectures you might give. You can do the same ones at the three universities, of course.'

I suppose I should have consulted Fred before committing myself, but Simon was in a hurry. It was a Friday afternoon and he was anxious to secure a stand-in for the injured lecturer before the offices in London and Warsaw closed. He was off skiing himself for the weekend. ('Cross-country,' he said, 'quite safe.') I couldn't bear the thought of the opportunity going to somebody else while I dithered; and no doubt subconsciously I didn't want to give Fred the opportunity to talk me out of it.

When she came in and I told her I was going to Poland, she put all the arguments against the idea that I had suppressed in agreeing to go. She reminded me of the frustration and exhaustion I had complained of on returning from my last few trips abroad, mostly caused by not being able to understand what people were saying to me, not only in Q&A sessions but on every social occasion, and pointed out what an inauspicious time of year it was for such a trip – Poland would be freezing in January and travel difficult. Three places in little more than a week sounded like a gruelling schedule. I would probably catch a cold and/or succumb to a stomach upset from eating and drinking too much, as I nearly always did on such trips in the past, when I was younger and fitter and able to throw off minor indispositions. In short, she thought it was a bad idea.

'Well, I can't get out of it now,' I said.

'Of course you can,' she said. 'Just pick up the phone.'

I told her it was too late: I couldn't get hold of Simon again until Monday and I would feel I had really let him down, withdrawing at that point.

'Then I've wasted my breath,' she said, with a shrug. 'You'd better tell your father, I don't want to have to deal with his mad phone calls while you're away.' I said I would visit him in London before I go, and I would ask Dr Simmonds to look in on him while I'm in Poland.

6th January. An email from Alex today attaching what she called a 'preliminary draft' of a chapter entitled 'The Absence of "suicide" and Suicide as Absence', with my quote from Borges as an epigraph, and a few pages of argument more or less repeating my off-the-cuff remarks in the car on Boxing Day. She asked me to tell her if I thought she was heading in the right direction and said, 'Feel free to fill out my sketchy ideas and add any more that occur to you' – her most blatant attempt to date to get me to write her thesis for her. I took some satisfaction in telling her that I had been invited at very short notice to give some lectures in Poland and would be fully occupied for the next two weeks preparing for that. I expected a miffed response but she replied serenely: 'That's OK, it can wait. I may be busy doing some preparation myself – I'm applying to do some teaching this term. Dr Rimmer is on sick leave and they're hiring a postgrad to take over her tutorials. Congratulations on the invitation. Have a great time.' I'm surprised that she thinks she has any chance of getting teaching work in the English Department, since it would have to be approved by Butterworth.

*

7th January. I made my usual Sunday evening telephone calls. Dad is now totally confused about his income tax rebate, his savings certificates and his Premium Bonds – they are all hopelessly mixed up in his mind, as is the geography of Great Britain. 'That letter you sent to the geezer up north, you gave me a rub – you know what I mean by a rub? [he meant a photocopy] – about the competition, well it's not a competition exactly, but you know what I mean, you buy them at the Post Office, the money multiplies itself over five years . . . I haven't heard from him lately, I don't know if I will get something or nothing . . . they're such a lot of thieving bastards up there in Blackpool, I don't mean Blackpool, it's one of those islands off the west coast of Scotland, the Isle of Sheppey or the Isle of Scilly or the Isle of Man . . . I'm going to go through my papers again tonight, see if I can pin them down . . .'

'I wouldn't do that Dad,' I said. 'Leave it till next time I see you.' To change the subject I asked him what he had had for his dinner today. 'A very nice bird,' he said. 'You mean a chicken?' I said. 'It might have been a very small chicken,' he said. 'I got it at the market yesterday. You just point and they give it to you.' 'How did you cook it?' I asked him. 'I bunged it in the oven, and took it out when it looked cooked. I had mashed potatoes with it, and half a tomato, and some . . . What is it? A green one.' 'Cabbage?' 'No, not cabbage, it's like cabbage, but you don't cook it.' 'Lettuce?' 'No, not lettuce . . . it's got a hard skin like a crocodile . . .' 'Cucumber?' 'Yes, that's it, cucumber, I cut it up, you know, and sprinkle a bit of pepper and salt on it . . .'

I reminded him that he had an appointment to see Dr Simmonds tomorrow, and his tone immediately became melancholy. 'I think he wants to get me into hospital for an operation,' he said. 'No he doesn't, Dad,' I said. 'It's just for a check-up.' 'What's he going to do, then?' 'He'll probably take a blood sample –' 'That's a needle, innit? I hate needles' '– and a urine sample.' 'Oh, well, no problem there, I produce one of them every five minutes.' I thought it was a good sign that he could still crack a joke.

I phoned Anne. She is OK, apart from backache. I told her I was going to Poland, but would be back in plenty of time for the arrival of the baby. 'Were you thinking of giving a hand with the birth, then, Dad?' she joked. 'No, I'll leave that to Jim,' I said. 'But I'd like to be around.' She was supportive about my trip. 'It'll do you good to have a change. I feel you've been getting into a bit of a rut lately.' 'It's called rut-irement,' I said. She groaned. 'You always loved making terrible puns, didn't you? And you encouraged us to do the same when we were kids – I remember it used to drive Mum mad.' 'It was an educational device,' I said, 'to give you a feeling for language.' 'Well now you could get a retirement job making up jokes to go in Christmas crackers.' 'Thank God we've seen the back of all that for another year,' I said. Fred and I spent this afternoon taking down the Christmas decorations, putting them back in their cardboard boxes for storage in the attic, carrying the moulting Christmas tree through the French windows into the back garden and hoovering up the needles in the drawing room.

I phoned Richard, and got through to him for once, instead of just his answerphone. I told him about the trip to Poland. 'I expect you've been there,' I said. 'Yes, I went to a conference at Cracow a few years ago,' he said. 'It's very beautiful – it was hardly damaged at all in the Second World War – just about the only city in Poland that wasn't. Wonderful churches of every period – Romanesque, Gothic, baroque – it's an architectural anthology.' Richard is a cultured scientist, and knows much more about architecture than I do. 'And of course Auschwitz is quite near,' he added.

'Is it?' I said. 'I didn't know that.'

'Yes. You should go.'

'Well, I don't know if I shall have time . . .' I said.

'You shouldn't miss it,' he said. 'Everyone should go if they get the chance.'

I told him about Dad, and said that if he happened to be in London with some time to spare it would be nice if he called at Lime Avenue, especially when I would be away. He said, without great enthusiasm, that he would try. 'Be sure to phone him first,' I said, 'or he might not recognise you. He might not even open the door.'

I wish Richard hadn't told me about Auschwitz. It has cast a kind of cloud over the prospect of my trip. I've read about it, of course. I know about the glass cases full of shoes and hair, the gas chambers and the ovens . . . but I'm not sure I want to see them. There's something wrong, it seems to me, about making the site of such appalling atrocities into a museum, a tourist attraction. I've read enough about the Holocaust – Primo Levi's books, other memoirs, histories of the Third Reich – to convince me that the systematic cold-blooded murder of millions of Jews by the Nazis was a deed of unprecedented evil. I don't know what visiting a kind of heritage site, with turnstiles and guides and coach parties, which I presume Auschwitz is like today, could usefully add. But perhaps I'm being lazy and cowardly. There was an implication that it is a kind of duty, a moral obligation, in Richard's 'should': *'You should go . . . Everyone should go, if they get the chance.'* This is almost certainly the last opportunity I shall have in my life, so I suppose I will have to go, if only to be able to hold up my head in the presence of my son when I get back. I've looked at the itinerary Simon sent me and there seems to be a free afternoon in Cracow on my last day, but it's not the climax to my trip I envisaged when I agreed to it.

8th January. I was going through my lecture notes and seminar papers this morning, sorting out material that I might use for my trip to Poland, and rather enjoying being focused on a purposeful intellectual task once again, when I was interrupted by a phone call from Colin Butterworth. 'I'd be very much obliged if I could see you some time today,' he said. He sounded tense and wound up. I told him I was rather busy and explained why – I was rather pleased to have the opportunity to let him know that I wasn't altogether an academic has-been – but he said the matter was urgent. He was willing to come round to my house if that would be more convenient, at any time that would suit me, but the sooner the better. I asked him if it was about Alex, and he said it was but he would rather not elaborate on the phone. I invited him to call on me in the afternoon, any time after two.

He arrived on the dot at two o'clock. He had never been in our house before, and made some complimentary remarks about it as I led him into my study. I said Fred was mainly responsible for the internal decor. He seemed relieved to learn that she was out. I sat him down in the armchair and took the desk chair myself, moving it near to him to be sure that I heard what he had to say. He was dressed in his usual smart-casual style, but there was dandruff on the shoulders of his suede jacket and he had not shaved well. His eyes looked tired. He took out a pack of cigarettes and asked if I would mind if he smoked. I said I would.

'You're quite right, it's a filthy habit. I've kicked it several times, but when I'm stressed . . . Frances is furious with me.' He put the cigarettes back in his pocket. 'I gather you're still seeing a good deal of Alex Loom,' he said. 'Quite a friend of the family, she tells me.'

'I wouldn't say that,' I said. 'She came to a party here on Boxing Day. She was supposed to be going home for Christmas, as you probably know, her father sent her the money for the fare, but she was fogged in at Heathrow and gave up.'

Butterworth looked surprised. 'Is that what she told you – about her father?' When I confirmed it, he said: 'Her father committed suicide when she was thirteen.'

I wasn't sure that I had heard him correctly, and asked him to repeat this astonishing piece of information.

'That's what she told me – who knows if it's true? She says that was why she got interested in suicide notes. Her father didn't leave one, you see. She's trying to discover why he killed himself by reading other people's. At least, that was one therapist's theory.'

'She told me she got interested in the subject through a boyfriend who was doing psychological research on suicide,' I said. 'The one who wrote that article.'

'Yes, well, he may or may not have been her boyfriend . . . Anyway, that's not what I came here to talk to you about. She's applied for a tutorial assistantship we've advertised internally, because Hetty Rimmer is off sick with ME. It's out of the question, of course. We couldn't possibly let Alex loose on a lot of undergraduates, and anyway there are several more deserving candidates. The trouble is, she doesn't see it that way, and she's convinced the job is in my gift. Well, perhaps once upon a time it would have been, but there are procedures now . . .' He paused and looked at me. 'I must ask you to treat this conversation as strictly confidential.'

'All right,' I said, my curiosity now thoroughly aroused.

'Last summer term, not long after I started supervising her, and before I realised what an unstable character she was, I did a very foolish thing. I got into . . . er . . . an inappropriate relationship with her.'

'You mean a sexual relationship?' I asked.

'Ex-President Clinton would say not,' he said with a wry smile. 'But I think the Grievances subcommittee of the Staff-Student Relations Board would take a different view. As would my wife.'

The story as he told it was a familiar one, of a charismatic, intellectually dazzling professor seduced by an admiring and attractive young student who had something to gain from the relationship. 'It was wrong of me, of course,' he said, 'but she made all the running, and it wasn't as if I was taking advantage of some innocent undergraduate. She's twenty-seven after all. She's a mature adult – at least I thought she was. And at the time things weren't going too well between Frances and me . . .' He took the cigarette pack out of his pocket with an automatic gesture, remembered my objection, and put it back. 'I first crossed the line when she gave me a kiss at the end of a supervision, and I kissed her back instead of telling her not to. The next time it was a longer kiss, with some stroking and groping, and so it went on. It was very exciting, because when she came for a supervision we both knew how it would end, with an almost wordless snog by the door before she went out, and because it was so risky. One day she knelt down and unzipped my trousers and sucked me off, with the door unlocked and people walking up and down the corridor outside. She would do pretty well anything except proper sex. Even when I started going to her flat – she has a flat in one of those new buildings on the canal – she wouldn't do penetrative sex. She liked to be spanked. That was when I began to get worried about what I was getting into. And to be honest I was fed up with never having a proper fuck. I was glad when summer vacation started and we went – Frances and I – to our place in Spain for a couple of months. When we came back I told Alex the sex had to stop. I apologised, I blamed myself, I didn't accuse her of anything, but she wasn't happy. I thought of trying to transfer her to another supervisor, but I was afraid she might shop me. Which in fact is what she's threatening to do now, if I don't get her the tutoring job.'

So that was why he had come to see me in such a hurry. 'I wrote her the best reference I could manage without perjuring myself,' he said. 'But I couldn't argue her case when we had a meeting about the appointment this morning. She's perceived as an enigmatic character and she hasn't produced any evidence of competence in linguistics. She was the first candidate to be eliminated. The job will be offered to someone else, as she will soon discover.'

'Why are you telling me all this?' I asked, though I had a pretty good idea.

'I was hoping you could persuade her not to make a complaint against me. I know she likes you, respects you. She always speaks very warmly of you. I think she would listen to you.'

'I see,' I said, and fell silent, thinking.

'You might well ask, "*Why should I?*"' he said.

'The question does occur,' I said.

'You hardly know me, you don't owe me anything, you probably disapprove of what I've done –'

'Yes, I do,' I said.

'But this could destroy me, you know. Not just my career, but

256

my marriage, my family . . . Frances would be shattered. And I have two teenage daughters, thirteen and fifteen. Imagine what their lives will be like if this ever becomes public.'

'Do you really think Alex would make a formal complaint?'

'I wouldn't have told you all this otherwise.'

'Why would anyone believe her, since she's such a compulsive fantasist?' I said.

He grimaced. 'She's got tissues with my DNA on them, or so she says. She certainly had plenty of opportunities to obtain them.' He must have caught an expression of distaste on my face, for he said, 'I'm sorry to burden you with this sleazy tale, but I'd be incredibly grateful if you would speak to her. As soon as possible.'

I said I would see what I could do.

9th January. I met Alex by arrangement at Pam's Pantry this afternoon. This time she was waiting for me, sitting in the same seat at the back of the café where I had sat before, nursing a cup of coffee in her hands. The place was almost empty. I bought myself a latte at the counter and joined her. She looked even paler than usual, and her blonde hair was lank and lifeless. Perhaps it was her period, but more likely it was the stress of the dangerous game she was playing. I came straight to the point, and summarised what Butterworth had told me about their relationship, without going into the sexual details. She listened impassively, and then said: 'I didn't know you and Colin were buddies.'

'We're not,' I said.

'But men stick together in these situations, don't they?'

'Listen,' I said, 'I don't like Colin Butterworth, never have. It wouldn't bother me in the least if he were publicly reprimanded, or had to resign. I think he behaved quite improperly towards you, even if you initiated the affair.' I noted that she didn't deny this. 'But if you make an official complaint, he won't be the only one to suffer. His wife and children will too. He has two teenage daughters. You could break up a family – and for what? It won't get you the job. The job will be given to somebody else.'

'How do you know that?' she said sharply.

'Butterworth told me.'

Alex swivelled her head and addressed the wall. '*Asshole*,' she hissed.

'Believe me, there was no way he could have got you appointed, even if he tried. So you see there's no point in your shopping him. You would come in for some very unpleasant questioning – he'd have a lawyer, provided by the UCU – and he will accuse you of trying to blackmail him. Which you did. You would be disgraced too, and expelled from the University.'

'There's nothing in writing,' she said, turning her head to face me again across the table. 'I could deny it. It would be his word against mine.'

'But your word isn't very reliable, is it, Alex?' I said.

'What do you mean by that?' she said.

'You told Fred that your father sent you an air ticket to go home at Christmas. You told Butterworth that your father committed suicide when you were thirteen. Which is the truth?'

Alex looked down and stirred her coffee, though it was cold and the cup half-empty, and murmured something through a limp curtain of hair.

I leaned forward across the table. 'What did you say?'

'My daddy did kill himself,' she said.

I said I was sorry to hear it, but didn't understand why she had made up the story about the air ticket. She said she had been sitting around with some of the English Language postgrads after a seminar and people had been talking about going home for Christmas and when somebody asked her what she was doing she instantly made up a story about going back to the States to spend Christmas with her folks, because she didn't want to admit that she would be spending it alone in her flat. 'I do that sometimes,' she said. 'I make up a story, or I tell a lie, or I play a trick, on the spur of the moment. I can't help myself. It's not as if I cared about being alone for Christmas. I have no folks. My mother died of cancer five years ago, my grandparents are dead, apart from one who has Alzheimer's . . . I'm estranged from my sister. I have no home to go to in the States. But I didn't want to be pitied or patronised, so I made up this idyll about going back to my family for Christmas, it was like an old *Saturday Evening Post* cover. I figured nobody would know I was holed up in my apartment with a stack of TV dinners.' When she received Fred's invitation to our party she desperately wished she could accept, but she had to keep up the pretence that she was going back to America for the holiday. 'I thought it would be nice if my daddy sent me the money for the flight,' she said. 'Since I was inventing an idyll, I thought I might as well make the most of it. So I put that in my letter to Winifred. It seemed to make it more believable. Then when Christmas came, and I saw all these people fogged in at Heathrow, I thought I had the perfect excuse to go to your party after all.'

'You mean you made up all those stories about the hell of Heathrow from watching the TV news?'

'It wasn't difficult,' she said. 'I read the newspapers too.'

'You know, you ought to put your talent for invention to better use,' I said. 'You should try writing fiction.'

She smiled faintly. 'Maybe I will one day,' she said.

I asked her why she had given Butterworth and me two different explanations of how she got interested in suicide notes. 'They're not incompatible, they're both true in different ways,' she said. 'It was the guy at Columbia who first gave me the idea of doing linguistic research on suicide notes. But of course I had a psychological motive too. It always bugged me that Daddy didn't leave a note. We never knew why he did it. We weren't aware that he was depressed. We never found any motive, like he'd done something terrible and was afraid of being found out, or that he'd been diagnosed with some dreadful disease, nothing like that, nothing at all. He just went out in a rowboat in a lake near home one evening and shot himself with a hunting rifle.'

'Perhaps it was an accident,' I said.

'He had the barrel in his mouth,' she said, 'and he used his toe to pull the trigger.'

Is this the truth? I really have no idea, though I pretended to believe it, because it would have been incredibly hurtful not to. On the whole I am inclined to believe that it is true. Such a traumatic event in childhood would explain a lot about Alex's behaviour besides her obsession with suicide notes: her fantasising, her attraction to older men, her pleasure in manipulating them and making them suffer. It would also explain the rather callous, even contemptuous, tone of her remarks on the subject of suicide, and her comments about the Writer's Guide website, whether it was her own work or not. It's obvious that as a teenager she loved her father but was deeply angry with him for his deed, and still is. 'How could he do that to us?' she said. 'Killing himself, without a word of explanation. Leaving us to wonder for ever why he did it, whether it was our fault in some way we couldn't guess. It meant we could never have closure. Never.' I think her psychological motive for research into suicide notes is more to relieve anger than to solve an enigma.

When I got home I called Butterworth and told him that I had spoken to Alex and I was pretty sure she would not proceed with a complaint. I could have been more positive, but didn't feel inclined to let him off too lightly, or too quickly, from the pangs of apprehension. In any case, he was hugely relieved and effusively grateful for this much reassurance.

11th January. In the fraught circumstances of my life at present, the lip-reading class is a haven of peace and innocent distraction. The new term started today. We began with a session about the January Sales. Beth handed us slips of paper on which was written a sentence, '*I bought . . . in the January Sales*', and we had to fill in the nominal group (though of course she didn't call it that) and lip-speak it to the others. I said I had bought some shirts at the January Sales, which made me wish I had, I could do with some new ones for my trip to Poland. Beryl said she had bought something none of us could lip-read. It turned out to be a Chinese carpet. It was the 'Chinese' which threw us. If it had been 'Persian carpet', I think we would have got it, but 'Chinese carpet' is not a familiar phrase or concept – though everything in the shops is made in China these days, including Persian carpets probably.

Then we had a session on New Year's Eve, but fortunately were not asked how we celebrated it. Beth went through the requirements for First Footing, without voice, and then with voice. The man who crosses the threshold first after midnight must be tall and well-built, mustn't be lame or have a squint, must carry a piece of coal, a piece of bread, and a bottle of whisky, but not a knife, must not be flat-footed or have eyebrows that meet in the middle, must not wear black or speak until he has put the bread on the table, the coal on the fire and given the whisky to the head of the house, after which he says 'Happy New Year' and exits by the back door. It seems that he doesn't have to be able to hear anything said to him, so I would qualify.

Then we had a quiz on applications of the words *Scot, Scotch, Scottish*, which we had to try and answer by lip-speaking with a partner. I had Gladys as a partner again. I think she tries to sit next to me because she knows I'm well-educated and she's very competitive – so keen to be the first to complete the quiz that she often forgot to speak to me without voice. The clues were pretty easy: *An egg encased in sausage meat . . . A famous explorer . . . A game played by children . . .* One that foxed everybody was *A customary tax*. I pretended I didn't know the answer: 'a scot'. Nothing to do with Scotland of course – it's Old English, now obsolete, though it survives in the expression 'scot-free'.

After the tea break we had the talk about hearing dogs from Trevor, a deaf man who has one. He brought it with him, a winning Jack Russell called Patch who sat at his feet and seemed to follow the talk, which it had no doubt heard many times, since Trevor goes around the country addressing groups like ours on behalf of the organisation which trains these animals. It costs £5,000 to train a dog because it takes a long time and a lot of patience. They learn to recognise and distinguish the sounds of an owner's alarm clock, cooker timer, telephone, smoke alarm and fire alarm. On hearing a sound they identify its source, then attract the owner's attention by pawing them and lead them to it. If it's the smoke alarm or the fire alarm they paw and then drop to the floor, signalling danger. Hearing dogs seldom bark for obvious reasons, though Trevor has been told Patch sometimes barks in his sleep. He carries a passport and ID for Patch stating that the dog is legally allowed into restaurants and food stores, though he says he has been refused entry on occasion. Would a shop or a restaurant refuse a blind person's guide dog? I doubt it.

Trevor implied that he is single, and on reflection, if you had a spouse or live-in partner you wouldn't really need a hearing dog. Obviously the companionship of Patch is as important to him as its practical assistance. It is pleasant to think of this network of clever dogs and dedicated trainers and grateful owners, from which all parties both take and give something valuable, quietly accomplishing its mission, day after day, year after year, unknown to the majority of the population.

15th January. I haven't had time to keep up this journal for the past week – I've been too busy preparing for my Polish trip, which begins the day after tomorrow. When I looked over my unpublished papers and lectures none of them looked entirely satisfactory as they stood, so I have spent a lot of time revising three of them and bringing them up to date.

Yesterday there was worrying news about Anne. She's had some bleeding, so they've taken her into the maternity hospital for observation and rest. I spoke to her on the phone, and she said it was just a precautionary measure. There's nothing wrong with the baby, but they want to avoid a premature birth. Still, one can't help worrying.

I left it late to tell Dad about my trip – deliberately, because I knew it would upset him, and the less time he has to brood on it the better. 'Poland? *Poland?* What in Gawd's name d'you want to go there for? All the Poles are desperate to come over here, from what I read in my paper. I never heard anything good about

Poland. Anyway, I thought you'd given up that lark.' I explained the circumstances and said, with more enthusiasm than I really feel at present, that I was looking forward to the trip. 'Well, rather you than me, mate,' he said. 'How are you getting there – flying? Not on a Polish plane I hope.' 'No, British Airways,' I said, though in fact I shall be coming back from Cracow by LOT. I'm flying from Heathrow on an early morning flight, and have booked into an airport hotel for the night before, so I will go down to London tomorrow, and make a detour to visit Dad on my way. This seemed to placate him.

18

18th February. I haven't written anything here for the past four weeks, because I've been away from my PC most of the time, and when I was at home I was either too preoccupied or too tired to bring this journal up to date. While I was in Poland I made handwritten notes on my tour but I can't be bothered now to transcribe my impressions of Warsaw, Lodz and Cracow, or of my encounters with Polish academics and their students. These topics seem of trivial interest in the light of what happened at the very end of my visit, and subsequently back in England, which is what I'm going to recall now. Of the tour, it's enough to say that my talks were well received and I coped with my hearing problem reasonably well – it was more difficult in informal social situations like restaurants and receptions than at the lectures and seminars. Most of the Poles I met spoke good English, though sometimes with disconcerting accents, like Estuary or Brooklyn, depending on where or from whom they had learned it. I ate a lot of meat and game and sausage and drank too much wine and beer and vodka. The Poles and the British Council between them worked me hard and I was beginning to tire by the time I got to Cracow.

The city is as beautiful as everybody says, but I didn't have much time to appreciate it, being kept busy at the Jagellonian University and the British Council Centre. I did manage to see the inside of St Mary's Church, with its astonishing carved and painted high altar, and the outside of the Cloth Hall, and Leonardo's *Lady with an Ermine* in the Czartoryski Museum, and a few other famous sights, but I had reserved my one free afternoon for the visit to Auschwitz. That was my first mistake, because in January the site closes at three, a fact I discovered belatedly in my guidebook on the way there. Nobody in Cracow pointed this out to me when I said I was going to Auschwitz on my last afternoon. Or more likely somebody did tell me and I pretended I had heard them but I didn't. I was left very much to myself for this excursion. There were plenty of volunteers to show me the sights of Cracow, but nobody offered to accompany me to Auschwitz. Not surprising, I suppose: if you've been there once you probably wouldn't want to go again. But I wondered how many of the Poles I met had in fact visited it themselves. When I told them I was going they nodded politely and changed the subject. I got the impression that it was a bit of an embarrassment to them, living in this lovely old civilised city so close to a place whose name is a metonym for genocide. It has been declared a World Heritage Site by UNESCO, but it's not one that Poland wants to claim as part of its heritage, even though a lot of Poles died there.

I gave a lecture at the University at ten in the morning that Friday, followed by coffee with some of the faculty, and didn't get back to my hotel till 11.45. I had been advised by Simon Greensmith to hire a taxi to take me to Auschwitz and bring me back because the public transport is slow and inconvenient, and I had ordered it at the hotel reception desk for 12.15, giving myself time to have a sandwich in the bar. I had acquired a false idea of how near Auschwitz was to Cracow – that was my second mistake. When I asked the young woman at Reception how far it was I thought she said 'thirty minutes', but as the journey dragged on and on I decided I must have misheard – perhaps she had said 'thirty kilometres'. After a few miles of motorway towards the airport, the road to Oswieçem (the Polish name of the town of Auschwitz) became a congested single carriageway. There had been a fall of snow in the night, and the fields and trees were virgin white, but the road was slushy, impeding progress. My taxi was an old black Fiat with a noisy diesel engine and worn-out shock-absorbers. The thick-set, leather-jacketed driver spoke little English and seemed disinclined to improve it by practice. 'How much longer?' I kept asking, and he would shrug and grunt and lift his hands from the wheel in a gesture signifying, 'It depends on the traffic.' Near Oświęcem we were held up for several minutes at a level crossing, while an enormously long train of closed goods vans rumbled slowly past, a grimly appropriate prelude to my visit, but another frustrating delay. In the end the journey took well over an hour, and I found I had just one hour and forty minutes to assimilate the reality of the most appalling mass murder in recorded history.

At the entrance to the site there is a Visitors' Centre with photographic displays, a cafeteria, and a cinema showing film footage of the camp when it was occupied which I couldn't spare the time to see. Admission is free unless you want to hire a personal guide, which I declined. I was going to have to proceed at my own pace, which would be almost indecently brisk. The famous, or infamous, gate to the camp proper, with the slogan *Arbeit Macht Frei* inscribed above it in wrought iron, is surprisingly small, and the camp itself is physically something of an anticlimax after the dread with which one approaches it, out of scale with the enormity of the crimes committed there. It resembles a grim London housing estate built between the wars, or a military barracks – which it was originally. Uniform three-storey brick blocks are laid out in a grid pattern, with trees planted along the paths or roads between them. I hadn't expected trees. There were not many visitors moving around the site, because of the time of year I presume, and I followed the imprints of their footsteps on the thin layer of snow that covered the paths and roadways instead of puzzling over the map in my guidebook.

A number of the blocks have been turned into museums dedicated to particular aspects of camp life – bleak dormitories, beds with straw mattresses, minimal washing facilities, the coarse striped prison clothing – or particular ethnic and national groups who suffered there. The walls are lined with portraits of prisoners, photographed with typical German efficiency full-face and in profile. The faces are haunting: some look impassive, some angry, some mad. A few even smile faintly, perhaps hoping this would ingratiate them with their captors. Block 11 was the punishment block. Here are the cramped 'standing cells' in which it was impossible to lie down, and rooms with benches for floggings and hooks for hauling prisoners off their feet by their arms tied behind their backs. Here men and women condemned to death were forced to strip naked and marched outside to be shot against a wall, the windows of the adjoining block being boarded up so that no one could witness the executions. Just outside the boundary wall of the camp is the crematorium where their corpses were burned, and which also housed a gas chamber. Somebody had left a wreath of flowers beside the ovens. And there was the block called 'Extermination', with the heartbreaking heaps of women's hair, children's clothing, and shoes, displayed behind glass.

I knew from my guidebook that Auschwitz comprised two camps – the one I was in, designed as a concentration camp, which worked its prisoners to death and treated them with great brutality, but was not dedicated to killing them, and a bigger camp called Auschwitz-Birkenau, where the policy of extermination was carried out. I had supposed they adjoined each other, but discovered from my driver that Birkenau was two or three kilometres distant. He said that he would wait in the car park outside the Visitors' Centre to drive me there. As the light of the winter afternoon waned I hurried my pace around the main camp, fearing I would be too late to get into Birkenau. I felt stupid and incompetent, having steeled myself to make this reluctant visit and then given myself insufficient time to absorb it, and I cursed my defective hearing which I was sure had caused the miscalculation. It was a quarter to three by the time we left the main camp, and I could only hope that I might be allowed five minutes in Birkenau, or if not, be able to view it from outside the perimeter fence before darkness fell. Five minutes for Birkenau: the phrase seemed to encapsulate my folly.

By the time we got there it was already three by my watch.

The place was almost deserted, with just a few vehicles in the featureless car park. There was no Visitors' Centre, there were no turnstiles, no visible staff, and few lights in the windows of the redbrick building which forms the entrance, its outline familiar from films and photographs, and its design so banal that it might have been modelled with a child's building blocks: a square gatehouse, with a pitched tiled roof and one-storey wings to each side, which squats over an archway through which the railway line passes into the camp and seems to continue straight on to the horizon, to infinity, which is where nearly everybody who arrived there by train was going, very soon. There was an iron grille across the archway. 'It's closed,' I said dejectedly to my driver. 'No, you can go in. I wait,' he said, and pointed to an entrance on one side of the building.

It seems that although Birkenau officially closes at the same time as the main camp, visitors are allowed to stay on and roam about the site unsupervised. I joined the few who were still there that cold afternoon. What first strikes you when you enter the place is its sheer immensity, stretching out of sight to the right of the railway line, rows and rows of huts marked only by their foundations and the brick chimneys that rise from the centre of each oblong like elongated tombstones. Most of the huts were destroyed by the Germans before they left, or plundered by Poles for timber after the war, or have been worn away by wind and weather over the years, but a few have been preserved to give one an idea of what it was like to occupy them. Flimsy structures with gaps in their clapboard walls, mud floors, rough wooden bunks and just one small stove, they must have been stifling in the heat of summer and bitterly cold in winter. These were the living quarters of prisoners deemed strong enough to work, but they were not habitations designed to keep human beings alive for very long.

A path stretches alongside the railway line and the platform where the trains discharged their human cargo, and information boards explain in several languages what happened next: the separation of men from women and children, and then the separation by SS doctors of those who would be allowed to live for a while from those who would be marched immediately to the gas chambers at the far end of the camp, believing, or wanting to believe, what they were told, that they were going to have showers, which, after days in a crowded cattle car with one bucket for a latrine, must have been a welcome prospect. Within hours of their arrival they would have been gassed and cremated, thousands in a single day, well over a million in all.

It has been said often enough that there are no words adequate to describe the horror of what happened at Auschwitz, and in other extermination camps whose traces were more thoroughly obliterated by the retreating Nazis. There are no adequate thoughts either, no adequate emotional responses, available to the visitor whose life has contained nothing even remotely comparable. One feels pity of course, and sorrow, and anger, but these feelings seem as superfluous to the immensity of woe this place evokes as tears dropped into an ocean. Perhaps tears would in fact be some relief, but like Richard I do not weep readily. In the end perhaps the best you can do is to humble yourself in the face of what happened here, and be for ever grateful that you weren't around to be drawn into its vortex of evil, in either suffering or complicity. By chance – through my own incompetence – I experienced this place of desolation in a way I knew I would never forget.

At first I saw other visitors, mostly in small groups or couples, walking beside the railway line, or moving between the wooden huts that have been preserved, and several passed me making their way to the exit. But as I moved deeper and deeper into the camp, as the natural light faded, darkness fell, and the temperature dropped to zero, there were fewer and fewer of them visible, the sounds of their voices ceased, and eventually it seemed to me that I was all alone. Normally in such a situation I would have removed my hearing aid to give my ears some relief; but I kept the earpieces in, because I wanted to hear the silence, a silence broken only by the crunch of my shoes on the frozen snow, the occasional sound of a dog barking in the distance, and the mournful whistle of a train. Arc-lights mounted at intervals on tall poles lit the path and shed some light across the railway and over the snow-covered foundations of the nearer huts. The black silhouettes of their bare chimneys stood out against the white expanse in receding rows until all visible features became lost in darkness. It was impossible to see the perimeter of the camp – it seemed to go on for ever. Eventually, at the end of the railway line, I came to the memorial to the victims of Auschwitz, and on each side of it the purpose-built gas chambers and crematoria, which the Germans dynamited before they retreated from the advancing Russian army. These structures have been left untouched, mounds of brickwork and jagged slabs of ferro-concrete. In a niche in the ruins of one of them somebody had placed a small votive candle or lamp, of the kind you see in churches, and perhaps synagogues, in a red glass vessel. Its feeble flickering flame was the only light in this part of the camp, and the only sign of life in the landscape of death. I hoped it would last through the night. I stood for some minutes watching the flame, until the cold began to chill my bones; then I retraced my steps. My taxi was all alone in the car park, its engine running to keep the heater going. I was the last person out of Auschwitz that day.

I apologised to the driver for keeping him waiting. He gave a grunt and shoved the gear lever into first, making the back wheels sashay in the snow as he accelerated away. I was grateful for his taciturnity on the way back to Cracow. I wanted to go over in my mind all I had seen that afternoon, ensuring that it was safely stored in my memory. I was engaged to have dinner with the British Council's Language Officer in the evening, but I decided to call him and cancel it. It was to have been nothing formal, just the two of us, a dutiful offer to keep me company on my last evening, but I didn't really want to talk to him about Auschwitz, and I didn't want to talk about anything else. Suddenly I was impatient to get home and tell Fred about it. I had called her only twice, from Warsaw and Lodz, and we didn't talk for long. If I use hotel phones with my hearing aid in place I get a feedback howl in my ear, and it's a struggle for me to hear what she's saying without it. She told me that Anne had been sent home by the maternity hospital and advised to take things very easy – no reason for alarm there. She had phoned Dad, and he seemed disorganised but OK. He asked her who Richard was. *'Bloke called Richard says he's coming to see me – what d'you think he wants?'* She told him. I was glad that Richard had responded to my hint.

I nodded off in the back seat on the return journey: the car was warm, and I was very tired. I woke as we stopped abruptly at an intersection near the city centre. It was Friday evening, the pavements were crowded, and lights blazed from shop windows stacked with food, laptop computers and designer sportswear. Auschwitz seemed as far away as the moon. When we got to my hotel I paid off the driver and gave him a generous tip, which provoked his first smile of the day. The girl at the reception desk smiled too. 'A message for you, Professor,' she said, plucking a folded piece of paper from the pigeonholes behind her. 'I take the call myself. Congratulations!'

I unfolded the message form. *'Mrs Bates phoned at 3.15 p.m. Your doghter birthed a baby boy today. Mother and baby both fine.'*

I went to my room and called Fred, who gave me all the details she had received from Jim: the baby was born that morning, four weeks premature, smallish (five pounds seven ounces) but perfect, the labour lasted about six hours, Anne tired but blissfully happy, Jim present throughout and over the moon, in short all good news. 'And how are you, darling?' Fred asked, when we had exhausted this topic. 'I'm all right,' I said. 'I went to Auschwitz today.' 'Did you?' She sounded surprised: I hadn't told of her of my plan in case I changed my mind. 'Was it awful?' 'It was unforgettable,' I said. 'I'll tell you about it when I get home.' 'Yes, do, darling, not now,' she said. 'Let's not spoil the birth of your first grandchild with such a gloomy topic. They're going to call him Desmond, by the way.' 'Poor kid,' I said, though in truth I was pleased.

I called the British Council chap and cancelled the meal. He knew where I had been that afternoon and was understanding. 'A lot of people feel they'd rather be on their own for a while after they've been there,' he said. I told him about the birth of Anne's child. 'Well, that's great!' he said. 'That should cheer you up.' And of course it did, but I didn't know quite how to balance this private joy against the experience of Auschwitz, one new life against a million deaths. It didn't feel quite right to celebrate all on my own with champagne from the minibar. Instead I ordered a room-service dinner with a half-bottle of Bulgarian red, and while I was waiting for it made some notes about the afternoon which I have drawn on in writing this.

My flight next day was at 1430 hours, so I had some free time in the morning to do some shopping. I bought an amber necklace for Anne and an antique silver brooch for Fred and some cute wooden toys from a stall in the market square for Daniel and Lena – an articulated camel that waddled down a ramp by its own momentum particularly took my fancy. I returned to the hotel pleased with these purchases and went to reception to tell them I would be checking out soon. The man on duty gave me a message slip: *'Please call your wif as soon as possible. Urgenty.'*

My first thought was like a blow to the heart: *something wrong with Anne's baby*. I'm afraid I uttered a silent petitionary prayer as I hurried up to my room, and I suppose one could say that it was answered – but not in a way that brought relief from anxiety. It wasn't Anne's baby – it was Dad. 'Your father's in hospital – they think it's a stroke,' Fred said when I got through to her. I didn't catch everything she said through the wretched hotel telephone, but I got the gist. Richard had gone to Lime Avenue that morning by arrangement, banged on the door, got no answer, enquired of the Barkers, who knew nothing, climbed over the back gate of the house and looked through the French windows into the dining room and saw Dad lying on the floor next to the television, which was on. Richard got a heavy chisel from the toolshed in the garden and levered the windows open, found Dad unconscious and called an ambulance. The paramedics thought it was a stroke rather than a heart attack. Richard had called Fred to tell her he was going with Dad in the ambulance to the local hospital and she had called me immediately. She didn't know any more. 'Thank goodness I caught you, darling. You'll be able to go straight to the hospital from Heathrow.' I had already had the same thought.

It was evening by the time I got to the Tideway Hospital, sweating inside my heavy winter overcoat in London's unseasonably warm weather, and dragging my wheeled suitcase. The reception desk said regretfully that they couldn't look after it, for security reasons, so I had to lug it with me up to the geriatric ward where Dad had been placed. The old people propped up in their beds in various states of debility and dementia regarded me with alarm as I passed them in my black overcoat, my suitcase rumbling on the vinyl-tiled floor behind me, as if they feared I was an undertaker come to measure them up. Richard, who was sitting beside Dad, said that he had only been in the ward for an hour or so, and that they had had to wait for hours in A&E before he was examined by a doctor. Dad was a pathetic sight: his face was bruised down one side where he had banged it against the sideboard when he collapsed, and he had a dressing on his forehead. He looked haggard and dazed, and his false teeth had been removed. A drip was attached to the back of his hand, and a notice at the foot of the bed said, 'Nil by mouth'. Apparently stroke victims have difficulty swallowing and can swallow their tongues. He seemed to recognise me, and mumbled a few words. I thought I heard 'bloody bad', or perhaps it was 'bloody sad'.

Richard gave me a more detailed account of the story I had already heard from Fred, and then said he had better be on his way back to Cambridge. I thanked him warmly for all he had done. I had never thought of Richard as a man of action, who would clamber over a back gate and jemmy his way into a house, but he had coped splendidly with the emergency. There was no way of knowing how long Dad had been lying on the floor of the dining room, though the fact that the TV was on suggested that he collapsed in the evening. Fred had last spoken to him by phone on Thursday evening and the Barkers next door had seen nothing of him on Friday, so he could have collapsed on Thursday after Fred's phone call, or on Friday evening. But he might have lain there for another day if it hadn't been for Richard's visit. 'Goodbye, Granddad,' Richard said, taking Dad's unencumbered hand, and received an answering squeeze and mumbled words, perhaps of thanks. I stayed for a while with Dad, reminding him that I had been away in Poland, and telling him about Anne's baby, but he paid no attention, not even responding to the phrase, 'You're a great-grandfather now.' Instead he stared fixedly at the tube bandaged to his wrist, turning his hand back and forth in puzzlement, as if wondering how the tube got there. There was no doctor available for me to speak to, so I told the ward sister that I would come back in the morning. She asked me if I would bring some toiletries, a dressing gown, cardigan and slippers for Dad.

I spent the night at the house in Lime Avenue. I knew where to find a spare set of keys, buried in a tin box under the lavender bush near the front door for just such contingencies. The house seemed more than usually cheerless as I let myself in: gloomy, chilly, fusty. I turned up the central heating, and switched on a transistor radio in the grease-coated kitchen to relieve the tomb-like silence, as I made myself supper with some bacon and a tin of baked beans. I called Fred to tell her how Dad was, and then Anne, in *her* hospital, to give her an edited version of the same report and to congratulate her on the safe arrival of the baby. She was of course very sorry to hear about Dad, and sorry not to be able to help, but I could tell that what most concerned her in the whole world at the moment was getting the baby to take the breast.

I made up the bed in the back bedroom which I had occupied

as a child and teenager, and as a university student in the vacations. After I left home for good Dad had taken it over for his various hobbies, evidence of which was displayed or stored around the room: an easel, oil paintings of rural scenes carefully copied from postcards, and still lifes assembled by himself; 'antique' ceramic vases and bowls, one or two of them cracked or chipped; a heap of old golfing magazines; books on calligraphy, a paperback *How To Make Money on the Stock Exchange*, and a picture of himself on West Pier at Brighton, grinning and holding up a large sea bass, the biggest fish he ever caught. Above the picture rail over the mantelpiece and the boarded-up fireplace there was still a trace of my own occupancy – a kind of mural of the red-and-white shield of Charlton Athletic, the football team I supported as a boy, against a green football-pitch background, executed in poster paints from the top of a step ladder when I was aged fourteen. Dad was rather fond of it and could never bring himself to obliterate it under a fresh coat of white emulsion when he redecorated the room. It was the last thing my eyes fell on before I turned out the bedside lamp. The mattress of the single divan bed felt soft and lumpy, but I had warmed it up with a hot water bottle and, exhausted as I was, I had no difficulty in falling asleep.

I returned to the hospital the next day, taking the things I had been asked to bring. Dad was sitting up in the chair next to his bed, wearing a faded towelling robe someone had found for him, and wedged in behind a movable tray-table that had been jammed under his bed. The ward sister told me this was to prevent him from trying to get up and walk, which he had showed signs of attempting. Also he had caused some disturbance in the night by pulling out his drip and trying to hit the nurse who replaced it. He was still staring fixedly at the tube bandaged to his wrist, and turning his hand from side to side. He seemed to recognise me, but looked with much more interest at the tea trolley when it approached his bed. He was allowed to have drinks with supervision, and I held a non-spill cup of tepid tea to his lips. He sucked thirstily, but much of the liquid dribbled from his mouth and down the front of his hospital pyjamas. He said very little, and that was unintelligible.

I met Dr Kannangara, the geriatric consultant responsible for Dad: a short, plump Asian with rimless spectacles and a round, impassive face, who confirmed the diagnosis of stroke. He said they would keep Dad in the ward for a few weeks and then he would be moved into a local geriatric unit with nursing care. There was a procedure for this which the hospital's welfare department would explain to me. I asked if he could be moved by ambulance to a private nursing home near us, if I found one, and he looked surprised but said he thought it was feasible. I asked if Dad would recover his speech, and he said probably not to any great extent. He has some paralysis down his right side, indicating that the stroke affected the left lobe of the brain which controls language functions.

It was depressing to reflect that I would probably never have a proper conversation with my father again, but it was a consolation that when I had called on him two weeks earlier on my way to Poland he had been calmer and much more lucid than of late, and surprised me with feats of long-term memory, like sunbursts through cloud suddenly illuminating small patches of a dark and obscure landscape. I asked him what his earliest memory was, and he said it was being carried on his father's shoulder to the tobacconist to buy cigarettes. 'He asked the man in the shop for twenty Wills' Gold Flake and the man took them down off the shelf and gave them to him. Well, my father was called Will, remember, so I thought the cigarettes were made specially for him. That made him laugh. And he had a brother called Alf, who had a real boozer's nose, you know, all broken veins, and I called him "the uncle with the writing on his nose". That made them all laugh too.' He even dredged up some stories about his early musical career that I hadn't heard before. 'For a time I used to do two jobs of an evening – the band at the 53 Club off Regent Street, which opened at about nine o'clock, and before that, on my way to the West End, I used to do a session at a dance school at the

Elephant and Castle – they called it a dance school, it was really a way of running a dance hall without paying entertainment tax. It was just a three-piece band, piano, drums and me on sax and clarinet, strict tempo stuff, quick quick slow, I could play the tunes in my sleep, in fact I used to read a book while I was blowing, had it propped up on the music stand, nobody on the floor could see . . . but the money was useful. I was saving up to get married. Not that I was in a hurry, but your mother was. One day, she said to me, "When are we going to get married? Mum and Dad want to know." So I named a date, and then I had to think about putting a few quid in the bank. But I gave up the dance school when we got married. I wasn't seeing enough of Norma.' The thought seemed to make him melancholy. 'I suppose she never had much of a life, being married to a musician, out at work every evening, and Jewish weddings most Sundays. Especially after you came along. But she never complained.' I remembered how sorry for my mother Maisie had been when she was introduced to our nuclear family and realised what a limited, home-bound existence Mum had led for most of her life, living vicariously on the anecdotes her musician husband and scholarly son brought back from the wider world. 'She made herself a slave to you two men,' Maisie used to say, and in retrospect I think she was right, but it was much too late in the day to say as much to Dad, and I didn't want to strike a discordant note in what was the best conversation I had had with him for a long time.

I stayed on at the house, uncomfortable and depressing as it was, for a few more days, in order to visit Dad regularly at the hospital. It is a pretty typical NHS hospital in an underprivileged bit of London: overcrowded, in need of refurbishment, and not as clean as it should be. The medics and senior nurses seemed harassed and anxious, the other staff stoical and slow-moving. You could sense the fear of MRSA and the latest super-bug, *C. difficile*, in the overheated air of the wards. Petty pilfering is rife. Dad's lambswool cardigan, which I gave him as a Christmas present, disappeared two days after I brought it in, and I found him wearing some horrible acrylic garment with two buttons missing, probably left behind by a deceased patient, which the staff had found him as a substitute. The ward sister apologised and said she would make a search for the lambswool one but wasn't hopeful of recovering it. I wanted to get him out of there as soon as possible, and decided to go home and look for a suitable nursing home near us.

Returning to Rectory Road after spending several days shuttling by bus between Dad's dingy domicile and the geriatric ward of Tideway Hospital seemed more than ever like entering a haven of civilised comfort. Fred was out, but the house did not seem empty: the pale light-reflecting walls, the familiar pictures, the surfaces and textures and artfully blended colours of the floors and furnishings, the carpeted staircase with its brass stair-rods and polished wood banister, were welcoming presences, like a team of mute, discreetly smiling servants welcoming the master home. I unpacked, tipped a load of soiled clothing into the laundry basket, took a long hot bath in a warm, spotlessly clean bathroom, and dressed in fresh clean clothes. When Fred came in we hugged and kissed speechlessly for a minute or two. There was much to talk about, and we did that over a supper she had prepared in advance. We went to bed early and made ardent love. Driven by desire and long abstinence, I had no difficulty performing the act. We both slept deeply afterwards.

The petty offences and recriminations of the Christmas and New Year holidays, and the chilly relations between us up to the time when I left for Poland, were all forgiven and forgotten. Fred was sympathetic and supportive of what I had done and planned to do about Dad, quickly drew up a list of possible nursing homes from the Yellow Pages, and made appointments to view three of them. We arranged to visit Anne, who was already back home with her baby, at the weekend. I responded gratefully to Fred's help and empathy with these family concerns, but there was another contributory element in our reconciliation, though I wasn't fully conscious of it at the time, and Fred not at all. When

I told her about my visit to Auschwitz, she listened attentively, shuddered at my descriptions, and said she admired me for facing such a harrowing experience; but she seemed relieved when I finished my tale, and glad to move on to another topic. I realised that I could never convey to her in words the impression the place, especially Birkenau, had left on me.

When I returned to London on the following Monday I bought a paperback about Auschwitz and the Final Solution at the station bookstall, and read it on my journey and over the following days, filling out my sketchy knowledge of the history of the place, and acquiring some sense of the individuality of its victims and their experiences. Many of them, knowing they would never survive, left letters to their loved ones buried in jars or canteens in the camp, hoping these documents might one day be discovered and delivered, or at least read by somebody. The most moving of those cited in the book was a letter from Chaim Hermann, a Sonderkommando, to his wife, which was written in November 1944 and dug up from a pile of human ashes near one of the crematoria at Birkenau in 1945. The Sonderkommandos were able-bodied prisoners who were compelled to work in the extermination process itself, ushering the unwitting victims towards the gas chambers, removing their corpses afterwards and burning them in the ovens of the crematoria. To refuse the work was to invite instant execution; to perform it brought better living conditions – for a finite period. In a way the Sonderkommandos were the most unfortunate of all the victims of Auschwitz. The great majority of those who died there went unsuspectingly to the gas chambers. The Sonderkommandos lived for months with the certain knowledge that sooner or later they too would be killed, because the Nazis could not risk allowing them to survive as witnesses, and in fact their first duty was likely to be disposing of the corpses of their predecessors on the ghastly production line of death. Chaim Hermann described Auschwitz as *simply hell, but Dante's hell is incomparably ridiculous in comparison with this real one here, and we are its eye-witnesses, and we cannot leave it alive*'. He also said that he intended to die *'calmly, perhaps heroically (this will depend on circumstances)'*, hinting at a final act of resistance, but it is not known whether he achieved that. He himself had no way of knowing whether his wife would ever receive his letter, but in the midst of all this diabolical evil he asked her forgiveness for not sufficiently appreciating their life together, and this was the sentence in his letter that most affected me: *'If there have been, at various times, trifling misunderstandings in our life, now I see how one was unable to value the passing time.'*

We looked at three private nursing homes. The only one that didn't smell of urine nauseatingly mixed with air-freshener, and was in other respects acceptable, was horrendously expensive, but I decided that Dad's life expectancy must now be limited, and that what time was left to him should be made as comfortable as possible. They had a vacancy, and were prepared to keep it open for a week or two, but when I went back to the hospital after the weekend the news was not good. Dad's condition had not improved over the previous few days, in fact it had deteriorated. Dr Kannangara was not available, but I spoke to a young doctor, a houseman I suppose, who was his chief assistant, and asked him if Dad was likely to be fit to make the journey north by ambulance in the next week or two, and he shook his head doubtfully. Dad was still having difficulty swallowing, and losing weight through lack of real sustenance. He continued to require an IV drip, and was plucking at it feebly again with his weak right hand, sitting in his wedged-in chair beside the bed, when I greeted him. I showed him the brochure of the nursing home and talked in a cheerful tone about moving him there soon, and he stroked the glossy paper with its coloured photos of the bedrooms and the conservatory, but I had no way of knowing how much, if anything, he understood. Even sadder was that he clearly didn't understand when I told him what a thrill it had been to hold my grandson, his great-grandson, in my arms the previous Sunday, when we visited Anne and Jim. I was nervous of doing so, the baby seemed so tiny and fragile, but Anne gently insisted on placing him in my cradled arms, and having just been fed he looked up placidly at me with unfocused eyes, drunk with breast milk, until a bubble of indigestion moved his mouth into the semblance of a smile. 'There, he smiled at you!' Anne exclaimed, and I accepted the fiction. 'He has Maisie's mouth, like you,' I said. 'And your nose,' she said. 'I suppose I get the ears,' said Jim. 'They seem to stick out like mine.' I relayed all this to my indifferent auditor because it was better than sitting in silence, and anyway I enjoyed recalling this happy visit.

Dad seemed drowsy as well as inattentive, and when I commented on this to a nurse she said, 'That's because he fought us this morning when we got him up.' They used an ingenious kind of crane with a canvas cradle to lift him off the bed and into the chair and back again. I began to develop a great respect for the nurses in this crowded ward, who do a difficult job with patients whose minds are going and whose bodies are collapsing, and many of whom seem, like Dad, ungrateful for their care.

There were no set visiting hours in the ward: visitors were allowed to come and go at almost any time, presumably in the hope that they would keep the patients stimulated and help with tasks like feeding and giving drinks. I got used to holding a non-spill cup of the kind used by infants to Dad's lips, and occasionally spooned a little fruit yogurt between them, reflecting that sixty-odd years ago he would have been doing the same for me (or, on reflection, perhaps not; male/female roles were more differentiated then). One morning that week I happened to be sitting with him when the ward nurse, Caroline, came up with an Afro-Caribbean auxiliary in tow and began drawing the curtains round the bed. I asked if I should get out of their way. Caroline looked at me in a slightly challenging way and said: 'No, I'd like you to help Delphine wash your father.' I was taken completely by surprise. Inwardly I recoiled from the idea, but I could think of no way to refuse that wouldn't discredit me in their eyes. 'All right,' I said. 'What do I do?' 'Delphine will show you,' Caroline said, and left us to it. Delphine put on a waterproof apron and a pair of latex gloves taken from a sealed pack, and looked at me sceptically. 'Better take off that nice jacket,' she said.

It was an extraordinary experience, which took the reversal of the infant-parent relationship through the taboo barrier. Basically I was helping to change a nappy on an eighty-nine-year-old man, but he happened to be my father. First we had to take off his pyjamas and vest, which entailed helping him to sit up, and rocking him from side to side. His body looked painfully thin and wasted, but being a tall man and big-boned he was still a heavy dead weight to support. He was wearing a diaper under plastic pants. Delphine covered his loins with a towel while she washed his upper body, and I dried it; then she removed the pants and the paper diaper. He had passed a small bowel movement, but it did not smell too bad, perhaps because of his bland diet. She washed and powdered his private parts, in a respectful but matter-of-fact way, then attached a tube to his penis and strapped a reservoir for the urine to his leg. Then we put the pyjama trousers back on him, and a vest, and the pyjama jacket. What a relief it was to see the bare forked animal clothed again. My arm ached from the effort of supporting him. Throughout the operation Dad was mostly passive and obedient, though once or twice I had to take his hand when he tried to push Delphine's away. 'He normally give us more trouble,' Delphine said laconically. 'Must be 'cause you're here.'

When we were finished, and Dad was lying back against the pillows, she stripped off the latex gloves and tossed them in a pedal bin. 'Thanks for your help,' she said. 'I've never done anything like that before,' I said. Even when she was very ill Maisie was never as helpless as Dad, and she was always able to get to the bathroom with my help or the nurse's. 'I don't think I will ever forget it,' I added. When Caroline came to check that everything was OK, Delphine repeated my remark to her. 'Now you know what we do every day,' Caroline said. At the time I assumed that she was just seizing the opportunity to off-load a routine chore and attend to something more important, but I wondered later whether she wasn't deliberately giving me a lesson in what would be entailed in Dad's long-term care. When I told Fred on the phone that evening (I was staying in the Lime Avenue house again) that I had helped to wash Dad, she said, 'I don't believe it.' I said that I could hardly believe it myself. I was glad to have done it, but I wasn't anxious to repeat the experience, and my dominant emotion was a fervent hope that I would never require such a service myself, from anyone.

Dr Kannangara was very elusive that week, and to my annoyance I missed his ward visit on the Thursday. I did however see the young houseman, Wilson by name. He took me aside and led me into a store room off the end of the ward, and spoke in a quiet confidential tone. He told me that the specialist would make another assessment of Dad's condition on the following Monday and see me afterwards. 'He'll probably suggest inserting a PEG tube,' he said, and explained that this was a device which fed sustenance directly into the stomach. 'Your dad's had an extension of his stroke, which has further reduced his ability to swallow. If he doesn't get more nourishment he'll gradually get weaker and weaker.' 'And with this tube he'll get stronger?' I asked. 'Let's say he'll remain in a stable condition. The same as he is now – unless he has another serious stroke, of course.' He looked at me speculatively. 'Your father's achieved a good age, nearly ninety. In cases like this we like to be guided by the family. We can keep him alive, but without much quality of life. Or we can make him as comfortable as we can and let nature take its course. It's really up to you.'

I didn't like being presented with this choice. I didn't like it at all. When I told Fred about it that evening, she could hear the stress in my voice, and decided I needed moral support. 'I'll come down to London tomorrow, and stay for a few days,' she said. 'Jakki can look after the shop. Ron will help out.' I didn't try to dissuade her, though I did warn her the house was a tip.

I met her the next morning at King's Cross, and we took an extravagant cab all the way to the hospital. Dad didn't look too good. Somebody had tried to shave him earlier and I guessed he had made the operation difficult, because he had a couple of cuts, and patches of his stubble were untouched. He didn't seem to recognise Fred, though when she began to speak to him he looked sharply at her as if the sound of her voice triggered some faint memory. I wasn't sure that he recognised me any more. While Fred and I went through a pantomime of hospital visitors chatting away to a responsive patient his eyes were following the uniformed nurses and ancillaries who went to and fro past the end of his bed with a kind of feral attention, as if he knew that these were the people on whom he depended for food, drink, and other physical needs. It seemed to me that he had regressed even past human infancy on the evolutionary scale and that his reflexes were disturbingly like those of an animal in captivity.

Fred was shocked and dismayed by what she saw. Afterwards, when we were back in Lime Avenue, sitting in front of the electric fire in the dingy dining room with cups of tea, we discussed the issue of the PEG tube. She said she didn't see the point of keeping anyone in Dad's condition alive by such an intrusive and artificial procedure. 'Of course the doctors have to offer to do it, since it's available, but the houseman gave you a heavy hint that they think nature should take its course now.'

'But that puts all the onus on me,' I said. 'I have to decide whether he lives or dies.'

'We're all going to die sooner or later, darling,' she said, and her 'darling' was gentle and sympathetic. 'Do you really want him to be lying in a hospital bed for perhaps months, unable to speak, unable to recognise anyone, looked after like a baby, fed through a hole in his stomach? It would be kinder to let him go.' I nodded agreement, but I must have looked unconvinced, because she added: 'What would you want *me* to do, if you were in the same condition?'

'Oh God, let me go!' I said. 'No PEG tubes, no life-support machines, please.'

'Well, then,' she said, as if resting her case.

'I suppose the reason I find this so hard,' I said, 'is that it's the second time in my life I have held another person's life in my hands.' And then I told her what I have told no other person, that I helped Maisie to die.

That last Christmas she was very ill, very weak, and in pain, though she bravely concealed the severity of it from the children. The cancer had metastasised all over her body and she knew there would be no remission. When I arranged for the kids to go on the skiing holiday, she saw a window of opportunity, to leave without fuss a life that promised nothing but more suffering, physical and emotional. She didn't want to die in a hospital, or a hospice, looked after by strangers, however kind. 'I've had enough, Des,' she said. 'I'm not sure how much longer I can stay in control. I'm tired. It's time to go, and you've got to help me.' I think our GP guessed her intention and decided tacitly to cooperate. Her principal means of pain relief was a battery-operated syringe driver – a fairly new device in those days – which administered a continuous supply of diamorphine subcutaneously, refilled by the visiting nurse as required. Maisie was able to increase the supply herself according to need, but only up to a safe level. She also used Distalgesic tablets when the pain was very bad. Towards the end of Christmas week our GP wrote a prescription for a larger than usual quantity, 'to see you through the New Year holiday', and as he handed it over he looked me in the eye and said: 'Too many of these combined with alcohol can be dangerous.' On the last night of the year I crushed twenty Distalgesic tablets and helped Maisie swallow them in a mix-ture of warm milk and brandy. She turned up the syringe driver to maximum. I kissed her, lit a night-light candle beside the bed, and lay down beside her, holding her hand, until she fell into a deep sleep. Then I sat in an armchair and watched her breathing until I fell asleep myself. When I woke at 4 a.m., the candle was out, and she was dead, her face quite peaceful, her limbs relaxed. I called the doctor at six and he came round. He didn't ask any questions, and in due course he signed the death certificate. Later that morning I phoned the ski resort in Austria to tell Anne and Richard.

'You poor darling,' Fred said, when I had finished my story. While we had been talking daylight had faded outside the windows and the red glow of the electric fire was the only illumination in the room. She came across and knelt on the floor and took my hands in hers. 'How awful for you. And how brave you were.'

'Not as brave as Maisie,' I said. 'But would you do the same for me?'

'I don't know,' she said hesitantly. 'Catholics aren't supposed to, of course . . . but if it came to the point, and you asked, I probably would. What you did for Maisie was an act of love.'

'I'd like to think so,' I said. 'But the trouble is, I wanted her to die. I wanted the whole miserable business to be over – almost as much, I believe, as she did. I had to struggle to conceal my relief afterwards, disguising it under grief. It left me with a residual sense of guilt that I think I've never entirely got rid of. And now it's all happening again. Of course I don't want Dad's life to drag on pointlessly – but not just because it would be horrible for him. Because it would be horrible for me.'

We talked for a long time, and Fred did her best to convince me that I had no reason to reproach myself over the death of Maisie, nor would I if I decided against the PEG procedure for Dad. She invoked some abstruse Catholic casuistry about 'double effect' – if you did something with a good reason but a bad side effect then it wasn't a sin, something like that. I wasn't sure how it fitted my case, but I was grateful for her support. In the event I was spared the decision. Dad developed a chest infection over the weekend and by the time I had the interview with Kannangara it was obvious that he was in rapid and irreversible decline. Meanwhile Fred and I camped out in the house in Lime Avenue. Neither of us felt like sleeping in Dad's bed, or sleeping apart, so we took the mattresses off both beds and made up one for ourselves on the floor of the lounge, the one room in the house that still looked in any way inviting. We did not attempt to make love, but we caressed each other and drifted off to sleep in a comfortable embrace, my hand between her warm thighs. Sooner or later that is what our sexual life will dwindle to, I suppose, if we live long enough – a tender intimate touching; and one might as well accept that prospect as infinitely preferable to nothing at all (while hoping it will happen later rather than sooner, of course).

Between hospital visits Fred bought cleaning materials and we set about scouring the kitchen of its coating of grease, and the rest of the house of its coating of dust, just to have something to do; and within a few days living there was no longer the queasy ordeal it had been. I visited Dad every day, sometimes with Fred, sometimes alone. Eventually she decided she would have to go back home and relieve Jakki, who had been running the shop largely on her own. Richard came to the hospital one day, and when he spoke to Dad and held his hand I saw the last gleam of recognition in Dad's eyes, perhaps sparked by a dim memory of how Richard had found him and accompanied him to hospital. By the end of the week he was a pitiful sight. His left wrist was bruised and bloody from the repeated insertion and displacement of the IV tube, which was now attached to his stomach. He was too weak to sit in his chair, and lay in bed in the same position until the nurses moved him, breathing noisily with the aid of a mask which supplied his lungs with humidified oxygen. He seemed to find the mask, attached to the back of his head by an elastic band, irritating, and made periodic attempts to pull it off, sometimes successfully. If I was there I would hold the mask to his nose and mouth and grasp his hand at the same time, and he became more peaceful. But one afternoon when I tried to do this he brushed the mask away again and again until he was exhausted, then closed his eyes and submitted to the mask being replaced with the elastic band. That evening back at the house I had a call from the ward nurse that he was sinking rapidly and I had better come. I called a minicab and was at the hospital in under half an hour, but the ward sister told me he had passed away five minutes after we spoke on the phone. She left me with him behind the curtains drawn round his bed. He looked stern, almost noble, in death and I was not sorry that I had missed his last laboured breaths. I wondered whether his stubborn resistance to wearing the mask that afternoon had been a sign that somewhere in his ruined consciousness he had decided to give up the fight for life, and let go.

19

22nd February. Dad made the long journey north after all, not in an ambulance, but in a hearse. Tonight his body reposes just up the road in the mortuary of B. H. Gilbert & Sons, Funeral Directors, whose men fetched it from Tideway Hospital today. The local cemetery for Brickley, where Mum was cremated, is a dreary place, hemmed in by a council estate and a railway line where trains rattle noisily past every few minutes. I remember her funeral as a profoundly depressing occasion. There was a municipal strike on at the time, and a lot of uncollected garbage was blowing about the site in the strong March wind, and there were heaps of flowers all over the place, rotting inside their cellophane wrappings. There weren't many mourners, and I knew there would be even fewer for Dad's funeral if it were held in London. His two cousins, to whom I have written about his death, are both too old and infirm to travel from their seaside homes, and I can't think of anyone in Brickley who would have come except perhaps the Barkers. When I drew up a list it mostly consisted of Fred's family and mine, and the thought of inviting them back after the service to the house in Lime Avenue, even in its cleaned-up state, or hiring some place in Brickley, a district not noted for elegant licensed premises, was dispiriting. So we decided to have the funeral up here, and the reception at home. It's been arranged for next Monday at twelve. It will be a cremation, and in due course I'll take the ashes back to Brickley Cemetery where Mum was cremated and scatter them in the Garden of Remembrance where Dad scattered Mum's. He left no instructions about his funeral, needless to say, but I think that's what he would have wanted.

I saw his body once more after he died, next day in the hospital's chapel of rest, but I rather wish I hadn't. There must have been some delay before his body was laid out, by which time rigor mortis had set in, and they obviously had trouble fitting his false teeth, because his mouth was open and his teeth bared in a ghastly grimace. I found it uncomfortable to look at him, and sat behind his head as I thought about his long life. I had spent the previous evening going through old photographs I found in his chaotic desk, and it was pleasanter to fill one's mind with those creased and dog-eared images in sepia or black-and-white: youthful Dad with his tenor sax slung round his neck, posing with the other members of a five-piece band, the Dulwich Dixies, its name emblazoned on the bass drum; Dad and Mum together, young and good-looking, on holiday somewhere flat and sandy in Thirties beachwear; Dad in the back garden at Lime Avenue, with me aged three straddling his shoulders and holding on tightly to his upstretched hands; a studio portrait of Dad looking deceptively heroic in his RAF uniform and angled forage cap; Dad and Arthur Lane in their tropical shorts, sunburned and grinning into the camera; Dad's agency photos for modelling and TV work, wearing various costumes and expressions – here a comic Cockney in a flat cap, there a sober businessman in a chalk-striped suit . . .

Afterwards I registered the death at the local registry office, a tedious process because the staff were in a tizzy about a new computerised system (I glimpsed 'DEATH MENU' on a monitor screen); then I locked up the house and came home to make arrangements for the funeral. Fred has got her parish priest to officiate at the service, which is nice of her – and of him, considering that Dad was barely a Christian, let alone a Catholic. But it seems that the Catholic clergy are fairly easy-going about such matters now, accepting, I presume, that their main function is to bring comfort to the bereaved, and if that involves a little prevarication about the beliefs of the departed, so be it. It will be a short service, since there are funerals every half-hour at the crematorium. Fr Michael has given us a free hand in filling in the basic Catholic template. Anne and Richard will do readings. I'm going to say a few words – eulogy seems too pompous a word – about

Dad, and I've tape-recorded some of his favourite classical music for the service. I thought of playing a few bars of 'The Night, the Stars and the Music' too, but Fred vetoed that.

I have given very little thought to Alex Loom in the past few weeks, having other things on my mind. Fred told me she had left messages on the answerphone a couple of times when I was in London, wanting to speak to me, which I didn't bother to follow up, and when I came back to Rectory Road I found several emails from her in my inbox, saying she was very sorry to hear that my father was ill, but she urgently needed to see me as soon as I could manage it, and was willing to travel down to London if necessary. Today when I came in from delivering the music tapes to the undertakers Fred said that Alex had called again, and she had told her of Dad's death. 'She said she was very sorry to hear it, and she'd like to come to the funeral.'

The information disturbed me. If she came to the funeral we could hardly avoid asking her back to the house afterwards. 'I hope you didn't invite her,' I said. 'It would be quite inappropriate. She never even met Dad – he was upstairs sleeping off the booze when she turned up on Boxing Day.'

'No, I pretended the arrangements weren't settled yet. I should put her off, if I were you. And while you're about it, darling, you might tactfully remind her that she still owes us for her curtains.'

'You mean the ones she bought from *Décor*?' I said, surprised. 'That was quite a long time ago.'

'Exactly,' Fred said. 'She paid a small deposit, and the balance was due when Ron fitted them for her in mid-January. She's had a reminder.'

I asked how much was outstanding and Fred said it was four hundred pounds – 'As I remarked at the time, she has very good taste.'

I went to my study to send an email to Alex and found a new one from her in my inbox, commiserating with me over Dad's death and reiterating her wish to attend the funeral. I replied, thanking her for her condolences, and said that the funeral was to be a small private affair for the family only. I decided it would compromise the formal and distant tone of my message to mention the matter of the curtains.

23rd February. Alex called me this morning, after Fred had gone into the city centre. She said she understood about the funeral, but she was very anxious to meet me to discuss something. I said I was far too busy, and would be for some time, sorting out my father's probate, and disposing of his possessions and the house. I asked her what it was about, and she said she would rather explain in person, at her flat. When I said that wasn't possible, she suggested Pam's Pantry, and when I rejected that proposal too she reluctantly told me over the phone why she had been trying to reach me ever since my return from Poland.

'I can't go on being supervised by Colin Butterworth,' she said. 'It's impossible, for obvious reasons. It's the only thing we agree on. He asked me if there was anyone else in the Department I would like to transfer to, and I said no, there isn't, but I would love to be supervised by you. He thinks it's a brilliant idea, and he's sure there won't be any problem getting the University to approve it. You'd get some kind of payment, not a lot I guess, but something. And I don't need to tell you I'd be absolutely thrilled.'

'No, Alex,' I said when she had finished her pitch.

'Why?' she wailed. 'When I asked you before, you said it would be an insult to Colin, but that doesn't apply any more.'

'I just don't want to,' I said.

'But why?' she persisted.

'If you really want to know, it's because I don't understand you, I don't trust you, and I seriously doubt whether you are capable of writing a PhD thesis. I'm afraid I would end up writing it for you.'

She was silent for a moment.

'I guess you're upset about your daddy's death,' she said. 'I can understand that. I'll let you think about it for a while.'

'I won't change my mind,' I said, and to change the subject I added: 'By the way, Fred tells me you have an outstanding account with her, for some curtains. It would avoid embarrassment if you could settle it.'

There followed another of Alex's enigmatic telephonic pauses. 'Yeah, I'm sorry about that. Fact is, I'm short of cash at the moment. You wouldn't lend me the money, would you?'

'You mean lend you the money to pay my wife?'

'Yeah. It's only four hundred and fifty pounds.'

'Fred said it was four hundred.'

'Oh yeah, right. I paid a deposit of fifty, I remember now.'

It was my turn to pause for rapid thought. I was pretty sure her mistake had been deliberate, and pretty sure too that this loan would never be repaid. Her cool cheek amazed me, but for a moment I was tempted to pay her off, so to speak, with this favour. Then I thought of what mischief she might make with a cheque for £400 signed by me, unknown to Fred, and handing her a brown envelope full of used banknotes under the table at Pam's Pantry might be equally compromising. 'No, Alex,' I said, for the third time, and rang off.

Later today I got an email from Butterworth saying that, for reasons I was aware of, it had become impossible for him to continue supervising Alex, and that he had tried without success to find a colleague willing to take her on. She herself had suggested I might be approached, indeed urged it with great enthusiasm, since she had already received valuable informal advice from me. He could think of no one better qualified than myself to supervise her, and was sure that there would be no problem about appointing me as an external supervisor with an appropriate stipend. He himself, needless to say, would be extraordinarily grateful if I would act in this capacity.

I replied that I was sorry, but, for several reasons which I didn't want to go into, it was out of the question.

26th February. The funeral today went off well. There was a decent number of people present in the crematorium chapel:

293

Anne and Jim of course, with baby Desmond, and Richard; but I was grateful that so many of Fred's family made the effort to come, not only Marcia and Peter and the children, who live near, but Ben and Maxine and Giles came up from London, and even Cecilia made the long journey from Cheltenham, which considering how little joy she got from Dad's company was really very nice of her. There were also a few friends and neighbours who had met him when he stayed with us, and remembered him affectionately as a 'character', whom Fred thought of inviting. I was surprised and moved by the turn-out. The service was a success – it sounds rather flippant to say so, but a funeral is a form of theatre, it can be a flop or a hit, and frankly it's an advantage to have a minister of religion running the show. I went to a humanist funeral once and I wouldn't want to have one myself even though I'm a humanist. When Fr Michael asked me if Dad had been baptised, I said yes, though I couldn't swear to it, on the assumption that everybody was christened in respectable working-class society in his day, so we began with the language of Christian prayer. The loop system in the chapel was about the best I have ever experienced, and I heard every word:

The grace of our Lord Jesus Christ and the love of God and the fellowship of the Holy Spirit be with you all . . . In the waters of Baptism, Harry died with Christ and rose with him to new life . . . Confident that God always remembers the good we have done and forgives our sins, let us pray, asking God to gather Harry to Himself . . .

There is something seemly about the language of transcendence, even if you don't believe in it, at a funeral. They were, I suppose, petitionary, or rather intercessionary, prayers we were saying 'Amen' to, but what after all is a prayer but a wish – a wish, in this case, that there might be an afterlife in which the evil and suffering and mistakes and disappointments of this one will be redeemed – and wishing is only human. Do animals wish? Do computers wish? I think not. According to tradition, Beethoven's last words were: *'I will hear in heaven.'* I don't suppose he actually said them, but they express our wish for him.

Richard struck a more bracingly materialist note by reading a powerful passage from the journal of Bruce Cummings, an early twentieth-century naturalist, which I photocopied before he went back to Cambridge:

To me the honour is sufficient of belonging to the universe – such a great universe, and so great a scheme of things. Not even Death can rob me of that honour. For nothing can alter the fact that I have lived; I have been I, if for ever so short a time. And when I am dead, the matter which composes my body is indestructible – and eternal, so that come what may to my 'Soul', my dust will always be going on, each separate atom of me playing its separate part – I shall still have some sort of finger in the pie. When I am dead, you can boil me, burn me, drown me, scatter me – but you cannot destroy me: my little atoms would merely deride such heavy vengeance. Death can do no more than kill you.

Fr Michael pursed his lips a little as he listened to these words, but I heard him say to Richard afterwards in his Irish brogue, 'That was a very inter-resting passage you read. Who was the fella that wrote it, now?' Anne spoke tenderly about her memories of Dad when she was young, and finished by reading a short poem she got off the Internet:

> *Where do people go to when they die?*
> *Somewhere down below or in the sky?*
> *'I can't be sure,' said Granddad, 'but it seems*
> *They simply set up home inside our dreams.'*

Not the greatest poetry, perhaps, but it expressed a truth: I have dreamed several times of Dad since he died. Then we sang that least dogmatic of hymns, 'To Be a Pilgrim', and it was time for my few words. I spoke of Dad's indomitable spirit, the way he had adapted himself to changes and setbacks in his long career, and his determination to live his own life in his own house, which he almost achieved to the very end. I explained that I had chosen Delius's 'Walk to the Paradise Garden' for the entrance to the chapel, the slow movement of Rachmaninov's Symphony No. 2 for the committal, and 'Nimrod' from Elgar's Enigma Variations for the exit – because they were all favourites of his, which he liked to listen to on his music centre, reclining in an armchair with a handkerchief over his face to keep out the light and other visual distractions. It was a habit carried over from the time when he worked in nightclubs, and managed to sleep through the hours of daylight by having a pillow over his head as well as one under it.

When we got back to the house and had had something to eat and drink, I played my tape recording of Dad's scratchy old record of 'The Night, the Stars and the Music'. Although it was only a demo recording, not commercially released, it was made with the full Arthur Roseberry band, perhaps supplemented for the occasion. After a long swooning, swooping introduction with harmonised saxophones, muted horns, a piano solo and even a few bars of what sounds like a mandolin, Dad's voice breaks in, incredibly high, effortlessly sweet, his pitch perfect, his enunciation just a shade over-anxious.

> The night, the stars and the music,
> The magic of a tryst with you.
> Romance, a dance and the music,
> The loveliness of you,
> My dream of dreams come true . . .

Something like that, anyway. It was impossible to make out all the words from this second-generation copy of a very imperfect original, but it didn't really matter. What we heard, from beyond the grave, as it were, was a voice, the voice of a young man, eager, alive, and capable of simulating the rapture of romantic love. When the record came to an end, there were sighs and murmurs of appreciation from the listeners, and a patter of applause, which little Daniel instantly imitated, clapping his hands vigorously. I had been slightly surprised that Marcia and Peter brought him and Lena to the funeral, but very pleased. It was good to have these children, and the babe in Anne's arms, to represent the beginning of the human life cycle at an event focused on its end. They had been very well behaved in the chapel, attentive and not apparently disturbed by the proceedings. I asked Daniel what part of the service he liked best, and he said: 'I liked it when he went down,' referring to the slow descent and disappearance of the coffin at the committal, which I suppose must have seemed rather magical to his infant perception. I was interested to note that Daniel has begun to use the first-person pronoun.

28th February. I opened my email at about ten this morning to find a message from Alex, with one word in the subject box: 'Goodbye'.

> *Dear Desmond,*
>   *You're absolutely right of course. I am flaky, deceitful, and incapable of completing a doctoral dissertation. My life has been one long series of failures, frustrations, and follies, so I have decided to end it. I've read too many suicide notes to try to write one that wouldn't seem another, final failure, but perhaps this is the first one to be delivered by email. On reflection it's probably not, but I'm betting that you don't get up in the middle of the night, as I have been known to do, to check your email, so that by the time you read this I will be gone and never bother you again. Don't feel bad about it. I've taken the pills and cut my wrists and now I'm going to press the Send button while I still have the strength.*
>   *Goodbye Desdond.*
>   *Alex*

I looked at the time on the dateline of the message: 03.21. Nearly seven hours ago. I ran to my car without bothering to set the house burglar alarm, and drove to Wharfside Court as fast as the traffic permitted. I had no idea whether the message was genuine, or some kind of joke – whether I would find Alex unconscious, or dead, curled up on her blood-soaked bed, or lolling naked in a bath full of red-tinted water; or whether she would open the door with a smile, smart and svelte as usual in her black top and pants, saying with a flick of her glossy blonde hair, 'Hi! Come in. I thought that would bring you running.' Was her use of the word 'suicide' – avoided, as she had told me, by most people who committed it – a hint that her note was a hoax, or on the contrary a guarantee of its authenticity? Was the uncorrected typo, 'Desdond', evidence that the pills or loss of blood were beginning to take their effect, or a cunning device to give just that impression?

A speed camera flashed as I passed it on the way to Wharfside Court, and I wondered if I could avoid three penalty points by pleading an emergency. If the note was genuine, I might; if it was a hoax, probably not. I sent up a petitionary prayer that it was a hoax, not just for Alex's sake, but for my own. I had a vivid premonition of the consequences if she were dead: an inquest, the contents of her hard disk submitted in evidence, her emails read out in court, the coroner's questions ('What exactly was your relationship to the deceased, Professor Bates?'). 'Don't feel bad about it,' she had written, but the opening of that email had been designed to make me do just that: 'You're absolutely right, of course. I am flaky, deceitful, and incapable of completing a doctoral dissertation.' ('What remark of yours does this refer to, Professor Bates? Would you say it might have precipitated Miss Loom's decision to take her own life?')

I squealed to a halt in the parking lot as near as possible to the building's entrance, between a saloon car and a large van, and ran to the lift. It was evidently stuck on the third floor, so I strode up the stairs and arrived panting at the door to Alex's flat. Two men in jeans and sweatshirts were manoeuvring her sofa through the doorway.

'What's going on?' I gasped.

One of the men said something. I realised that in my haste I had forgotten to put in my hearing aid before I left the house, and that it was now reposing on my desk, zipped cosily into its little purse.

'What?' I said.

The man said something again, and when I didn't appear to understand, jerked his head towards the interior of the flat. They moved off, carrying the sofa towards the open lift, and I entered the flat. A youngish man in a dark suit was standing at the window of the almost empty living room, looking out across the canal. He wheeled round as I entered and said something with a politely questioning air.

It was fortunate that Jeremy Hall, as he told me in the course of our conversation, has an elderly father who is pretty deaf, so he is used to raising his voice and speaking clearly. Thanks to that, and with a tolerable amount of repetition, he was able to explain into my cupped ear what had happened. The bailiffs had arrived that morning to repossess Alex's furniture, all of which had been bought from a single megastore on credit terms on which she had defaulted. They had arrived very early to be sure of finding Alex at home, but found the door of the flat on the latch and the place unoccupied. Most clothing and other personal possessions, apart from some books, had been removed, and a neighbour reported seeing Alex getting into a cab with two large suitcases three days ago. The bailiffs had contacted the estate agency which manages the letting of Alex's flat, and asked them to send someone to witness the authorised removal of the furniture and secure the flat after they had left. Hall had been given this task. He told me Alex was three months in arrears with her rent and that they were in the process of taking legal action against her. 'It seems she's done a runner,' he said phlegmatically.

He asked me, reasonably enough, why I had come to the flat, and I said I had received a disturbing email from Alex that morning, suggesting that she might do herself some harm. 'But it can't have been sent from here,' I said looking round the now nearly empty room.

'Probably sent from America,' he said. 'She was American was-n't she? My bet is she's gone back there.'

'Will you pursue her there?' I asked.

'Not much point,' he said with a shrug. 'It would cost us more than it's worth. Her name will go on a list, and if she tried to get back into this country she'd be in trouble, but I imagine she's too smart to risk that.'

The senior of the two bailiffs came into the room and said to him, 'We're finished here, then.'

Hall looked around the room and nodded towards the window. 'What about the curtains? A nice bit of material.'

'They're not on the inventory,' the bailiff said. 'They don't belong to our client.'

'No, they belong to my wife,' I said.

Hall laughed. 'How's that?'

When I explained he said, 'I know that shop, in the Rialto mall, isn't it? Good-quality stuff. Why don't you take them?'

I thought: why not? The material, a rich velvet brocade in tones of red and black, could be used for cushion covers. Hall did-n't seem to want any proof or receipt – just my name and address – and he helped me to stand on the window ledge to unhook the curtains from the runners.

I was putting the curtains into the boot of my car when a Volvo estate came into the parking lot at some speed and drew up in the space vacated by the bailiffs' van. Colin Butterworth got out of the car and gave a start as he recognised me. He looked pale and tense, and he was unshaven, though he was dressed in one of his smart suits. He said something as he came up to me.

'You'll have to speak louder,' I said. 'I'm not wearing my hear-ing aid.'

'Where's Alex? Is she all right? I just got back from Paris this morning and found a message saying she was going to kill herself.'

'Me too,' I said.

I related to him briefly what had happened. He almost crum-pled to the ground with relief. 'Thank God!' he exclaimed.

'Thank God.' He fumbled in his jacket pocket for a pack of cigarettes and a lighter, lit up, and inhaled deeply. 'Is it possible that little bitch is out of my life for good?' he wondered aloud. 'It seems too good to be true.' Then a dismaying thought struck him. 'Suppose she's written emails to other people?'

'You mean, to the chairperson of the Staff-Student Relations Board, for instance?'

'Exactly.' He dragged on his cigarette.

'Well, you'll soon find out,' I said unsympathetically. He shot me a resentful glance, but said nothing. I relented a little, and said: 'Anyway, as I understand it, she can't return to this country to give evidence against you without being arrested for debt.'

'Good,' he said. 'I wonder what she's going to do next? Talk her way into another university and fuck up some other poor bugger's life I suppose.'

'She might try writing fiction,' I said. 'She's got the imagination for it. It wouldn't surprise me if we both turn up lightly disguised in a campus novel one of these days.'

I was joking, but he seemed to take the threat seriously. 'Christ, I hope not,' he said. If I had felt before that he got off lightly, with my help, from his involvement with Alex, I now saw that he would never be entirely free from the fear that one day she would pop up again to cause him trouble.

I am of course, as relieved as Butterworth at Alex's sudden removal of herself from my life, and my disapproval of his conduct is not as righteous as he thinks. If I turned down opportunities for kinky shenanigans with her, that was as much out of timidity as principle, and even so I wove a web of deceit around my dealings with her from which I have been lucky to escape unscathed, with my wife's trust intact. When Fred comes home this evening, I shall be able to tell her the story of the morning's events without compromising myself – or Butterworth, for that matter, since it's entirely plausible that Alex should have sent a fake suicide note to him too. She will be shocked and astonished by Alex's conduct, of course, but I think she was already beginning to have reservations about her character. And she will be amused by my resourcefulness in recovering the curtains. I am a lucky man.

As for Alex, it is hard to know whether she is mad, or bad, or a bit of both; but now that she has gone I can feel a little sorry for her, and hope that somewhere, somehow, her unquiet soul will find some peace.

20

7th March. I've been down in London for a couple of days, and slept for the last time in that soft, narrow, lumpy bed in the back bedroom, glancing up, before turning out the light, at the Charlton Athletic shield above the picture rail, which the next owner of the house will certainly paint over. I can't put it on the market until I've got probate, which will take some time in the absence of a will, but I've cleared it out ready for that process. I drove down here, so that I could bring back a few mementoes: a couple of Dad's nicer, undamaged ceramic pots, and the best of his paintings for Anne and Richard to choose from. I put his old clothes into bin bags for the refuse collection, and gave the good stuff to the Salvation Army. I called a firm in the Yellow Pages that does house clearances, and the proprietor, a well-dressed man with a handlebar moustache that seemed to quiver like a diviner's rod in anticipation of rich pickings, presented himself at the front door within the hour. If my educated voice had misled him into imagining a house full of fine antique furniture, he was quickly disillusioned. He strode from room to room tutting and sighing, and announced at the end that there was nothing of any value except the cherry-wood gate-leg table in the dining room, worth about £120. In exchange for that, and an additional £300, he offered to take away the entire contents of the house and dispose of them as rubbish. I accepted the offer without demur, and his men came with a van the next day. The house looked incredibly bare and bleak after they had gone, and when I took a last look round before I left it, my footsteps making a hollow sound on the bare, dusty floorboards, I felt a wave of sadness flood through me, at the fragility of our grip on life, the ease with which the marks we leave on the surface of the earth are erased. Tony Harrison said it all, in a few lines:

The ambulance, the hearse, the auctioneers
clear all the life of that loved house away.
The hard-earned treasures of some 50 years
sized up as junk, and shifted in a day.

Our house was not loved by me since childhood, and not I think loved by Mum, who hankered after something more modern and commodious, in a better area, but deferred to Dad's hatred of change and expenditure. He loved it though, I really think he loved it, hard as it is to believe anyone could love a jerry-built inter-war semi. I had an estate agent come round to value it, and he estimated, incredibly, £250,000. I found the cash Dad had hidden away under loose floorboards in two places, his bedroom and the cupboard under the stairs: fat brown envelopes containing about £500, all in old banknotes, probably payments for gigs which he didn't declare on his tax return. I doubt if they are legal tender any more, and will have to take them to the bank, getting some curious looks from the cashier no doubt. It pains me to think of the value they have lost lying there through decades of inflation, perhaps nine-tenths of what they were worth when he earned them. The money in his estate will, of course, come in useful, as money always does, and I shall give some to Anne and Richard, but my main emotion is regret that he left so much behind, and had so little pleasure out of it while he was alive. It was, I'm sure, the result of his impoverished childhood, growing up in a milieu where nobody had savings, and when the state offered no safety net for the unemployed and the unfortunate: he had seen the consequences of poverty and he was conditioned all his life by the fear of it.

I brought his ashes down to London with me, and took them to Brickley cemetery yesterday. I had collected them by arrangement from the undertaker's in a plain metal canister (when I asked on the phone how big it was, the woman who took my call said, 'Think of a sweetie jar,' and I feared it might be transparent). I handed over this container at the crematorium, and was joined shortly afterwards by a man in a dark suit who had transferred the ashes to a 'scatterer', i.e. a small urn, metallic gold in colour, with a trigger on the top which releases the ashes from the bottom. It was almost the anniversary of Mum's funeral, another cool March day, but calmer and sunnier, and the cemetery looked much more tidy and less depressing than I remembered. The ugly council flats that used to frown down on it have been demolished and replaced by an estate of small town houses, though the electric trains still rattle past in the cutting on the other side. My escort led me to a lawn surrounded by trees and rose bushes – 'very nice here in the summer, when the roses are in bloom,' he remarked – and suggested that I scatter the ashes in the pattern of a cross. I could see faint traces of one or two other crosses on the lawn where ashes had sunk into the earth between the blades of grass, but not yet disappeared. I made a cross on the lawn with two sweeps of the scatterer. The ashes were surprisingly light in colour, almost white, and more like grit than ash in consistency. I wondered if the ash of cremated human bodies is naturally like this, or whether they put something in the ovens to produce these clean, sterile, free-flowing granules. Did the ash-heap beside the crematorium at Auschwitz in which Chaim Hermann's letter to his wife was found look like this? Somehow I doubted it.

The events of the last couple of months keep provoking echoes and cross-references like that: the votive candle flickering in the dark on the rubble of the Auschwitz crematorium and the night-light I put on Maisie's bedside table when she fell asleep for ever; hospital pyjamas and striped prison uniforms; the sight of Dad's wasted naked body on the hospital mattress when I helped to wash him, and grainy photographs of naked corpses heaped in the death camps. It's been something of an education, the experience of these last few weeks. 'Deafness is comic, blindness is tragic,' I wrote earlier in this journal, and I have played variations on the phonetic near-equivalence of 'deaf' and 'death', but now it seems more meaningful to say that deafness is comic and death is tragic, because final, inevitable, and inscrutable. As Wittgenstein said, 'Death is not an event of life.' You cannot experience it, you can only behold it happening to others, with various degrees of pity and fear, knowing that one day it will happen to you.

> The sure extinction that we travel to
> And shall be lost in always. Not to be here,
> Not to be anywhere,
> And soon; nothing more terrible, nothing more true.

Philip Larkin, the deaf bard of *timor mortis*.

I keep thinking of that header on the registry office computer screen, 'DEATH MENU', and wondering whimsically whether if such a thing were offered, like the *carte* in a restaurant, by the Angel of Death, what one would choose. Something painless, obviously, but not so sudden that you would not have time to take it in, to say goodbye to life, to hold it in your hand, as it were and let it go; but on the other hand not so long-drawn-out as to be tedious or terrifying. Something painless, dignified (no bedpans and catheters), fully conscious, all faculties intact, not too quick, not too slow, at home not in hospital, so not a heart attack, not a stroke, not cancer, not an air crash or a car crash – oh, what's the point, nothing will do, the fact is we don't want to order death at all, in any shape or form, unless we are suicidal. (Suicide bombers order for everybody.) You could say that birth itself is a sentence of death – I expect some glib philosopher *has* said it somewhere – but it is a perverse and useless thought. Better to dwell on life, and try to value the passing time.

8th March. Back to the lip-reading class today, after a long interval. I had written to Beth to explain the reason for my absence and the group welcomed me back with sympathetic smiles as I took my place in the semicircle of stacking chairs. There's a lot of mutual kindness and compassion here on Deaf Row. We began with a puzzle, a picture of a young girl's face, and three utterances: *'Philip plays football.' 'Barbara likes to watch football.' 'Sharon hates football.'* If the pictured girl was going to say one of these sentences which would it be and who was she? I couldn't make sense of it, but the others seemed to find it easy, perhaps because they had played the game before. The correct answer was Sharon, about to say, *'Barbara likes to watch football'*, because she was forming her lips to make a 'b' sound. Then we had a session on gardens. Garden gnomes were originally images of earth spirits, introduced into Britain from Germany in the 1840s by an eccentric baronet, and were not mass-produced here until the 1920s. The lawnmower was invented by Edward Budding, a weaver from Gloucestershire, who got the idea from watching the blades of the cloth-cutting machines in the local textile factory that had put him out of a job. There is an English vicar who has mowed his 200-foot garden in the shape of the British Isles.

We had a session on homophenes which could cause misunderstanding, for example, *married* and *buried*, *wet suit* and *wedding suit*, *big kiss* and *biscuits*. Much laughter. Members volunteered their own stories of misunderstandings. Marjorie was asked at the supermarket checkout if she would like a 'free gateau' and eagerly accepted the offer, which turned out to be a free catalogue. Violet was baffled when her friend enthused about 'laxative porridge', which turned out to be 'wax-free polish'. I told my story of the 'long-stick saucepan'. We had a short talk on towers. Apparently the leaning tower of Pisa began to lean when they reached the third storey, and the succeeding storeys were made progressively smaller in diameter to compensate. The Eiffel Tower was built as a temporary structure for the 1889 Paris Exhibition, and was much criticised at the time. It was supposed to be demolished afterwards, but the populace became fond of it and it was saved when a wireless transmitter was put on the top. I always learn something new at the lip-reading class.

Acknowledgements

The narrator's deafness and his Dad have their sources in my own experience, but the other characters in this novel are fictional creations, as is the nameless northern city where most of the story is set, and its university. The only source for Alex Loom's PhD topic, apart from my own imagination, is an article by Charles E. Osgood, 'Some Effects of Motivation on Style of Encoding . . . based on research using samples of suicide and pseudicide notes', in Thomas Sebeok ed., *Style in Language* (1960). I read that book more than forty years ago in preparation for writing my first work of academic criticism, *Language of Fiction* (1966), where it is mentioned in a footnote. I did not cite Osgood's article, which was irrelevant to my subject, but it must have struck me as an idea capable of fictional development because it stayed half-buried in my memory, and with this novel its time had come. When I was about halfway through writing *Deaf Sentence* I heard by chance of a doctoral dissertation in progress applying linguistic analysis to suicide notes, and learned that other linguists are currently engaged in research and publication on the same subject. To avoid any confusion between my fiction and fact I deliberately avoided acquainting myself with any of this work or its authors. The character of Alex and her observations regarding suicide notes are entirely invented.

The brief quotations from suicide notes in chapter 7 are, however, taken from a documentary source, Udo Grashoff's anthology *Let Me Finis* (Headline Review, 2006). Other publications I have found useful in writing this novel include the following: J . L. Austin, *How To Do Things With Words* (2nd edition, 1962); John Carey, ed., *The Faber Book of Science* (for the passage by Bruce Frederick Cummings quoted in chapter 19); Jean Francois

Chabrun, *Goya* (1965); Malcolm Coulthard, *Introduction to Discourse Analysis* (1977); Peter French, 'Mr Akbar's nearest ear versus the Lombard Reflex' in *Forensic Linguistics* (vol. 5, no. 1, 1998); Brian Grant, ed., *The Quiet Ear: Deafness in Literature, an anthology* (1987); Peter Grundy, *Doing Pragmatics* (2000); Neil Mercer, *Words & Minds* (2000); Laurence Rees, *Auschwitz: the Nazis and the 'Final Solution'* (2005); Peter Roach, *English Phonetics and Phonology* (3rd edn. 2000); Thayer's *Life of Beethoven*, edited and revised by Elliot Forbes, (1964); Michael Stubbs, *Discourse Analysis* (1983) and *Text and Corpus Analysis* (1966); Antonina Vallentin, *This I saw: the Life and Times of Goya* (1951).

I am very grateful to Charles Owen and Vijay Raichura for information and advice concerning linguistic and medical aspects of the novel respectively, and to several others for their notes and comments on various drafts: Bernard Bergonzi, Tony Lacey, Julia Lodge, Alison Lurie, Geoff Mulligan, Jonny Pegg, Tom Rosenthal, Mike Shaw, Paul Slovak and, as always, my wife Mary. And thanks to my granddaughter Fiona for a pun on Marks & Spencer.

D. L.
September, 2007

By the same author

THERAPY

A successful sitcom writer with plenty of money, a stable marriage, a platonic mistress and a flash car, Laurence 'Tubby' Passmore has more reason than most to be happy. Yet neither physiotherapy nor aromatherapy, cognitive behaviour therapy or acupuncture can cure his unidentified knee pain or his equally inexplicable mid-life angst . . .

'Full of delights . . . His view of our stultifying neuroses is sane, intelligent and amused' *Sunday Times*

'Lodge remains one of the very best in English comic novelists of the post-war era; and *Therapy* is good for you' *Time Out*

'A real treat. It's a Bumper Book or Hit Parade of all his comic devices . . . The result is a joy' *Observer*

By the same author

PARADISE NEWS

Bernard Walsh, agnostic theologian, has a sort of professional interest in Paradise. But, having come to Hawaii to escort his reluctant father Jack to the deathbed of Jack's estranged sister, he does not, like his fellow package tourists, hope for a heavenly holiday.

But Hawaii holds surprises undreamed of in overcast Rummidge. As honeymooners, professional freeloaders and amateur cameramen avidly pursue their earthly visions of paradise, Bernard discovers the astonishing possibility of love ...

'Amusing, accessible, intelligent ... the story rolls, the sparks fly' *Financial Times*

'Further proof that Lodge is master of ... scintillating satire' *Daily Mail*

By the same author

SMALL WORLD

Philip Swallow, Morris Zapp, Persse McGar-
rigle, the lovely Angelica – the jet-propelled
academics are on the move, in the air, on the
make, in

Small World

'Academic infightings, couplings touching,
funny and frightful, set pieces, dark humour,
sharp wit and plain farce – here is everything
one expects from this author but thrisefold'
Sunday Telegraph

'Sex, romance, thrills, burlesque, satire, farce
. . . most enjoyable' *Daily Mail*

'A wonderful tissue of outrageous coincidences
and correspondences' *Observer*

Small World is also published, with *Changing
Places* and *Nice Work*, as *A David Lodge Trilogy*.

He just wanted a decent book to read ...

Not too much to ask, is it? It was in 1935 when Allen Lane, Managing Director of Bodley Head Publishers, stood on a platform at Exeter railway station looking for something good to read on his journey back to London. His choice was limited to popular magazines and poor-quality paperbacks – the same choice faced every day by the vast majority of readers, few of whom could afford hardbacks. Lane's disappointment and subsequent anger at the range of books generally available led him to found a company – and change the world.

'We believed in the existence in this country of a vast reading public for intelligent books at a low price, and staked everything on it'
Sir Allen Lane, 1902–1970, founder of Penguin Books

The quality paperback had arrived – and not just in bookshops. Lane was adamant that his Penguins should appear in chain stores and tobacconists, and should cost no more than a packet of cigarettes.

Reading habits (and cigarette prices) have changed since 1935, but Penguin still believes in publishing the best books for everybody to enjoy. We still believe that good design costs no more than bad design, and we still believe that quality books published passionately and responsibly make the world a better place.

So wherever you see the little bird – whether it's on a piece of prize-winning literary fiction or a celebrity autobiography, political tour de force or historical masterpiece, a serial-killer thriller, reference book, world classic or a piece of pure escapism – you can bet that it represents the very best that the genre has to offer.

Whatever you like to read – trust Penguin.